RESOLVE OF STEEL

Book Two of the Halloran's War Series

By J.R. Geoghan

WAR WITHOUT HONOR is a work of fiction.

All names, characters, organizations and situations depicted in this novel are fictitious within the context of larger historical events or drawn from the author's imagination. Sometimes both. Any resemblance to actual events, names, or persons living or dead, is entirely coincidental.

Copyright ©2019 J.R. Geoghan and Adventus Press. All rights reserved. No part of this publication may be reproduced, distributed or transmitted in any form or by any means, or stored in a database or retrieval system, without the prior written permission of the publisher. If you would like permission to use material from this book (other than for review purposes), please contact info@jrgeoghan.com. Thank you for your support of the author's rights.

Adventus Press supports the right to free expression and the value of copyright. The purpose of copyright is to encourage writers and artists to produce the creative works that enrich our culture.

First U.S. edition, April 2019

Dedication

To everyone who reads my stories, and especially those who enjoy helping me make them better.

www.JRGeoghan.com

"I wish to have no connection with any ship that does not sail fast; for I intend to go in harm's way"

– John Paul Jones

Resolve Of Steel

Part One - Rumblings

Resolve Of Steel

Chapter 1

Planet Tavar - Struve System
11.53 LY from Earth

The howling wind competed with the ice particles whipping at his face mask for attention. With one hand lifted to shield his eyes from the white blast, he tried valiantly to concentrate on the valley before him. With his other hand he grasped a set of enhanced binocs.

After a few moments of naked eye, he placed the binocs against his mask and waited for the software to pair up between the two devices. When that desired result failed to materialize, he began to wonder if the intense cold had finally overpowered the batteries within them. He was about to lower the binocs to holster them when the sync beeped in his earpiece.

Grumbling, he leaned out over the retaining wall and ran his scan of the ravine and opposite sheer wall of ice. For the thousandth time. And, for the thousandth time, the scans all registered nothing. No life, no heat, no growth. Just galeforce winds rising up from the valley with enough force to lift a man bodily and throw him half a kilometer before releasing him to fall to his death. Mladin had been there when it'd happened. Holdar had been a buddy from Initial.

Mladin stepped back, scanning the swirling sky above. The thick cloud cover blanketed the frozen planet as always, its moisture and the ultra-low surface temperature causing a vicious ecosystem of frigid extremes. No one using such visible-spectrum equipment could hope to penetrate that blue-white maelstrom. He turned away from the observation post as he holstered the binocs, making a mental note to have the batteries checked before his next shift.

The entrance to the side of the mountain had auto-locked behind him, its triple-barred innards hardened against any and all incursions from without. This was always the part that Mladin hated; the specter of his access code failing or some sort of mechanical/computer glitch causing the unlock sequence to not initialize. He knew that, even fortified as he was against the weather in a military exposure suit, the cold would get him before anyone could reach his remote location.

As part of the planetary garrison, his unit was assigned to patrol duty throughout the incredibly large maze of tunnels and access points that made up the colony of Tavar. That meant that most of his comrades were out of touch with one another and their superiors very often. Even the most sophisticated comm systems found the unique rock formations surrounding the underground facilities virtually impossible to penetrate, forcing the guard substations to rely on old-school fiberline tech physically run through the hundreds of kilometers of conduit installed over a century ago.

Mladin placed his gloved hand on the locking panel, shifting his weapon higher on his shoulder; the mil-spec straps were too thin to get a good purchase on the exposure suit uppers, causing the rifle to slip from time to time. *One more annoyance,* Mladin thought as he keyed the code into the mechanism and held his breath.

The nearest substation—his—was almost ten kilometers away. And not an easy 10K, either. Several narrow passageways that required careful threading when fully laden with full pack. This spot was one of the lowest in the colony, and one of the least visited by anyone, whether garrison or civilian.

Mladin had rotated down only the week prior, grumbling and cursing at the wisdom of his Commander. He'd been scheduled for rotation to the spaceport above, located in synchronous orbit directly over the ground facilities. More bars, more possibilities of the female nature, more warmth…but instead he and several other career soldiers had been reassigned to the bowels of the colony to investigate anomalies in the readings.

For almost a year, techs had been chasing gremlins in the colony science systems, or so Mladin had been told at the briefing. Unexplained drops in power output from the life support reactors. Fluctuations in telemetry from the mining operations, deeper still within the core of the planet. At last, the smart people had isolated the anomalies to this sector of the colony. But—and this was a big but for Mladin—the absolute remoteness of this sector convinced the smart people to only send an extra squad to bolster the three-man substation. Fifteen warm bodies to patrol these catacombs and keep an eye out for the odd broken piece of something that would signal the source of the anomaly.

The hatch was taking a while to open, Mladin's mind screamed silently in his ear. He rekeyed the code and allowed the scanner to register his biochip a second time; the security systems on this godforsaken planet were almost as old as the colony itself. Ancient, but tough and hard to crack.

Just like the colonists, Mladin thought as he forced his mind to relax and let the unlock mechanism do its work.

He was reaching for his comm unit, which he knew could reach all the way to the orbital station if needed, when the rock face shifted to the side a few centimeters before curling inward. The resulting opening was just a fraction taller than his two meters, and barely wide enough to fit his gear-laden form. But with the strength of a man who'd nearly been condemned to die in the merciless cold, Mladin shoved on the rock and forced his way into the warmth of the passageway within.

Silly, he told himself as he smacked the locking pad on the inner surface of the hatch and stepped further into the interior to allow the door to complete its closing cycle. Mladin knew intellectually that he was never in any real danger; he was nearly positive that a shuttle would be dispatched at his comm call should he have truly been stranded outside. Nearly. The fuel required to fly halfway around the world, just to pick up one underpaid grunt who'd lost his way... After ten years, he had better rate a full charging of ion fuel. Still, the re-entry always spooked him.

With a sigh, he lowered his face mask around his neck and extracted a wipe from his pocket, rubbing around his face vigorously. The exposure suit included a full mask for vacuum operations, but nobody used those on the surface teams, opting instead for the partial-cover mask that held a small supply of air— maybe half and hour's worth. The low O2 count in the planetary atmosphere necessitated an augmented supply, but no one liked the bulkiness of the full cover. The price they paid after two minutes outside was numbed skin; after ten it was time for medical treatment to avoid skin loss.

Done resuscitating his epidermis, Mladin replaced the wipe and unslung his weapon to give it a quick check and clear it of any frost that might have built up outside. The cold particles stuck to any metal surface and clung on for dear life. Almost impossible to remove without a significant temp rise. But his rifle looked nominal. He glanced at the charge indicator on the side; full capacity...fifty bursts of clean, cutting plasma on tap. *Not that I get to fire it much outside of a range.*

He re-slung the rifle and looked up and down the passageway. All quiet.

After a moment, Mladin realized what it was that bugged him. It was *too* quiet. The quiet rumbling of life support that pervaded the mountain range was hushed...perhaps altogether missing.

He stopped in mid-stride and held himself as silently as he could. Nope, nothing.

"Huh."

Mladin half-lifted his all-but-useless comm unit, glancing at the signal strength meter on its top. An empty readout returned his gaze.

"Figures."

He turned around to head back up the tunnel toward his substation, wanting to report the issue as soon as possible. Not that he was in any immediate danger; the air pressure in the tunnels gave anyone needing breathability many hours of cushion.

Clunk.

Mladin paused in mid-stride yet again, listening intently.

After a minute of nothing, the odd sound repeated itself.

Now, Mladin's senses were extended, his training kicking in. He crouched low, deftly removing the rifle and holding it at the low ready. He edged forward, downward, toward where he'd heard the sound from. Fifteen meters away was a slight bend in the passage, and it was toward this juncture that he now padded, his boots making little sound against the stone floor.

Although he knew that the atmosphere was still quite viable, his mind began ticking off a list of the ways a man could die in these catacombs; dropped down a previously unknown or recently opened chasm, stranded by an impenetrable rockfall, exposed to an open vein of the volatile mineral that made this planet so prized—precious yet immensely dangerous to human life in its raw form.

But when he peeked around the corner, none of those horrid eventualities presented themselves. Instead, he saw what looked like a man-made hatch standing open in the wall of the rock below him, perhaps thirty meters away. *Impossible,* he told himself. The garrison was well-versed in the old mining layouts that formed the infrastructure of the colony. Down, here, there were no chambers. No nothing…just empty and unused access points created multiple decades ago to provide options to the colonists should they choose to try new avenues for exploration. But there it was.

Then, before Mladin's eyes, it swung shut with a *clunk*.

Now he was angry. With rifle in position, Mladin moved forward to where the door should be. It was set very tightly in the rock face, that much he realized immediately. The gap was almost invisible to the unknowing eye; indeed, had he not just seen the door open moments ago, he would not have picked up on its presence. "Nice," he murmured to himself as he felt around its perimeter. The thought of retreating into comm range of his substation crossed his mind, but Mladin was a man on a mission now. His fingers ducked in and out of crevices, searching grooves left by the century-old laser excavators.

There it was. The small, ever-so-slightly discolored patch of stone, that gave under the pressure of three fingers. He stepped back, gun barrel trained, as the hatch made its quiet noise and swung open.

Nothing.

The space behind the entrance was dark and narrow. He nosed in, looking around it. Tall, too.

Finally, and not a moment too soon, discretion took over for valor and Mladin decided that it was time to get back to where the reinforcements were. It would be a long ten kilometers uphill, but he wanted gone—now.

With his rifle still angled toward the silent, clever opening, he began backing away. At the corner he paused, never taking his eyes from the threat vector. With a final glance he turned to sprint up the passageway, back to the outer entrance.

But a huge form blocked his way, and he stumbled in confusion.

It loomed over him, filling the passage and blocking the light emanating from the nearest wall fixture located near the outer door. He ducked instinctively, seeing more motion in the passageway behind the thing immediately before him. In fact, the passage was teeming with silent, moving apparitions. And he saw, just as the thing reached down and plucked away his rifle as though taking sweets from a naughty child, that the outer door stood open.

And then the cold and dark washed over him like an electric shock and he was slammed with brutality against the nearest wall. Sometime later—probably only moments—he felt the hardness of the rock floor beneath his exposed cheek. The pain overwhelmed his senses, crushing him beneath its weight. He guessed that his skull had been crushed by the force of the impact.

Before his eyes closed forever Mladin had a moment left to curse this frozen planet one more time…

Chapter 2

Aboard USS Serapis, formerly Prax Warship Trellixan
Luyten System - 8.73 LY from Earth

"It just won't work."

"Try it again." Chief John Parker was leaning hard on a valve set into a large elbow, putting all his weight on the handle. Though Parker was normally a substantial individual, his weight—as was true of most of the crew—was down from the lack of hearty Navy food. Parker's energy was low as well. "I've got my whole weight on this thing now."

Machinist's Mate Al Nunez's voice filtered back from the tight access tube he was currently crawled into. "Not seeing any flow back here, Chief."

"Now?"

A moment passed. "Wait, I see that this meter is registering something."

Parker exhaled slowly, feeling the edge of the valve lever pressing into his ribs. "Giving it all I got, Nunez."

"Hold that…right there, Chief!"

Parker glanced up in annoyance, his tired muscles aching with the exertion. All he could see of the other man was the soles of his boots protruding out of the tube over his head.

"Okay. Okay. Will it stay like that?" came the muffled question.

Parker gingerly let the pressure off. The valve appeared to stay in the same position. "I think it is." He took his calloused hands off the valve lever gingerly, exhaling in relief.

"Hang on a moment."

More than a moment later—maybe thirty seconds, actually—Nunez had extricated himself from the tube and dropped nimbly down to land on the decking beside the Chief. He tapped the valve. "Seems to be holding. Not full flow, but call it eighty-five percent."

"Better'n nothing." Parker gathered up the tools he'd dropped during their repair session at this end of the B deck mechanicals compartment. "We'll have to check the showers again."

Nunez took some of the tools and set them in a bag he'd found in a crew cabin. It was a prized possession now for the life support specialist; everyone was making do with ad hoc tools and equipment, attempting to regain a semblance of military order and discipline in their tasks. The bag was a simple but strong mesh, not unlike something he would have picked up at the local big-box home improvement store, designed for handymen.

But there was no supply depot. Or big-box store. No handymen. In fact, no planet to have big-box stores on. For Nunez and the other three-odd dozen humans aboard this alien spaceship, virtually everything was foreign…as in *totally* alien. Gauges read backward, upside down and using characters that constantly needed deciphering. Every hatch, access tube and lever was labeled neatly in lettering that was incomprehensible to humans.

Nunez prized his bag.

Parker handed him one last tool, something that acted like a screwdriver but vibrated when you held it a certain way. Unnerving. "Your bag is cool."

"You can't have it. Chief."

The Chief shook his head as he turned to examine the valve one more time. "I don't want your bag, Nunez. I want a hot shower for a change."

"I'm going up to A deck now to find Bert James—he said he needed some help figuring out a set of relays that he was afraid to test without a second opinion. Want me to stop by the bridge and tell the Old Man that we may have fixed the hot water flow issue?"

Parker tapped the valve, nodding meaningfully. "You realize that we're recycling water for the showers? That's—."

"—Washing up using our own bodily fluids. Yep, figured that out early on, Chief."

"Yeah, now we've got to find out where the component is that actually purifies the stuff. Hate to have *that* go on the fritz and not know it." Parker grinned. "You stop and tell the Captain, that's fine. Thanks for crawlin' up there—no way I'd fit in."

Nunez started off down the passage, ducking underneath a low-hanging bit of equipment. "I don't know, Chief. At the rate we're all going we're going to waste away to nothing in a few more weeks."

Parker watched Nunez go, rubbing his temples at the sudden pain. *Hunger.* "What I wouldn't give for a cheeseburger."

Directly below those two, on "C deck" as named by the human crew, Missile Technician Karen Flagler and Machinist's Mate Frank DeBartelo were working down opposite sides of a long, menacing barrel that was ringed with coils of wire and innumerable electronic sensors and connectors. It was low to the decking and set in a section that actually slid outward, deploying the barrel through a port in the hull where it could change elevation and deflection by up to thirty degrees. The entire assembly was massive. The two were running their hands along the electronics and calling to each other softly.

The hatch into the ship's interior passageways opened and a man with a pockmarked face stepped in. Though he wore the same green camo US Navy coveralls worn by everyone else originally from 2029, his visible undershirt was the traditional black and white-stripe of the Russian Navy. He walked over and knelt down. "Getting a better understanding of how it works?" Though the English was acceptable and rendered the translator device unnecessary, his Slavic accent was noticeable.

Flagler glanced up and nodded at Executive Officer Pyotr Antonov. "Morning, sir. Not really, to be honest. Everything just looks like it's supposed to be there and is in working order."

DeBartelo grunted in agreement from his side of the barrel.

Antonov laid a hand on the thick cabling circling its length. "When do you want to test-fire it?"

Flagler shrugged. "I'm okay with anytime. I'd hoped to find the damaged relay before then."

Antonov sighed; they'd taken more damage during their first hectic engagement than they'd initially realized. Systems had been punctured in dozens of places by the projectiles thrown by guns such as the one he had his hand on; in fact, probably exactly the same since they'd come from other Prax warships—ones actually crewed by aliens. The projectiles themselves were more like elongated pencils made of hardened metals rather than bullets. Their ship had a ready supply of them in all sizes in magazines just below each gun mount. The technology was basically that of a massive rail gun, as they would have been known in the twenty-first century. They drew lots of power and there were eight of them, mounted around the lower midsection of the ship, directly at the outer edges where they could have the most room to adjust fire direction.

This one, mounted on the aft port quarter of C deck, was malfunctioning according to the systems-ready monitors up in the weapons substation. The alien Axxa had interpreted the readouts for them. "I'll tell the Captain when you're ready for me to do so."

Flagler looked up. "Thanks, sir."

Antonov stood and wandered past Flagler to the port at the mouth of the gun; it looked so much like an ancient cannon port to him. Of course, when deployed and port opened this compartment would be in the vacuum of space.

The ship was well-armed. Aside from the projectile guns, they had found another eight plasma weapons and sixteen beam weapons that Axxa explained were used to super-heat enemy sensor emitters, frying them and rendering the opponent blind. They also acted as a point-defense against missiles, a role in which they are particularly effective at. According to the Prax, the role of missiles in space inter-ship combat had dwindled to almost nothing due to the effect of the beam weapons.

The plasma guns were the most devastating of the three main armaments, though. Antonov and Halloran had listened as Axxa described the way the emitter fired an amorphous slug of super-heated plasma matter that traveled at an extremely high velocity, its passage marked by a blinding ray of light. The matter would shear off entire sections of ship and tear gaping holes in hulls and possessed a significant range. The power requirements were greatest for these pieces of main armament, however, and at close range a spread of meter-thick projectiles would actually do more damage by passing deep into (or entirely through) an opponent's hull. But when they fired nearby the plasma guns were fearsome.

Antonov, like everyone else from 2029 aboard this ship, were ex-submariners. They knew torpedoes and ballistic missiles. And, like the rest, Antonov had always poked fun at his contemporaries in the surface fleet. Now, he was one of them…

Flagler sat up, wiping a sheen of grease from her hand to her coverall legs. "They working on the cloaking device, sir?"

He turned and came back toward her. "Yes, Lieutenant Carruthers is in charge of that device's operation. I believe that she has interpreted the schematics with the Captain's help."

"We should test it, sir." She turned to DeBartelo, who was also rising from his side of the barrel. "That reminds me, Frank; I need to stop up and congratulate her on her promotion."

"Yeah, she jumped rank nicely. From PO to full LT."

Flagler got to her feet with an assist from Antonov. "She earned it."

"We all did. What do you think, sir?" DeBartelo addressed the Russian. "How 'bout combat pay increases and battlefield promotions all around? When I get back, I have a family to feed."

Antonov smiled at the man. "If you were in the Russian Navy, we'd be sure to at least give you double rations of Borscht for combat service."

"Seriously?"

Flagler shook her head at her partner. "No, you idiot. He's kidding."

Antonov headed for the interior hatch. "Perhaps not. But I suspect we shall have a hard time making this dish in our current time. I do have an excellent recipe in my head somewhere."

The Missile Tech stared wistfully after him. "That sounds *so* good." Her upbringing had been in suburban Denver, Colorado. To her knowledge, she'd never had nor seen Borscht.

"Someday, perhaps?" Then he was gone through the hatch.

DeBartelo looked up at her. "He's not bad for a Russky."

Nunez had just left the bridge after reporting the restoration of hot water when Elias Whitney entered, looking soberly around him at the watch crew, all busy at their stations. He walked forward to the Captain's command seat. "Sir, got a moment?"

Captain Thomas Halloran half-turned in the large, imposing seat and recognized the ship's Corpsman. With a grunt, he got to his feet and stepped around the chair, stretching mightily. "Elias." He tapped the chair. "I think this chair is meant to be a torture device, not a plush Captain's chair."

"Sir. Can I talk to you, out in the hall?"

Halloran waved. "Lead on."

"Captain leaving the bridge!" Called Lieutenant Carruthers from her station.

Halloran caught her eye. "You have the conn, Lieutenant."

"Aye, sir."

Outside the bridge, Whitney turned and walked a few paces down from the hatch. When Halloran caught up to him he lowered his voice. "Sir, the food situation is getting worse. Morale is going, too."

"What've you got?" Halloran placed a hand on the red-painted piping near his head, leaning in.

"Well, Yeoman Butler and Bert James have been all over the galley systems, trying to find out what the issue is. Nothing seems to work."

Halloran sighed. "I've heard that several times…in the last hour, as a matter of fact. What does Axxa think?" He knew that the Prax officer had been down on B deck with the human crew members, translating what he could from the equipment labels from his own language and generally trying to be helpful.

Whitney shrugged. "He means well. And since this is one of their ships…thing is, he wasn't an engineer."

"What about Kendra and her sidekick? Traver something."

"I haven't met the other guy. He's hiding out in Engineering with Wyatt. The lady officer, she won't even acknowledge the alien."

Halloran frowned. "Have you seen this in person?"

Whitney straightened. "Sure, sir. Whenever he comes into a compartment, she leaves. Like, *right* away." His eyebrows went up to accent his point.

"We've got to get the food processors online ASAP, Whitney."

"Sir, I'm a medical tech, not an Electrician's Mate. And even *those* guys can't figure out how this Prax stuff is supposed to work."

Halloran laid a hand on the younger man's arm. "I need you down there to test the food immediately, in case some eager hand goes after it before we can test its safety."

"I know, sir. I'm hanging around them."

Halloran nodded with a smile. "Try to make yourself useful in the meantime. How are the injuries?"

"That's one area where we got lucky; two broken arms and half-dozen lacerations. The med tech on this ship made short work of that. Frankly, it's amazing stuff, sir."

Halloran had heard about the future-tech that Whitney was referring to. They'd been schooled in its use by their resident alien, Axxa, who actually knew how to work most gear in the infirmary. Bone-healers, using a beam that instantly knitted the broken sections together without cutting through skin. Flexible tissue-wraps that somehow bonded with the skin below and caused it to heal at an amazing rate. If he had any one of the gadgets back in 2029, he would be able to leave the Navy and retire early.

But, of course, 2029 was a long, long time ago and neither him nor Whitney were going back anytime soon.

Halloran nodded again, stretching. The passage was tall for humans; it would have normally had to accommodate the Prax crew who stood half a meter taller. "Good to hear. Keep me in the loop the moment you see any light at the end of the tunnel. I'm getting sick of that liquid nutrient solution, too."

Whitney smiled. "It's keeping you alive, sir. I'm just glad we figured *that* device out. Imagine if—."

Halloran held up a hand. "One miracle at a time, Elias. Speaking of which...apparently we now may have hot water showers in the crew quarters."

"That'll help morale, sir."

"Let's hope so. Dismissed."

"Yes, sir."

When the Corpsman had gone, Halloran turned and wearily trudged up the length of the passage, passing the bridge door and turning left into his cabin. Closing the hatch behind him, he leaned against it, exhaling. It was taking everything he had to keep the crew together and any semblance of forward progress. If something didn't get better soon, he might have a mutiny on his hands.

Someone interrupted his self-pity by tapping with a heavy hand on the cabin door. With a sigh, Halloran turned and unlatched it.

Seaman Jeff Kaufmann was there. "Sir, you need to come to Operations Center. Now."

Chapter 3

Halloran barged into the Ops Center—so named by the crew after its function as a central node of control for many onboard computer systems—looking for trouble. And he found it.

Several crew stood to one side and watched without interfering as Axxa the alien soldier and Kendra the human officer punched at each other. He was big, much bigger than his female opponent, and fast. But she was apparently proving faster still and was in the process of landing a solid punch to the red-skinned creature's gut as Halloran stepped through the hatch.

In between them, a civilian man darted and waved in a vain attempt to separate the two combatants. His name was Deacon, and Axxa was technically his charge; Deacon was the one who'd convinced the Prax to defect to the human side of the war. But here, the disheveled young man was not having much luck as he was shoved aside by the much larger alien in his anger at the woman.

Axxa's long arms were just encircling Kendra's body when Halloran sucked in a breath. "As you *were*, people." His tone was slightly louder than normal and firm.

Every eye swiveled to the Captain in the entrance. Axxa's turned shifty and avoided the man's. Kendra's eyes slitted and her hands went to her hips, her shoulders heaving with exertion and defiance.

After several moments of nothing, Halloran looked around the room calmly. "US personnel out of the room."

As the half-dozen spectators filed out, eyes down on the deck, Halloran kept his own eyes on the two combatants. Deacon had slipped and got to his feet to step back, apparently not wanting to be in the middle of what was to come.

Kendra was breathing hard; obviously she wouldn't have been able to hold off her huge opponent much longer. As Halloran looked on, trying to radiate calm, she backed slowly away from Axxa, looking around her. Her eyes avoided his until he caught them in a glance; then she locked on his with a subdued fury that smoldered. Finally, her voice caught up with her as she swiped a lock of jet-black hair aside. "What?"

Halloran was furious. With a quick glance to ensure that the door was securely shut behind him, he moved forward into their personal space. First, Kendra. She was backed up several more steps, attempting to avoid a bodily collision.

At the last second he pulled up short, staring down at her. "What are you doing, *Captain?*" His emphasis on that last word stung her; her eyes averted again. "You're getting into physical altercations *now?* In front of my crew? Who do you think you are?"

Kendra's mouth opened as if to shoot back a barb, then it shut just as quickly.

"Hmm. You told me you rose through the ranks as an officer. Was this—," he waved to point out Axxa, "—How you demonstrated your cool under pressure?!"

She waved her own arms, low. "That's not how it is. You don't understand these things, what they've done to our people for decades. *Your* people!" He saw the intense fire behind those dark eyes, marveling at her power of will. To go up against a being such as a Prax in hand-to-hand…he was impressed but kept that underneath his anger.

He turned on his heel, stalking over to the alien in question. "And *you.*" He cast a glance at Deacon, as if to say *and you too for not nipping this in the bud.* "You and I are already on less-than-ideal terms."

He heard the Praxxan language translated in his linguistic implant. The voice was calm. The alien wasn't winded in the slightest. "Captain, you know I understand this. Captain Kendra—."

Halloran's voice was low and menacing. "Axxa, how many Captains are there on this vessel."

The Prax was tall, but Halloran was nearly his equal. The alien's eyes narrowed in defense, then wavered. They never left his, though.

"One."

"Correct."

"We're just not going to see eye-to-eye, Captain," Kendra said from behind Halloran.

He stepped back to address the two of them. "You don't need to; what you need to see is that this crew is on the edge…it won't take much to completely deflate their will to live. And I won't stand for it."

Kendra pointed at Axxa. "This race brutally conquered Earth and murdered millions upon millions to secure control and create a staging base to subjugate the entire solar system. There's not a human alive in the galaxy today—let alone in the Fleet—who would stand to even be in the same proximity of a Prax without trying to kill it. In self-defense, yes. But also in revenge for what they've *done to humanity!*" She looked down, spent by her tirade. "I for one won't be a part of it."

Halloran was calmer. "Understood, Kendra." When she looked up into his eyes he himself wavered from her intensity. Gathering himself, he continued with a huge exhalation of breath. "This is the situation. Our ship is wounded, and my crew—though willing—desperately need help. From *both* of you." He looked pointedly from one to the other. "I need Axxa's interpretive help with every label, readout and control on this vessel. And I need Kendra's knowledge of engineering and how things work in the human world of whatever year this is."

Axxa nodded solemnly, watching Kendra. "I will be pleased to be of assistance, Captain. I owe you," he glanced at Deacon, "both of you, for rescuing me from my forces on Earth."

Halloran allowed a small grin. "I seem to remember you saving *our* bacon."

"Bacon?" Apparently the translator wasn't picking up on the arcane reference.

"They don't have bacon in this time? Just great." Halloran looked at Kendra. "Thoughts?"

After a long moment, the woman nodded slowly. "I'm not going to like it, but I see your point here."

"That's all I want from you." He turned to the door, then paused with his hand on the frame in the act of unlatching it. "I'm glad this is behind us, because I want to call an officer's meeting in the conference room. As soon as you both can get there." Then he was gone, nodding to the crew gathered outside the hatch.

One of the green-uniformed crew leaned in, looking around as if checking for blood. "All right for us to get back to work?"

As the three headed for the exit the same human asked Axxa, "Can you stay to translate?"

The Prax looked down at him as he passed. "I cannot; your Captain has summoned me."

The man nodded. "Afterward then, sir."

When they were gone the other crew members came in.

"All clear, PO?" asked Seaman Don King.

"I don't know, you tell me. They sure looked like they would fight it out," answered Petty Officer David Chapan.

"Sure did. That lady officer is a tough one. You see her eyes?"

Chapan was already studying the nearest computer panel, motioning to Electronics Tech Jack Stacey. He spared a meaningful look in King's direction. "You keep your eyes low and focused on the task, Seaman."

"Aye."

"Now, let's figure out how these red nutjobs wired their panels, shall we?"

The conference room was just down the passage from the Captain's quarters, and clearly that was its function; a cylindrical projection in the center of the triangular table was a holographic image generator, according to Axxa, designed to show three-dimensional images of speakers or a rendering of a star system. Three seats were set along each face of the triangle, and several more were arrayed along the one wall of the room. Halloran walked to one point of the triangle and waited patiently as the officers filed in. He knew that PO Gerry Wilson had gone through the ship, in the absence of a working loudspeaker, to find and summon them.

Gail Carruthers sat at the "foot" of the triangle, chattering quietly with the other non-US human officer aboard, Lieutenant Travers. No last name. Halloran frowned at the oddness of the lack of last names for humans in this time. Or was it the lack of first names?

On the opposite side of Travers, Petty Officer Trigg Wyatt sat listening intently to the exchange between the Lieutenants. Halloran had asked for him despite his rank, acknowledging that Wyatt's engineering brilliance was sorely-needed right now.

On his left, Pyotr Antonov sat quietly, talking to no one. Halloran watched him out of the corner of his eye, thinking for a moment about the sturdy Russian Captain. The man had had the misfortune of choosing the last cruise of Halloran's old ship, the USS Bonhomme Richard, as the one he'd join as a passenger. True, the Bonny Rich had been the Navy's newest and most powerful ballistic missile submarine to date—back in 2029—but now it had been reduced to a rusting hulk in what remained of the Egyptian desert back on Earth. And Antonov had survived the brutal culling of the time-traveling crew by the Prax and crappy circumstances, ending up as Halloran's chosen Executive Officer aboard their commandeered Prax warship. The USS Serapis.

Next to the taciturn Russian sat Lieutenant Mark Hummel, who kept his eyes down and his thoughts to himself. Formerly the Bonhomme Richard's supply officer, Hummel had taken over broader duties aboard this new ship, beginning with watching over the engineering project underway by Wyatt and Travers. Halloran trusted the young, aspirational officer to keep order as was in his DNA.

Across from them, on Halloran's right, were two empty seats with one occupied strategically between them. Master Chief Petty Officer Abran Reyes returned Halloran's look and secret grin with a slight nod. Reyes had been handpicked by Halloran as the Chief of the Boat for Bonhomme Richard. The stocky, intense Cuban was his closest confidant and the unquestioned leader of the crew. Even the massive Axxa hesitated in the face of the Chief's wrath despite having nearly a meter in height advantage.

I'm so glad Abran had not gotten to that altercation before me, Halloran found himself thinking with humor. *He'd have beaten both of them into a pulp rather than negotiating with them.*

"Something funny, sir?"

Halloran came back and shook his head at Reyes. "I'll tell you later. I like where you're sitting."

"Our two lovebirds?"

Halloran caught himself staring. "How'd—." It had been less than fifteen minutes.

Reyes shrugged. "My job."

Moments later the door swung open and admitted Captain Kendra, who paused only for a moment to scan the room before pointing herself at one of the remaining seats next to Reyes.

Lastly, the Prax entered—most likely had timed it so he wouldn't be in the doorway at the same time as Kendra—and all eyes went to him. Despite his clearly humanoid appearance, the Prax were an imposing presence when in a confined space such as this. Axxa's skin was a dull rust-red and his hair dark charcoal in color, with bright, focused green-tinted eyeballs. His physique was impressive, and like all the other Prax Halloran had had the misfortune to encounter, he was pushing two and half meters in height. Still, the room had been constructed for his people and he fit in easily, sliding into the only open seat. Several of those around the table stared openly, clearly still less-than-comfortable with the alien's presence even after the weeks they'd spent in his presence.

Rather than take his own seat, Halloran paced up and down a few times, lost in thought and setting the mood somewhat. Finally, he stopped and placed a fist on the point of the Table. "Mark, Trigg, talk to me about engineering."

Hummel glanced at Wyatt before answering. "Well, sir, the main reactor appears to be functioning within normal parameters. Axxa here tells us that the jumpdrive is in working order."

"It is," the Prax commented, his language translated by the devices everyone wore at the base of their skull on the right rear. They hurt when implanted.

"We have full normal-space capability as well. For all intents and purposes, the engines themselves escaped any major damage in the battle." Hummel looked up at Halloran. "I just want all of us on the team to be thoroughly familiar with the equipment going into our next situation. No engines, no go…sir."

Halloran nodded. "Agreed." He looked at Travers pointedly. "Thank you, Lieutenant, for your assistance down there. I hear you're a whiz kid."

The young man noticeably flushed at the compliment delivered through his translator. The language spoken by all humans in this time was called 'Standard.' He nodded. "I...appreciate that, sir. You have excellent officers."

Halloran caught Reyes' amused look. *Buttering up the junior officers.*

He glanced down at Antonov. "XO, Chief, we've got damage issues."

Antonov nodded slowly. "Several large holes in the outer hull from the prior engagement that will need a dockyard, according to Captain Kendra." He nodded across the table at her. "Numerous system outages—we just don't know how to chase down the break points. Those projectiles passed clean through the ship in places, poking holes as small as twenty centimeters through eight or ten inner hull walls along with everything in those compartments. Nasty weapons," he ended with a frown.

Reyes spoke up. "Crew is working 'round the clock, as you know, sir. Rations are non-existent; I've got people poking around those systems, and it's a priority."

"Yes, yes it is, Chief. The Navy always has the chow." Halloran caught Kendra's puzzled look before continuing, sitting in the single remaining seat. "We have the ability to run and gun at the moment—if we need to. But, our damage and overtaxed crew necessitate corrective steps. Then there's the significant hull damage." He looked around at the group, catching each eye. "I'm open to suggestions."

Hummel spoke up. "I guess Pearl's out of the question. One drink at Wiki Waki Woo and I think I'd get my strength back."

Halloran shook his head. "Not helpful." Reyes grunted something that sounded like "officers" under his breath.

Kendra was looking at Travers. Halloran watched them communicate with their eyes before interrupting. "Do the Fleet officers have an idea?"

She faced him. "Tavar."

"Tavar."

"It's the planet where the material needed to create Tavarran steel was discovered. In the Struve system—I'd have to double-check the distance from our position but it would be the logical place to seek replacement Tavarran steel hull sections. Unfortunately, you can't mate Tavarran with Terran steel. Or Praxxan that I understand. In a hull at least."

Halloran nodded slowly. "Tavar."

She nodded at Axxa. "Although it's never been explained how a Prax ship is composed of Tavarran steel. That planet and system is crawling with Fleet protection."

Hummel leaned on the table, hands out in front of him. "And this place is the only source of the material?"

She folded her arms. "Well, you could fly up to a Fleet station and demand a refit, but I don't think that would go too well for you."

Hummel frowned at her. "We could hold our own."

Her snort set the atmosphere around the table on edge.

Halloran regained control. "So how is Tavar a better option? You say it's well-protected."

She caught his disapproving look as she glanced his way. "Um, well. The miners are an independent colony.

Very independent. I bet they'd be willing to trade with us privately if we could get to them."

Travers nodded when Halloran looked to him for corroboration. "I've heard this as well, Captain."

Trigg spoke. "That would mean using the jumpdrive." He sounded awestruck at the prospect.

Halloran pursed his lips as he looked around the table one more time. It felt good to have a wardroom talk—even if the tension between Kendra and Axxa could be cut by a knife, poisoning the goodwill that could be growing through comaraderie. He'd have to do something about that. For the first time, Halloran considered dropping Kendra somewhere rather than keeping her aboard. But there was nowhere.

The scans showed that they were outside the star system and heading on a general course toward Sol, but they needed to do something to fix the ship. And maybe these Tavarrans could help with repairing other components… "We will use the jumpdrive to proceed to Tavar and attempt to insert ourselves without detection, seeking to investigate the mining operation and make friendly contact without poking the hornet's nest in the process." He glanced at Carruthers. "Lieutenant Carruthers and I are working on understanding the Hidden Claw device and I plan to engage it the moment we arrive near Tavar. And we can all offer our congratulations on her promotion."

The chorus of well-wishes passed around the table until Travers piped up. "'Hidden Claw?'"

Carruthers shrugged. "We found its name in the schematics." She looked at Axxa somewhat timidly.

The alien's face didn't register any emotion. "A reference to one of the many birds of prey on our world."

After a few more moments Halloran said, "Dismissed, and thank you."

Chapter 4

Prax Homeworld
26.8 LY From Earth

The heat was intense this morning, the high season reaching its apex of the cycle. The guard booths stationed around the Center were recessed into cooled alcoves, out of the burning rays of the competing suns. Reddish dust rose in the air, swirling in clouds that seemed to take on a life of their own, twisting this way and that as if in anguish before dissipating and reforming. The Corpus troops who served as the honor guard for the Great City and Center of the Praxxan mission of Conquest were well-trained and more than smart enough to avoid activities that took them outside the facility unless a deployment was ordered. Which every now and then was done by a mid-level officer attempting to gain favor within the strict military system.

The guards at one booth in particular were currently standing aside, quietly watching the visitor to their station out of the corner of their eyes as they remained stiffly at attention.

The visitor's hand motioned for them to relax. "Please, you're making me nervous. I just like to watch the sun's rise. I'll be away shortly."

Ryax, the lead guard at this station, motioned for his group to disperse. As they drifted away, eyes still on their well-known guest, he moved closer instead. "You find the view from this station preferable, Lord?"

The Premier of the Praxxan Empire cast a side-wise look at the officer. "Don't you?" He returned his gaze to the red horizon, beyond the city, where the immense mountain range rose in the hazy pink sky. "So how is my old friend's youngest son?"

Ryax stood next to his ruler, unafraid. He knew that his men would understand. "I am well, Lord." After a moment he added the question. "What brings our Premier to my humble station this morning?"

The Premier chuckled. "I know that my wife prefers this location, and now I begin to understand her occasional diversions to visit her son's closest friend." He waved at the view through the window.

Ryax nodded. "And what of my friend Axxa?"

The Premier turned to the young man, sparing a look around at the soldiers in the room. Aside from Ryax's unit, he was alone. *Not wise for a Premier to move alone.* "He is, as usual, enmeshed in affairs beyond the scope of his ability."

"Sounds like my Axxa…Lord."

"I have my own challenges dealing with a new threat—from within."

Ryax stiffened. "It cannot be."

"It can and is. I am here to enlist you to my cause."

"Lord, you have my loyalty, unto death."

The Premier nodded understandingly. "I am sure of it. But a See'r has foreseen the exposure of a plan, a wide-ranging one, that threatens all of us. I would ask you to assist me in investigating this concern within the Center."

"Of course—."

The Premier raised a hand, stopping Ryax. "Slow, and sure. Do not raise awareness. Your ability to move within the system and justification for requesting information shall be your strength. I will clear away any remaining roadblocks to collecting data." He laid the hand on the officer's shoulder. "Axxa is presumed lost in the Sol system, Ryax."

The young man's intake of breath showed his regard for the Premier's son. "May it never be."

"I too, feel that way. There have been other developments there that buoy my hopes that he yet lives, however."

Ryax's eyes were serious. "Lord, whatever I can do."

The Premier nodded. "We shall talk later, after you have begun with your task. Any transactions, conversations recorded that might be of interest to me. You know how to proceed."

"Yes, Lord."

With a last look at the still-rising suns, The Praxxan ruler tapped Ryax on the shoulder and turned away, striding through the entrance and disappearing into the passage beyond.

One of Ryax's troops sidled up to the officer. "Commander, what did he want?" The soldier was clearly awestruck by the leader's presence.

Ryax looked at the Prax. "The same thing Lord Sar'yana always wants when she stops down here; a good look at the morning sun."

"Sir..."

Ryax waved a hand. "Back to your post. Excitement's over."

As the guard walked off shaking his head, Ryax took in the suns rising for himself. Beautiful. And dangerous for all caught in their heat. *Just like the High Family of Prax.*

The Premier could feel the eyes upon him as he entered the council chambers. Hundreds of representatives from the many Conquered Worlds were arriving daily, in advance of the Rite ceremony and the strategy meetings that accompanied it. Already there were many here, mostly Prax of the strong families who had a member who'd ascended to Prime in a conquered system. And their extensive retinues of servants and advisors.

As he advanced toward the Center Circle he stopped often to exchange pleasantries with those he knew well. During his tenure as Premier he had determined to win over coalitions of support from the Conquered Worlds using frank, open communications and ample military supply—a sharp departure from past Premiers who'd ruled through intimidation and assassination. Not that he hadn't strayed at times and ordered a disappearance or two…he had his own approach to assessing threats.

And the threats today were real.

A hidden force was whispering in the background, winning Lords over among the strong families and organizing a coup. He had become aware early on and long suspected Talxen of the Sol system as its root. Now, as he surveyed the immense, high-ceilinged chamber and the groups of those present, a chill of danger ran down his spine and cooled his naturally hot blood.

A large, intimidating Warrior-Lord was before him, bowing slightly. Too slightly. "Premier, it is good to see you again."

The Premier assented with a nod. "Haryx. I trust your long trip wasn't too arduous?"

Haryx flashed his teeth in what passed for a Prax grin. "The flight from Gliebe system took twice as long with our malfunctioning drive."

The Premier nodded gravely. The Praxxan jumpdrives were still inferior to the original human designs they had captured. "I am glad to see you here."

Haryx glanced around. "I stand with you."

This Lord was in his column yet, thought the Premier as he laid a hand on the Prax's shoulder and passed by. But many standing around and nodding as he passed were more likely to side with the coup; the ones who were older or more militaristic.

Not that he lacked prowess or courage when it came to affairs of the Conquest. He firmly adhered to the long-held mantra of "Conquer to thrive" that gripped the Praxxan psyche. An honored warrior from a long line of leaders on the battlefield, the Premier had cemented his status within their society many cycles ago. His two sons were, in their own right, lauded heroes of the Conquest.

It was his approach to governance within the society that angered many. Negotiation rather than domination by force, including Conquered Worlds into Prax culture, empowering the Primes to effect more open changes and avoid repression once a world was cleansed of opposition.

He reached his seat at the head of the Circle. This assembly would be a discussion of how to address the current shortages of supplies arising from the war with the humans.

As he settled into his seat, he wondered once again where Axxa was. He resented those females who held access to the Sight so closely, desiring the ability for himself to sense the movements of destiny and the figures caught up in it. He would inquire about Axxa, who he had come to realize was most likely a victim of assassination by that schemer Talxen on Earth.

Talxen came from a strong family, of course, and though he'd been part of the human war in the early days, he'd far from proven himself. But, upon his return to Prax he'd lobbied—successfully—for an appointment to Prime status based upon his military record. The Premier had had little choice, in the interests of keeping peace with Talxen's family, than to capitulate. An unfortunate sign of weakness. He'd attempted to mitigate things by giving Talxen the Sol system as his jurisdiction, in the hope that the active conflict with the humans there would give Talxen opportunities to shine.

The head of Talxen's family, Terxan, sat across from the Premier at that moment. Their eyes locked across the space, but no nods were exchanged. Old rivals, Terxan and the Premier shared no love either.

The Sol system was a problem, and the humans were far more tenacious than the Prax had originally planned for when launching the Earth invasion. The human space fleet was powerful even as the Prax secured the human homeworld and began eliminating pockets of resistance around the star system. Talxen had failed to score a conclusive victory over the human force, despite the leadership of the Premier's old friend Xylan at the head of their fleet in-system. And now, Axxa was gone. The Premier knew that Talxen and his family was weaving a web around him. But how far had it progressed?

Sar'yana. He would go to her afterwards, probing her further about the visions she'd been experiencing recently. Something about a new presence, a force within the Sight that had interacted with Axxa in some way. Perhaps an assassin? His consort was wise far beyond her years, but the Premier gave her too little credence in his quest to rule.

The page stood, looking slowly and officiously around the seated council members, eyes resting lastly on the Premier. "We have the required number to begin, Lord."

The Premier nodded his assent.

As the young Prax—who was a rising member of his family—opened the morning's meeting, the Premier remembered his early days in these very chambers, seeking to build his own coalition. Many were seated here today, but many—too many—were gone now, lost to battle and disease.

Fools fail to calculate the cost. He had faithfully adhered to the time-worn Praxxan maxim and calculated everything for so many cycles that he'd grown accustomed to seeing plots in every deferential answer, finding double and triple meanings in every seemingly careless word spoken. But was he uselessly fighting a destiny that he could not escape? *These are the thoughts of an old fool,* he told himself as he watched Terxan confer with an advisor over his shoulder. But still, he couldn't shake the growing sense of foreboding.

The blazing sun had no effect within the High Family residence where Sar'yana sat behind a thick wall of transparent material, gazing out across the valley and Great City below. But her eyes didn't truly see the vista before her, and her hand held the section of food she'd cut away long ago, now forgotten in mid-lift as the Sight had taken her.

Instead, her glazed-over eyes saw shapes, colors, faces, lives intertwined, blackness replaced by a blinding light and then darkness returning, voices both near and distant. The panoply of civilizations seemed to parade before her mind in a balance between madness and incredible clarity.

She felt the presence of many humans, forcing their way into her vision. Distorted faces, anger...rage. Disgusting. And many more of her own race, the Prax matching the humans in hate and anger. War. This was nothing she hadn't seen for as long as she could remember in the Sight; the conflict with the humans had been ongoing since her youngest years. The Sight sucked her in without notice, as if it had a will of its own. Which it did. Trying to show her something.

Sar'yana stilled her racing thoughts to focus on the visions, to isolate events or individuals that seemed important. The cacophony of action crystallized into the face of a human, seemingly in the act of bending over her, concern written on his face. She recognized the name Thomas once again—this human was a recent addition to the parade of human faces and one she'd recently seen in the company with their son, Axxa. Sar'yana leaned closer in her mind, trying to talk but knowing it wasn't real, but a phantasm of this human. She repeated her entreaty over and over to the wavering face, trying to capture the moment. Then, as he leaned even closer and his pale face filled her view, she felt a shock of recognition at the face reflected in the human's glistening eyes.

Sar'yana blinked. Exhaled. Her hand registered the weight of something in it, and she looked down, feeling as though she'd just woken from a deep sleep. The food was in her hand, held there throughout the whole reverie. With a sigh, she set it down and placed her hands in her lap, trying to remember the details of the vision as they had been placed before her by the Sight. Over the cycles since discovering her gift she had become adept at making some sense of the images and twisted sounds. Her skill, in fact, surpassed that of any of the other Praxxan females who were of the See'r order.

She stood and stretched after a time, attempting to feel the life within her flow back into her aging bones. After that she placed a hand on the thick, clear wall and watched the Great City bustle below her, seeing the Center in its midst and wondering what was happening down there. Her mind was now scorched with the memory of what she'd seen in the Sight, her concern slowly building. She must speak with her husband soon.

Chapter 5

USS Serapis

Petty Officer Gerry Wilson was in quiet conversation with Chief Reyes and Yeoman Christina Butler as Halloran walked up the passage. When he arrived, Reyes nodded as Butler and Wilson saluted. "Morning, sir," said the Chief of the Boat.

"Morning. Where are we with things?"

Yeoman Butler said, "I've got the crew organized into decent sections: Electrical, Engineering, Life Support, Ops, Weapons and Security. Plus Whitney as Corpsman and Richards as Mess under ops of course."

"Is Mess a thing yet?"

Reyes shook his head grimly. "Not yet, sir. Still can't find the cause of the processor failure."

When Halloran didn't reply, Wilson said, "Weapons I've got PO Flagler leading; she's crawling all over the equipment with DeBartelo and Cochran. When the time comes to fire, I think they'll be ready. But...three crew plus me isn't much to cover the size of this ship, and thirty weapons stations that could fail or be hit, needing repair in a fight."

Halloran nodded. "Well, we're sitting at least thirty percent of the full crew complement, based on my translation of the Prax documents Axxa and I looked over. It'll have to do."

Reyes said, "I gave them a brief of your proposed plan, sir."

"I'm heading to Engineering now to talk to them directly about it."

Reyes slitted his eyes. "Sir, if you can get Bruce Brown to one side, pump him up a bit. He's been moping about his brother."

Chief Scott Brown, Bruce's older brother, was one of the 12 men left behind on Earth when they—namely Halloran—had to choose to save weight on their escape shuttle. "I think about them every time I wake up, Chief. We could use them right about now, in fact."

"You'll get them back, sir," Reyes offered helpfully.

"Want me to come along to Engineering?" asked Wilson. "I can talk to Brown, too. We go back in the boats, his brother and me."

"Sure. Thanks, Wilson."

As the two walked to the lift, Wilson asked, "What do you think about Captain Kendra, sir?"

"Meaning?"

"She's angry. Like dangerous angry."

Halloran enjoyed Wilson's frank assessment of people. With a chuckle, he said, "Kendra is an Admiral's daughter."

Wilson cocked an eyebrow at his Captain. "Oh, yeah, sir?"

"She likes to be in the action, you see." Halloran tapped the lift button to summon the car. "Our kidnapping her is just slowing down the process of her getting back into the war."

"We kidnapped her?"

"Well, sort of. I think she was already in trouble with somebody back there." He waved Wilson into the lift ahead of him, following after. "For now, she's content to be heading in the right direction, I think."

"She's not acting content about much around the crew, sir. You heard about the dust-up with the alien?"

Halloran nodded. "I did."

"The two of them hate each other."

Halloran looked hard at Wilson. "Don't forget, Gerry. In this time, humans have been crushed by the Prax and anyone alive now is going to hate—I mean really hate—them. I'm surprised she or Travers haven't tried to grab a gun and just shoot Axxa yet."

"Um, understood, sir."

Halloran poked the man's shoulder. "That's *your* job. Keep the guns locked up and an eye on everyone aboard…for our safety."

The door opened on C deck.

"After you, sir."

After walking through the plan to jump to the Struve System with the Engineering section and encouraging them to keep the ship running, Halloran met Gail Carruthers and Sonar Tech Chapan in a corner of C deck. "Who's at your station?" he asked the two.

"Malone, sir," answered Carruthers.

Halloran nodded, pointing at the bank of equipment that was before them. "This it?"

Chapan began running his hands over the various readouts and tapping things for emphasis. "This is definitely the main control panel for the Hidden Claw system. You can see here that it's drawing power direct from the reactor. Doesn't appear to be tied to the ion drive, but only the jumpdrive." He grinned at Halloran. "It's ingenious, according to Mr. Travers. It actually routes the light around us rather than moving us through it."

Halloran thought a moment. "But the sensors? The Fleet ship that was shooting at us lost sensor contact with us when you turned that thing on. Otherwise they could've kept firing in the blind."

"The bubble the Hidden Claw creates works like a reflector. Signals of all sorts bounce off of it. Bend around it." He looked apologetic. "We're still figuring it out, sir."

"But we can see out?"

"Yes, sir. It radiates outward somehow. Travers seemed to grasp the physics better than I." Carruthers grinned. "I'm used to salt water, sir."

"I get it." He fixed her with a stare. "Are your people ready to operate this device and the other comm equipment and sensors in a combat situation?"

The new officer sighed. "I've been working on the language with Mr. Axxa, sir. I think I'm getting better at reading the prompts in the system when I boot it up." She looked at Halloran. "You know, we're lucky that it was already booted up when I hit the engage button for it during the battle. Someone had kindly left it set up for us."

"Just make sure you're more in control of the situations and outcomes next battle, Lieutenant."

She straightened at the mention of her rank. "We'll make it happen when you need it, sir."

On his way back to the bridge, Halloran paused by his favorite window at the rear extreme of A deck. It was a quiet spot, and the stars twinkled in the black expanse beyond the transparent material of unknown origin.

He placed his hands on the material, feeling the cool of its surface on his palms. Closing his eyes, he tried to clear his mind and relax it.

So many details. So much left unknown. He needed three more of him to grasp all of the advanced concepts and inscrutable technology that made up a spaceship—and an alien one at that. They had gotten so lucky in their first, harried engagement with the enemy; the element of surprise had carried the day rather than their tactical prowess. Now the ship was holed, compartments vented to space, and important repairs undone. Yes, the crew had rallied to their new ship well, setting aside concerns for loved ones and focusing on the tasks assigned to them. But that was what Navy did. It didn't make the heart ache any less.

He thought of his kids. Where would they have gone in life? What had been said about his—his ship's—disappearance? He would assume that, after a lengthy investigation, the DoD would've listed them as lost at sea. *On eternal patrol.*

Halloran exhaled slowly, feeling the tightness in his chest and realizing that he was carrying too much on his shoulders. *I need to give these people a boat they can believe in. And get back to my crew left on Earth. The ones I abandoned... Then we can decide our own destiny, be it going back to 2029 or staying here. But staying alive and defensible are my top priorities.*

He forced his feet to take him forward up the passage. Passing the bridge, he glanced in. Djembe, the human smuggler who was now their pilot, was showing the Deacon how to operate something. The two seemed to get along, which Halloran appreciated. Deacon had seemed perpetually out of sorts since leaving Earth.

The young man with the hard eyes had never been off the planet and the time in space hadn't worn well on him. Halloran understood that the guy had been a smuggler and spy on Earth, two unsavory enterprises but necessary for survival on their grim homeworld. Deacon needed something constructive to focus on.

Antonov sat in the Command station, watching the pair himself. Sonar Technician Yusef Malone manned the comm station and was studying a screen in front of him. All seemed quiet enough. Halloran made the decision to keep walking and continued on to his cabin, thinking that a short nap would do him good.

The last thing he remembered as he hit the pillow was thinking how big the Prax Captain's bed was.

Twenty minutes later he sat bolt upright on the still-made bed, groggy and mind racing.

He'd dreamed of a series of tall ridges that seemed to go on into the hazy distance. Every time he crested a rise, the destination seemed just as far away. They reminded him of the hills in Central Pennsylvania where he'd grown up.

There'd been Cindy. His wife had urged him on, declining to follow him while she cradled their infant child in her arms. Him, begging her to accompany him…but her turning away. His grown kids, Tom Jr. And Laura, waving at him from the nearest hilltop only to vanish as he arrived, panting.

And a woman, watching him as he toiled but not aiding him. She was dressed strangely and he couldn't make out her face, only seeing her height as she towered over him in flowing robes. He'd seen her before, in other dreams.

But what had woken him was when the hills turned blood-red and sky burned like fire, and the specter of a Prax—it had to be one of them—lying bleeding on the ground before Halloran. Bending over and frowning, assessing his wounds but not seeing sources for the blood everywhere, staining the dust in an expanding circle that encompassed Halloran's boots. Then the Prax's head rolls to one side, being cleanly severed by a lance of some sort embedding into it...

Halloran pulled up a corner of fabric and mopped his brow, shivering. *Am I losing it?* The dreams had started when they jumped into this time about a month prior, but this one had been the most violent and stressful yet.

The loud "alarm" sound that reverberated the hull walls shocked him back to reality and he leapt for cabin door, straightening his uniform as he did. He immediately noticed how close it sounded to the "general quarters" onboard ship back in 2029.

As he pounded down the short passage to the bridge, a voice came over hidden speakers along the way. "Captain to the bridge. Captain to the bridge."

With a snort, Halloran calmed himself as he stepped onto the bridge. "What's the meaning of this?" He walked directly to the pilot station where Djembe sat, looking up in sudden indecision at the clearly-annoyed Captain.

"Captain on the bridge!" called Malone.

The pilot half-smiled and lifted an eyebrow. "We figured out the shipwide announcement system. And the battle stations siren. Ummm."

Halloran stood glowering down at him. "I suppose I should be thrilled, Pilot?"

A chuckle sounded behind Halloran. "Told you he wouldn't like it."

Halloran spun on Antonov. "That created an unnecessary distraction from work that needs to be done," he said firmly with fist clenched at his side.

The Russian looked him up and down, slowly and deliberately, pausing his gaze on the Captain's fists. Then he looked up. "Can we speak privately for a moment? Mr Malone, you have the conn."

"Aye, sir."

Halloran felt the anger drain out of him, realizing he'd overplayed the moment. As he followed Antonov across the bridge he half-turned to Djembe. "Good job figuring out the intercom."

The pilot nodded gravely as he turned back to his work.

"Captain leaving the bridge!"

In the passage outside, Halloran held up a hand immediately. "I know."

Antonov leaned against the bulkhead. "In my Navy we have a man—usually a senior enlisted officer—aboard ship whose assignment is to watch the Captain and Executive Officer. But mostly the Captain." He raised his eyebrows at Halloran. "His job is to tell them when he thinks they are pushing themselves too hard, getting close to making bad decisions that would affect the crew, the ship."

"Interesting." Halloran could figure where this was going. "I have Reyes, to be honest."

"An excellent choice for Senior Chief. But, he is overtaxed by his current assignments, as are all the others at this time."

"Okay. Look, Pyotr, I appreciate—."

"I will be your man, Captain." He glanced down. "You need a fresh uniform and a nap…but not in that order, yes?"

Halloran stretched. "I tried a nap. Didn't work out too well."

"What is the problem?"

"I have…nightmares."

Antonov looked sympathetic. "About your family?" Halloran's wife and infant child were killed in a car crash just months before the day they were abducted. *Hundreds of years ago now,* Halloran reminded himself. It was all so weird. "No. Yes. Maybe." He smiled faintly. "Maybe I just haven't given it enough of a try. There's so much to understand about this time we are in, this ship." Halloran waved a hand at the passage around them. "I have this sense of dread that the situation is going to disintegrate before we're ready."

The Russian shook his head and crossed his arms, still leaning against the conduits set into the wall. "We will never be ready, Captain. This is too much for our people, and we must recognize that. You wish to have a ship of your own back, but this vessel does not belong to either the US or Russian Navy. Or even the twenty-first century." He smiled tightly. "All we can do is our duty to each other now."

He was right. Despite Halloran's burning desire to restore normality, it would never return for them. *At least in this century.* And whether they could ever return to theirs was still an unknown.

Halloran exhaled, rubbing his temples furiously. "Okay, okay. I'll try some more sleep. Then we plan the jump to this system with the metal we need."

Antonov's smile morphed into a small grin. "This is already plotted. Djembe is a very good pilot, sir."

Halloran took the good-natured rebuke on the chin. "To bed with me, then."

He was halfway back to his cabin when he had a thought, turning and walking backward a moment to see Antonov. "Who's assigned to watch the Executive Officer?"

The Russian paused with his hands on the bridge entrance rim and looked in his direction. "No one…yet." Then he was gone.

Chapter 6

Kendra sat in the corner of the officer's wardroom, arms crossed tightly and reveling in the solitude of the empty space. Like a steel coffin…knowing that the prior crew had been decimated by some unknown disease had given Kendra some uneasy moments when pondering their fate in the few weeks since she'd ended up aboard.

The ship was mid-sized, perhaps frigate-class in the Prax fleet. Not a design configuration that she immediately recognized, though. For a ship this small it packed a significant weapons punch, more than she'd ever heard of in the alien warship roster. The advanced jumpdrive and sensor-masking device made it a formidable tool in the hands of…Tomalloran. No, the man's name was two words—very odd—Thomas. Halloran. Like the rest of these odd military people from some other time. Two names.

Kendra frowned at the idea.

The man Halloran was hard to read; intense and stubborn one moment, then relaxed and thoughtful the next. For a human he was very tall, almost able to talk eye-to-eye with the Prax aboard. He had a cloud of mystery about him even though seeming completely approachable. Slightly graying brown moppy hair that had grown unkempt for a senior officer. But those eyes. She could get sucked into them…golden blue with a twinkle deep within their depths that seemed to be laughing at you—good naturedly. The man could command the respect of a crew; that much was true.

Kendra closed her own eyes. Travers and her had unwittingly hitched a ride with this crew following their abortive attempt to negotiate with Halloran under the direction of Captain Heres of the Valor. Heres—her old crewmate and rival—had basically sent Kendra on a suicide mission, rather than one of his own crew members. Then their shuttle had crash-landed aboard this ship as a surprise attack on the Agra colony had commenced, both her and Travers barely escaping becoming casualties themselves.

Then the most perplexing thing of all had happened; the moment the human ships had defeated the Prax, Heres had opened fire on this ship, knowing that not only was it crewed by humans—even if their loyalty was in question—and that two Fleet officers were potentially aboard. At the very least, he should have opened communications with Halloran to arrange a truce to continue the negotiation. But he'd apologized, veered off and fired a broadside instead.

Something was wrong. Within the Fleet. She didn't know what, but that hadn't been protocol for a ship's Captain—Heres had been acting on orders that made no sense.

Happily, one of Halloran's crew had unwittingly activated the sensor-masking device and they'd managed to get away from the larger Fleet cruiser without further damage. Now she found herself confined in a ship that wasn't hers, was commanded by little more than a rogue, and for good measure housed a Prax! Kendra felt the urge to vomit at the idea. And, to add more misery to the situation, they needed to go to the Struve system.

She felt the memories coursing through her brain yet again at the name…*Struve Six.* The tearing of metal. Bodies—pieces of them floating on the shattered bridge of the Goliath. The silence of lonely death, more deafening within her soul as all the violence of the action had been. Her resolve to not be among the dead…

Kendra's eyes popped open, and she wiped her hair back from her face where a slight sheen of perspiration had started. She *hated* the Struve system.

With a sigh and a dabbed tear from her cheek she realized that she had to be a part of this crew of humans who claimed to be from another time. Wherever they really came from, they were human and working hard to learn this ship and keep themselves alive. Travers had certainly seemed to integrate into their family well enough…*but he loves his engines,* she reminded herself. *It's a universal language among that group.* Kendra herself knew as much about modern engine systems as almost any engineer in the Fleet; it was what she came up in. Something had changed within her, she realized. Since the loss of her last ship in action in the Sol system, and her unfortunate decision to go to Engineering rather than stay on her bridge, she'd resolved to stay the course consistent with her rank. There was no going back.

Father would certainly love to hear about my new professional commitment, she smiled to herself. Admiral Kendall commanded the Sol system defenses and found Kendra a source of frustration. Not so his other daughter, Kaela, who stood in the literal center of the intelligence group on Mars and ran the Fleet's brain, so to speak. Their father had always looked favorably upon her older sister. That had become more obvious after Kendra took her path into the Merchant Arm, preferring immediate space duty to wiping desks in some fancy station for tottering old officers who should've retired to Coloran long ago. It had only been a freak accident of being in the wrong place at the wrong time—at Struve Six—that had bumped Kendra into the "real" Fleet and ultimately the Captain's chair.

And now, she was a hanger-on in a motley crew on a ship provided by Haulers, no less.

Kendra found herself chuckling at the idea.

"What's so funny?"

Startled, she looked up to see one of the junior officers staring down at her.

After a moment, he turned away. "Whatever. Ma'am."

"I had the funny vision of your—our—Captain as a Hauler."

The man stretched out on a low padded bench along the far bulkhead of the wardroom. "Like those nasty types we got the ship from? Doubt he'd appreciate that. But, you never know."

He tapped the base of his head. "These translation devices are pretty cool." She regarded the prostrate form. "You serve with him long?"

The man put his hands behind his head, staring up at the ceiling. "The Bonhomme Richard was my first assignment with him. But I knew who he was, of course."

"Of course?"

He lifted his head to look briefly at her. "We all know the Captains in the service."

"What service was that again?"

He put his head back. "Boomers, we call 'em. Ballistic missile subs. Only twenty-eight."

"That's not much of a fleet."

He snorted. "Each of us carried enough firepower to wipe out half a continent. There are only…" he thought a moment, "Seven continents, including our own of course."

"On Earth."

His eyes flicked her way again. "On Earth. That sounds so weird."

"And this ship of yours, it's on Earth now?"

"Yep. High and dry with holes cut into her."

"'Her?'"

"Yes, we use that pronoun for ships."

Kendra tightened her crossed arms a bit. "Hmmph."

"What's your deal?" The man asked. When she didn't answer, he looked at her again. "Why are you…like *that*.?All the time?" He used his eyes to indicate her body posture.

"You wouldn't understand. I'm not where I planned to be."

He sat up slowly, never taking his eyes off her and resting his hands on the bench in front of him. "Ma'am, I have a wife and three kids. Fifteen, fourteen and nine." He tapped the bench with one hand. "I haven't seen them in two months,and have no idea if I will ever see them again. I might as well be dead right now," his voice cracked a bit, "but I'm not. So guess what, ma'am? This place? It's basically hell for me…for all of us. We never died back in 2029, we just disappeared." He made a gesture with his hands, spreading fingers quickly apart. Then he lay back. "So yeah, I get it."

She just watched the man, thinking, for a few long moments. Then, "I'm Captain Kendra, by the way."

"Is that your first name or last name, Kendra?" He didn't look at her.

"Um, neither. We don't use whatever name you're referencing.

"The man sighed. "Well, I'm Lieutenant Mark Hummel."

"I'm sorry about your family, Lieutenant."

"Me too, ma'am. Me too."

The command station in the center of the bridge was composed of a seat built into a low bank of display monitors, many of which repeated the view of the crew stations in front and to the sides of the command perch. One of the screens ran through a series of camera views that covered the main compartments and passageways; by toggling a small button below the screen, Halloran could scan back and forth through the feed order, stopping on any given feed in order to focus on it. It was pretty intuitive, which he appreciated.

He thought again about the alien Captain, Traxxus. The guy had clearly been on a war mission against humanity so Halloran wasn't broken up that he'd been destroyed. And, the death of the Prax crew at the hands of the unknown illness had seemed so clean and quick that Traxxus had probably gotten off easy. *But the Captain of this ship would've rather gone out in battle, making a difference,* Halloran thought. *Easy isn't the way of the warrior.* Now he had the opportunity to leverage this warship against the very enemy who had created it. Halloran was under no misconceptions; whatever would happen next wouldn't be easy. People were going to die. If there was one thing he'd learned since leaving Earth, it was that life and death in the vacuum of space were balanced much more finely even than life and death in the waters of his home planet.

Time to give the order.

"Pilot, ready in all respects?"

Djembe nodded. "Jumpdrive is available at your command, Captain. Coordinates set as discussed, for the outer edge of the Struve system."

"XO, anything I'm forgetting about?" He spared Antonov a glance.

The Russian was sitting in one of the work tation seats, with Kendra next to him and looking pensive. Antonov checked a panel in front of him. "All compartments report to be as ready as they can make them." He punctuated the remark with a shrug which succinctly communicated the rest of his emotions.

Halloran turned back to Carruthers. "Hidden Claw prepared to engage should we meet undesirables upon re-entry into space there?"

"I've got my hand hovering over the red button, sir." He could hear her forced levity mixed with strain.

He sighed to himself. "Time to get this ball rolling. Engage the jumpdrive, pilot."

"Engaging."

Trigg Wyatt was anchored at the main control for the jumpdrive, waiting for the order to engage it. Seated next to him was the new officer, Travers. Wyatt liked the young and nerdy man, easily finding his groove alongside the other as he systematically worked through the foreign—alien—engine systems and cataloged them. Wyatt had been initially completely out of his depth, but made up for it through raw enthusiasm to finally have machines of his own to work on again.

Poor Bonny Rich, he thought as he glanced around the Engineering space once again. He missed his ship. Everything's so…weird. His eyes met those of the alien seated against the far bulkhead, whose reddish face revealed no anxiety over the impending engine run. *Old hat,* Wyatt mused. The thing was certainly not forthcoming with its emotions, even when that freaky confrontation between him and the woman officer happened right here in this compartment. They'd almost shot each other before the Skipper broke it up.

Travers chuckled next to him. "You worried about him?"

Wyatt saw him flick his eyes toward the red form. "Nope. I've seen enough crazy stuff in the last month to fill two horror movies."

"What's a 'movie'?"

Wyatt lifted an eyebrow. "A…movie. I don't know, it's a story told on a screen by actors. I like the classics. Top Gun, Hunt For Red October." He elbowed Travers. "Great sub movie."

"Sub, like as in your last ship? You explained about the water."

"Yeah. Our Navy was powerful. Is powerful." Wyatt frowned. "Whatever."

"But the 'sub' could only travel within the water. How limiting."

Wyatt shook his head. "No way, man. The ocean is a true, living thing. A thrill to be immersed in."

Travers looked at him. "It is alive? Sentient?"

"No…sort of. The ocean has a heart…a mind of its own. It could never be tamed. Centuries of manmade travel and nope, never tamed." He warmed to his topic. "See, our boat—the Bonhomme Richard—it was the absolute greatest oceangoing vessel of all time. Could travel faster at a greater depth than anything ever made by man before. Not counting the bathyspheres that charted the ocean bottom, of course."

Travers was trying to keep up. "Bathees—what?"

"Bathyspheres. They were basically hollowed-out bowling balls with two-foot thick hulls that could touch down in the deepest corners of any ocean. Really cool stuff. But they just basically went straight down and back up, on a cable mostly. Now us, we could burn through the water with our nuclear engines and hit nearly a thousand meters if needed."

Travers seemed dubious. That doesn't sound like much. A thousand meters is not a large distance…"

Wyatt waved him off. "I get it. But the water pressure, see, it is *intense*. Like nothing you've used to in space, where you have the opposite problem."

"So your ship had a thick exo-hull."

"Yep, we call it a 'pressure hull.' Crazy strong."

Travers sat back, crossing his arms. "You love this ocean." It was a statement, not a question.

Wyatt blew out an exhalation. "Yep. I surfed it from as young as I can remember. Dove in it. Surfing, now that's something I'm going to miss."

"What is this, a sport or recreation?"

Wyatt snapped his fingers at Travers. "Exactly!"

Electronics Technician Jack Stacey poked his head around a nearby partition of instruments. His duty station had been set at the main relays adjoining the reactor space. "What are you two going on about out there?" His voice was tight and his face pinched with stress.

Wyatt outranked Stacey but ignored the man's outburst. "Educating this fine young officer as to the merits of Salt Life."

Stacey look from one of them to the other, clearly unsure what to respond. Then he glanced over at Axxa and back to them. He shrugged. "I'm all for reminiscing, but the Captain should be calling for power any moment now."

Wyatt waved at him. "You get back there, Jack. I'll take care of Mr. Travers here while we wait." His sandy hair, grown long in the past month, fell between his eyes and he flicked it away as Stacey disappeared with a grunt. "Now where was I?"

Their moment was broken by the short, shrill tone of an incoming command from the bridge. Travers leaned in and tensed. "They're calling up the jumpdrive." Now, even his voice had a bit of an edge to it. "Command successfully relayed. The reactor AI is handling the request. Drive powering up."

Wyatt rubbed his hands gleefully, smiling widely at the alien. "Here we go, buddy!"

Chapter 7

Mars Command

"I want a full workup as soon as it can dropped on my desk, Commander!" Admiral Kendall stormed from the adjutant's office, annoyed that the soft-closing entrance door couldn't be slammed. He wanted to vent his frustration. Even if most of that annoyance would ultimately fall upon the shoulders of his daughter.

The intelligence group had botched the job of recording the apparently massive nuclear blast on the Earth's surface. Several of the clandestine Earth-monitoring sensors installed on the Moon had been active and trained properly on the human homeworld, but mysteriously failed to track the moment of the explosion in the western hemisphere…not to mention several critical time segments immediately afterward, as the event faded.

He barged into his own office atrium, startling his assistant Satra as he marched past, entering his own space and proceeding straight to his desk. As the entrance door softly closed he dropped into his chair and leaned back, rubbing his temples.

Something was wrong. The explosion was the first of its kind in decades, and no military action was ongoing on the planet surface to warrant an attack. So it was a test.

He stared at the overhead. Of course it was a test. That Captain Halloran had tried to warn him. The ancient weapons somehow brought back from the past. It was all incredible.

The flotilla sentry ships had all immediately reported the immense vapor cloud rising into the Earth's upper atmosphere following the magnetic pulse. All cursory indications had confirmed that the explosion was the largest magnitude in recorded history. That history only reached back just over four hundred years. Kendall had no way of knowing what this blast represented in comparison to old-Earth weaponry. Either way, it represented a clear and present danger to the Fleet around Mars.

He stared at the tablet in the center of his workstation, its notification icon silently blinking yellow to register unfinished files.

Intelligence. The adjutant had been sent to find out exactly why the moon-based sensors, sophisticated monitoring pieces the size of a small shuttle and mounted discreetly away from the annihilated colony facilities, had failed to operate without warning. Had they been sabotaged by the Prax? After the invasion, the aliens had summarily launched missiles at the Earth satellite that blasted the research facilities and garrison quarters. This was in the early days, when the Fleet had been ill-prepared and far-flung in humanity's quest to conquer the star routes. Then the close-quarters bombardments and execution of anyone surrendering. By the time the first flotilla arrived in force and retook the Moon, there was nothing—nobody—left to save. The area was abandoned and Mars became the rallying point for the gathering warships. For all the years following, however, the sensors had faithfully recorded the Prax ship movements above the Earth.

He pushed the tablet away in disgust, then on a second thought pulled it back and picked it up. "Open file Halloran."

The device showed a file photo, clearly ancient in nature and complete with evident scratches indicating a scan from another, physical medium. He studied the man's lean, intense features. The photo was him in uniform of an old Earth military, light-colored shirt with breast decorations that meant nothing to Kendall. Halloran's cap rode high on his forehead, indicating a slight disregard for dress. He smirked. Some things really never did change... The photo was undated, but the file notes at the bottom had a caption. "Halloran, Thomas Captain USN. Lost at sea old Earth dating 2029-08-21. Image coded date 339.09.09.50, recovered from Telos Archive."

Kendall snorted. "Telos Archive." He tossed the tablet onto the desk and stood up. 339 was almost fifty years before he'd been born on Coloran. So the man Halloran seemed to be telling some truth; no one lived that long, even if the photo had been faked back at that time.

He stepped to his favorite spot in front of the clearsteel window facing the red vista of Mars. So Halloran had slipped through the capable fingers of none other than Captain Heres and the Valor, a top-of-the-line warcruiser. Either this mythical man was incredibly good or incredibly blessed... The Admiral's jaw stiffened in memory of his daughter. Kendra. Missing in action, presumed dead, even by her own sister. But he had his doubts. Something like a father's intuition. But where was she? He hardly dared to hope that she'd ended up with this Halloran fellow.

His door chime sounded. "Enter."

"You wanted to see me, sir?"

He turned to face his daughter. "No, not really."

Her already-pale face lightened somewhat. "I came anyway. You ordered a review of my department—."

He held up a hand to silence her as he returned to his desk. Once seated he looked up, seeing Kaela through tired eyes. "I need to understand why this miraculous error took place at the exact time needed to fail us in monitoring the planetside explosion."

Kaela began to protest but his hand went up again. "Commander, you and I both know that an egregious mistake in either the tech or the monitoring thereof occurred. This matter is closed for discussion until my adjutant completes his investigation. His eyes narrowed. "For the record, I'm disappointed with this turn of events." His eye said the rest. *You've failed me.*

Knowing better to respond, she moved to the window and faced away from him. "Father, you grieve over Kendra."

"Your point?"

She turned to him. "May I speak freely?"

"You may."

"You are blaming me for her death. May I remind you that *you* ordered her onto that shuttle to Coloran, not me?"

"I fail to see your point."

She smoothed her uniform and clasped her hands behind her back, looking over his right shoulder. "I would prefer to be treated as a Fleet officer on my own merits, not as a scapegoat for your grief."

His eyes were hard. This was not a view of Kaela that he enjoyed. Part of him wanted to reprimand her;

the other desired to go to her and hold her close. He had always chosen the former—all her career—in an effort to toughen her up for command. *Perhaps I have neglected her. Both of them.* He noticed something else, too; her stance, her defiance, it lacked the accustomed deference that she always showed him as a senior officer.

Something was wrong.

Finally, he spoke. "The matter at hand is far more important to the safety of our people than your or my pain of loss. There are clear initial indications that your department failed in its duty—and this is *not* my *personal* assessment." He glanced at the tablet on his desk, then back up to her. She was still rigid, not meeting his eyes. "Commander, thank you for coming. My advice to you is to get your house in order, ASAP. There *will* be scrutiny. And," he added, "get a crew out to the Moon to check those sensor arrays and find out what happened."

After a moment she saluted. "Yes, sir. Am I dismissed?"

Kendall sat back in his chair, suddenly feeling his age. "Yes, Commander."

She had her hand on the latch when his voice stopped her. "Kaela."

She dropped her head and listened without turning. "Yes, Admiral?"

"Get Kendra out of your head. Wherever she is, dead or alive, we can't help her. We've got to help ourselves now."

When she was gone he leaned forward and steepled his fingers, elbows on the desk and thinking. After a minute or so he pinged Satra in.

"Sir?" She asked from the door.

He waved her in and motioned for her to shut the door. It closed softly behind her as he waited for it to seal. Then he crossed his arms on the desk and said, "Use my authorization to inquire into Commander Kaela's most recent med evals."

Her eyebrows went up fractionally. "What am I looking for?"

He pursed his lips. "Any signs of stressors or aberrant readings—even if the medical tech noted it as within tolerances."

Satra made a note. He knew she'd keep everything out of the record that directly pertained to his family. She'd done a whole lot more than this in helping Kendra avoid the brig over the years. "Anything else?"

"I want you to use your connections in intelligence to ask around. Probe for unusual conversations, issues with decorum or security that stand out. You know everybody on this red ball."

Satra nodded. "I'll see what I can find out, sir."

Alone again, he wondered what he was missing. He didn't have much time, though; his comm channel buzzed with an incoming call from Commander Tarsa of the flotilla. "Tarsa," Kendall answered. "Your analysis?"

His most loyal man's voice was tight. "My analysis, Kendall, is that your intelligence group botched the job."

"Tarsa—."

"Anyway," Tarsa continued, "The picket ships got a half-decent scan of the atmosphere at least. The weapon obliterated a two-hundred kilometer section of the western ocean. Untold billions of tons of water evaporated into the atmosphere. The techs say the blast wave and water wall probably devastated the island nations."

"Any estimate of the power factor? Its been a long time since we dealt with nukes."

He could hear Tarsa on the line, breathing. "Kendall, it's much more than a nuclear weapon. It literally scorched the planet with its power. If the Prax have more of these, we need to radically alter our plans for Mars defense. If just one got through to you…"

Kendall was truly feeling his age now. "Agreed, Commander. Set your flotilla on high alert. Get your top people back for a conference in my office."

"And Kendall."

"Yes."

"You've got a problem closer to you."

"I know. I'm taking steps."

"Remember, we're *all* your responsibility."

Kendall knew what his old friend was saying without saying it. "Just get back and let's regroup."

"Tarsa out."

Kendall put his head in his hands, wishing his wife were there to talk with him. But she was far off in the Tau Ceti system and he was here, trying to reclaim the Sol system before it was lost to the Prax invaders. On his own.

He stood and walked around his desk a few times, thinking. If the Prax had indeed reclaimed ancient United States weaponry, there would be better data available *somewhere* in the galaxy about it.

Telos Archive.

Kendal groaned at the prospect. But his old comrade was his best option to find out if anything could be learned. He walked to his door and into the atrium. Satra looked up from her workstation with a quizzical eye.

"Prepare a courier drone to receive an informational request from archival human data."

"Oh? Which archive?" Her half-grin indicated she had an inkling; if Kendall really wanted ancient intel, there was only one archive to go to.

He sighed. "Telos."

"As you wish, sir. Check your tablet for the message input screen."

"I'll do that. And Satra?"

She looked back up. "Yes, Sir?"

"Thank you for keeping things low-key. Sometimes I wonder who *really* runs this star system."

She smiled sweetly. "You do, Admiral. And I like it just that way."

"Thank you."

Back in his office he picked up the tablet and looked at the blinking message option. Telos. He wondered if the old man was dead by now. No matter. Kendall began tapping out the message rather than dictating it as would be his norm. After a minute he recognized his own growing paranoia and shook it off. "Telos, we need your help. Any info you can dig up in your maze on either this Captain Halloran, his service record and most importantly the weapon in question, please return ASAP within this drone. Signed Kendall."

He sent the message and put the tablet down. *Now we wait.*

Part Two - Arrivals

Resolve Of Steel

Chapter 8

USS Serapis
Entering Struve System

The ship shuddered, and Halloran gripped the rest beneath his arm to steady himself. He looked around the bridge, scanning each person present quickly for anything unusual. Seeing nothing, he consciously loosened his grip and exhaled. "We there?" He asked to Djembe.

The pilot was hunched over his instrument panel, his gray-haired head swiveling as he took in the information the ship was showing him. Halloran wondered how old he really was; in 2029 he'd have looked all of seventy.

Djembe glanced over his shoulder. "Successful exit from jumpspace."

"Excellent. Up 'scope."

"Captain?"

Halloran got up, feeling the hardness of the seat edge in the back of his thighs; he'd been clenching. "A joke, pilot. Can we see what is out there at least?"

Carruthers spoke up from her station. "Captain, sensors are picking up…ships! Lots of them!"

Halloran stepped to her. "Show me what you're seeing."

The Lieutenant looked up at him. "I…can't, sir. It's a neural interface."

"A what?"

She tapped a block of controls on her station. "It's fed by the sensors through some sort of AI into my head through a set of plugs." She tapped her ear. "I can interpret the readouts with the aid of the ship's computer. It's pretty freakin' cool, sir—."

He leaned over her and put a hand on the station, looking down. "Lieutenant. The ship readings."

She pointed past him at the same time that several gasps sounded around the bridge. Halloran turned to see, and the breath left his body in a rush.

The space in front of them, stretching from edge to edge of the huge monitor, was a mass of broken ships.

"Report, Carruthers." Halloran couldn't tear his eyes from the scene. "Pilot, increase magnification. Prepare for general quarters!"

"Sir." The objects leapt into clearer focus. Immediately Halloran saw the situation; dozens—hundreds—of ship fragments littered the black void ahead of them.

"Belay that last order. Slow to one third, Pilot."

Djembe had worked out what Halloran meant when he asked for these arcane expressions of velocity. Apparently the ancient sea vessels used measurements such as "full ahead, half ahead" and so forth. He translated the Captain's request into the propulsion controls and hoped it was close to what Halloran needed. "One third, sir."

"Halloran stepped to the middle of the bridge, in front of the command station. "They look like hulks." He looked over at Carruthers. "Is your head telling you anything different, Lieutenant?"

She shook her head in response. "Sensors are not picking up any energy output from that graveyard."

He shook his head. "And that planet in the background?"

"Struve Six. Sixth planet in the star system. We emerged precisely where we planned to." Djembe looked over his shoulder. "I'd forgotten about the battle here."

"Battle?"

Djembe looked past Halloran, then nodded. "I think she knows more than I do."

Halloran felt the presence at the rear of the bridge. It was Kendra. He glanced at her, motioning with his head in the direction of the monitor. "You know about this?" As he asked, Axxa entered the bridge and made his way across to his station.

Kendra stepped forward and nodded slowly. "I was in this battle. Many years ago."

Halloran said, "Can we navigate around that mess?"

"Executing at one-third, Captain."

"Thank you." He turned and reseated himself at the command chair. When she glanced his way, Halloran turned a palm up in her direction. "Go on."

With a sharp eye movement in Axxa's direction, Kendra began. "I was a First Officer in the Merchant Arm. We were part of the crew of a good-sized intersystem freighter." She sighed. "It was the biggest thing with engines back then."

"Goliath," breathed Djembe. "I begin to understand."

"Okay." Halloran's raised eyebrow posed the question.

She looked tense. "We were jumped near here by a Prax assault force. Their goal was to hit Tavar as it is a major source of raw materials for the Fleet." Another flick of the dark eyes toward the alien who sat quietly in the back of the bridge.

Halloran appraised the cloud of debris as they crept past it on the starboard side. "That's a lot of blown-up derelicts, Captain."

Her eyes were a thousand kilometers away. "Goliath did a lot of that."

"I thought it was a cargo ship?"

She looked evenly at him. "It was, until the Prax killed my Captain and the bridge crew. I detonated its reactor system in the middle of the red murderer's fleet."

Djembe had turned and was staring at her. "So it *was* you."

Kendra shrugged. "I did what needed to be done."

Carruthers cut in. "Passing the derelicts now, sir."

Halloran looked at the blackened hulks, each spinning in a different rotation, creating a sensation of movement while the mass of ships held their relative positions. "What about anything we could use for repairs?"

"Haulers would have picked this place over a long time ago," said Djembe. "Anything worth salvaging is gone."

"It was indeed a significant battle, Captain." Axxa spoke up carefully from where he was seated. "The humans defended their territory with great resolve. Although I was not present for this, the stories were told of the great ship exploding and turning the tide against our forces." Even he was looking at Kendra differently.

Halloran caught the quiet guffaw that fell from her lips.

Djembe spoke into the sudden stillness on the bridge. "Past the derelict fleet, sir. Course laid in for Tavar. Transit at two-thirds speed is eight point five hours."

Halloran looked away from Kendra's vacant stare toward the front of the bridge. He wanted to hear more of this battle at Struve Six…clearly she had been significantly impacted by it. "Any readings of warships there?"

Djembe glanced at Carruthers, who took her cue. "Too far out for sensor readings, Captain. Tavar is the third planet from their star and we'll need to halve the distance first."

Halloran assented with a nod. "Proceed at two-thirds."

"Two-thirds."

"There will be a defensive force at Tavar," said Kendra at length.

Petty Officer Gerry Wilson was standing on the other side of the command station. He'd been so quiet in the last minutes that Halloran had forgotten about him. "Sir, recommend a weapons test? And perhaps a test of the Hidden Claw?"

Halloran stared at the man, considering the request. They were in what looked like dead space near Struve Six, but the danger of detection by others would rise dramatically as they penetrated into the inner system. It was now. "Proceed with weapons test."

"Aye, sir." Wilson nodded and walked over to his security station on the rear half opposite of where Axxa sat. He tapped a comm unit there. "Weapons, bridge."

"Bridge, weapons, aye." It was Frank DeBartelo on the other end.

"Fire starboard plasma batteries. Target the nearest derelict for effect."

"Sir, which one? Sensors show a lot of targets."

"Choose the nearest sizeable hulk."

"Firing now."

Djembe had just shifted the monitor to a view off the starboard drop of the hull. In the next moment a bright yellow-blue beam emanated from four points along the ship, two in plain sight on the rear quarter and two from out of view ahead of the camera. The beams intersected on a large chunk of ship in the near distance as they slowly pulled away. The resulting blast of light, silent but brilliant, burned into the bridge crew's eyes. Then it faded away and the black returned.

"Starboard batteries operational, sir. The computer targeting is amazing. Imagine what we could have done with this tech back home, sir?"

"Keep the commentary to a minimum, thank you." But Wilson grinned slightly as he looked over at Halloran. "Projectiles, sir?"

Halloran shook his head. "Let's not waste the ammo, Wilson."

"Aye, sir." He hit the comm switch. "Weapons, bridge. Secure the main plasma batteries. Good shooting."

Halloran motioned to Carruthers. "Hit the magic button again, Lieutenant. Engage the Hidden Claw device."

She smiled slightly and reached for her panel. "Engaging the Hidden Claw, sir."

Moments later Halloran felt a ripple of energy pass through his body, as though he'd received a mild shock that lingered too long. "That was interesting. I don't remember that from the battle."

"We were distracted, sir." She didn't glance up at him.

"Are we, er, cloaked?" It felt like a cheap science fiction term, but it was descriptive.

"The device appears to be functioning. The ship's computer is telling me that the energy being pulled from the reactor is stable. Significant usage, however."

"Well, that sounds somewhat promising."

"We have no way of know what we look like to everyone around us, however." Carruthers examined her readouts again. "I'm still getting used to this, sir."

"Stow the Hidden Claw. Lieutenant, I want you go over the system until you're comfortable with it."

"Aye, sir."

"Stepping out for a minute. You have the conn, Lieutenant." Halloran motioned to Kendra to follow him.

"Captain leaving the bridge!"

A moment later, in the outer passage, he turned to her with hands behind his back. "You're having trouble with all this."

She leaned back against the bulkhead and crossed her arms, head down as though in thought. He waited patiently until she looked up.

"Captain, have you ever been in combat?"

Halloran shook his head slowly. "Not like what's happening in this time. I've been in the Navy most of my adult life, and we had a number of close scrapes in the last few years with the Chinese. But no, I haven't had combat casualties…" He swallowed, feeling the sudden constriction in his throat. "…Until all this happened."

She wouldn't break his stare. "I've lost a lot of crewmates. Friends. This place," she waved a hand around her, "is a graveyard. There are many. Those red killers," she pointed toward the bridge where Axxa was, "Are relentless. Merciless. They blow our ships to pieces and kill the survivors in the pods afterward. It's a sport to them!" Her naturally pale face was colored with anger now. "Captain, all I've ever known is combat. And my father before me."

There didn't seem anything to say. He'd had to counsel men under him who'd lost loved ones while under his command, and even a few who'd lost friends on other boats when accidents happened. But, Halloran realized, nothing approached the level of ferocity that these future humans had had to endure.

She apparently noticed the softening in Halloran's eyes. "Don't go all sentimental on me, Captain. I'm telling you this because you seem to exist in a bubble where the Prax brutality and the death hasn't happened. But it has." She pointed at his chest with her finger. "You need to keep us alive and use this ship to hit them where it hurts."

He nodded. "I did promise that."

"You did."

For a moment their eyes lingered on each other before she shrugged off the moment. "Anything else, Captain?" She asked as she gathered up her hair and knotted it.

"No. Thank you."

She glanced at him again, then turned and went back to the bridge entrance, leaving him alone in the passage.

Chapter 9

"**Tell** me more about this planet." Halloran sat back in his chair at the conference table, arms crossed, looking around at those assembled from under his brown eyebrows.

"Not much to tell, Captain." Lieutenant Travers shifted in his seat under the older man's gaze. "I personally haven't been there. They say Tavar is one of the coldest planets that are inhabited. It's all underground."

"It's a mining colony?" Halloran looked at Kendra.

"Yes, one of the first systems visited during the expansion."

"The expansion?"

Travers shrugged. "That's what we call it. When humanity began to explore the systems. 300."

"Is that a year reference?"

Travers looked patient. "Yes. The beginning."

"Of what?"

Okay, the patience was wearing. "Of the expansion, Captain."

Halloran nodded. They'd all noticed the use of terms like 'year,' 'week' and 'day' in this future lexicon, which gave them some comfort even if it was obvious that there were differences in the definitions. Halloran had noticed that a 'week' meant six days aboard ship. And that a day was three shifts of six hours; all familiar for the most part. But the actual year had eluded them so far. Here, Travers was referring to a beginning year of 300. *But what did that signify?*

The young officer was continuing. "Tavar was inhospitable, but while doing planetary scans they discovered the material. The element that became Tavarran steel."

Halloran was interested and leaned forward and placed his elbows on the table. "They refine it there as well?"

Travers nodded. "The Fleet has stationed a perpetual guard flotilla in the inner system since the battle. I image it's still there, but with the war going on everywhere else the Fleet may have pulled them away."

"Chief, how much of this steel do we need?"

Reyes tapped the table, remembering. "Figure on fifty square meters at thirty centimeters thickness."

Halloran had heard these figures before from Antonov's report a few days prior, but wanted to lay everything out. "That's a lot of material. How do we get it from the surface to the ship in orbit, without being picked up by the Fleet sentinels and surface monitoring?"

"The ship's shuttle is tiny, but I think we could tow it up. I wish we still had the shuttle Captain Kendra and Travers came in. Much bigger." After those two had crash-landed in the shuttle bay during the action with the Prax raiding ships, that shuttle had been dislodged through the blasted bay door and lost.

"Does it have the horsepower to lift that much steel, Chief?"

Reyes glanced at Travers. "Sir, tell him what you told me."

"The Prax engine on the shuttle is small; it's really only sized to carry several of them to a planet or station and back. This ship wasn't intended to have a detail of troops aboard, apparently." Travers pursed his lips. "But I told the Chief that we could tweak the power of that thing a bit and use it as a lifting force to get the material through the atmosphere. However we'd be under the eye of every sensor within the gravitational well of the planet."

"No way to extend the Hidden Claw somehow to cover the shuttle?"

Kendra said, "The shuttle is tiny and I don't think you'd be spotted dropping in, as long as the ship is undetected to that point. It'd be almost like a meteor falling into the atmosphere. Once it fell into the lower airspace it would be only seconds until you touched down. Of course, then you've got to get inside the facility somehow without freezing to death."

Antonov spoke up from the other side of the table. "A happy thought."

Kendra ignored him. "Let's assume you retrieved the metal and managed to attach it to the shuttle. The moment you popped into the upper atmosphere, every ship in the area would pick you up. And, the moment you re-entered the shuttle bay and secured the metal our position would be revealed."

Reyes said, "We'd be cloaked."

"Yes, but everyone would have our last known coordinates. Unless we broke orbit within a minute, their targeting computers would have all they need to let them fire on us." She stared at the Chief. "And they would, without hesitation. The Fleet is dead serious about defending that planet."

Halloran said, "Tell us about the Tavarrans."

"I don't know much; haven't actually been there either. They're miners. Fiercely independent. Don't take much assistance from the Fleet or outsiders."

"They manage to be self-sufficient somehow, on that inhospitable planet," Travers added.

"Don't they profit from the sale of the steel?" Antonov asked.

"They do receive funding from the Fleet and mercantile companies that trade with them, yes. The Fleet protection is in part a form of payment itself," Kendra answered.

Halloran steepled his fingers and touched them to his chin, noticing the grizzled beard underneath them. "We know they're independent and make the final product. What do we offer them? Or do we try to steal it?" He found himself remembering Antonov reporting on the state of the weakened hull, the assessment by both Axxa and Travers that the weakness if not patched would lead to a catastrophic failure in an inopportune moment. He sighed. "I don't want to steal anything, but what do we have to offer?" He looked around the table.

Reyes said, "We've been talking about that, sir. Other than the stealth tech—which is substantial but not particularly desirable to a planet—there isn't anything aboard of perceived value to them."

"We could give them the Prax," Kendra offered.

"Would they find that useful?"

She shrugged. Clearly ridding herself of Axxa was the priority in her mind.

He looked around. "Would bringing Axxa have value?"

Travers frowned. "I think that would send the impression we're a Prax raiding party of some sort."

Halloran exhaled. Stealing the metal was sounding more and more likely. "Could we offer them the blueprints of the Hidden Claw system?"

Reyes nodded. "We do have access to those files in the computer."

A plan began to form inside Halloran's mind. "So we don't know how much ground defense we'd be dealing with?"

Travers replied, "Since this is a Prax ship the computer records are pretty much useless." He took his turn looking around the table. "Still, the fact remains that this ship was manufactured with Tavarran steel."

"And there're no references to that fact in the ship's logs or records?"

Antonov shook his head. "I've leveraged Axxa heavily in translation of the files we have access to. Nothing on the construction phase. There are sealed records that are eyes-only for the prior Captain, could be orders or perhaps those directories. No way of knowing."

"But the fact remains that either the Prax found an alternate source of a remarkably similar material for their construction, or they have access to the material located within Tavar."

Reyes spoke up. "Sir. What if the Tavarrans have gone over to the other side?"

No one spoke for a minute as everyone digested the possibility of humans turning traitor to their own race.

At length Halloran sighed. "No way to know until we're boots on the ground."

"Not much of a plan so far," Kendra muttered to the tabletop.

"I wish we had some Marines along, Chief. Sorry."

Reyes snorted, but nodded all the same. "We're already shorthanded aboard ship, sir."

"Can we scan for possible entry points, Travers? Once we're in orbit."

"Yes, sir. Should be able to."

The plan was fully formed in Halloran's head now.

"Captain, sensors are now picking up warships in orbit around Tavar," Carruthers announced.

Halloran leaned forward in the command station. "Give me the bad news."

Travers' voice filtered up from Engineering through the comm unit at his elbow. "I recognize the signatures. There are six light cruisers and two patrol-class frigates." His low whistle carried across the bridge. "Lot of firepower."

Carruthers spoke up. "Sensors also read an additional three of the smaller configuration ships outside the Tavarran orbital plane. They appear to be acting as pickets, stationed approximately four hundred thousand kilometers away at spaced intervals."

Travers added, "Those are probably sensor-enhanced frigates. We employ those in defensive schemas."

"So I should be glad we engaged the Hidden Claw earlier, you're saying, Lieutenant."

Yes, sir. I'm sure they could have picked us up by now."

Axxa spoke from the rear of the bridge. "Do we have assurance that they have indeed not scanned us as of yet?"

Halloran said, "What about it, Lieutenants?"

Carruthers shook her head. "I don't know, sir."

"Sir," Travers called, "I'm watching their plot tracks now and they don't appear to be on any sort of heightened state of awareness or alert."

Halloran looked for Kendra, but remembered she had asked to be moved to Engineering instead of the bridge for their approach. "And this is…good?"

A moment's silence on the comm, then, "I don't think their commander would be this cool a customer if he knew that Prax ship was approaching from the outer system."

"Thank you, Lieutenant."

Halloran nodded Antonov, who in turn spoke to Djembe. "Proceed on your current course and speed to the planet, Pilot."

"Proceeding, sir. Expect to reach orbit entry in three hours, twenty-five minutes."

"Thank you," replied Antonov. "Everyone keep on their guard; we're now officially on silent running until this mission is over."

Travers had left the comm line open and now Halloran heard his voice, speaking to someone else with him. "'Silent running?'"

"Act like a hole in the water, Lieutenant," Wyatt's voice answered.

Halloran grinned and close the comm channel, leaving those two to finish their discussion down belowdecks.

"Captain, do you truly understand the tactical advantage this ship affords you?"

Halloran twisted in his seat to see Axxa. "You mean the Hidden Claw."

The alien nodded. "If our forces truly possess this technology, the balance of power in the war will be drastically altered."

"You mean the relative parity of weaponry and ship counts."

Axxa nodded. "The damage that even a few such vessels as these could do…"

"Fly right in and drop a weapon into a command ship inside the screen. Nuke a planetary base without advance warning. I get it, Axxa."

"I specifically refer to the weapons your old ship was armed with."

"The pure fusions."

Another nod. "One wonders if any other Prax ships are even now arming with your weapons, bound for Mars or even Coloran."

To Halloran, much of the larger strategic overview was dark. As an outsider in this time, he'd only been exposed to small windows of the bigger picture. A half-destroyed Earth civilization. The protracted engagement between human and Prax fleets in the Sol System. The skirmishes and larger battles scattered through the systems between Sol and Tau Ceti, where a second human homeworld had been established and was unmolested to date. It seemed as though the Prax were overextended from their own home system, wherever that was. The humans more mobile and in force along their systems of influence. But stealth tech like the Serapis possessed would indeed allow for a shift of power favoring the Prax. "Thank you, Axxa. Your insight is…appreciated."

The Prax dipped his head in response. Halloran still resented the alien deeply for the hand he had played in the killing of Halloran's best friend back on Earth. But here, millions of kilometers away and in a tense time, he needed him.

Halloran shook his head, rubbing a temple to relax it. "You have the conn, Mr. Antonov. I'll be in my stateroom."

"Aye, sir," the Russian answered from his station. "Captain is leaving the bridge."

Resolve Of Steel

Chapter 10

The dream was particularly vivid this time. As he sat bolt upright on the bed, Halloran tried to recall the details as best he could. Cindy, TJ and Laura were posing in front of a huge waterfall—Yosemite, he recognized. They'd visited the park years ago. 2015? The four had climbed the steep path to the peak above the waterfall. In the dream, they were together, out of breath and laughing, taking in the incredible views of the valley as they ascended. The dream seemed to last forever, while also seeming to end in the blink of eye all the same. It ended with Tom falling from the path, reaching for their grasping hands as he slipped away…feeling the warm, thundering halo of spray enveloping him as he became one with the pounding water flow…expecting and dreading the eventual crush of the bottom as the moments passed and his speed increased.

He sat on the edge of the bed and put his elbows on his knees. Frowning.

The lesson—the message—he was receiving in these dreams was inescapable. His family was lost to him. Like the waterfall, he had been carried inexorably away from them.

He was the one who died on *them*.

Halloran shook his head to clear it. *Cindy* had died. Only months before the…whatever this strange trip could be called. In a car accident in the Jetta. He remembered the night, of course. The notification, the tension during the drive to the hospital. Hearing the news, there in the lobby with the smells of sickness and medicine in the air. He remembered it, but somehow those recollections seemed fuzzy, fading.

Then there had been the funeral, the crush of white Navy uniforms, everyone from enlisted crew to the Navy Joint Chief. Cindy had touched them all during Tom's career. But he realized that only a few people alive—now—actually knew her—had known her. Terry Singletary, his XO. Where was Terry now? Halloran had left him behind on Earth when they got away. It'd been Terry's decision. He would've made it for him but his friend had done it himself.

I need to get back and save Terry and the men I left behind.

Halloran felt the familiar wash of helplessness that was the constant companion of a Navy man at sea. The complete inability to influence what happened back home while on duty. Everything from unmowed lawns to dying loved ones…

With a grunt of annoyance, Halloran reached for his boots and slid them on, lacing them up with a sense of renewed purpose.

And there was something else. He found himself thinking about Kendra, what she'd said about losing people in combat with the Prax. There was a flat finality about their anger, these future humans, toward the Prax. Their destiny was set, and it was intertwined with this brutal warrior race.

But he rejected that. As he stood up, Halloran's mind was resolved toward this time. He would do what was necessary to bring his people home. He would use this ship, and anyone who would help, to force his way into the history yet to be written of this conflict. His military background might not be tinged with the blood of fallen comrades, but he was ready to show them what he was made of.

A tap sounded at the entrance. "Come," Halloran answered.

The hatch swung open to admit Antonov, who paused halfway in with a hand on the lever. "We're entering the inner system proper. Just over an hour to Tavar. No signs of enhanced defensive postures among the Fleet units present in orbit."

"Thank you." Halloran glanced around for his cap, remembering that he didn't have one anymore. Then he noticed the steaming mug in the man's hand. "What is *that*?" he asked incredulously.

Antonov grinned. "Your Chief Parker got the food processor working, and not a moment too soon. We've started it spitting out slabs of something gray that tastes like steak for all hands."

"Wow." Halloran was impressed. "Just in time to hopefully raise morale before we go in."

"He said all we needed now was something called an 'auto-dog,' but I didn't understand the reference."

Halloran chuckled. "Soft ice cream machine."

"Aha." Antonov shrugged. "It's edible solid food. This," he offered up the mug toward Halloran, "is Parker's concept of chicken soup."

"I'll take it. Thank you, Chief Parker."

"I trust you got a good nap in?"

Halloran walked over to Antonov. "Not bad."

The Russian nodded. "This is good."

He took the mug from Antonov and put his nose to the yellowy goo, feeling the familiar tickle. It smelled okay, so he took a sip. "Love it. Now we need coffee."

Antonov smiled. "He's working on it."

Halloran said quietly, "Pyotr, let me ask you something. You see combat?"

Antonov regarded him seriously for a moment before looking away. "During the Chinese conflict, we encountered two of their subs monitoring our fleet. My vessel was detailed to screen. One of their Captains had an itchy trigger finger and fired a torpedo at us. We went deep, and the countermeasures worked to shake the torpedo loose from us."

Halloran nodded. "A close shave."

"The torpedo acquired a nearby destroyer and sank it. Two hundred crew died."

"That I *do* remember reading about. The cause of the sinking was never revealed by your government."

Antonov turned back. "Also never spoken about is that I fired a spread at their sub the following day, unprovoked. One torpedo hit at great depth."

The two Captains stood close together, watching each other warily in the background hum of machinery.

Finally, Halloran nodded. "I understand."

"With due respect, Captain. You do not. It is the Russian way."

"I'll try to remember that, Pyotr." As he began to head for the bridge, he glanced back and waved the steaming mug at Antonov. "By the way, I'm glad you're on *my* side."

The planet loomed large in the forward monitor as Gerry Wilson stopped at the command station. "Sir, the shuttle is prepared and ready to drop."

Halloran looked up from his panel where he'd been reading the atmospheric sensor. "Thanks, Wilson.

Those exposure suits going to be enough?" Wilson and Flagler had tweaked the clothing processor to spit out a bulky coverall-style outfit that was many centimeters too tall—a holdover from the computer's insistence on Prax dimensions they couldn't figure out how to program away—but thick and gray-colored. Everyone would wear two of them in layers over their normal uniforms.

"I think so, sir. Those readings," he pointed at the numbers on the command chair readout, "aren't promising, but we'll manage. As long as we find a point of egress quick."

"Captain."

Halloran turned his attention to Djembe. As he did so he realized that the pilot hadn't left his station in what seemed like days. "Yes?"

"I've got the ship in vector to enter a low orbit as ordered. We'll need to begin decel in five minutes. Should I proceed as directed?"

"You may, pilot." Halloran turned to Carruthers. "Any of the other ships nearby?"

She pulled up a holographic display of the planet that showed a large number of rings around it, each with a colored dot in the ring at different points. Some orbits took the dot over the poles, others were closer to the equator.

"Nice, Carruthers."

She smiled back at him. "The three green dots are Fleet units. You can see how they are in the same general equatorial plane of orbit. This one," she made one of the polar orbits blink, "is one of their sensor-enhanced frigates. And the other one seems to be the command ship." One of the equatorial orbits blinked.

"They're in some sort of a defensive pattern of orbits."

"Yes, sir. Obviously they aren't tracking us, but I didn't want to take any chances so Djembe and I plotted a route that drops us in underneath their altitudes in a weak spot between their projected sensor cones." She lit up the space around the planet in two different colors. "This is us." Another bright line glowed to indicate their entry into the atmosphere.

Halloran was impressed. "Nice work, you two. I like the tech."

Carruthers was clearly pleased with the compliment. "Figuring out new stuff every shift, sir."

"So the other ships departed as we entered orbit. Not because of us, I assume?"

"All we could tell was that they formed up and headed out-system at what seemed like top speed."

"Hmm. Three warships to one. Us."

"At the moment, sir. We'll keep them at arm's length."

"You people and your expressions," snorted the Pilot. He seemed on edge.

"Djembe, you need a break?" asked Halloran.

"I am not in need."

"Seems like you're pushing yourself a bit."

Djembe turned and looked back at Halloran, his brown skin bunched up in a grimace of annoyance. "Are you requesting that I call for relief?"

Halloran felt the man's hurt pride and shame, but kept his face carefully neutral. "No, Pilot, I'm suggesting that you plan to take a break once your orbital insertion is complete and things stabilize. You've been hard at it and I appreciate that; but everyone needs the down time. Make sense?" He wasn't accustomed to explaining his reasons to crew, but Halloran knew that this man was long out of active service and used to operating outside of protocol.

Djembe studied Halloran's face for a moment before nodding. "I will have Patredes take my position for a short time once I am satisfied our orbit is stable and your shuttle is away."

"Excellent. You fit right in with our renegade crew, Djembe."

He turned back to his instruments. "This is an excellent ship, but I miss my Imani."

"I'm sure. We'll get you back, Djembe." The Imani was the man's own spaceship, the one that had hauled Halloran and his crew from Earth to the edge of the solar system. "I miss her, too, in a way."

A short nod from Djembe indicated his agreement. "Ten minutes to orbital insertion. Beginning decel now. Prepare for burn."

Wilson was still standing there. "What would we have done without him, sir?" he whispered.

"Figured it out ourselves, Wilson. I'm glad we don't have to."

"Agreed, sir."

"Carry on. Have the landing party assemble in the hangar bay in an hour. That'll give us time to survey the planet, I think." He looked up at the Petty Officer. "Pray we find a back door they left open."

Lieutenant Hummel stalked back and forth between the main engine panels and the artificial gravity modulator controls, watching Travers making adjustments to the one and passing orders to Trigg

Wyatt at the other. The transition from forward motion to deceleration for a ship this large was a complex balancing of opposing energies and controlled burn sequences involving the attitude thrusters and four main engine outputs at the stern of the ship. Hummel tried to take every detail in, learning and internalizing as best he could with the realization that if this guy from the future were incapacitated or not available, he and Wyatt would need to be able to replicate the procedure.

In the back half of the Engineering compartment, Travers' buddy Kendra was watching over Jack Stacey as he monitored the reactor. Hummel still wasn't sure about her, but she seemed supremely tough. She certainly knew her way around the engine spaces of a ship. He envied these two with their knowledge of spaceships and modern equipment.

XO Antonov had pulled Hummel aside earlier, when they'd been a few hours out from their destination, to ask Hummel on the QT to keep one eye on the woman officer. To notify him the moment anything sideways happened. Especially if the alien showed up in Engineering.

"Lieutenant, can you stand here and watch this level reading?" Travers was waving him back to the engine controls.

Hummel saw it was the nozzle pressure regulator—it had been explained to him already—and he positioned himself by the bank of lit readouts. "Here."

Travers had moved over to another area several meters away, focused on yet more controls. "We're reaching max burn." He looked up at Hummel. "You see the pressure climbing?"

Hummel frowned at the gauge. "Yes."

"Over the red line?"

"No. Wait. Getting close."

"Good. Trigg!"

"Sir," replied Wyatt from the gravity controls across the compartment.

"Engage the fluctuation dampeners now. Just like I showed you."

"To full?"

"Yes. Lieutenant Hummel, adjust that large central control by rotating to your left, slowly."

Hummel did as requested. "So, I'm easing the pressure on the main engine housings during max burn?"

"That's correct, Lieutenant. Well done." Travers smiled at him. "We're running this ship at full ahead, to use your Captain's parlance. But in order to slow our velocity down. The main engines don't care which direction we're headed but the artificial gravity hates these maneuvers and wants to throw everyone against a bulkhead with enough force to flatten us instantly. Nothing like a merchant ship; this vessel is powerful for its size." Hummel watched Travers lovingly pat the panel in front of him.

"Watch out, Travers. You're falling for her."

The other officer raised an eyebrow. "Your time's affectation of ships with female attributes is…mostly correct, interestingly."

"Would your Captain Kendra agree?"

Travers grinned. "Oh, yes. They remind her of her mother."

Wyatt called, "Hey, should I be doing anything else right now?"

Travers shook his head. "The decel burn is proceeding perfectly. Now we wait for the bridge command to slow our rate." He looked around at the other men wistfully. "I only wish we had another six or seven crew down here. Operating this short-handed is challenging."

Hummel looked down at his assigned gauge, watching the level hovering near the red. "Yeah, well, they didn't make it," he said softly.

Chapter 11

Prax Homeworld

The new day on Prax brought an even hotter wind to the Great City. Only those who truly reveled in the furnace outside ventured to the surface, while the rest moved through the maze of lower passageways filled with the crush and noise of marketplaces. As always, the soldiers drilled in the heat above, their lungs growing more acclimated to the extreme climate as they labored to improve their readiness for battle.

Far above the red deserts and valleys of Prax, in high orbit, hung the great shipbuilding and command station for the vast military power hub of the empire. From tip to tip it measured over ten kilometers, and was half as much around at its thickest point. The station rotated slowly in an antiquated system of artificial gravity, approximating the same forces as below on the planet. The station was purpose-built to produce spacefaring ships of war, and the brightest minds of the Empire were brought here to work on new projects and perfect older designs. The Prax scientists were behind those of other worlds, in particular those of the human race. However, time had proven them more adaptable and able to clone enemy designs and improve upon them.

It was toward these science facilities that Ryax now traveled.

The shuttle ride up from the planet had been rougher than typical, the warm season bringing the usual atmospheric upheavals. After the pounding of the initial ascent, the calm of space soothed Ryax's anxieties. Although he'd not served in the space forces, he'd been part of the bloody assault on Tritor as a young foot soldier. Forced to watch many of his fellow troops die under the vicious counterattacks of the Tor beasts, Ryax had quickly developed the thick skin of combat. But his place was boots on the ground, not floating through the blackness. Now, moving through the crowd of workers on the station, Ryax felt both tension at being far from the planet and security at being among the crowds.

No matter his feelings, Ryax needed to get to one scientist in particular. Ysarx was of his old unit, since gone into the sciences after testing well in aptitude. Ryax's initial message had been met with hesitancy, but his old compatriot would speak to him out of deference to the fallen they shared.

Checking the signage, Ryax took a lift down many levels before exiting. Here the crowds were thin and individuals walked with more purpose. He felt suddenly alone, standing out with his soldier's attire.

Eventually he located the module Ysarx had left in the message. It was part of the construction yards, and Ryax paused along the gangway to admire the sleek hulls in various stages of completion in the ways below. The space was truly immense, with the overhead virtually lost to the eye, even with the direct lighting that flooded the station here. He saw what seemed like thousands of workers moving around and over the warships. Each of the vessels bore the same Prax design hallmarks—forward-swept winglets, hornlike protrusions at the bridge deck. Even the transports he'd traveled to battle in many cycles ago were built in the same fashion.

At the end of the gangway a large compartment entrance awaited. As Ryax approached, the hatch swung open before him. Two armed guards stood watch at the other side, their plasma rifles cradled carefully. He nodded to them, aware of his military ID scanchip and his obvious Prax military identity. If they wondered what a planet-side security officer was doing on the station, they didn't ask.

It took another few stops along a series of smaller workspaces before he caught sight of Ysarx bending over another scientist-type, gesturing at a monitor set in the station before them. When he drew close, Ysarx glanced up and registered the visitor's presence with a short nod.

Ryax waited patiently in the corridor while Ysarx completed his discourse, which Ryax now recognized as a harangue of a lesser worker. Eventually, his friend stood straight and patted the seated scientist on the shoulder, looking to where Ryax stood.

"To the Fallen," he said as he grasped Ryax's hand tightly.

"To the Fallen."

"You surprise me with your desire, Ryax. We are a long way from your comfortable billet in the Premier's Hall."

Ryax grinned. "Anything to see an old friend who fled the mother planet to bury himself in books."

Ysarx motioned for Ryax to follow. Without a word, the scientist led him to a nearby workstation that had an even grander view of the building quays. "Do these look like books to you, foot soldier?"

Ryax batted him on his shoulder, noting the tough muscles that still lay beneath the civilian uniform. "Are you a fleet Captain now? Bah."

Ysarx turned to him, arms folding. The time for remembering was past. "What are you looking for, Ryax? Something brought you up here."

Ryax had considered this moment for the entire trip to the station. How much should he divulge? The Premier had held him to strict confidence…but Ryax had to trust in bonds forged in fire. He sighed.

"The Premier has approached me privately."

"I see." Ysarx's stance remained, but his eye sharpened somewhat.

"He sees betrayal as imminent."

"And you thought of me."

Ryax waved at the ship hulls below. "You have served the military for many cycles. The ships built for all Lords come from this yard. I need people I can trust, who are loyal to our Premier." His gaze didn't waver.

Ysarx nodded, ever so slightly. "You know we both owe our allegiance to the one who saved us on Tritor."

Ryax leaned in closer. "Have you seen unusual behavior among the shipyard representatives for Lords? A buildup?"

Ysarx considered the question for several long moments, pausing to look out at the vista before returning his eyes to Ryax. Finally he motioned with a hand.

Ryax obediently followed the scientist down the remaining length of the labs area and into a stairwell at the far end. Down they descended, level upon level, and even Ryax's legs began to burn before they reached the bottom.

"I imagine you didn't realize how many levels there were, even in this mid-bay portion of the station." Ysarx held a hatch open for Ryax.

"To be true, I did not expect the sheer size of it."

Outside on the open way, the noise assaulted their ears. The buzz of untold numbers of pieces of construction equipment filled the metallic hangar. Ysarx leaned close, needed to speak loudly to be heard. "In here, many things can happen which are out of the sight of those overseers from Prax. Cameras go offline so often that the security force gives up the maintenance of them after a time." He pointed across the bay toward a far wall. "What one wishes to hide may indeed remain hidden."

Ryax nodded, following his friend's lead as the other moved off in the indicated direction.

Eventually they reached the far bulkhead and Ryax immediately noticed the alert-looking guard who began to approach them.

"State your business here," announced the Prax, whom Ryax noted was garbed in a nondescript uniform of the Primes, not the Prax military.

Ysarx intervened. "This soldier is here to evaluate the crew quarters for suitability."

The guard scanned Ryax's chip. "He is of the Corpus Guard."

Ysarx nodded. "Yes. He is here on my authority."

The guard looked dubious, but clearly Ysarx held more than enough authority to cow him. With a dip of his helmeted head he turned on a heel and moved away.

Ysarx shrugged. "I get what I want."

"After you, Lord."

Ysarx coughed with feigned indignation as he scanned his chip at a nearby entrance to something. A large hatch slid back, and the two entered the chamber beyond.

Ryax stood for a moment, taking in the ship before him. Finally he turned to Ysarx. "What is it?"

"This, my friend, is the future of our fleet."

The vessel was several hundred meters long—Ryax guessed about Frigate-sized. It was unlike any Prax hull shape he'd seen outside in the ways, its slender and tapered main fuselage featuring two winglike extensions that flared out.

But it was the ship's hull itself that drew his attention. It was black—deep black like the space around the station. Light seemed to disappear into it. "The metal hull. It absorbs the light somehow."

Ysarx clapped his hands once. "This metal you see—it is a true marvel. The humans created it, but we have perfected it!"

"What is it?"

"The composite we had been looking for. It is virtually alive. The molecules rebond upon separation."

Ryax walked toward the ship, which although large didn't dominate the bay. It had a low, thin meanness about the design which, combined with the ghostly-black coloration, gave it a menacing sleekness.

Ysarx followed. "This is the third such vessel of this class."

Ryax turned. "And what of the first two."

His friend's professional pride wilted somewhat under scrutiny. "They were built—spec'd out by—the clans."

"Which ones?"

Ysarx held out his palms in mock surrender. "Clans which are loyal to the Premier, my comrade."

"So you say."

"These vessels, they are destined for the fleet fighting the humans directly. How much more loyal could that make them and their gallant crews?"

Ryax stared. "You mean the Sol System? That's Terxan's clan—Talxen his son is the Prime there."

Ysarx nodded. "The first was delivered to the trials crew a season ago, and is in service as I understand it. The second is in trials now with the clan crew. The third sits before you."

Ryax saw the craft in a new light. "These ships have advanced tech?"

"The most advanced." He leaned in conspiratorially. "One device in particular that we recovered and re-engineered from a destroyed warship that a patrol discovered in deep space."

"Interesting."

"Come, let me show you aboard it. You will be amazed at what we've accomplished here!"

In the Great City below on the surface, The Premier sat in his place to hear the opening ceremony of the Rite, where the clans and families of the Prax as well as the Conquered Worlds renewed their vows to the common defense of the empire.

Sar'yana's latest vision had him disturbed beyond measure. She had seen something—something incomprehensible. The image of himself in the eyes of another, prostrate on the ground. She had seen it so vividly, the scene, and so concerned for his safety that she prevailed upon him to double his bodyguard.

This human she kept referring to. The man who had been envisioned alongside their son. The Premier wondered at his identity. As a Prax he was conditioned to despise that ragged race, one and all, but his figuring so prominently in the visions of a Prax See'r intrigued him.

The noises of the beginning of the Rite reached his ears, and he set aside the musings to concentrate on the proceedings.

A young leader of the Conquered Worlds, Praxxan by birth and a rising force in his clan, gave the prerequisite greetings to the assembled entourages. The Hall was filled to capacity as he rambled through the history, recited since a young age, of the conquests of the empire and the Conquest as a mission. The Premier nodded in appreciation of the young one's timbre of voice and obvious confidence. For his part, the Prax took note of the nods and colored somewhat under the scrutiny of his Premier. But he finished well.

Then several moments passed as the leader stepped down from the dais and bowed before the Premier's seating area. All eyes looked from the exchange to the next speaker, Terxan.

Terxan gazed impassively down at the Premier for several beats, then cast his proud head in a broad circle to take in the assembly as he greeted them. "Honored guests, celebrated families of the Prax, many have traveled far to attend this Rite of re-dedication. The Empire owes you a debt!"

The applause that thundered shook the hall.

"Virtuous comrades, this Rite shall take days to fully attain to. Most of the clans have attended Rites since the founding of the empire. Many have attained to the role of Premier." Terxan glanced down at the Premier momentarily, nodding deferentially. "Many clan leaders have had the high honor of seeing their own sons ascend to the throne during their lifetimes. Should it not be so among the Prax?" Terxan thundered out those last words, creating yet another furious response from the crowd.

After a moment's pause, Terxan looked down at the Premier again, and this time the leader felt the gaze of the hunter upon him. "But alas, our own Premier's son is unavailable to attend this Rite." He looked up and around. "Where is the great Axxa?"

The Premier felt his cheeks warming.

Terxan threw up his hands. "We would inquire of this assembly; what of Axxa?"

The huge crowd had fallen silent. Murmurs now began in the background.

"My own son, Talxen, was given charge over the warrior Axxa, but." And Terxan clipped the 'but' short. "*But,* he has disappeared from his post on Earth—in the midst of the gallant struggle to rid the system of the human infestation. Again, I must inquire…does anyone know of this great warrior's whereabouts?"

The Premier found himself on his feet. About to speak, but his Advisor was there next to his ear. "He is baiting you, Lord. Let it pass."

Terxan cast a baleful glance at the two, standing alone in their booth. "It is my sincere wish that the Premier's noble son be found, and that he might return home to a hero's welcome. Long live our Premier!"

The applause was deafening, and should have reassured the Premier, who had remained standing as Terxan stepped down to relinquish the podium. Only when the next speaker stood to ascend, looking uncertainly at his Premier standing as if to speak, did the Premier slowly sit with a nod for the proceedings to continue.

The rest of the opening ceremony passed in a blur to him. He found himself appreciating the fact that the Premier didn't address the gathering until later in the Rite—he needed to understand what Terxan was up to.

As he left the Hall, long after sundown after many, many greetings and conversations, an aide handed him a comm unit. "Private, Lord."

He took the device and connected it to his ear. The voice of Ryax filled it. "Lord, I must make my first report to you. Please, if you may, meet me at her favorite location at the sunrise."

He deleted the message and handed the device back to the page. As the vehicle rose into the air to return him to their home, he looked out at the city and longed for the clarity of battle rather than the intrigue of leadership.

Chapter 12

USS Serapis

Carruthers was studying the surface readouts with all the excitement of a first-year student. Every few minutes a short chirp of interest would usher from her station, eventually causing Antonov to walk over, hands behind his back. "What is so engaging, Lieutenant?"

She looked up briefly, then over at Chapan who had the pilot's position at the moment. "Well sir, it's just that, um, this is all amazing. I spent my career learning sonar, radar and UF/HF communications. Now here I am, instructing a supercomputer to analyze a frozen planet from orbit." She grinned. "It's pretty awesome. Sir."

Antonov smiled very briefly. "Understood, *Lieutenant.*"

Carruthers looked from him back to Chapan, who'd suddenly developed an interest in his controls. "Yes...no report at this time, sir. I'll keep my enthusiasm to myself in the meantime."

Antonov returned to the command seat, noticing Axxa in the process. The alien was in his normal spot at one of the unused workstations, watching the rest of them. "Do you find it frustrating," he asked on an impulse, "that you weren't chosen for the shore party by the Captain?"

The red face stared back. "As you weren't, either, Captain."

Antonov sat in the chair. "On this ship, I'm not a Captain. I'm the Executive Officer. You may address me as such."

"To answer your question… No, I am not dissatisfied with the Captain's decision."

The words coming from the Prax's mouth sounded odd to Antonov, but the translation device embedded at the base of his skull smoothly converted the Prax language into Russian for him. Antonov was continually surprised at how adept the software in the device was at providing exact language elements—emotion, grammar, almost dialectal in nature.

Although he had spent most of his life in the Navy as a submariner, Antonov had been a closet linguist, enjoying the study of language through his interactions with naval counterparts from other countries. After the Chinese incident, he'd been moved carefully into a staff role and out of the boats, much to the chagrin of his crewmates and supporters within the Navy. But he had understood, and used the time to involve himself in the Intelligence Directorate. His proficiency in English won him several investigative assignments in the US, most recently his part in the ill-fated Bonhomme Richard incident. Basically, he'd swapped out his sub credentials for those of a spy.

Now, the irony of his position as ad hoc XO to the very American he'd flown to the US to study weighed on him. He was aware of the need for a competent senior second officer, and logically he'd been the best choice. *I'd have done it myself.* Although, to all rights, it certainly looked as though his assignment from Russia was on a semi-permanent hold, his training and patriotism kept him in check from engaging too much with the Americans, should the day come when he had the opportunity to return to his country with the astounding news of the future. Personal relationships must be subordinate to the mission.

He understood the Americans. But this alien, he was a mystery to Antonov. But maybe not so much as he would like to think. In a recent conversation the Prax had admitted his race's penchant for conquest, their constant need to expand their territory. *So Russian of them.* Their society was one of hardship, extremes, unblinking dedication to their future. In a way, Antonov rather liked them.

He half-turned to Axxa. "That is wise of you. It is most likely true that a Prax among the party might incite distrust among the local population."

"As I said, Executive Officer, I have no quarrel with the decision."

Antonov turned back, pretending not to notice Chapan's quick spin back to his work. "Please call me Mr. Antonov, Axxa."

After a moment, Axxa spoke form behind him. "I, too, am a Commander in rank."

Antonov didn't turn this time. "Oh? Would you prefer to be addressed as such?"

Another pause. Then, "No."

"As you wish, Axxa."

"Mr. Antonov, I think I've found something," called Carruthers.

In the shuttle bay, the shore party went over their gear again. Chief Reyes was the lead rating for the assignment, and despite the presence of the Captain he held forth as though he outranked everyone. Now he was pointing to Frank DeBartelo's belt. "Cinch that thing up, Frank. You'll lose your drawers in the first drop."

In addition to the burly Machinist's Mate and Reyes, Halloran had selected PO Gerry Wilson, Seaman Rick Patredes, Chief John Parker and Elias Whitney, the Corpsman. Like DeBartelo, Wilson and Patredes were larger men who had weapons training. Those three carried the heavy plasma rifles. Parker was the metal whiz who'd be needed to work out specifics once Halloran negotiated…whatever he ended up negotiating. Assuming they didn't freeze outside the facility before gaining access. Reyes' job—and Whitney's—was to keep them all alive. Rounding out the group was Captain Kendra as the shuttle pilot.

The weapons were still a novelty. Unfortunately, Travers had warned them that firing the plasma weapons onboard was dangerous to everyone's health, so testing them was off the table until they arrived on the planet. Halloran and Reyes carried small projectile pistols similar to the ones they'd first tried back on Earth. Halloran felt comfortable that, in a pinch, he could get off a few rounds of the uber-thin projectiles expelled via electromagnetic force—mini railguns. Other than that, Reyes had procured a wicked-looking knife from a crew cabin, and Parker had a set of pry tools in a bag over his shoulder. Rudimentary housebreaker equipment. When Halloran had poked his head into the bag, Parker had shrugged, adding, "We may end up locked out of the house. Plus a crowbar is as good a weapon as any in a tight fit."

The Prax shuttle was going to be a tight fit. From the looks of it, the ten-meter long craft was meant to ferry just a small group of Prax at a time. The eight humans were nowhere near as sizeable as the aliens, but they weren't the smallest crew and were chosen for their physical ability, in case hauling a slab of steel became a reality somewhere along the line. By pressing a wardroom bench into service as a second row of seating, and rigging a spare cable across the rear of the cabin in an attempt to provide seatbelts, the ship was barely ready to go. One saving grace was that Travers and Kendra had tweaked the output of the shuttle's single engine, claiming that the small ship would be able to lift the requisite steel out of the planet's atmosphere when needed.

Halloran stood back and let Reyes do his thing. The Chief of the Boat was impeccable, unflappable in action. Outside of the minor breakdown he'd suffered on Earth initially after watching his beloved crew mowed down by that demon Talxen, Reyes had truly been the glue that held the Serapis together. Halloran had long ago learned that the Chief of the Boat must be allowed to own his crew, without impediment from the officers. It was somewhat backward to the outside untrained observer, but the best-run ships were the ones with proper understandings between the senior noncoms and the officer team.

At the end of the day, however, the fact remained that he was leading them into a difficult scenario. The situation on the planet was hardly a known quantity. The weather looked downright deadly. The odds that the local miners would take kindly to someone sneaking in the back door and having an invisible spaceship that needed their particular brand of steel were certainly low. Not to mention the distinct lack of bargaining power Halloran possessed.

Basically, he was winging it.

But hey, they all had just enjoyed a steaming cup of passable hot cocoa from the newly-functioning processors. And they had hot water showers.

"Captain, getting a call from the bridge." Seaman Don King stood to one side, waiting to relay instructions. Now he pointed to the comm unit near him, set into the bulkhead.

Halloran motioned to Reyes to follow him and walked over. On the line was Antonov. "Captain, Lieutenant Carruthers has found three access points that look promising."

"Go on."

The line clicked as Antonov passed the channel over to Gail. "Captain," she began. "The whole mountain range in the equatorial belt of the planet is studded with subterranean facilities. A lot of the reading come back as mining operations, which makes sense. However, there seem to be large areas below these active levels which are less-used, with little energy signatures. Several exits to the outer surface exist on these levels."

"Seems too easy."

"Yes sir, it is. The reason I located them was the existence of energy weapons located in those points of egress. They're well-defended."

Halloran looked at Reyes. "But the three?"

"There are three sites with what I would define as 'intermittent' energy signatures. One, in fact, seems undefended."

"Why do you think the readings are intermittent?"

A pause on the line. "I think they might be patrols with energy weapons passing by the entry points."

"So," Halloran leaned in to the wall unit. "Tell me about the unguarded point."

"It's located in a rough spot, sir. A deep canyon with no access for a shuttle to put down. You should see the cartographic—."

Halloran smiled patiently at the comm unit. "Later, Lieutenant. So, the other two look better for a landing?"

"Yes, sir, the one has a broad, level plateau outside that shouldn't be a problem for setting the shuttle down safely."

"Getting shot down by a surface-to-air missile would be unfortunate, Captain," added Antonov, who was still on the open channel.

"Sir, the site I've selected seems to have reasonable access to the upper levels where we can see the most density of human population. Life forms the computer denotes as human, at least."

"All right, Lieutenant, you've sold me. How do we get the coordinates into the shuttle computer?"

King spoke up from nearby. "Sir, I can get Lieutenant Travers over from Engineering."

Halloran nodded to the young man. "You do that."

Carruthers said, "From our orbital path, you can drop and glide right into the mountain range with minimal flight alterations, sir. But I would suggest you go soon."

"How soon?"

"Optimum positioning in ten minutes, sir."

"Get Travers the coordinates to feed to the shuttle." He looked over at Kendra, who had come up to their group but looked unusually subdued. "You're up, Captain. Get us on the surface in one piece."

"Yes, Captain."

After a second look at her, Halloran walked back to the party.

"I think we're ready, sir," announced Reyes.

"Let's hop aboard then." He looked at Chief Parker. "Last chance, Chief. Any way we can get by without the Tavarran steel sections?"

The red-faced Irishman shook his head. "I went and checked the holed areas again, thinking the same thing, sir. The steel is frayed beyond repair and getting worse every time we engage the engines. The jump was really bad—."

Halloran held up a hand. "Message received, Chief. We go in. Serapis needs to be a fighting concern."

Reyes waited and watched the group board, first Kendra and then the rest in turn. "You're in next, sir," he motioned when only the two were left in the bay.

"Chief, if I get knocked down and out of this…"

The Cuban smiled sweetly. "Then I'll carry your sorry ass back myself, sir."

Halloran chuckled. "You fill me with a determination to get back in one piece."

"After you, sir. Clock's ticking."

Chapter 13

"Serapis, Shuttle 1-5, ready for departure."

Halloran leaned over. "1-5?"

Kendra pointed to two Prax numerals on the ship's dash control panel. "One.Five."

"Sounds as official as anything else," Halloran admitted.

"Shuttle 1-5, Serapis conn." Antonov's voice held the slightest edge of humor in it. "Lieutenant Travers is opening the bay doors now."

"Understood, Serapis. Please be advised that we will be operating under comms blackout until we've reached the surface."

"Serapis understands, shuttle. Doors are open, you are clear to launch."

Chief Parker was the other man in the forward seating. He asked Kendra, "Do you think that our shuttle will attract attention?"

"Let's hope not, Chief Parker."

Halloran saw her at the controls as she lifted the small craft and flew it out of the bay, angling it down and away. She was a pro. "Can you pull up the rearview camera, if this thing has one?"

She flicked a few switches. "Probably one of these. There."

The view from where they had just left was…empty. Nothing but the twinkling stars. But…as Halloran watched, an area of the starfield moved oddly and seemed to get hazy for a moment before reforming.

Parker said, "You see that, sir?"

"I did. You'd have to be staring right at that spot, though, to pick up it. Incredible camouflage." Halloran thought of the words with Axxa about the Prax having more ships with this technology. It didn't bode well for the human side.

"Your Lieutenant Carruthers is picking up the sensors and nav very well, Captain," said Kendra as she manipulated the controls. "This flight path is clean and quick, right out the bay doors and dropping into that plateau as if she's been plotting all her life."

"I'm glad you're impressed, Captain."

She looked at Halloran. "Should you be referring to me as 'Captain?'"

"You're a Captain. You earned it, correct?"

"Very much so."

"Then I'm okay calling you that for the moment. If you come up with a better title, let me know and I'll take it under advisement." Halloran flicked the switch to return the view to the forward camera. The ship had no viewports.

She glanced at him. "How long were you in the…Navy? That's the term, right?"

"Yes, and twenty-six years."

"So it's your life's work."

He cocked his head at her. "Interesting way to phrase it."

"My family is all Fleet. Other than my father, my mother was a Commander in the Coloran defense flotilla for much of her middle years."

"And your sister, too," Halloran offered.

She nodded.

"You're more like your father." It was a statement, not a question.

She didn't answer for a minute as she handled the shuttle. Then she nodded. "In his younger years, perhaps. Before my sister and I were born."

"No family of your own?"

She glanced at him again. "None. But you do."

"I do."

"Coming up on the inner atmosphere. The ride will get rough now, everyone."

And rough it got. Within seconds the small craft was tilted on its side and an ominous shaking began, accompanied by a growing moan and rising temps in the cabin. Everyone held firmly to the nearest solid point of contact, no one talking as the tension suddenly ratcheted up.

Just when the shaking seemed to be ready to twist the hull in two, and the noise simply couldn't get any more deafening, the ship righted itself and dropped like a chunk of wood going over a waterfall.

"In the lower atmosphere," choked out Kendra.

Everyone's heart was in their throat for a few more long, drawn-out moments before the ship pulled up suddenly. Halloran felt his throat constrict as his stomach firmly settled as low as it could go in his abdomen. He pulled in a ragged gasp of air just as the ship began to fly level and the motion abated.

"At the proscribed elevation. Sorry about the dive, I wanted to get us out of the clear shot from any ground-based defenses or line-of-sight sensors."

Halloran could only nod. He heard DeBartelo rumble from the rear, "Now we know what the shuttle pilots went through with re-entry."

Whitney replied, "It couldn't have been as bad as that."

"You're probably right, Doc."

"Range to target site twenty-five kilometers. I plan to land as close to the coordinates as possible, Captain." Kendra adjusted a control and the forward monitor re-lit, bathing the compartment in whiteness. They were flying through a blinding snowstorm. "Getting even a few extra kilometers further away could be detrimental to our health."

"Agreed, get as close as practical, Captain."

She glanced at him again. It was sort of funny, the way she did that with the eye twinkle. "What's a 'shuttle pilot?'"

He found himself mildly distracted. "Hmm? Oh, that's from the early days of controlled space fight in the US. On Earth. Our country had vehicles that would launch using booster rockets to get through the atmosphere, then the orbiter portion would detach and set up for whatever mission they were on—deploying a satellite, visiting the space station."

"A space station, orbiting Earth?"

"Yes. You seem surprised."

She shrugged. "Prax destroyed dozens of stations orbiting Earth in the first days. Hundreds were killed instantly."

"Oh." There didn't seem to be anything to say to that, so Halloran went back to staring at the mesmerizing snowfall whipping by the ship.

"Coming up on the optimum landing site now. Our altitude is two hundred meters."

"Wow, that's low," Chief Parker commented. "Isn't it?"

"Our friends in the Air Force do it all the time, I bet, Chief."

"I just prefer being at a thousand meters down, Sir."

"Agreed."

"Flaring out now. Prepare for debarkation!" She smacked a control with the flat of her hand, then pulled back on the control stalk and Halloran felt the ship shudder and fall a bit. Then the landing skids obviously touched ground with a *thwump*. Kendra cut the power, and the engine began to whine softly down. Within moments, everyone could hear the wind groaning over the hull. It was going to be cold out there.

Reyes was on his feet. "Let's go, people. Get your gear ready and have those face masks up!"

Halloran asked Kendra, "What heading to the entrance?"

She tapped a screen on the dash and a small map displayed—more like a radar repeater. The ship was the center and a small dot glowed to the left of it, not far off. She pointed to the dot. "About half a kilometer. Heading would be…exactly one-eight-zero magnetic."

"That's great, how do we manage to stay on course in this blow?"

She pressed a wide button below the screen and the entire display popped loose from the dash. She lifted it and handed it to Halloran.

"Aha. Thanks, Captain."

She pulled her coat tight around her face, slipping the mask up to cover her features. But a stray lock of that black hair fell free as if in revolt. "I got us here. You're in charge now."

The outside was even worse than anticipated. The shuttle, after they'd locked it down and walked off a few paces, disappeared in the white swirling mess.

Halloran put the mapping device close to his face and turned, trying to fix a direction without any points of reference. He found himself hoping that the thing had great batteries.

Reyes was there, putting his face close. "Gotta move, sir!"

Halloran nodded, pointing along the indicated heading.

Without further attempts at conversation the group moved off, staying very close together at arm's length to avoid separation in the inky whiteness. Several times the wind threatened to upend them. The cold was intense. Halloran took the lead with the tracking device, followed closely by DeBartelo with rifle at the ready. There was virtually no way that voices would be heard, so the men held their peace.

At length Halloran saw from the glowing device that the destination was just ahead. He held up, going to one knee in the thin snow layer. Immediately his knee grew cold from the permafrost beneath.

Reyes came forward and got down next to him. Halloran pointed at the spot on the device and saw the Chief's head dip in understanding. It was now or never for their back-door plan. If anyone was waiting, they'd know it shortly.

The Chief and Halloran moved forward, at first more quickly and then slower, with arms outstretched. *It has to be right here.* Halloran was attempting to tuck the device into his coat pocket, cursing the smallish opening—a side effect of the quirky clothing replicator—when he literally ran into the wall of rock.

Recovering, he looked up and around as the others gathered again.

Reyes was gesturing to their right. Then pointing at DeBartelo with his gun. The big man passed the shorter Chief, weapon up and ready as they followed the wall of ice-coated stone.

A massive gust of wind slammed Halloran hard against the unyielding surface and a sharp protrusion jammed into his side. The next instant, the wind reversed direction and tossed him to the ground effortlessly. The hammer of air carried him for several meters, sliding along on the icy permafrost. When the storm was done with him for the moment, Halloran got to his knees, immediately feeling the stab of pain in his midriff. Inhaling lightly, he noted that several others were strewn around him. As he stumbled to his feet, he saw a motionless lump of gray nearby.

Reyes was there, the short man moving quickly through the disoriented group. He knelt next to the still figure as Halloran came behind.

He stuck his head in next to Reyes. "Who?"

Reyes turned and pressed his face close. "Parker."

Another man appeared and forced his way in between them unceremoniously. From the shape of his pack Halloran recognized Whitney and got out of the Corpsman's way. With a last glance at the sad knot of figures, he rejoined those who huddled against the rock wall. The wind howled louder than ever above them.

Someone came very close to Halloran. It was DeBartelo. "Sir! I scouted the entry. About twenty meters." The hooded head shook. "No guards outside."

Outside. Halloran motioned to the others to hunker down while Whitney and Reyes worked on Chief Parker. No need to overexpose themselves to the mercy of those nasty gusts…

The cold seemed into his body like a cancer. It seemed as if the rock of this planet had a supercooling property—or the place was just *that* cold. Halloran was starting to understand why the colonists had chosen to tunnel into the mountains than brave this every day.

He thought of the Serapis above, wondering if anything was happening. He imagined Antonov sitting in the command chair, stoically watching the others with that small smile playing across his lips from time to time.

Halloran had been taken aback by the man's admission of the attack on the Chinese sub. He knew the name of Antonov's victim, in fact. The Zenshou. The Chinese had never publicly announced the loss of the ship, but US intelligence had quickly gathered that the older-style sub had been lost at sea. The fact that Antonov would do what he did, using his crew in the process, said a lot about the man's character. He may be tough and dependable as Halloran had originally thought, but there existed also an inner identity that operated on its own. But he *had* admitted the attack, and their current circumstances had the inexorable tendency to draw men together against common adversaries. Having thus reconsidered Antonov, Halloran concluded that the man would do what was necessary to keep the ship and crew safe in his absence.

Then there was Kendra. A highly skilled pilot and Fleet lifer with that cold exterior but a burning desire within…revenge. Or something more?

Someone pushed against him hard, and Halloran looked up. Reyes was there with an arm outstretched. He followed the man's gesture to see two others nearby, leaning on each other. *Must be Parker and Whitney.*

Reyes lowered his arm and offered it to Halloran, who gratefully grabbed it and hauled himself to his feet. After a moment, he motioned to proceed.

The group filed along the rock wall, now more wary of the vagaries of the wind. Quickly, though, they reached a corner and DeBartelo held up, peering around it gingerly. Halloran wanted to get a look and came up, pressing into the sailor and looking around his shoulder.

It was a recess in the wall, cut cleanly and with a solid, flat floor. At the perimeter was a low wall that extended out in a semicircle away from them. Everything, of course, was coated with a layer of whitish ice.

DeBartelo's voice carried to him. "See, sir? Unguarded."

Halloran looked back to see Reyes behind them, then tapped DeBartelo on the shoulder to propel him forward. They climbed briefly over the wall and Halloran's side pinched him again. *A broken rib, most likely.*

They stopped at the entrance and appraised the door. It was a massive affair, and reminded Halloran of the watertight doors between sections in a submarine, only larger. No way it would just swing open at a knock or a gentle touch…

The group spread out and examined the door and surrounding wall. Quickly someone spotted the cameras mounted in opposite corners of the area. No indicator lights glowed to show someone or something was watching. Halloran felt sure that there had to be some kind of external detection system that would register their presence outside the entrance. Or perhaps no one much worried about who was freezing to death outside.

The way in was the plainly located keypad next to the door. Without a hacker in residence, they had no way to cleverly decrypt the entry code like in the movies. In truth, Halloran had quietly hoped that there'd be the ability to communicate with the inside so they could bargain for entry. He walked over to where he was clearly in view of the camera nearest him and began to wave his arms. When someone from the group came over, he pointed them to the other camera. Soon all of them were jumping up and down for the benefit of those on the other end of the video signal.

Tired, Halloran walked over the keypad and mashed on it for a few seconds. Nothing.

A few minutes passed before Halloran motioned Reyes over. "Thoughts?"

The Chief tapped the door. "My guess—." The wind drowned out the next few words. "—waiting inside."

Halloran looked up and around them. The unforgiving white rock encompassed everything. There was nowhere else to go. They needed to get back to the shuttle and find a new way in.

He gathered everyone together and indicated they should huddle. "We need to go back to the shuttle!"

Heads bobbed in understanding.

At that moment the air was filled with light, flashing out into the swirling snow. Halloran spun as best as he could in the bulky clothes.

The door stood open and a group of better-dressed troops, some kneeling and some standing, trained rifles on them.

Halloran pushed DeBartelo's gun barrel down and raised his other hand, stepping forward from his team toward the light.

The muzzles pointed at them flashed as the soldiers fired.

Chapter 14

Tavar, Struve System

For a hundred years since the first scientists arrived from Earth the colony had steadily grown. Each year—as measured to Sol and enshrined in a time system people loathed but adhered to—more people arrived and added to the ranks of of the closed system entombed within the crust of the planet.

Merchant ships and military fleets, all came and went throughout the year. Virtually all traffic, however, was strictly controlled by the Fleet. Since the bloody battle in the outer system with the Prax some fifteen years prior, Fleet ships populated the space around Tavar. But people still arrived, uninvited.

Some were stowaways from other colonies. Some were disaffected crew off merchant ships, deciding to hide away until their ship left them for dead and flew off. Still others were relatives of citizens, coming in from somewhere else to claim citizenship of their own.

The citizen system dated back to the founding of Tavar, when the leadership had had to beg Earth to send more bodies. The "new gold rush" as the discovery of Tavarran steel had been proclaimed in the media, had turned out less of a rush than a slight trickle as people also discovered the harsh existence on the planet. It had taken forty years just to get the colony self-sustaining. Then the war had come and eventually their product became a critical military asset. Over half a century of "protection." There were days that Jackson wondered how much worse the Prax would truly be than their human overlords.

As he stood on the balcony of the control level and watched the crowds moving along the main street below, he crossed his arms and pulled them in tight, thinking about the citizens of Tavar once more. Twenty-two thousand, eight hundred and twelve at last count. The planet groaned under the weight of them, but most had earned their keep. The mines required more and more as they aged and began to collapse, defying the equally aging technology of the colony. Despite the Fleet's intense concern for continuing the flow of Tavarran steel into its shipbuilding program, the local representatives held a pronounced disdain for Tavarrans and mostly left them to themselves.

And Jackson would have it no other way. He himself had grown up in the colony, the son of the last Governor. After his father was killed, the citizens had elected him to the office at the tender age of eighteen. That had been ten hard years ago.

His government was solid. He'd been lucky to get Arienda, a lawyer from Coloran who'd run off to see the galaxy, as his Vice-Governor several years back. Between the two of them, they'd purged any remains of the insurrection that had claimed his father's life years prior. Tavar was a mercurial place, filled with people who struggled daily with the planet and co-existed in an environment free of all outside influences. They were an independent colony made up of independent citizens who sometimes formed unhealthy alliances. The insurrection had been an ill-advised effort of a group from Bethel Mountain who'd formed protests and ultimately stormed the control level to convey their anger.

He exhaled slowly through pursed lips. Captain Orris was inside now, awaiting their monthly requisition meeting. Jackson was keeping him waiting. It was one of his little games to pass the time.

Being the leader of an underground colony in a remote star system wasn't all that glamorous.

He reached out and grasped the steaming mug on the railing in front of him. The coffee was too hot to drink, so he sipped at it and inhaled the aroma. He remembered the stories of the beverage's origin on Earth and wondered idly if they still made it there, in the green forests on tall hills below a blue sky. He wondered what was left of the planet their race had originated from.

At length he tried a deeper sip but was rewarded with a burn on his tongue. Grimacing, he gave in to the need to get the impatient Captain on his way back to his ship and out of the colony, and turned to the open door behind him.

The control level was where the main colonial security facility was housed. As the Governor, Jackson had direct access to the Chief of Security and his staff. It was here that the Fleet representatives liked to meet—they didn't feel safe down in the bowels of the facility. Jackson didn't blame them. Fleet wasn't all that revered by the masses here.

Captain Orris was standing at the far end of the battered conference table along with two of his lackeys—officers by the look of them. In their formal gray uniforms. Sitting at the table and clearly ignoring the Fleet people was a large, sloppily dressed man with unkempt hair and a worker's hat set at a deliberately rakish angle. Jackson smothered a smirk as he slid in next to the man and sat intentionally erect. "Gentlemen."

Orris was annoyed. "Governor Jackson. Did we spoil your morning coffee?"

Jackson waved at the seats standing vacant across from him. "Hardly. It was too hot. Burned my tongue."

"You have my sympathies." The Captain's dry tone indicated his lack of compassion, but he grabbed the back of a chair and glanced down to check its cleanliness. Satisfied, he slid into it and shot a pointed look at his subordinates. One of them, a young woman, looked about to let a grin loose but Jackson watched her sublimate it under the senior officer's glare. She and the other one took their own seats facing Jackson.

"Let's get right to it, Governor. Your last shipment was delayed by six days, and the one before that five. I fail to see why the Fleet should wait even a day beyond the agreed-upon interval for finished, rolled product."

Jackson was impassive. "We're aware of the concerns. However, my office has assured me that the delays will be dealt with by the next shipment."

Orris didn't look placated. "I'll pass your assurances on to Fleet command. In the meantime, I want to discuss the laxes in security that have come to my attention."

Jackson blinked at the sudden shift of topic. He wasn't aware of any such concerns. "And you have this on what authority?"

Orris had the look of a predator who'd cornered his prey. "The Fleet has its sources. So you don't deny the loss of a security team of two officers last week?"

Jackson heard the man next to him sit up straight and clear his throat. "Those 'sources' of yours, Orris—they turncoats on my security team? If so…" The man slammed a palm on the thick wood tabletop. "I'll find 'em."

Orris hadn't flinched. "Ah, the vaunted Chief of Security has a voice." The officer's words dripped with sarcasm.

Jackson leaned in. "Captain, we're supposed to be on the same side."

Orris leaned in himself, matching Jackson's posture. "If we were on the same side, you'd be sharing your security concerns with the flotilla assigned to protect this rock from the Prax."

Jackson held the man's gaze. "This is first I am hearing of a security failing in my colony."

Finally, he'd made an impression. Orris' eyes faltered. "You're serious, aren't you?"

Jackson sat back, nodding. "Apparently, *someone* isn't sharing everything with the proper authorities. Max?"

The Security Chief fidgeted under the two leader's glares. "It was last week. The roving patrol found the signs of a struggle in a lower passage. The two missing men are suspected to have ties to smuggling operations within the colony."

Orris' look hardened. "My understanding was that that was dealt with a year ago."

Jackson intervened. "Captain, I appreciate your concern, but the governance—including security—of this colony is my administration's responsibility. We'll conduct the necessary investigations and be *sure* to include your staff in the conclusions." He didn't need the Fleet crawling up his backside at this point.

After a few moments of resolute silence, Orris placed his hands on the table and slowly stood. His eyes met Jackson's. He exhaled slowly. "The two of you think this is a game. That you can play the Fleet and collect your payments for this super-steel."

Jackson wanted to burst to his own feet, but made himself sit still. The goal was to let the Captain go.

Orris stood completely and looked down at him. "There's a shooting war going on out there. Our forces are taking a pounding in several systems, most notably the Sol system. People are *dying*, Governor. And my ships are stuck in orbit watching over your frozen rock. Most days, I don't think you appreciate my restraint as much as you should."

Jackson nodded. "Your concerns are noted, Captain. The people of Tavar do appreciate the protection your ships afford us."

Orris regarded the two Tavarrans for another few seconds before pushing the chair aside and stepping for the door. His two juniors leapt up and followed him. The door was opened smoothly for him by Jackson's aide; he'd been waiting in the hall.

When the door closed Jackson got to his feet and paced across the room.

"Go ahead. Say it," prompted Max.

Jackson turned on him. "What do you think you're doing? And in front of Fleet?"

Max raised both hands in supplication. "Wait, wait, Governor. The men in question are almost guaranteed to turn up in a back-alley den any day now. You know how those off-worlder grunts are."

"But you need to bring me in on these situations. *All* of them." Jackson smacked his hand on the back of a nearby chair. "Max, you may be my cousin, but I can remove you at any moment."

"Your uncle may see it differently."

Jackson closed both eyes and rubbed his hands across his bare head, massaging it. "Tell me what you *do* have."

"The two men were part of the Delta Level team."

Jackson stopped and looked at him. "*Now* you mention this?" The Delta Level team had been detailed to monitor a remote level in the lower mountain range after the science team felt more strongly that the disruptions were emanating from that area of the colony. Those sections were notoriously dangerous and virtually all citizens shunned them. Someone could legitimately get lost down there and not turn up for months. When their body *was* found.

Max drummed his fingers on the table. "The rest of the team has been combing the lower levels, but nothing. The log in Egress 256 shows the passcode for one of the missing men, Mladin, was used to open it right around the time he should've checked it on patrol. After that, nothing."

"The other guard?"

"Anders. He was slated to relieve Mladin. When neither checked in the team went on alert."

"Did either have any family in the colony?"

Max shook his head. "Don't think so. Both were part of the Delta Level team for a reason."

Jackson dropped in a seat. "No chance they skipped up to the port for a girlfriend visit?" He asked hopefully. The spaceport above their heads in orbit was technically a fleet facility but a thousand more adventurous citizens had set up living quarters among the ship docks. The port was the one place at Tavar where citizens could interact—nominally—with the outside world.

"Don't think so."

"We have to assume that this is connected with the disruptions."

Max's gaze sharpened. "You think we should send a team down in force? Dig the whole region up?"

"It's something to think about." He waved in the direction of the door. "The Fleet is getting more and more insistent about the delays. We can't keep pretending that the issue will resolve itself." For almost a year now, the planet had seemed to be fighting them at every turn. The electronics would fry in odd places, often deep in the bowels of the mining levels. Ore lifts would fail for no reason, causing days of diagnostic and repair delays. And yes, several workers had gone missing or been found dead beneath cave-ins. After years of steady progress, the mining ops seemed cursed. Despite the frustrations, everyone carried on.

Max shifted. "Those lower levels scare even me, frankly. And I don't scare easy."

Jackson nodded. That was an understatement. As they were growing up together in and around the mines, he would watch his cousin do incredibly stupid things almost every day. The fact that he was alive today itself was a minor miracle. "Start putting a force together. Include some guys from the ops, I want miners with them. Plus some old-timers who remember more about the lower level construction."

"I know a few," Max offered.

"Good." Jackson got up. "And please, stop trying so hard to antagonize the Fleet people with your attire at these meetings."

Max stood as well. "A Tavarran's got to have a *little* fun, *Governor*," he teased.

"That's what you've always said, as long as I can remember."

Max followed him to the door. "Yep."

Jackson watched his cousin's back as he receded down the long hall outside. *He's actually a good security boss, despite his non-existent political skills,* he thought.

His aide was at his side. "Sir, your next meeting is here."

"Lead the way."

He had his hand on the hand on the entry lever to the other conference room when he heard a commotion and looked. Max was running back up the corridor toward him, now with another security officer behind him.

Jackson and the aide exchanged alarmed looks. The other's eyes were wide.

"I've never seen him run like that," Jackson admitted.

Part Three - Citizens

Chapter 15

Tavar, Struve System

Cold.

Halloran felt consciousness returning, and with it an intense sensation of numbness combined with pain. It was several long minutes before he felt gathered enough to pull himself into a seated position. He felt his hands raw with the temperature and realized that his gloves were off. An exhalation came out as a cloud of semi-frozen droplets.

He was not outside, that much was obvious at first glance. And not alone, either; men were piled in heaps around him. Light was in short supply, but the lumps of gray were clearly familiar.

Halloran tried to stretch, feeling the lethargy in his bones and muscles. A supreme effort of will and he found himself on his feet.

"Captain."

He bent at the waist, trying to stretch his midriff, and looked for the voice in the gloomy space. "Here." His back ached, too.

"Wilson over here, sir. Thought it looked like you."

"Any idea where we are?" Halloran tried to remember the chain of events; the cold wind, the aches, the door opening. Other men. Guns. "I thought we got shot."

"I think we did, sir. But not bullets or those plasma weapons."

Halloran stood straight and rubbed his temples. That *hurt*. "What hit us?"

Wilson was up now, moving through the inert forms and placing his hands on shoulders, shoving and tugging.

"Ugh," said a voice from the pile.

"Here now, Frank. On your feet. The Skipper's waiting," encouraged Wilson.

Halloran stepped over the nearest body toward the shaft of light emanating from the wall. His outstretched hand met cold stone and, several inches to the left, metal. They were dumped in a storage room or something similar. "Wilson see if you can get everyone up."

"Workin' on it, sir. Do you see any of our packs or weapons?"

Halloran moved around the perimeter of the space, searching with his eyes and toe tips for anything solid. "Nothing."

"Figures, sir."

"Keep at it." He saw Chief Reyes staring up at him with sightless eyes. Stooping, he slapped the man on the cheek with some force.

That worked; Abran blinked and groaned. "Ouch…sir? What hit me? Gawd, I think I'm drooling!" He swiped the back of a meaty hand across his cheek.

Halloran shook his shoulder. "Welcome back to the land of the living, Chief. And yes, you were." He stood back up and extended a hand to the Cuban, whose eyes locked on and a hand reached up in a viselike grasp.

When they were standing together, Reyes looked around. "We need to get these boys up from their naps. My head is *killing* me, sir. You?"

"Same, Chief." Halloran had a thought. "Seems like we were tasered or something."

"Makes sense, sir. Let me do some rousting while you get a lay of the land."

Halloran went back to the door and a crack of light that shone through the gap. His side ached from the fall out on the surface. Finding no evidence of a handle, he pried his fingers into the space as best as he could and gave an experimental tug. Nothing. So they were definitely locked up. He wanted to rap on the door and demand that they be released, but decided to wait until his people were back at their best strength.

"Sir," Reyes called softly. "No sign of Captain Kendra."

"Thanks, Chief."

Several minutes later everyone was up and, other than splitting headaches and limbs numbed by the pervasive cold, no injuries were reported by Corpsman Whitney. Not that he could have done much for a wound; his med bag was missing as well. Parker was cursing a blue streak under his breath about his missing tool bag, leading Halloran to deduce that even he was better following his fall.

They gathered by the door. "Any luck with this, sir?" asked DeBartelo.

"It's not a tight fit, as you can see from the light getting in. But the frame is solid and in the rock. See what you can do, Frank."

The burly sailor tested the metal, flexing his muscles against the unyielding door. "Oomph. Pretty secure, sir."

Halloran crossed his arms. "So we wait."

Turned out that the wait wasn't all that long. Everyone had just settled into positions sitting or squatting when the light flashed briefly and the sound of the door latch being operated brought everyone to their feet.

"Stay sharp, everyone," warned Halloran. "If we see a chance to make a break for it, follow either my or Chief Reyes' lead and don't hesitate."

A chorus of "ayes" sounded as the door clanked and began to grind outward. Light now blinded them and filled the room. Halloran held his arm up to shield his eyes and acquire a better view of the forms standing in the entrance.

Halloran wanted to assert his authority before anything else happened. "Everyone, show them your hands."

A looming shadow was in his face, now shoving him back a step.

"Get 'em up!" said a gruff voice from the entrance. "Let us see them clearly, or we'll knock you all down again and start over."

So these are humans at least.

The form in front of Halloran grabbed him by the collar, lifting him to his toe-tips.

"Bring him," ordered the gruff voice. "The rest of you, hold where you are!"

"You can't take the skipper," someone said from his group. There was a cold fury in the voice and booted feet shuffled on the stone floor.

"We'll take who we please. You keep still or it'll cost all of you."

Halloran, trying to limit his struggle against his oversized captor, intervened before anyone did something stupid. "Belay that. I'll be fine."

The gruff voice had stepped back from the opening. "Yeah, he'll be *fine*. So sit down."

Halloran was dragged by his toes through the doorway and he blinked in the bright light of the corridor. The door closed behind him as he was shoved against another wall of stone, lightly smacking the back of his head against it with a wince.

The monster of a man held him pinioned against the rock, regarding him with an expression that bordered on boredom. The eyes were cold. He wore a thick parka with a blaze of orange down both sleeves. On his massive head sat a too-small helmet that looked a lot like the old kevlar lids. The man's cheeks were thick and droopy, as if he was ill-nourished. But his grip and arm strength certainly wasn't lacking.

"So you're the officer, eh?" Said Gruff Voice from behind the monster.

"Captain Thomas Halloran, USN, at your service. We're here to meet with your senior officer. To discuss—."

"Grillo, shut him up."

Grillo reached out with his other paw and placed it across Halloran's mouth, adjusting his fingers as an afterthought to clear Halloran's nose opening so he could breathe.

"That's better. Let me get a look at him."

A much-shorter man moved around Grillo and leaned in. He was a good foot shorter than Halloran and was a fraction of the size of his hired monster. He had his helmet off and his seriously matted brown hair was clearly going gray. The jaw was scarred and looked like it had taken a large number of beatings over a lifetime. The eyes were dark and hard, matching his deep gravelly voice.

"You're a tall one for a human," Gruff Voice said. "Lucky I've got Grillo along." He frowned at Halloran. "You're coming with us. Grillo, bring the 'officer'. The rest can wait."

Grillo released his planted hand and wadded the fingers into a pointed fist gesture as if to say "no talking," in conjunction with a scrunching up of his rumpled face. After a moment, he used his other hand to grab Halloran by the upper arm and propel him forward on the heels of Gruff.

Fifty paces up and they turned left into another stone-cut corridor, then down a short ramp and right into an open door. They passed several men who stopped to watch them pass; all wore similar shabby uniforms to Gruff and Grillo. So it was a military facility.

The march ended in a room that was clear of furniture except for a solitary table and several chairs. When Grillo shoved him in the direction of one, Halloran discovered that they were screwed into the floor. The fresh pain in his side reminded him of his losing battle with the wind outside, and the shuttle and ship in orbit. He needed to regain control of this shore party...soon.

"Sit," ordered Gruff as he took up station along the wall next to the door. Halloran decided to play along and lowered himself into one of the chairs, which were made of a dull metal that was surprisingly warm to the touch. Grillo shot him a last warning glare and turned his huge back on Halloran, stomping out of the room and turning to the right in the corridor outside.

Halloran looked around; other than the table, chairs and several cameras mounted up high there was nothing. Obviously an interrogation room. He crossed his arms and looked at Gruff without saying anything.

"You're a tough one, aren't you?" Gruff shifted his feet, the thick parka pants making a rustling sound as he did.

Halloran smiled but said nothing. Clearly, they were waiting for something.

"Do *not* push me like that!" Kendra's voice.

The woman herself followed the voice moments later, led in by Grillo. He towered over her and had his hand on her shoulder, keeping her moving at an arm's length. Halloran immediately picked up it; the hulking man was trying to show her respect. A good sign. Not that Kendra liked it much.

He couldn't help himself; his mouth turned up in the slightest of grins and a part of his heart warmed suddenly, without urging. *I'm relieved to see her okay,* he told himself.

Her eyes met Halloran's as Grillo propelled her all the way to another seat at the table, then held her there expectantly. Her hair was down again; that stuff sure had a hard time staying in place.

"Morning," Halloran offered, letting the grin stay. "I think."

Kendra shrugged off the now-slack hand of Grillo and dropped into the seat. "Is it?" Halloran could tell she was still ticked off about being handled.

"I suspect we'll know in a few minutes."

Gruff stepped forward. "No talking."

Grillo looked at Halloran and his eyes said "that means you, too." Then he turned and loped out of the room without another glance.

An uneasy silence descended on the room and Halloran closed his eyes, feeling his aches and sores and taking stock of the situation. Everything depended on the superior officer who was coming to interrogate them being open to reason. Halloran wanted to be ready. As part of his training over the years was resisting interrogation techniques. Breathing and focus were two of the top things he remembered about it.

Kendra stirred in her seat. "My head is screaming at me."

Halloran didn't open his eyes. "We were stunned by some sort of weapon."

A low chuckle came from the other side of the room. "A nice, locally developed way of keeping the peace," answered Gruff.

Kendra fidgeted. "How long are you going to keep us locked up?"

"That depends, my friend, on how forthright you plan on being with me about your clandestine visit to our planet."

Halloran's eyes came open at the new, in-charge voice in the room. A powerful-looking man with a bald head and clean-shaven features looked down at him from the doorway. His expression was carefully guarded and obviously adept at not showing emotion. His voice had been pleasant with an undertone of resolve. The eyes were a steel-gray. Halloran was impressed. "My I assume I have the pleasure of speaking to the man in charge?"

The bald man cocked his head to one side, eyes widening fractionally. "You are speaking English. I had thought I heard that in the hall, but didn't believe it." And his lips were forming the words in the same language, not the translator speaking in Halloran's head.

Halloran started; no one he'd yet encountered in this time spoke English.

The man smiled and stepped into the room, deliberately choosing a seat and settling into it. He fixed Halloran with an icy stare. "I see you're impressed."

"No one here speaks English."

The man leaned forward. "No one *anywhere* speaks English. How is it that *you* do?"

Halloran shrugged slightly. "It's our native language."

The man's face betrayed his confusion—for a moment. Then the mask of civility returned and he leaned back again, glancing over at Gruff. "Leave us," he said in the new language used by humans called Standard.

"But, Governor…" The translator worked for Gruff, who apparently didn't speak English.

The bald man—the 'Governor,' apparently—waved. "Go. I'll be safe."

With a hesitant nod, Gruff stalked out.

"And close the door."

Without turning, Gruff shut the door behind him.

"He and his team may be rough around the edges, but they are loyal." The man's eyes went hard. "And that is *everything* on Tavar."

"So you're the Governor? Of this planet?" Halloran said.

"I am indeed. And I do speak your language. What I am most interested in is how *you* speak it. It is an ancestral language of our forefathers here on Tavar, now only used by those descended from the original settlers."

"Where I come from, like I said, it's the primary language."

The man looked unconvinced and glanced at Kendra. "And you?"

She replied in Standard. "I don't speak that language."

The man nodded. "Interesting. You're Fleet, aren't you?"

Kendra's eyes narrowed, but she said nothing.

The man turned back to Halloran. "Fleet. But you, you're *not* Fleet. But military. And I understand that men report to you."

"Yes, and they are being unfairly imprisoned near here. I'd like—."

The man tapped the table with a finger. "What you'd like is irrelevant. Your party was caught attempting to infiltrate our facility, armed with advanced weapons with Prax markings on them. I have good reason to just lock you up for a month and see who cracks first among your group." The tone and body language brooked no misunderstanding; this man wasn't playing games.

Halloran was impressed again with the man's skills. "I appreciate the gravity of our situation, Governor. All I ask is a few minutes to outline the reasons for our visit and the low-profile approach."

"I would enjoy hearing it." The bald man sat back, looked them both over, crossed his arms and furrowed his brow. "You may begin."

Chapter 16

Prax Homeworld

Ryax decided to take the walk from his quarters to the guard station outside this morning, instead of through the passageways. The heat was oppressive but tolerable, and he wanted to clear his head with fresh air.

From the moment he stepped outside into the sizzling Prax atmosphere, his center began to radiate a calming effect to his entire being. It was well known to the denizens of this planet how the air cleared the mind and calmed the center of being. Particularly for soldiers; which was why he now saw several exercising in the open square near him. Ryax knew there would be many others scattered about the city at this early hour, preparing their bodies for the long star journeys and battles beyond. As he moved along at a purposefully brisk pace, he focused his mind on what he would say to his Premier.

That the house of Terxan was building a force of its own was obvious. Ysarx had as much as admitted to being on the family's payroll, despite his claims to the contrary. Ryax had realized that his old comrade was blinded by loyalty—not an uncommon trait among the old soldiers. *Or the young ones. Perhaps they are worse.* While it was common for clans to have their own security teams, the scope of the tech and pace of construction Ryax had seen at the station had been unprecedented. The house of Terxan had quietly moved in and was using military resources…which meant that officers had been co-opted along the way. And probably ships with their Commanders. It sickened him to even think it.

What all this meant for the Premier or the empire was beyond Ryax. He was well aware of the limitations of his ability for intrigue. His lot was to be a faithful lieutenant in a larger game.

He glanced at his chronometer and realized that he was going to arrive at the gate later than he had planned. It would leave him little time to shuffle his men off to other stations while he conferred with the Premier. Ryax picked up his pace, breaking into a quicker jog and enjoying the muscle work.

As he approached the complex he decided to enter from the gate rather than the guard's entrance, which was further away. He changed course and arrived at the gate slightly out of breath, but it had felt good to clear his head. He scanned himself in through the security system portal outside and stepped through the opening door, expecting to surprise his guards with his unorthodox approach.

The passage was empty.

Frowning, Ryax went forward and turned into the guard station with a rebuke prepared for their laxness at this early hour. He had only been away for two shifts; how quick they took advantage!

The first thing that washed over Ryax as he opened the door was the stench of blood. The second was the state of the station walls, which were liberally splashed with the stuff. As his eyes moved over the scene his mind grappled with disbelief at the sudden change in circumstances.

Bodies in various states of dismemberment—and chunks of bodies—were strewn about the space. Ryax reached for his weapon only to remember that he'd had to relinquish it for the journey to the station. It sat in his storage locker only meters away.

"Ah, the Prax himself. I was beginning to wonder where you'd gotten to."

Ryax's eyes snapped to the Prax standing to one side of the room, closest to the inside entrance. *The one the Premier would be arriving at shortly.* It was a Xu assassin, that much was obvious from his attire and stance. Part of a nomadic order of devotees of focused combat, the Xu were rare in the Empire but appeared occasionally at the side of a clan leader. To the military, they were rarely an ally in the Conquest.

That they were skilled in their art of death was unquestioned.

Ryax realized at once that he was severely outmatched, as the bodies of his comrades attested to. He tensed up for the anticipated attack.

Instead, the Xu flicked his longblade in Ryax's direction and he felt the slap of blood strike his face and clothing. He resisted the urge to wipe at it, eyes focused on his unit's killer.

"That's better." The Xu wiped the longblade on the clothing of a dead soldier at his feet. His hooded head shifted as the folds changed their shape around his face. "I see that you're ready to fight. It's not in the plan for you to die, however. I had hoped you could have seen this." The assassin waved the blade at the corpses. "They fought—if that was the word for it—with gallantry." He pointed the blade at Ryax. "But the traitor Ryax dispatched them all before assassinating our glorious Premier."

Ryax forcefully exhaled to clear away the surging emotions within him. The thick smell of blood filled his mind with warlust and an overpowering desire to rush the Xu, to kill him. It was the Prax way and Ryax knew the assassin was counting on it.

The other taunted him. "Come, does your blood not boil within you? Attack me!" With a swift movement he scooped up a dead soldier's battle knife and tossed it at Ryax, who flinched. But the weapon embedded itself in the wall next to his head. "Take it. Strike me down!" He said.

All the faithful soldier could picture was this Xu falling upon the hapless Premier who'd be arriving unguarded. He saw that this would be the Xu's plan. And he desperately wanted to withdraw the knife from the wall and fly at the murderer with all the force of his hatred.

But Ryax was no fool. He knew that, in the face of a calculated plan, planning of his own was was required. *Fools fail to calculate the cost.* If he attacked now he'd be badly injured, deliberately by this killer and left alive to be held up as the assassin. His first duty, however, was to his Premier. He must intervene, warn him somehow.

His comm would be off. He'd come alone or with one trusted guard. It would be no trouble for this Xu to dispatch them both in moments.

The bigger picture splashed across Ryax's mind; *this is a coup, and I am being molded into the instigator.*

Terxan.

"You are not the brave warrior I had heard about when inquiring after you, Ryax," announced the Xu as he leaned on his longblade, point into the floor. "How disappointing."

Ryax ignored the insults—and bitter insults they were to his Praxxan soul—and focused on the mess at his feet, without moving his eyes from the enemy. A severed arm. Sections of armor. He'd caught some in the midst of suiting up for duty. Several blades.

There it was. The handle of a plasma rifle butting out from underneath a corpse, several meters to his right. The Xu favored the blade weapons over modern energy ones. Ryax could imagine this one slashing his way through the unit, hardly seeing the guard fall with his duty weapon in his attack. Knowing that the guards carried energy weapons but not fearing them as he should, given his infinitely superior Xu speed.

But Ryax had trained and fought with a plasma rifle since he was a young recruit. He knew the rifle as he would a loved child. And he was an advanced marksman, a minor legend among his men.

As Ryax inhaled, he realized that everything depended on the Premier being accompanied by a guard—a poor soldier who'd pay with his life for that of his master.

In his chamber not far away, clan leader Haryx prepared for the day's events with grave misgivings. As he dressed he processed the message received from Terxan that he suspected the Premier of a plot to destroy the clans. That his missing son Axxa was in fact behind the effort from the shadows. The encouragement for Haryx to watch his own family security.

Haryx had known The High Family to be loyal to the Conquest for generations and the Premier generous in his dealings with the clans. This threat from Terxan confused him more than anything else, but he'd ordered additional guards up from the garrison near his ship.

His wife called from the outer chamber. "Are you ready to go? I have a meeting with Sar'yana I do not want to be late for."

"On my way." Haryx handed his page his coat. "Take this with you." It was the armored one. He would wear it during the Rite sessions, just in case.

"Yes, Lord."

Haryx motioned him to move on and followed him into the main rooms.

"Lord," called his wife from the entryway. "There are new guards here."

"Yes," he answered as he picked up his case. "I requested them."

"But they wear the colors of—."

Haryx's blood ran cold as a strangled sound emanated from the front of the residence. *Female.* He desperately grasped for the pistol tucked in the side of his case.

But it was too late. Several unfamiliar guards dressed in High Family livery burst into the room, firing indiscriminately at the entourage gathered there. In moments all had been cut down by the plasma bursts, save Haryx himself who took down two of them with his own pistol before he felt a barrel jammed against the side of his head.

It was his own page. "It's better this way, Lord." He pulled the trigger.

"**Ah,** we are about to be graced with the presence of your dear leader," the Xu said as he lifted his longblade casually and spun it in a hand.

Ryax subtly shifted his body position as he said, "I didn't know the Xu were murderers of their own kind."

The assassin grasped his blade in mid-spin. "We're taking cues from our old enemy the humans. They turn on each other at the slightest provocation." He pointed the blade at Ryax. "And you shall be remembered as one of the most hated of assassins."

"Show your face."

The Xu cocked his head to one side, then shook it. "Ah, but that is not in the plan. They come!"

The door to the station from the inner corridor slid open, and a heartbeat passed before the face of a guard appeared in the opening.

Several things happened at once. The guard stepped into the room, his eyes going wide as he saw the blood everywhere. The Xu slashing with his blade from his position next to the doorway. Ryax diving toward the plasma rifle, hands outstretched and ready for the familiarity of the weapon's grip.

He slammed into the ground, sliding on the blood, as more was added to the wall and the now to the face of the appearing Premier, framed in the door behind the hapless guard.

The Xu brought his blade around in a sweeping arc from his uppercut across the guard's chest and face to cleanly decapitate him. The burst of blood splattered the Premier as Ryax felt the gun was in his hands, coming up as the Xu pivoted and threw his longblade with precision accuracy toward where he lay. He had lined up the weapon and pulled the trigger.

The plasma bolt and the longblade passed each other in mid-flight. Ryax closed his eyes, knowing that it was over.

An extra heartbeat extended his life a bit longer than Ryax had expected, and he felt it lug a third time in his pounding chest. Cautiously he opened one eye.

The blade had embedded itself in the corpse in front of him on the floor. His eye followed its shaft as it pointed back in the direction of flight.

Beyond, the Xu stood motionless, hooded head turned toward him and hand still outstretched from the throw. As Ryax's heart beat another several beats of life, the figure toppled forward, revealing a blast mark on the wall behind it with splatters of gray matter surrounding it.

He looked to the Premier and saw the shock and surprise written on his red-stained face. This awoke Ryax from his battle-focus. "Lord!"

The leader's eyes darted to his face. "Ryax?" His lips formed the name but no sound came out.

Ryax came up, still gripping the weapon and looking for more enemy forces. He slipped on some blood as he made his way quickly to where the Premier stood and pushed past him, checking the hallway.

"What…" The Premier had regained his voice but not his comprehension.

Ryax, who'd had just a little more time than his Lord to process what was likely happening, grasped the man by his bloodstained shoulder. "We must get you away."

Chapter 17

Tavar, Struve System

The Governor sat through most of Halloran's relatively short exposition without comment, arms crossed and a scowl on his face. But the eyebrows had definitely gone downward at the point where the Captain made mention of a Prax ship utilizing Tavarran steel.

Only at one point did he interrupt Halloran; when the self-proclaimed Earther had talked about escaping from his supposed home planet in a pirate shuttle, the Governor had turned to Kendra and asked, "And you were with him during this?"

Kendra had shaken her head. "I met him later."

"Hmm."

After that he just listened, and once Halloran came to the part about landing on the planet surreptitiously he stood up and put his hands on the table in front of him.

"When your security people zapped us with whatever those guns were, we became your honored guests," Halloran concluded.

My story seems nutty even to me, he thought as he watched the Governor regard the tabletop for several moments.

Finally the other man looked up slowly to Halloran, then to Kendra. "I'll admit that you and your crew are having quite an adventure, if even half of what you just told me is true."

Kendra smiled. "More like a nightmare."

He fixed her with a look. "You…you're a Captain in the Fleet?" He sounded conflicted about something.

"That's correct."

The man raised his voice. "Guard!"

Gruff promptly reappeared in the entrance, gun at the ready.

"Put this man back in confinement."

"But—." Halloran began to object.

Without looking at him the Governor pointed a warning finger in his direction to silence him. "And make sure they're comfortable in there. Get them a heating unit and something to eat."

"Will do, sir."

The massive bulk of Grillo loomed behind Gruff. Halloran sighed.

"See you 'round," he smiled at Kendra as he passed.

She only nodded in return, looking lost. He felt his heart skip a beat and strongly considered putting up some resistance. But, no; this Governor had potential. *Breathe, Tom…*

Gruff marched him down the return way and popped the cell door. Now, Halloran could see that the room they were stuffed in was actually one of a row of identical compartments—storage. "No wonder we're freezing."

"Ha," Gruff said. "You don't *know* freezing." As the door opened he lightly shoved Halloran in.

"Sir, glad you're back," Reyes said from the other side.

Halloran turned. "He promised us a heater."

"Give it a few minutes. We'll be back." The door closed on Gruff's face.

The others crowded around. "What happened, sir?"

"I'm not exactly sure. But I got our story out."

An hour later, Kendra was in her cell—which was actually a decent, small bedchamber of some sort—contemplating the ceiling when a guard knocked on the door and cracked it open. "You're wanted."

What followed was a long walk to a lift, which the two of them took up enough levels for Kendra to lose track. "Where are we going?"

The man didn't look at her. "Control."

"Alright." It was pretty much what she had figured anyway, so she kept to herself until the lift finally stopped and another guard was standing at the entrance. This one was dressed in a formal uniform of gray and orange, and looked professional. Without a word, he motioned for Kendra to step out and join him. As she followed him down a metallic-paneled hall, Kendra heard the lift door close behind her.

This level was much better; the warmth filled her body, and she realized just how chilled she'd been up to this point. The neat furnishings and uniforms reassured her.

The man deposited her in a normal-looking conference room and closed the door without a word. She wandered around the old, battered wood table that suddenly she noticed seemed out of place here where everything was made of metal or stone.

She was running her hand across its surface when the Governor entered the room, nodding on the way to the guard who was apparently stationed outside. Behind him was a less-intimidating man in one of the official uniforms.

"Sit," the Governor motioned to the table. He pointed to another seat for the other man and pulled out a chair at the head of the table closest to the door.

Kendra wished for a moment that she still had her official uniform; the Serapis' clothing generator had done a passable job replicating the cut of it in creating a replacement for the battered official wear she'd had to discard, but the colors were all off and wouldn't have passed for regulation anywhere. Anyway, she self-consciously smoothed the top and tugged it at her waist as she sat down; a practiced motion from years of staff meetings with men.

The Governor twisted slightly in his seat to give himself a better view of her. "So…Kendra, is it?"

"Yes."

The man glanced at the smaller man on the opposite side of the table. "Captain Kendra."

The other man had produced a tablet and was looking intently at it, then up at Kendra. Finally, he turned the tablet around and showed it to both of the other people at the table. It was a file photo of her in Merchant Arm uniform, her hair in a regulation bun, drawn up tall. It was taken at the medal ceremony. After that day on Goliath. After she'd recovered for two months in medical.

The Governor took the tablet and looked at it for a moment, then handed it back and laced his fingers together and stared up at a corner of the room for another few seconds. Finally he came back to her. "So, I was right when I thought I'd remembered your name from somewhere. You were the one from the battle of Struve Six."

She dipped her head and raised an eyebrow. "There were a lot of us there."

The man's eyes narrowed briefly. "But you're *her*—the one from the Goliath."

"Like I said, there were many of us who did what had to be done. I survived to get a medal for the rest of them."

The Governor sighed and nodded to the other man. "You were right."

Kendra looked from one to the other. "Right about what?"

The other man stood. "I'll see to it." He turned to the doorway.

Kendra found herself on her feet as well. "What?" She demanded.

"By the way, we haven't been properly introduced." The Governor waved her back down. When she was planted again, still looking after the disappearing lackey, he continued. "My name is Jackson, and I'm the Planetary Governor of the Colonial Republic of Tavar. You are an honored guest, Captain Kendra. The government of this planet does not long forget those who defended our system against invasion and certain death."

She focused on him. "So you're the boss of the whole system?"

He smiled. "Well, your Fleet would probably disagree with that assessment, but since Tavar itself makes up ninety-five percent of the population of the system, it feels like semantics to me."

"You seem young to run a star system."

"I could say the same about you and your war hero stories."

She shrugged. "I started young."

He nodded, the overhead light reflecting off his smooth pate. "As did I. My father was the Governor before me. He died while in office and I was elected in his place."

"Quite a vote of confidence."

"And your family?"

"My father is Admiral of the Fleet."

Jackson smiled dryly. "Of course he is."

Another lackey knocked and came in, carrying a tray with mugs and a carafe which she set on the table. Kendra glanced over her uniform as she turned to go.

Jackson leaned over and grasped the carafe and a mug. "You need a fresh uniform. Coffee?"

She had smelled the drink but now it hit her. "That's real coffee." It was a statement, not a question.

He smiled again, this time more genuinely. He suddenly seemed more human to her. "I have a—special place—for growing Earth coffee." He poured her a cup and passed it across the table. "There's other ingredients on the tray, but personally I prefer it plain."

Eagerly, she sipped it. "Impressive. You sure know how to entertain a lady."

He waved his mug at her in salute. "Spoken like a true spacer. I know you people love your coffee." He took another sip. "I think half the time your officers come down just for the coffee."

She set the mug down warily. "Are they here now?"

He looked at her over his mug. "They were. Left earlier today."

The black liquid called to her. She lifted the mug for another whiff and sip. "Excellent."

He chuckled. "This is my personal stash."

Another, longer pull at the mug and Kendra set it down. "This table."

"From Earth. One of my ancestors brought it along during the initial colonization phase."

"It looks official. Beat up, though."

He set his own mug down and pushed it away from him, empty. "There is a seal of some sort on the top there," he nodded in the direction, "but the letters and symbols mean nothing. Now, we need to talk about your return to the Fleet and what to do with these strange people who had held you."

"What? No, they weren't holding me against my will. Well, not exactly."

Jackson said, "according the man's own story, he commandeered a ship and captured you and another Fleet officer."

Kendra stretched; the coffee was having the desired effect. "It was…chaotic. Captain Heres had sent us to negotiate with them and then the Prax attacked. I had little choice but to effect a landing aboard their ship. Afterward, something went wrong and Heres opened fire on us."

"Heres?"

She nodded heavily. "Yes, that one. He was there on the Goliath, too."

"Hardly expected for him to fire on you."

She ran her hand over the old table. "That's why I don't want to go back. Yet."

The silence stretched on a bit long.

Finally, he bent over and took the carafe, refilling his mug and hers. "So, you throw your lot in with these people?"

She pulled her mug to herself, letting the question hang as she drank it. After she'd set it down, she spun it slowly on the table by the handle with a finger. "Technically, my father expelled me from active duty. I was on a transport to Coloran, to play the returning hero daughter, when Halloran and his gang took over the ship." She looked up at him with a raised eyebrow. "At first I was…me…about it. I wanted him locked up. But he has a way about getting you to believe in him."

Jackson nodded appreciatively. "A worthy characteristic in a leader."

She leaned forward and put her forearms on the table. "Everything happens for a reason, right?"

He blinked, taken aback by her sudden directness. He set down his mug. "Yes, I think so. We believe that God created everything, directs everything."

Kendra nodded, thinking about the God reference. "Then, if that's even remotely true, then we were meant to meet. And there was a purpose for me to get kicked out of the military. And even for Halloran to be sucked through time."

"What?"

She remembered that Halloran had omitted that part in his narrative. "Traveling all the way from Earth to Agra to here," she covered.

Jackson stood up and paced to the window at the far wall, his back to her. "We need to understand how the Prax are getting quantities of steel." He turned back. "Are you requesting asylum on my planet? Or would you prefer to be repatriated to your military in orbit above?"

Kendra felt the weight of a momentous decision coming on. "So I can request asylum here?"

He nodded. "People come here all the time to find a fresh start in the mines, the businesses."

"But if I leave…"

"You'll be outside of our protection."

Memories came back to Kendra. "But Tavar is a nation-state."

"We are. With full rights granted to our citizenry."

Kendra stood, drawing in a large breath and exhaling it. Feeling the life she remembered slipping from her. She nodded. "Governor Jackson. I formally request asylum and citizenship of the Republic of Tavar."

The lift door opened and the largest of the armed guards prodded the group from the back with, "Let's go."

The room they entered was a cargo bay of some sort, and the first thing the men noticed was the concentration of soldiers at a far end. The group of at least fifty were busy loading bundles onto floating carts. Guns were everywhere.

Wilson was next to Halloran and Reyes as they walked. He nodded at the soldiers. "Wonder where they're going."

The guard prompted them. "This way." He led them through a doorway and down a short metal-walled hall to another room. The bright lights hurt Halloran's eyes as he squinted to look around.

The first he saw was Kendra. But she looked different. She was dressed in one of the planet's uniforms of gray and orange. More importantly, she had a sidearm strapped to her waist. His eyes went from her waist to the man standing next to her. He was a wild-looking one, with careless locks of hair spilling down over his uniform collar.

She saw the question in Halloran's eyes. "Good, you're here. We need to get to work."

He stepped to her. "What is going on, Kendra?" He asked without looking at the man next to her, who he noticed was smiling oddly at them.

Kendra put a hand on his shoulder, which he found interesting and comfortable at the same time. "The Governor of the Republic of Tavar has offered you and your crew asylum."

"Asylum!" exclaimed Reyes at his side.

She continued. "More than that, he extends the opportunity to become Tavarran citizens and continue under the protection of his government."

He saw her grin, one of pleasure, and found himself grinning back at her. "How did you pull that off?"

The man with the wild hair spoke up. "Our people owe Captain Kendra a great debt. This is the least we could do." He looked suddenly serious. "Now, you must decide. We move into the lower levels in force and need your assistance. Are you with us?"

Halloran took her hand in his and removed it gently from his shoulder, turning to his men who all stood around, looking expectantly at him.

"This is sudden," offered Elias Whitney.

Frank DeBartelo looked at the rest of them. "Whatever. We've done what is necessary to get home and this is just one more thing. No one'll ever believe when we get back, anyway."

Halloran shared DeBartelo's wish but had a feeling that getting back would be much harder. "Unless anyone has any profound statements to make, I'll decide for us all."

"You do it, sir. We're here with you," said Wilson.

With a nod of confirmation from Reyes, Halloran turned back to the waiting Tavarran. "What do you need from us?"

"For now? Just to repeat after me…"

Chapter 18

"**Man,** it's cold down here." Seaman Rick Patredes adjusted the stock on his weapon and tapped its side. "My hands are going numb even through these gloves." He held up the hand in question. "And these are *nice* gloves."

"Standard-issue down here. It's your offworlder blood that's not thick enough, that's all," replied the Tavarran soldier named Anders. He nudged the Earther with an elbow. "Stay tight with the man in front of you," he cautioned. "If the lights go out, it'll get dark real quick. You get disoriented immediately. Wouldn't want to shoot anyone in the back by accident out of panic."

Patredes glanced over his shoulder at the man. "You sound as though it's happened to you."

Anders shrugged without taking his eyes off of the Seaman.

"Quiet back there!" Hissed the group leader, an older Tavarran who seemed to have excellent hearing, thought Patredes. *He has to be fifteen yards in front of us.* The string of men moved through the tunnel, weapon lights on and comm units on live mode. They were hunting…something.

For Patredes and the others from the Serapis, the gear-up had been both familiar and foreign. The weaponry was unusual—plasma rifles and wands that fired a stun charge, the ones they'd been caught with—but the process felt comfortable. Gear check, comms check, cinching down belts and rigging. Slings. *Some things are always going to be the same.* He felt the light heft of the rifle in his hands. Lighter than the M6 he had qualified on as a new Navy recruit in 2027 but bulkier, apparently due to the plasma generator housed inside the business end. He briefly sighted through the remarkably familiar red-dot rig. It was supremely comfortable in his hands. Anders had explained the weapon's functions once they had been buddied up, explaining that the gun had been developed by the Fleet a generation ago.

When the Tavarran had asked Patredes about Earth, he'd remembered the Skipper's admonition to the group to keep the background chatter to a minimum—in particular any references to time-travel. Mr. Halloran had explained that the English language was, amazingly, still known within the colony and that everyone they'd interact with would immediately know they were from Earth. But the time travel bit was to stay off-limits.

So, Patredes had dodged the direct question. "We got off as soon as we could. It's a war zone."

Anders had pressed. "So what part of the planet were you raised in? The uniform says 'U.S.N.' on the insignia. What military is that part of?"

Patredes remembered thinking that he would have to get aggressive in his evasions, only to have Anders put up his hands in mock surrender with, "Hey, I understand. We see all types come through here. They want to disappear. I think you might want to, yes?"

Patredes had nodded emphatically, glad to have dodged the bullet.

He wondered how the others were getting on. The team from Serapis—the ship still another off-limits topic with the Tavarrans, according to Skipper—had been broken up among the colonial police soldiers. Four teams of twelve, as Patredes recalled. His team included Petty Officer Wilson as well as himself. After the decision was made to penetrate the deep levels in force and flush out whatever was hiding down there, everyone had put on their game face and got to work. But even Patredes knew that the story of the Serapis' hull, known only to the Governor and his select few leaders, would almost guarantee an encounter with Prax. For Patredes, that was all right. He thought of Wallis and Joyner, two close friends who died that first horrible day. Patredes wanted to kill some Prax.

"Stop here," came the order through his comm earpiece. He knew his own comm transmitter was set to 'off' so as not to distract from the leadership discussion. Patredes put up a fisted hand to signal Anders behind him.

"What does that mean?" Anders whispered. But he stopped.

"Team Three, are you at the waypoint?" He heard the officer up front ask.

"Team Four, we're there. How far are you?" said another voice on the channel.

"We're half a kilometer from your position."

"You're in a tight section there, Kalrod. You got Anders on your team, right?"

A moment, then his buddy keyed his comm. "Yes, sir. Anders here."

"Kalrod, Anders' family used to work that section of the mines. Get him up front and lead the way to our position."

Kalrod keyed an acknowledgment, then, "Anders and your buddy, come forward."

Anders tapped Patredes on the shoulder as he passed, their eyes making contact. They pushed past a dozen men dressed in Tavarran police gray and orange, several of whom patted Anders on his shoulder. *The man is well-liked,* Patredes thought.

He found himself recalling the time when he'd been on his first sea patrol, on the old Minnesota. He'd been asked to get a hundred feet of 'gig line' from Engineering by his PO. Once he arrived in Engineering, the watch officer had looked startled for a moment before nodding knowingly. He'd sent Patredes forward to the Torpedo Room where the gig line was stored out of season. Once at that location, the Chief Torpedoman had shook his head and directed him back to Maneuvering, since the gig line was actually stowed there on a temporary basis.

It was only after he noticed crew members sticking their heads out as he passed only to yank them back in, their grins obvious, that Patredes had realized that the joke was on him.

After confessing his annoyance to his team lead, that officer had smiled broadly with "That's because they like you. You don't want to know what they do to the ones they *don't* like."

Anders had stopped next to Kalrod and Patredes came up to a halt as well.

"You know where we are, son?" The officer asked.

"Yes, sir. Can I see the map?"

Kalrod passed over a tablet as Patredes sighted down the empty corridor in front of them. Even with the overhead lights cut into the tunnel, the place was deceptively dark. The sight illuminated the distant corner where the passage bent out of sight. Between them and the corner, several side passages showed by their black entrances.

Anders was looking at the chart on the tablet. "Sir, we're a level too low to get to that spot."

Kalrod pointed to a dot on the display. "We're headed there to link up."

"I understand, sir, but that passage is a level above us. This chart is incorrect."

Kalrod glanced at Patredes before leaning in to Anders and whispering, "You're sure about this."

"Sir, my family mined this section for ten years." I spent my childhood running around these passages."

Kalrod keyed his mic. "Team Three, we've got an issue here. Anders states that we're a level too low." He unclicked the comm and looked at Anders. "No way to ascend between here and there?"

Anders shook his head.

"We'll need to backtrack and attempt another go at your location, Team Three."

"Acknowledged, Team Four. Keep me in the loop."

Another voice came over the channel. "I'm looking at the same charts, Kalrod. Where is the error?"

Anders pointed again. "Here, sir. This whole section is off."

Kalrod tapped his comm. Anders took the hint and keyed his own. "Sir, the whole section is off. The tunnels I'm seeing don't exist—or at least they didn't exist on this level when we worked it."

Kalrod nodded. "Max, what do you want us to do?"

Patredes realized that the man on the other end of the conversation was the head of security, the one named Max who had sworn them in as citizens. Patredes wasn't sure exactly what that meant for him, but he had rolled with it after the Skipper had talked them through the reasoning.

"You're the man on the spot, Kalrod. Keep your eyes open and make best speed. Teams One and Two are already linked up at the far edge of level fifty-six."

Kalrod exhaled. "We'll keep the line open, sir." He pointed down the passage while looking at Anders. "Forward or backtrack?"

Anders frowned. "I'm pretty sure that if we go forward, we'll hit a main intersection. It should allow us to move back and around this mis-mapped area."

Kalrod motioned him. "Lead on." He gave Patredes a push to get him following the lead Tavarran.

The intersection arrived in short order and Anders paused, looking around. "Hmm."

Patredes came up and looked around him. "What?"

"Odd. There're signs of activity here. I don't remember these two tunnel branches. They're clearly new."

"Sir," Patredes turned. "Signs of activity."

"Weapons at the ready!" Hissed Kalrod through his comm.

"What is it, Kalrod?" Called Max.

"Not sure, sir." The officer pushed past Patredes.

The sounds of men yelling and weapons discharging filled everyone's ears—but it wasn't from in front of them. It was coming over the comms.

Max came back on. "Team Three, report!"

The live-mic cacophony of chaos continued unabated without reply from the other leader.

Kalrod grasped Anders by the sleeve. "Can you get us there *now?*"

Anders looked first at Patredes, who could sense his indecision, then at their leader. "I—I think so, sir." He pointed. "This tunnel wasn't there before. I think whoever is down here cut it. The only direction it *could* go is toward your other section."

Patredes said, "But the enemy could be waiting in there."

"It doesn't matter," answered Kalrod. "We go in. Our guys are getting cut up on the other side!" He called the rest of their team to the run and barged into the tunnel. His weapon light bounced and illuminated the passageway walls in an eerie fashion.

Anders was right on his heels, with Patredes and the rest coming up behind. The tunnel bent hard right and then sloped up; the walls dripping with gleaming ice formations that reflected the gun lights in crazy ways as the group passed. Kalrod had slowed and let them catch up, waving Anders and Patredes two abreast into the lead. Fear filled the back of the Earther's mind, crowding out his senses and fighting for control. Focusing on the tip of his barrel in front of him, he frowned and lifted the sight before one eye without losing step. The tunnel turned left about thirty meters ahead.

As Anders paused and stuck his head around the corner—wisely, it turned out—a plasma bolt burst against the outer rim of the tunnel. Patredes had a sudden memory of that moonbase near—*was it Pluto they'd said?*—and the plasma bolts cutting metal and flesh apart. It was like a waking nightmare.

Anders poked around the corner and let loose a blast of his own. Kalrod came up along with another Tavarran, pushing his way forward.

Wilson was there, hunching close to Patredes. "What's up?"

The presence of another Navy man calmed Patredes somewhat. "That wasn't our shot. Someone's up there."

"What team is getting hit on the comm?"

"Team Three, sir."

Wilson cursed. "That's Whitney and Parker's unit."

Several Tavarrans had bunched up at the corner, and Kalrod led them into the passage beyond, weapons firing bolt after bolt in a blinding display. Return fire from up ahead caught a man in the chest and threw him back against the tunnel wall.

Wilson grabbed Patredes' shoulder. "They stick together. Let's catch up to our buddies!"

They ran up the passage after the Tavarrans, leaping over another body—not Anders, Patredes noticed thankfully. Beyond that the tunnel turned again, and they both saw the devastation wrought from the concentration of plasma fire against the tunnel wall from the advancing Tavarran men.

The passage opened up and a stray bolt hit the overhead near them, shooting deadly shards of rock in every direction. Patredes felt the sting and warmth of a small sliver embedding itself in his cheek as he careened by the spot. Wilson was ahead of him by several steps when an arm reached out and shoved him to one side with great force.

Patredes saw the bolt coming directly at him, through the spot in the air where Wilson had been only milliseconds before. The light filled his vision as he tried to dive under it. Then everything went black.

He came to, flat on his back and looking up at Kalrod standing over him. The officer was hollering into his comm in a one-sided conversation as plasma bolts tore into the tunnel walls around him. "No, we're pinned down!"

Another retina-searing bolt. "I think we're doing that," Kalrod answered the unheard question. He ducked as a bolt got too close. "Sorry sir, can't get a clear look."

The face of Anders swam into view. "Buddy, are you unhurt?"

Patredes grimaced. "I—don't know."

Kalrod leaned over them. "He's fine. Took a plasma bolt past his head, damn near parted his hair!" The man grinned in a disconcerting way.

Anders helped Patredes up. "They've got a good defensive spot up ahead! Can't break through to the other team!"

"Are we close?" Patredes noticed the blood trickling down Anders' face in front of an ear.

Anders nodded, flinching as a bolt hit directly across from their spot huddled against the tunnel wall. Someone cried out nearby.

Kalrod yelled, "See to that man!"

Patredes saw Wilson prone on the ground, firing carefully aimed bursts at the invisible enemy blockade. He recognized that he wasn't doing much to contribute to the attack; in fact, he'd been mostly inept at combat so far.

And he realized that he was scared; more scared than he had ever felt before. Time slowed down. The plasma bolts slicing into the rock seemed muted in sound. Kalrod was calling something out but Patredes had difficulty focusing on the words. He tried shaking his head, but it just made the fuzziness inside worse.

He wanted so much to be of use. But the dullness spread in him and he dimly felt the wall thump him on the back…was it moving? He struggled to get steady but his legs wouldn't obey. Then a tremendous explosion nearby assaulted his ears and drove him facefirst into the stone floor, hard. Then he saw no more.

Light. It seemed too bright to be real. As it took shape in his mind, he tried to blink the brightness away. But his eyes couldn't work. He began struggling against some restraining force, becoming desperate to close his eyes. Close them!

"Whoa, hold up there, Seaman," Came a voice to his ears. He tried to turn his head to see the source, which seemed familiar.

A hand came into view, resting firmly on his forehead. "Stop that thrashing around or I'll sedate you again, Rick."

Patredes croaked, feeling the parched throat. "Whitney."

"Yep. You took quite a hit, Rick. Try to lie still now."

"What…"

The Corpsman's face moved into view. "Don't try to look at me. Here, I'll come 'round for you." He shifted closer. "That better?"

"Yes. Why can't…eyes."

"Your eyes? Oh yeah, they gave you some drug that freezes certain parts of your brain in place, somehow. You took a severe concussion—twice, judging from the bruising. Try to keep still and relax."

"Easy…you to say."

Whitney chuckled. "That's my boy."

"What. Happened."

Elias grew serious. "We found them, Rick. The Prax. A bunch of them jumped us while we were waiting for your team. Would've gotten us, too, if it weren't for a local guy who gave the warning. Got killed for his trouble."

"We win?"

"Don't try to look directly at me, I said. Keep those eyes up. After your team got pinned down we managed to break through their barrier and drive them off down a tunnel or something. Lost six guys in our team. Your team lost another five." He looked away. "Damn Prax."

"Mr. Whitney, please leave the patient alone. He needs to recover." A voice Patredes recognized as Chief Reyes preceded the man himself, who leaned in. "You holding up, Patredes?"

"Yes, sir. Can't close my eyes. Hurts."

Reyes nodded. "Suck it up, son. You did good out there."

Patredes searched his memory but couldn't come up with anything meriting that compliment.

Reyes patted him somewhere near his shoulder. "They say you'll be back on your feet in no time. Let 'em work on you and be a submariner." Then the Chief was gone.

Patredes sighed. He was alive. He would have another chance to really prove himself in battle.

Chapter 19

Halloran tapped the map on the tabletop display. "Well, we knew they were here somewhere. Now we know they are armed and ready to fight."

Max was across from him, arms crossed. "Tell me again that your ship is in orbit with our steel in its hull. It all seems incredible."

Jackson came into the room. "I was in Control when I heard about the fighting. So you found the source of the disruptions?" He asked Max.

Max looked at Halloran. "This man's claims appear to be proving true."

Jackson reached the table and looked down at the schematic. He touched the surface, and the legends popped into view. "Level sixty. They're deep." He looked up at Max. "What level did we lose those men earlier?"

"The egress was located on fifty-seven."

Halloran interrupted. "Look, these are Prax and they are infiltrating the colony and secreting out enough of your steel to build at least one stealth ship, which I am in possession of—."

Max leaned over the table. "Stealth ship? Tell us more."

Jackson got in between them. "I heard we took casualties. Max, the goal here is to secure the colony, and *now*. I want a full assembly of the police and security groups, geared up and ready to move into the lower levels. We need mass force."

Max was about to respond when the comm unit built into the table chirped. "Governor Jackson."

Jackson hit the channel indicator. "Jackson here."

"We just received a communication from Captain Orris that a message drone was launched from the planet a few minutes ago."

"Someone was signaling them?"

"No, sir. The drone jumped right after it cleared the atmosphere."

"They're phoning home," muttered Halloran.

"What was that?"

Halloran looked up. "The Prax are sending a message—they've been discovered."

The person on the comm spoke. "Should I tell the Captain anything, sir? He seems perturbed."

"Maybe we should ask for help after all," offered Halloran.

"No!" Jackson's fist came down on the table.

"Sir?" queried the man on the comm.

In a more calm tone, the Governor said, "Tell Orris we're investigating the source of the drone and will relay information soon."

"Um, I don't think—."

"*Stall* him, Bendis."

"Yes, sir."

Max was smiling. "Look at my cousin. His head is all red."

Halloran kept his expression neutral.

Jackson paced across the room and back again, returning to the table. His color had returned to a more normal state.

"You're not a fan of the Fleet," Halloran observed.

Jackson placed both hands on the table and looked at Max, then Halloran. "Actually, we owe them a debt. I place them high regard. But," and here he lightly tapped his fist on the display, "We *won't* be robbed of our sovereignty."

Halloran smiled. "Hey, I'm with you. We're citizens of yours now, remember?"

Max opened his arms wide. "Jackson! That means Tavar has a fleet of its own now!"

Jackson ignored his cousin. "Can your ship help us?"

"I don't know. I don't think so. We have advanced sensors, but I don't know if they could penetrate into your mountains down here."

"How did you know about the entrances?"

"The sensors. Carruthers did report the number of life forms…hmm."

"Can you talk to them?"

Halloran shook his head. "Total blackout. We didn't want to take any chances of the Fleet ships picking us up."

Max was interested. "Your ship cannot be sensed by them. How is that possible?"

Halloran looked evenly at him. "Advanced technology shields."

Jackson guffawed quietly. "That hide an entire ship?" He slapped the table and turned away.

But Halloran was thinking. "We dropped down quick into the atmosphere while on the away side of the orbit from the Fleet units. We could get the shuttle back up in the same way…bring the ship's sensors to bear on the mountains and look for intel."

"Who's your pilot?" Max asked.

"Captain Kendra. She's excellent."

"You don't say, Halloran."

Halloran felt a slight flush in his face and redirected it to a decision. "You want us to proceed with this direction, Governor?"

Jackson nodded slowly. "The Fleet is going to find out about your ship, anyway."

"We'll do it quietly. I have confidence in Kendra."

Max grinned mischievously again and turned to the door. "I'm going to work on the outfitting of our ground force."

When he was gone, Halloran and Jackson headed to the door after him. Halloran said, "So your name is Jackson."

"Yes, that mean something to you?"

Halloran shrugged. "One of my favorite Civil War generals."

"Your what?" Jackson stopped in the door, eyebrow raised.

"Thomas 'Stonewall' Jackson. My dad named me after him."

"I thought your name was Halloran."

"It is. My first name is Thomas. Middle name Jonathan…just like Stonewall."

Both eyebrows were up now. "You have…*three* names?"

Halloran laughed. "Yeah, we figured out that that's not something normal in this time."

"This what?"

Halloran realized that he'd overstepped. "On Earth, there are cultures that used to use more than one name, um, to name someone. We carry that tradition."

Jackson's brows came all the way down into a frown and he looked away, then back at Halloran with a serious face. "You're not being totally honest with me, Thomas Jonathan Halloran."

Kendra tapped the unlock code into the shuttle hatch, glancing at the three men guarding her as she waited for the computer to recognize the combination. The system had biometrics, but they were Prax; she'd managed to revert the locking matrix to numeric coding instead.

The cold seemed worse coming out than she remembered from their arrival. On the other hand, the shuttle's location had been actually quite close under the sheer rock cliff; she remembered *that* as being much further of a walk the last time.

After a groan of frosted metal the hatch jerked open a meter, then two. The shuttle was freezing solid. She hoped the engines would start. The techs inside had shared with her how they used similar-sized 'lift engines' to haul the refined steel up to the spaceport. The units were stored in a hangar every moment they weren't in space.

If I get back here, I'm parking this thing inside, she told herself as she tapped the nearest guard and pointed into the ship, then to herself. The guard nodded and stepped away, gathering up his fellow Tavarrans.

As she clambered inside the shuttle and stripped back her face mask, the vicious cold within gripped at her exposed cheeks. She made her way to the front and the pilot's seat. With a last look to check that the men had moved off to a safe distance, Kendra smacked the hatch close control and felt the sting of frigid metal bite her now-ungloved fingers. *Got to get the heat moving in this thing.* All instruments looked as she had left them.

The seat cushion was hard and frosty, and Kendra squirmed a bit on it as she worked through the pre-flight sequence. More than anything else, the increasing whine of the main engine warmed her heart. Glancing up, she noticed the warning light come on. It was for the fuel storage; the temperature was below operating parameters. "You'll get used to it," she addressed the indicator.

With Halloran's blackout on comms she was on her own to navigate up to the Serapis without being spotted. Thankfully, the inclement weather that ravaged the atmosphere playing havoc with sensors and she knew from past experience that the Fleet ships in orbit would have a hard time picking up her tiny craft before it disappeared within the perimeter of the Hidden Claw shield hiding the Serapis.

"That's if it's still there," She commented with frosty breath to herself as she took the controls and lifted the shuttle a meter off the surface, testing the craft's worthiness for flight. Satisfied with the response, she set an extreme-angle course directly at where the computer was telling her the Serapis should be.

The ship leaped up through the blinding whiteness. This was one of the parts Kendra loved; being pushed back into her seat by the forces overcoming the relatively weak artificial gravity put out by the shuttle's powerplant. As she had every time she launched from a gravity well, Kendra wondered what it must be like to fly an atmospheric-only craft. To sense the flow of molecules over a wing surface, the intuitive responsiveness of a ship that floated on the winds. Hers was a career of attitude thrusters and decel maneuvers. Even this small, nimble craft relied on such technology to overcome gravity and atmospheric variables. Still, she watched the snow thin before her eyes as the view gradually gave way to the dark of space. She was going home again.

At the tip of the upper atmosphere she cut power and leveled the craft off, angling toward the point indicated on the display coordinates. The forward view revealed nothing but the swirling gray-white below, morphing into the starfield at the horizon. Thankfully, no warships were in visual; she was more than close enough to be in visual range of the Serapis.

"Where are you?" She opened the comm as directed by the Captain when she'd lifted off.

A voice immediately crackled over the channel, the too-loud volume reverberating through the small cabin. "Shuttle, state your complement and intentions."

"Captain Kendra, flying alone. On return vector, requesting immediate clearance to land."

Several moments passed before another voice came on the comm. Antonov. "Shuttle, you are currently not on a vector to land at the colony." He was challenging her on the assumption that even their encrypted, short-range comm chatter could be intercepted.

She recalled the reply. "Received. If you can open the claw, I will find my way to base."

The original voice came back; the woman called Carruthers. "Continue on your current vector until notified."

"Acknowledged." Kendra cut the channel and sat back, still watching the horizon. This was a truly new experience; approaching a sizable warship that was completely hidden from view. She couldn't get past the amazement that the Prax had pulled the technology off. In fact, the more she thought about it, the more something seemed…off. The Prax was known for their ability to *copy*, not innovate. All the senior Fleet officers sat through briefings year after year about the technological capability of the enemy, but this "cloaking" device seemed far beyond the power of the aliens so thoroughly cataloged by the intelligence group headed by her own sister.

As if to punctuate her troubled thoughts, a shimmering haze leapt into view and washed over the shuttle quickly. She had moved through the event horizon of the Hidden Claw. Kendra's hands were already on the controls adjusting the thrusters as the Serapis suddenly became visible, not more than a few hundred meters away. She banked the shuttle to stay well clear of the larger hull and angled it toward the bay door.

"Clear to land," came Carruthers' voice over the comm.

"Acknowledged."

"The Executive Officer will meet you at the hangar." It sounded like a mild warning to Kendra, who grunted without replying as she chopped the remaining speed with a quick decel maneuver and glanced up to verify that the bay door was opening. The familiar decking awaited as she lined the shuttle up again and slowed to walking speed to let it coast into the bay. With twenty meters to the far bulkhead she cut power and felt the gravity dampeners from Serapis grasp the shuttle, dropping it to the deck. As she powered down the heads-up display illuminated, telling her that the atmosphere was pressurizing the bay outside her ship.

Her feet had barely touched the deck when Antonov stepped through the bay entrance and walked directly to her. He looked different somehow, Kendra noticed. More stiff. She crossed her arms to await whatever he had to say.

"Where is the Captain?" Antonov immediately demanded, his eyes hard.

"At the colony." She had a sudden urge to provoke the man.

"Be more specific. What is the team's status?"

Kendra looked toward the shuttle, patting the dark-gray hull. "Cold."

"Captain, I am not accustomed to being made a fool."

With her hand still resting on the shuttle—which *was* incredibly cold—she looked back to him. Antonov's face was very red, and she thought she caught a slight tic in one cheek.

Enough fun. Kendra exhaled slowly. "It's complicated, but the Captain and team are safe. There's been a battle, though, and we have wounded."

Antonov's fists balled. "Why didn't you evac them to the ship?"

"Medical care is underway with the best the Republic has to offer."

"The *what?*"

"It's a long story, Captain Antonov. Could I share it to the officers at one time?"

"Wait, are you telling me that the Captain swore allegiance to a foreign government? On behalf of all of us?" Hummel was incredulous as he leaned forward on the conference table.

Kendra feeling the need to pace the room. "Yes, I believe that is what he did. At least the ones who were physically present."

Travers whistled. "The Tavarrans are known to be fiercely independent. Not a lot of Fleet officers want to serve on a ship defending this system. Now you're a Tavarran," he remarked to Hummel.

The other was shaking his head. "I don't believe it. No way we'd sell out the US."

Travers was interested. "You've mentioned that before. The 'United States,' correct?"

Axxa spoke up from where he stood in a corner of the room. "Was the purpose of this profession on the part of Captain Halloran to effect a temporary alliance with the Tavarrans? Your non-lethal capture indicates that the Tavarrans may have similar principles to this 'United States' Lieutenant Hummel continually references."

Kendra frowned at the Prax, as usual uncomfortable with his presence in human discussions.

Antonov interrupted the stand-off. "But Seaman Patredes is injured and the assistance of the Tavarran medical resources rendered an alliance strategically useful." He looked over at Hummel. "I expect your good Captain is considering this to be dual citizenship."

Hummel's eyebrows went up. "Was that a joke, sir?" But he seemed to relax somewhat.

Carruthers pulled up a display depicting the planet that floated in the air in the center of the table, slowly rotating. "Our position relative to the Fleet units is as constant as possible, but that could change if they decide at any time to move. I think that may happen at some point." She looked at Travers. "Wouldn't it be some sort of protocol to adjust the location of the ship to avoid being targeted somehow?"

Travers nodded. "It's possible to be targeted, yes. Long-range projectile shots aimed to hit where the ship is expected to be based on its orbital track. We would adjust orbit periodically according to a randomized pattern to avoid predictive targeting algorithms."

Carruthers nodded. "Zig-zagging."

"What?" Deacon had been quietly leaning against the wall.

Antonov chuckled. "Good observation, Lieutenant." He smiled at Travers. "In our time, in ocean warfare, surface-only ships would employ a variable course to throw off any simple efforts to target them on the part of submarines with torpedoes—underwater missiles. However, if a target ship can be locked with a torpedo that can track it down by sound or magnetic field, 'zig-zagging' becomes less useful."

Travers considered the analogy. "The shielding currently in use can negate that targeting lock you speak of. In your example, if the targeted vessel has notice they can throw up shields and direct-energy screens and block incoming weapons as sophisticated as your 'torpedoes.' But projectile weapons travel at a very high rate of speed and can approach and strike a ship before it has time." He lifted his palms to Carruthers. "Hence the need for 'zig-zagging' while on station in orbit."

Antonov nodded. "Shields can't be up continuously due to the power resources needed. Understood. Lieutenant Carruthers, please coordinate with

Lieutenant Travers as to the likely course adjustments and our responses required to minimize the possibility of detection."

Kendra stopped by Antonov. "The moment she's done with that, we need her to begin scanning the colony for signs of Prax occupation."

The Executive Officer looked up at her. "Is the Captain and this Governor Jackson certain that the saboteurs are Prax?"

She leaned on his seat back. "Ask Seaman Patredes."

"They're Prax."

All eyes turned to the alien who had uttered the words.

Axxa continued. "It's the only logical conclusion. This vessel is the product of a significant covert operation to mine human resources."

Carruthers crossed her arms. "It seems unbelievable to think that the Prax could get a foothold on Tavar without…"

"…Human assistance. I fear you may be correct, Lieutenant Carruthers."

The silence in the room stretched on. After a time, Antonov stood. "Treachery. Some things remain the same always with humans."

Chapter 20

Prax Homeworld

Sar'yana sat alone, watching her planet disappear behind her. The red orb hovered against the growing field of black, its color growing fainter as her heart did the same. With a supreme effort of will she held her head up in response to the aide's query. "I am comfortable. See to the wounded instead."

As the young Prax nodded and turned away, Sar'yana looked across the cabin to her guard, the young Ryax of the Corpus. He wasn't paying attention to the exchange, intent instead on a display in front of him on the wall. She could make out the face of their Captain, an old veteran named Grysx.

The aide closed the door and Ryax noticed her attention in the reflection on the display. He cut the transmission and turned to her. "Did you have need of me, Lord?"

Sar'yana shook her head without saying a word. So much had happened in a short time; she continued to be overwhelmed at her sudden change in fortunes. But this Prax had surely saved her family, and she'd not burden him with additional woes.

"Very well. If I may take my leave; the Captain requests my presence on the bridge."

"Certainly."

He nodded. "I have guards at your door."

"Certainly we are safe on our own vessel, Commander?"

"Perhaps. But the last two days have proven that no one can be trusted, I'm sure you would agree, Lord."

When he was gone she went back to studying the receding red planet. What Ryax had said was certainly true; they had to take the precautions necessary given the betrayals of the recent hours.

It had started with a group of intense-looking Corpus Guards arriving at the residence. Immediately they had dismissed the staff and locked Sar'yana in her personal quarters. She remembered attempting to reach the Premier over and over on his personal comm, without result. Then the sounds of battle outside her doors, driving her to a safer location deep in their chamber storage rooms. Finally, the door to her quarters blown inward and Ryax himself storming in, weapons up and accompanied by several of his own guards, calling her name.

Ryax was known to her, of course, as he was one of Axxa's oldest friends. She'd come out to hear his tale of treachery throughout the Great City; the house of Terxan consolidating its power and assassinating the heads of clans gathered for the Rite. That her husband was safe but in hiding and attempting unsuccessfully to organize the military against the coup. Their flight to the private shuttle accompanied by a select few aides and guards, only to find the ship disabled.

Through the trial Ryax had been a resolute leader, forcing their pace even as he made every effort to defer to Sar'yana. She had realized, when the mountain shook and the report came that a missile had destroyed her residence, that he was her—all of their—lifeline.

At the last moment a loyal warship commanded by Grysx had sent a shuttle to scoop up their ragtag band of civilians and soldiers. The joyful reunion with her husband had been cut short by the attack of another warship under the flag of Terxan. Grysx had narrowly defeated the enemy with his superior skill, but the entire fleet and the orbiting station had gone dark, supposedly sabotaged and possibly even under the influence of Terxan.

So they fled with one solitary other cruiser for company. She felt her eyes dampen with the frustration of surrendering her world to others not entitled to it. On the ship they had all viewed the triumphant speech of Terxan, delivered earlier to the assembly even as her home was destroyed, as he declared his son Talxen the rightful heir of the Premiership.

Talxen. That revolting schemer who had caused such distress for her son. *Now his father declares him Premier.* She wiped a moist cheek as she wished revenge upon them both. Despite Axxa's appearance within her Sight visions, Sar'yana held little hope for his restoration to her.

"Wife."

She turned to see him standing in the entrance. "Yes, Lord."

"You watch Prax." He stepped toward her.

"Ripped from our family…oh, Lord!"

He caught her as she weakened, holding the smaller frame aloft easily. Pulling her close, he touched foreheads with her. "You feel chill." There was concern in his voice.

She lost herself in his embrace, laying her temple on his broad shoulder. "The cold of space. We are separated from our home. Oh, Krex…what will happen to us?"

The Premier kissed her hair. "We will seek shelter with loyal friends and plan our revenge."

She pulled back to look up at him. "But our friends seem few. Terxan—."

He frowned. "Do not speak the name."

She lowered her eyes in deference. "Our *enemy* speaks so eloquently of the need to re-engage the humans in all-out conflict, to end the war once and for all. The new technology he promised the people. How can these things be?"

He spoke softly to her. "It is true, my control over the narrative is lost for a time. Of the things he spoke I have limited knowledge, but Ryax has informed me of far-flung conspiracies within our military by agitators for increased aggression against the humans."

She nodded. "This seems to be the case."

He lifted her chin gently so her eyes met his. "But we will have allies of our own, my love. I sense it."

"You 'sense' it?" There was a playful smile tugging at the corners of her lips. She knew of his frustration with not having the Sight.

He smiled thinly. "You jest. But I feel…certain."

She grew serious. "As you wish, Lord."

"Now we flee. Our next steps *are* uncertain, and we must ascertain the extent of the uprising, but they have shown their hand. Now it will be our move." He kissed her slowly and carefully, as if to reassure her that he retained control of himself.

As she melted into his embrace, Sar'yana yearned to forget the visions the Sight had shown her of what lay ahead for them.

Ryax stood behind Grysx, studying the star map over the ship commander's shoulder.

The older man half-turned, a look of mild annoyance passing across his features. "Can you read a system map, soldier?"

"The concept is not completely foreign to me, Lord."

A grunt was the other's answer. "Call me Grysx, soldier. I know who you are and what you did."

"It is my honor."

Another grunt, this time of humor. Grysx tapped the map. "Our options are limited."

"Meaning that we have no assurance of safe passage?"

"Meaning that between Terxan and his son's influence, we are severely hemmed in. So much so that I fear we won't last long in Prax space with just two ships of the line."

"We need to jump."

"Agreed, but to where? The Premier has given me leave to make decisions for the high family. But the responsibility weighs heavy on me."

They studied the map for a while in silence, the sounds of the bridge crew behind them going about their routines fading into the background as they remained lost in their thoughts.

Finally Grysx tapped the map, zooming it in on a system with a huge, old star. The Captain continued enlarging it until a solitary planet stood out on the screen.

Ryax leaned in and read the label. "Garvin. Sounds human."

Grysx nodded. "Part of their early network of stations as they solidified their hold on the Earth—Coloran space lanes. Abandoned as being too far out of the way. We used the system as a marshaling point for our forces prior to the attack on the Struve system."

Ryax felt his hope rise. "Is it still abandoned?"

Grysx shrugged. "Unknown. But it's outside of Prax space. It could be a safe haven for a time."

"But what if the humans have retaken it? We'd be jumping into their arms with our Premier aboard."

The older Prax turned to him. "I share your concern. What would you have me do?"

Ryax felt his warrior blood boil, remembering the Xu and the blood of his soldiers on the walls. "We fight back! Surely you have many allies and friends among the fleet, Lord?"

Grysx nodded heavily. "I think I do, but we are cut off until I can communicate with them via jump drones, which will take time. And we do not know who has been compromised; I see treachery in every approaching ship now." He lowered his face. "No, we must get the high family to safety first. I will give the order to jump." He looked up at Ryax with the question in his eyes.

Ryax nodded. "Time waits not for the weak."

"Time waits not for the weak."

Mars Command

Kaela sat with hands resting on her lap, eyes front as the investigator read the last few lines of the initial findings report.

"…And the clear dereliction of duty by the maintenance officer charged with oversight of the sensor array group—Luna, in addition to the low standard of records accountability within the Fleet Intelligence Group that led to the failure of senior leadership to uncover the above-noted nonfunctional equipment." The young man sat the tablet he was reading from down.

Admiral Doren of the Mars staff group leaned forward in his seat at the head table. "And your recommendation?"

The investigator looked uncomfortable. "It's in our report, sir."

"I'd like you to read it aloud, son."

"Yes, sir."

Kaela slid her eyes to Senior Commander Krug as he sat against the far wall of the tribunal hall, arms crossed and head down as though he was asleep. Her fellow conspirator hadn't moved a muscle in the past hour as she'd been grilled for executing his orders.

The sensors on the Earth moon had indeed been strategically damaged—by a co-opted junior officer in her group. He'd done a good enough job of making it look like a maintenance failure that this investigation team hadn't picked up on it. Yet. And there was more damage done elsewhere, closer to Mars itself.

The investigator picked up his tablet again and cleared his throat slightly. Kaela knew that he was uncomfortable skewering Admiral Kendall's daughter in front of the man himself, who sat to Kaela's left in stoic silence. Other than direct responses to a few questions regarding Kaela's scope of responsibilities, he'd remained aloof from the questions that had flown in the tribunal chamber today. *Probably still pining away for his precious Kendra.*

"This board of investigation recommends that, based on the clear concerns outlined, Commander Kaela be suspended from active duty in her current leadership capacity until such time as a formal tribunal can be convened. Lieutenant Chowen of the Lunar Maintenance detail should be remanded for suspension until such time as a formal tribunal can be convened." The man cleared his throat again and fell silent.

"Thank you, Lieutenant." Doren seemed smugly satisfied; Kaela knew that the older man was a rival of father's.

The room was oddly silent for a moment, as if the assembled officers were pondering what had just happened. Then, people began to rise from their seats.

"I'm not going to relieve you," Kendall said softly at her side.

"As you wish, sir." As she stood, she smoothed her jacket.

"But, I want someone alongside you as an observer. A junior officer who can liaison between myself and your department."

Kaela stopped and looked at him. "Either you're relieving me or you're not, sir."

Kendall ignored her and motioned to Satra, who was there. "The name?"

"Alician, sir. Newly promoted Lieutenant."

Kendall nodded. "You remember Alician, Kaela? She was with Kendra for years. The Lieutcnant was assigned to your group after the Carillion...incident."

Kaela did indeed remember the short, stocky woman. She'd been aware of the reassignment but had taken little notice of her with all the focus of recent days. She grunted. "If you insist, sir."

Satra and Kendall exchanged looks. "I'll have her briefed on her responsibility. Kaela, I'm not sure what's gotten into you, but this is not the time to lose sight of what we're fighting for." Kendall waved Satra off and leaned in to his daughter. "I've always been there for you."

She resisted the urge to roll her eyes, looking for Krug. But the man had disappeared from his spot against the wall.

"When you and your sister took different paths in the Fleet, I did my best to help each of you—."

"Father, please. Kendra is the war hero…"

"—When you were in a hard place. You forget, Kendra almost died from her wounds at Struve Six; and neither you nor I were there to comfort her. But I helped her get back on her feet afterward." He laid a hand on her shoulder. "You're about to go through a hard time, Kaela. Let me help."

Kaela nodded. It wouldn't do to antagonize the Admiral.

He dropped his hand. "But you're in trouble here. The board *will* reconvene. Doren is concerned, and rightly so, about Mars security. There are tens of thousands of humans on the planet. I need you back one hundred percent, Commander."

"Yes, sir. I'll make sure that things are in order."

Kendall turned, then turned back. "Two things; get Luna back on line. I've got a bad feeling about the Prax making a move. We need all eyes and ears open."

"And the other?"

"I want any outbound communications to Fleet units under my jurisdiction run through my office first. No more 'assumptive orders' such as Krug's."

Krug had interposed an order under Kendall's name to the Valor for them to destroy the alien vessel carrying that Prax defector. Despite Kaela's misgivings about the possibility that Kendra was also on that ship, she'd passed the order on without hesitation. The gamble seemed to have paid off, for the mystery ship hadn't surfaced again. But Kendra may well be dead at her hands.

As she left the chamber she avoided going to the Intelligence Center, but instead went to a nearby food station for a hot drink. As she cradled the steaming beverage and stood before a viewport displaying the typical dreary red Mars terrain she asked herself if her own bravery for humanity would ever be recognized as Kendra's had been after that battle. It was true that her sister had been grievously wounded and needed a month in medical rehab. But what Kaela was doing would affect the human race as a whole.

Krug. She frowned. The disgusting man's motivations for spying on behalf of the Prax were his own. But ever since he'd lured her in to his web of traitors, Kaela had seen the opportunity within. By facilitating the Prax destruction of Mars, she would free humanity from their obsession with the "mother planet" and ensure the ascension of Coloran as the true homeworld of humanity's future. And by being the one to alert them to the Prax attack once the alien victory was assured, she'd earn the laurels so annoyingly bestowed upon her sister.

The time was near. Krug had made mention that the Prax were readying their new weapons and were working on a timetable that could be measured in days—weeks at most.

The notion that she was betraying the trust of her family and the Fleet nagged at Kaela, but as she always did, she brushed it away. *No, the galaxy will see that I was a hero. That I saved humanity from itself in its darkest hour.*

Kaela's comm unit buzzed. It was that woman Alician, no doubt looking for her new charge. An annoying wrinkle, but not insurmountable. Things were beginning to move swiftly to their conclusion, and neither Alician nor Kendall or Doren could stop them. Krug's and Kaela's plans were in place.

She dropped the drink in a waste recycler. *Just like I'll do with Krug when the time comes,* she mused. *The pig will share none of my glory.*

Chapter 21

Prax Sol System Center, Earth

Xylan disembarked and immediately felt the heat wash over him. It felt wonderful. For all his time in the Sol system, he'd only set foot on Earth twice. The atmosphere was oppressively thick, however, and he took a shallower breath to compensate. Better.

His aide, Commander Third-Rank Hrodax, accepted the Admiral's tablet from the shuttle pilot and tucked it under his arm. "The temperature is agreeable, Lord."

"It is." Xylan moved off toward the entry into the Center. His practiced eye ran over the various types of ships standing in the massive bay as well as the attending crews moving back and forth between them.

Hrodax kept with his Admiral's quick pace, but said nothing until they entered the passage, leaving the heat behind. "Communication between us and our fleet may be intercepted within this facility, Lord. Or dampened."

"Yes, I understand," Xylan answered. "We shall see very shortly if this is a problem for us. Keep that transponder ready."

Three armed guards awaited them at the far end of the passage. "Admiral Xylan, come with us," one announced overly officiously. Attempting to intimidate the elderly man.

Xylan eyed the Prax closely. "How old are you, son?"

"Lord?" The man held himself stiffly, suddenly wary of the officer. Xylan noticed his eyes shift slightly. *Trying to see if he's being watched somehow,* he thought. "You are to come—."

"I only ask," Xylan interrupted, "because I am not accustomed to being addressed in such a direct tone, with seeming disregard for my rank."

Their eyes held until the younger man relented. "My Lord," he continued with a now-bowed head. "Please come with us."

Good. Xylan saw the other two staring with awe at how the old Admiral had cowed the bully. When—if—the time came to seek allies, these three might do. He waved a hand. "You may escort my aide and I."

With a last glance of uncertainty as to what he'd done to himself, the guard moved off to lead. The other two fell in behind Xylan and Hrodax, who now walked side by side.

"I am glad of your company, Hrodax," Xylan said conversationally.

After a moment Hrodax replied, "The honor to be at your side in this hour is almost too much to bear, Lord."

The Admiral nodded. "Let us hope we live beyond it, that we may celebrate our good fortune."

They fell into a tense silence until the lead guard approached the heavy blast door that denoted the entrance into the core of the Center. Xylan had been in two other Centers installed on conquered planets, and the basic layout was the same. The facility was massive, larger than his biggest fleet vessel in sheer cubic volume. Level upon level, half of it excavated from the planet's crust, with the core beneath tapped for its thermal energy to power the base. An entire occupying army was stationed within, with every conceivable department of support needed to subjugate and police an entire planet for a generation. In fact, the soldiers and support staff housed within a Center typically spent a lifetime, a career, in the same star system. Sol Center was no different, even complete with the dictatorial ruler of a Prime.

He looked up at the high overhead ceiling as the guard addressed the Prax standing at the entrance in soft tones. *Except this Prime is committing treason.*

The first guard stepped up. "Lord, the Prime awaits you in his chamber."

Xylan nodded. "Are you a Prax of your duty?"

The guard stiffened. "Lord."

The Admiral pressed, leaning toward the bully. "Now and always?"

"Always, Lord," the Prax protested.

"Good." Xylan clasped his hands behind his back. "Lead on, and remember your duty."

The group passed into the core and turned into a wide, short passage that led to a closed door. As they approached it it opened for them and they passed in. The Prax who had opened the door ordered the guards to stay outside until needed.

Xylan glanced at the Prax as they passed him, seeing a senior commander in the Prime's ground forces on Earth.

"Admiral Xylan, so good of you to come on short notice."

The Prime was in his chair, pointedly failing to rise in greeting for the officer many years his senior. Despite the near-godlike authority granted a Prime in prosecuting his reign over a conquered system, the traditions of the Prax weighed heavily in favor of deference to older officers of rank. As Xylan approached the Prime's seat he noted Hrodax moving to stand next to the ground officer.

He stopped close. "It is my duty to respond when my Prime summons me."

The Prime tapped his steepled fingers together, not looking up at Xylan. "Ah, your duty. To *me*." He suddenly placed his hands on the arms of his chair and stood up, looking at Xylan intently before turning away and stepping off a few paces. "Admiral, you are nothing if not a loyal Prax. In fact, your personal association with the high family is well known." He turned around to face Xylan. "Does your allegiance—and that of your fleet—belong to the Premiership first?"

As the senior commander of all Prax warships in the Sol system, Xylan's authority was unquestioned. But he understood the game the Prime was playing. He'd seen it before. "My allegiance is to the rightful leadership of the empire, always."

The younger Prax had had enough of the cat and mouse already. He drew himself up and announced, "I have been chosen as the new Premier, Admiral."

When the revelation failed to make the hoped-for impression on the impassive officer, the Prime wagged a finger at him. "Your 'high family' has descended into treachery and abandonment of the empire, Xylan. The time for new leadership is here."

Xylan made to turn slowly, hands before him, as if to consider young Talxen's words. But his eye was for Hrodax standing beside the other officer. The nod was so slight as to be missed by the others but his aide closed his own lids in acknowledgment. Xylan then walked to the Prime's desk and placed a hand upon the smooth surface, as if appraising it.

"Say something!" the Prime burst out.

He let him wait another moment before answering, never looking up. "I find the sudden change of command and the odious charges leveled against a most honorable family repugnant," he said softly but clearly. "I have lived a long time, Talxen—."

He felt the younger man step close to him. "You shall address me as Lord!"

When the outburst had dissipated from the room Xylan ran his hand along the surface. "The house of Terxan is known to me." He chuckled to himself, remembering with a small smile. "Once I caught him fleeing from battle in his "flagship." My vessel's superior armament convinced him to re-engage the enemy."

The Prime grabbed him by the shoulders and shoved him against the desk, causing him to stumble and go to one knee beside it. He caught sight of Hrodax lunging forward, as if in slow-motion. Equally slow was the arm of the other officer coming up behind the aide, pistol in hand. The plasma bolt passed through Hrodax's head, blowing the body forward and into the desk beside Xylan. Gore splattered the Admiral as he grasped at the now-slippery desk surface to right himself. The body slumped into him and knocked him to the decking.

As Xylan gently pushed the body to one side he collected himself, thinking. Through the red mist he'd seen Talxen gloating, clearly exuberant. The Prime was past saving—that had just been proven beyond a doubt. Xylan's hands reached into the waist pocket of the body of his loyal aide to confirm the transponders activation;

yes, there was the light blinking. His warning had been sent.

"On your feet, Admiral." Talxen was standing over him, fists balled and spoiling for a fight in the presence of blood.

Xylan regained his footing and glanced down—the uniform was a mess. *Hrodax will be remembered with honor,* he noted deep in his active memory.

The door was open and the three guards were inside the office, weapons up. The officer's gun was in Xylans face. Everyone was looking extremely tense.

"Lord!" spoke the lead guard. "What has happened?" He looked from the crumpled form to Xylan, then to the raised gun. His own rifle came up to point at the officer. "Commander, your weapon!"

Talxen walked around the desk and pushed back the dripping chair with disgust, giving up on it. Instead, he crossed his arms and nodded to Xylan. "This officer has just murdered his aide in anger. Keep your weapons trained on him."

"You'll not find many allies in the fleet, Talxen," said Xylan carefully.

The Prime laughed. "My father has as many allies as you, old one. Your loyal officers are even now being removed from their posts with force. The fleet belongs to me."

Xylan was thankful that the jumpdrone from Prax with the news of the coup had reached him before responding to this summons. It had taken only an hour to get his most trusted commanders on the comms and planned the defense of key ships ahead of a possible mutiny. The blinking transponder in Hrodax' pocket had been the signal; *the coup was imminent, protect your vessels.* Now he said nothing, for nothing needed to be said. All would play out as fate dictated as it had so many times before in his career.

"Shall I kill this mutinous officer, Lord?" The Prax commander with the pistol asked.

Talxen looked from the astonished three guards to Xylan, then to the gun-toting officer. "No. Imprison him. But first, administer punishment for his crimes."

Xylan exhaled as the guards came toward him. The bully was smiling; the Admiral would receive no quarter in his beating from this one. That much had backfired, but Xylan's calculation that Talxen wouldn't kill him outright made the upcoming pain worth it. He'd live to fight again another day. *To the fallen.*

"Lord, we have secured twenty-six of the fleet. Fifteen cruisers, two of the heavies, nine smaller craft. Eight cruisers and the last heavy—the Dexellan—remain in the hands of the traitors."

"Too many!" The Prime pounded one hand with the other fist. "What happened?"

The Prax Captain on the screen looked unhappy. "Somehow the officers uncovered our forces and eliminated them quickly. All communications with them have been lost."

The Prime's face was contorted into a vicious combination of frustration and anger. "That's too many to defeat easily!"

"The nine traitorous ships have moved off and formed a defensive perimeter, overlapping their shields. It was if they had fully planned for our attack, Lord."

Xylan. The Prime's thoughts ran to murder, but came back to reason. He addressed the waiting aide.

"Please send word to Prax that Xylan's family be executed for treason."

The fleet officer's voice burst from the speaker. "Lord! No—."

The Prime pointed a finger at the screen. "—No, you listen, Horax. Re-establish communication with your compatriots aboard those ships! We must disable them from within. You will never convince the crew members of your own ships to fire on them openly. Loyalty to Xylan runs deep in your commands." It pained him to think of it as he cut the communication and shot a look at the aide, who scurried off to send the message. *Xylan and his house would pay for his insolence before the new Premier.*

"Lord, a word if you would?" One of his loyal officers stood nearby.

Talxen walked over, feeling spent and in need of libation. "What is it?"

"We have received a distress message from Tavar."

"The contents?"

"They have been discovered and are in need of evacuation."

"Evacuation! We *need* that steel, now more than ever!"

The Prax flinched in the face of the Prime's outburst. "Should I prepare a ship movement from the home system, Lord?"

"No," Talxen said firmly. "You should instruct Horax to form an attack flotilla from our loyal vessels and have them jump to the Struve system immediately. The humans only have three or four heavy units in that system—they're stretched too thin."

"But, Lord, they have a flotilla of their own within jump distance. We have avoided this battle for many cycles due to the strategic situation." The officer winced at his own temerity.

"Your objection is noted, and your insolence as well. Order the attack." Talxen rubbed his hands together with satisfaction. "My first victory will be the conquest of Tavar…at long last." The officer made to leave but Talxen stopped him. "And inform the medical unit; I want my son aboard the Horax' ship before they jump."

"As you wish, Lord."

"And prepare my personal escort; I will depart for Prax immediately; The First Advisor will assume the lead role until my return."

The Prax bowed and was gone.

The day was looking up. Talxen had no ultimate concern for the Prax infiltrators on Tavar; they could be easily mopped up by the humans now that they'd been found out. But the pretense for a Prax attack on Tavar and its valuable military resources was perfectly timed with the taking of the Premiership. Within a few days, his star will have ascended firmly over the empire for a generation to come.

Resolve Of Steel

Part Four - Resolve

Resolve Of Steel

Chapter 22

Tavar, Struve System

The shuttle angled in through the opening clamshell, bringing the cold in with it. Thankfully, the opening began closing again the instant the small vessel descended past the safety point.

Halloran stood with Chief Parker behind a thick window at the flight deck level, watching their craft descend. The close-in message from Kendra that she was on her way back had been received. As Halloran watched her land the ship next to another shuttle-style vessel, arms crossed as a defense against the cold that managed to find its way in everywhere, he said, "Let's hope this is what we needed." His chin was bare for the first time in a long time, and it was raw to the temperature. "Never thought a shave and a buzzcut could feel that good."

Parker also had a fresh shave that made him look decidedly Navy-like. In fact, they'd all grown accustomed to the beards over the last month. Now with access to shaving kits, everyone had availed themselves with gusto. Now the Chief looked at his skipper. "Sir, I am personally very ready to get back to work."

"Understood, Chief." Halloran glanced at the man with profound appreciation. "I want you to start on the steel project now. How much time will you need?"

"With the Tavarran help lifting the steel to Serapis and patch-welding? I can have her tightened up in forty-eight hours."

"What about our Fleet friends?"

Parker sighed. "Sir, that's above my pay grade. I think you need to figure out what to do about them. Just keep 'em from shooting my butt off while we're manhandling that chunk of steel up there."

Halloran nodded. "Take a man with you. Not DeBartelo; I want him with the assault team."

Parker considered the suggestion as they both saw Kendra coming across the deck dressed in her bulky snowsuit. The clamshell had closed above her. "I would have taken Patredes, but I'll go with Wilson, sir."

"Very well, let him know."

"Aye, sir. Um, permission to get going?"

Halloran nodded. "Granted, Chief. Keep me in the loop."

As Parker walked back the way they had come, the hatch door swooshed open and popped outward, letting in a blast of frigid air. Kendra stepped through the portal and glanced around for the controller. As she tapped the button to close the hatch Halloran said, "Welcome back, Captain."

She slid off the exposure suit headgear, giving her hair a shake to clear it. Halloran was struck by her rosy cheeks framed by that hair. "I see you received my message. Oh…" She was staring at him as he took her headgear from her hands.

"What?" He grinned.

Her eyes were on his crew cut, then down across his features as she took back her headgear. "You're shaved."

"Do you like it?"

She dropped her eyes and fidgeted in fishing out a data chip from a hip pocket. "Here's what you sent me out in the snow for. Antonov is worried about you." She held it out as if blocking the space between them.

He took it and grinned again, motioning down the passage. "This way." They shouldered past several colonists coming the other direction into the hangar. "I'm sure you like it better landing in a nice bay rather than blind out there."

She caught up to him and matched his pace in the widened corridor. "What's the situation down here? The comms blackout is frustrating."

"I think it's what is allowing us to plan this out ourselves. Remember, I'm still a renegade and you're technically dead." They came out of the passage and into a large, open chamber. Hundreds of colonists moved about the network of structures as they conducted their business of the day. "We're about to penetrate into the deep recesses of the mountain. Frankly, we've been waiting to get that chip from you. So?" He looked at her as he walked.

Two Tavarran women walked toward them. As they passed, both looked admiringly at Halloran and he smiled back.

Kendra coughed. "Lieutenant Carruthers and Travers did a full scan of the mountain in question. I think the Governor will find it useful. Faint but clear life-form readings that should help pinpoint their location on the colony mapping software."

"Good, that's good news. Nothing from the Fleet ships I presume?"

"The ship needs to alter course periodically to anticipate the defensive orbit patterns of the cruisers. Someone called it 'zig-zagging' as I remember."

Halloran nodded, then frowned. "Are they expecting trouble?" They reached a lift, and he pushed the control. "This one gets us up there, I think."

Kendra stepped in after him. "I don't think so, but it's standard protocol if the senior commander designates the threat level sufficient. Tavar would certainly qualify, in my mind."

As the car rose Halloran leaned against the wall, looking her thick clothing over. "You look frumpy," he said with a smile. He felt more peace here than he had at any time since the time jump. With her.

"Frumpy?"

"It's an Earth term. American. Means something like a ball of dough."

"Dough?"

He laughed. "Never mind."

She grew serious. "I'm sorry."

He cocked his head. "About what?"

"That you can't be there. Your home."

Halloran looked down, feeling the sense of peace freeze cold. After a moment he said, "Frankly, my home was gone before all this. When Cindy died, I planned to throw the rest of my life into the Navy; without them it was all I had left."

"You said you had other children?"

"Out of the house. Yes, I have them. Had them." Halloran shook his head. "I think we're all in denial that any of this really happened." He looked away. "Oz," he said softly.

"Oz?" She had moved closer.

"It was a movie. Made long before me. About a magical world that a kid gets sucked into." He chuckled. "Through a tornado. But she got to wake up."

Kendra laid a hand on his arm. "I don't know what any of that meant, but I do understand being stuck somewhere where you don't want to be, not knowing how to get back."

He was looking at her oddly. "Yes, I can bet you might."

She straightened and dropped her hand. "Anyway, I also know you can't talk about it with your crew. And that Jackson and the colonists are potentially unsafe. That leaves me, right?"

He grasped her upper arm, enveloping it with his long fingers. "Thanks, Captain. I might take you up on that once we get through this."

The car slowed prior to arriving. Halloran moved his hand to his belt and withdrew a new Tavarran security forces cap. He plopped it on his freshly cut head of hair and pulled it down snugly. "Now we help our fellow Tavarrans root out an infestation."

Aboard the Argon, orbiting Tavar

Lieutenant Treela kept her head down at her station both in an effort to study the scan data coming up from the planet surface and to avoid eye contact with the Captain, who was pacing the bridge directly behind her and currently experiencing intense frustration.

"Anything yet?" He was demanding of Tech Janyson.

"No sir, nothing new."

Orris paced over behind Treela and she heard him grinding his teeth as he stood nearby. She'd served with him on two ships so far in her career, first as a Tech and then as a commissioned officer. As the ship's sensor specialist, she was at the moment his focus of attention.

"New readings, Lieutenant?" he eventually queried the back of her head.

"Last pass shows the same data, sir."

He paced off a few steps then asked, "And how many were there?"

"One hundred and thirty-six, sir."

"And what levels?"

"Descending through level fourteen according to the colony schematic overlay."

He grunted and continued across the bridge. Treela glanced over the readings again, looking for new information that could ease the Captain's concern over not knowing.

Orris had stopped behind the communications officer. "Still no answer?"

The young Tech shook his head. "Sorry, sir. I'm hailing them on the usual channels, but no one's acknowledging down there."

"Irregular." Orris stalked back to his seat and dropped in. Treela glanced over and saw him, head in palm, lost in thought.

It *was* irregular. For all of the two months they'd been circling the planet, the Tavarrans had kept to a consistent pattern of behavior. The life-form readings would change locations on each pass of the sensors, going about their daily routine within the cavernous spaces of the mountain range that the sensors were attuned to. During the night cycles, only a few security personnel could be seen moving about. The computer recorded the total human count faithfully, and it never varied beyond acceptable norms given the traffic back and forth between the spaceport and surface.

But in the last day cycle things had changed dramatically. First, the sensor sweep had picked up a small craft somewhere in the periphery of its sensitively cone, alerting the bridge watch to extend the scan. But the blip had disappeared just as quickly and not reappeared. The event had been evaluated by the computer to be a cross between an atmospheric anomaly and a small patrol craft of the Tavarrans that had popped up too high into the atmosphere. Orris had dismissed the reading after reading the log.

But that was before the strange movements of groups of people deep in the colony. Energy readings had indicated that some weaponry was involved. When the groups had descended too deep in the planet for the scans to be reliable, Orris had called up the colony police and requested a conference with Jackson, but received only vague responses about needing more information before reporting in. Since then, nothing.

But things had become troublesome. Most of the population was on the move, heading up the lifts and stairwells to higher levels. To an observer it looked suspiciously like an evacuation. When Orris had seen the report of the large body of armed people were descending in force, it had been too much.

The last officer conference had entertained the idea of sending a shore party—also armed—to investigate. But Orris, always a cautious thinker, had elected instead to notify the Fleet and ask for additional ships to their three currently in orbit. He was beyond frustrated that the others on station had been called away just days before to the battle currently underway in the Epsilon

System. Two capital ships and three frigates, and two of those off in outer-system picket duty at that.

"Captain, communication coming in."

"Finally!" Orris jumped up.

The screen brightened over the tech's head and an officer's face and shoulders took form. Treela watched out of the corner of her eye, listening closely.

"Captain, Orris," the recording began. "Your advisory of unusual activity on Tavar has been received. Fleet leadership has appraised the current tactical situation in the Struve System and deems the threat level low."

Orris pounded the back of the tech's chair with a fist.

"However, we have a unit traversing to Sol system from an assignment in the Luyten system which we have directed to reroute to your location for as long as you deem it necessary. Valor will join Argon, Usar, Saranin, Borelin and Vanguard as part of the Tavarran defense flotilla. Please advise Captain Heres as to the updated situation upon his arrival and update Fleet as needed based on your discretion."

The comm screen went dark, leaving the Argon bridge crew waiting in suspense for the Captain's reaction.

After a moment of silence, Orris straightened and looked directly at Treela, catching her watching him. As she dropped her eyes he announced, "Recall the picket ships to Tavar; I want them close."

"Yes, sir."

"Pass the word to the watch crew to expect the arrival of a Fleet unit into the system. Track that vessel upon its approach to Tavar." He glanced down at the comm tech. "What class is the Valor?"

"Heavy cruiser, sir."

Orris nodded. "Thought so. Well, it's as good as we're going to get. Carry on, and keep me updated." He walked over to Treela's station and put a hand on the back of her chair. "Lieutenant," he said softly, "I want you monitoring the activity personally. Any additional anomalous behavior is to be reported to me immediately."

Aboard Valor, entering Struve system

"**Struve** system, sir," announced Grisa the sensor tech.

"Very well, set course for Tavar." Captain Heres slumped in his command station, looking to all the world bored out of his skull. He set his head back on the battle rest, staring at the overhead. "Renno, got anything interesting?"

"Sorry sir," answered the Lieutenant. "Scans indicate the Fleet units orbiting the planet. The spaceport is where the computer says it should be."

"Ugh. After all this we need an extra week's leave on Mars."

"Mars, sir?"

He sat up slightly and waved at the air. "Okay, I'll settle for patrolling between Mars and the belt. Anything but chasing ghosts around the shipping lanes."

Renno's chuckle was cut short as she made a short grunting sound.

"What?" Heres was out of his seat in a flash, standing behind her. He knew that sound.

"So, hmm. The sensors picked up something."

"What?" Heres leaned over her shoulder to get a look at what the ship's computer was telling her.

"The system is designating a target in orbit, but there's nothing there."

"What?"

She glanced up at him patiently.

He frowned at her. "Elaborate, please, Lieutenant."

Renno pointed at the holographic rendering of Tavar. The ship's targeting system had designated the three Fleet ships as friendlies. Two were identified as picket ships inbound from across the system but still hours off. But, there was another designate on the opposite side of the planet from the three in orbit. Renno knew what her Captain wanted and enlarged the imagery.

There was nothing there.

"Hmm."

"Exactly, sir."

"A bug?"

"It's possible, but unlikely. We just had the sensors calibrated less than a week ago. Reset them to shipyard defaults."

Heres straightened. "I knew that, didn't I? Seems like all we've been doing, calibrating things on a brand-new ship." He sighed, looking around the bridge. "It is interesting that the anomaly is running directly opposite to the Fleet ships, however."

"Sir, Argon is hailing us. It's Captain Orris."

Heres groaned audibly. The idea of being shunted off to Tavar and being placed under such an old-school flotilla leader as Orris bored him to no end. "I'll take it in my cabin. Let me know when we complete decel prior to orbital entry."

"Yes, sir," Grisa nodded at him.

He was halfway out the bridge entrance when Renno's call stopped him. "Sir!"

"Yes, Renno?" He set a hand on the door and looked back.

She was fully turned in her seat. "The computer has ID'd the orbital designate!"

"Really…what?"

"You better come look for yourself, sir. I don't think you'll believe me if I tell you."

Chapter 23

Tavar, Struve System

The first Prax casualty was sprawled across the tunnel floor with chunks of flesh splattered on the surrounding walls. Halloran stooped briefly to examine the body, wincing at the damage inflicted by the plasma bolts at close range. Picking through the gore he fished for pockets or any identifying items. The corpse was clear of anything, and he found himself wishing for Axxa's presence to advise him on the nuances of Praxxan attire. To his untrained eye, the dead alien was just a large lump of red flesh wrapped in winter clothing.

Wilson was standing there as he straightened, wiping his gloved hand on a pant leg. "Makes sense, sir. If they've been here over a year as I'm hearing from the locals, they're bound to be good at covering their tracks."

"Let's keep moving, Wilson. I want to stay with the group."

The Petty Officer nodded. "Aye, sir. Ain't leavin' you back here alone, sir."

Halloran gave the man a pat on the shoulder. "Lead the way."

The sounds of more shooting erupted down the passage as they jogged on.

"These rifles sure make an odd sound, sir," observed Wilson.

"Not something we're used to."

"They make a nice hole, though."

Halloran smiled tightly but didn't reply. As the two rounded a corner they came up on their unit, which was moving and firing into the darkness ahead.

A Tavarran named Anders was assigned to Halloran as the guide. He saw them coming. "More contact directly ahead! They are falling back."

Halloran nodded at him, then pushed Wilson forward. "Get back to your team."

Anders held up a tablet. "We are at this junction," he tapped the spot in question.

Halloran scanned the schematic. "And the other prong is coming down this shaft." He pointed to the corridor across the display.

"They will be coming into the lower level using a little-known accessway. I think they'll be able to get the Prax by surprise."

Halloran studied the man's earnest face; he liked the Tavarran. "I hope you're right. Seems like these guys have been under your noses for a long time."

"Moving up!" Called someone over the shooting up ahead.

Anders looked serious. "Now we know they're here. They're in our world."

Halloran's group numbered just over forty men; a nice complement of armed police and security who knew how to handle weapons. He admired their organization as they progressed steadily down the tunnel, clearing alcoves and keeping up a steady fire. When the first man got hit by a plasma shot—not center mass, thankfully—he was attended to by Elias Whitney as the rest moved on. Halloran paused over the duo, waiting until the Corpsman glanced up and nodded; the guy would recover.

After a protracted push of over an hour, the unit forced the defenders into an open cavern half-filled with covered pallets. Dust filled the air as plasma bolts exchanged between the two forces slashed through the tarps covering the pallets. As Halloran ducked behind one he peeked under the rough material. Crates.

Anders was there, tapping a crate. "Metals found during the mining. They wanted us to store it rather than incinerating it for some reason!" He yelled over the din of the echoes of plasma weapons around the cavern. "Been here forever!"

Halloran nodded. At least pallets filled with metal made good cover. He risked a look around the pallet and got a glimpse of tall figures darting between crates far across the cavern. There had to be a thousand stacks—excellent cover for *both* sides.

The battle went in their favor again as the Tavarrans showed considerable prowess in moving forward between the pallets, shooting and running as they went. Two were hit and killed by Prax fire, but they gave as good as they received and eventually the cavern was almost clear. Thirty of the Tavarrans took off into the far tunnel and Halloran jumped up to follow their lead.

"Sir!"

He turned to see Wilson waving at him and pointing at something. When he got there, he saw what the Petty Officer was gesturing at, and his jaw dropped.

A pallet had been knocked apart by a concentration of fire, ripping into the wood and splintering it. As a result, the contents were strewn out in a cascade onto the cavern floor.

Wilson picked up a chunk of the metal. It glowed in the artificial light illuminating the cavern. "Sir, is it?"

Halloran took the fist-sized piece from the other man and quickly examined it. "Sure looks like gold, Wilson."

Anders ran by. "We're on the move, Mr. Halloran."

Wilson pointed his rifle barrel at the piled gold chunks. "This is gold—is that what's in these crates?"

Anders frowned at the piece in Halloran's hand. "This is one of the storage caves for that stuff, yes. Do you know what it is?"

Halloran tossed the piece into the pile. "Nothing of value in this place, obviously." He pointed down the passage. "Let's go, Anders. Wilson, make a note to come back for your retirement fund later."

"Aye, sir."

Despite the narrow tunnels which hampered their advance, the men were able to force the Prax into another defensive position in a multi-leveled cavern deep within the mountain. A Tavarran leader named Lonergan was on the comm with the other force led by Max. "What are you finding?" Max asked him.

"New passages, widened passages with a lot of them leading here to this set of chambers."

"How far have you penetrated? We're seeing similar signs from our end."

"Not far. Mr. Halloran here wants to coordinate our final attack with yours. My people are hard to hold back, Max."

"Understood, Lonner. Give us fifteen minutes. Max out."

Lonergan shouted some orders to his men while Halloran pulled Wilson aside. "Remember," he said quietly, "let them do their thing. Once the area is secure, you are to be looking for information that may help us aboard Serapis."

"Aye, sir."

Anders handed Halloran a tablet. "Comm call for you, Mr. Halloran."

He carried it away a short distance to answer. It was Parker. "Sir, we're ready to go with the patch pieces. As a bonus, we're going to use one of their lift shuttles and Mr. Jackson has offered me three of his best welders with several bots."

"Robot welders, Chief?"

"Apparently it's the way to go. They say that based on my estimated specs, the cutting and welding should take less than thirty minutes."

Halloran nodded thoughtfully. "That sounds excellent, but what about the visibility of the lift shuttle to the Fleet ships?"

"Mr. Jackson says it may present a problem. Frankly, sir, he's still confused about our ship. I gather you kept some information from him?"

"Sorry, Chief. I suppose I made your job a bit harder."

Parker chuckled on the line. "No harder than it's been to work with these welders. Pig-headed lot all of them—they'd do any dockyard in the States proud. Sir."

Halloran thought a moment. "Thanks, Chief. Our plan will be to get back as a group and take the shuttle up. Kendra is guarding it and gathering intel from the Tavarrans right now. Our team takes the shuttle, you go in the Tavarran lift vessel with the steel. If we cause a commotion with the Fleet people, the Governor and I will attempt to stall them. Take anyone and anything you need to get that job done in record time, Chief. Clear?"

"On it, sir. Just get back safe first."

When he cut the transmission Wilson was walking over, cradling his rifle in his arms. "Do you need me, sir?"

Halloran relayed the rough plan.

"Makes sense, but what about Patredes? The doc says he's in no condition to be moved."

Halloran nodded grimly. "We will have to take him with us, or let the Tavarrans hide him until we can return."

Wilson looked serious. "You're thinkin' about Commander Chandler and the others, aren't you, sir?"

"I'm tired of leaving our people behind, Gerry."

"Me too, sir. Me too."

Rat City, Earth

The heat was oppressive. The people filling the streets were used to it and made their way to whatever subsistence they found in their daily struggle for life. For Lieutenant Commander Terry Singletary, the day only brought the dreary awareness that they were outsiders who'd be turned in for a pittance if the right local with Prax connections found them out.

Their ragged party stayed out of sight and moved only in the dark of night through the streets. The city was immense, and they seemed to wander for days in a single direction with painstaking care. The wreckage of humanity passed them by; people huddled in the streets, moments from starvation, or stumbling by without so much as a glance. There was the constant sense of eyes watching them, however, from every dark shattered window or dank alleyway.

The Navy men had long ago buried their uniforms and any identifying items in some rubble at Chandler's request. Their hosts were a band—one of several they'd crossed paths with—of "rebels." The twenty-odd people were unlikely to force their way into a Seven-Eleven, let alone that monstrosity of an alien headquarters that dominated the city's skyline. Armed with only a few small hand weapons they'd stolen from inattentive Prax and an assortment of knives, the humans were ill-equipped even to defend themselves.

Seeing this quickly after their rescue from the forcefield area along the water, Skip Chandler had found something for the Bonhomme Richard survivors to do; they'd started teaching the group about military routines of watch-keeping and reconnaissance. The leader was a thin, intelligent man named Granno. Granno's woman was called Jialar, and they seemed to have "adopted" the kid Boro who'd been part of their rescue—twice. Boro looked to be around thirteen but age seemed very relative in this desperate place. There weren't many kids on the streets; Singletary suspected that the Prax had done something to either irradiate or otherwise attempt to sterilize the population at some point.

In fact, Singletary spent almost every night wondering what the Earth was like beyond this slum of a city. Were there places where he could get to where the change wasn't so profound? Was his own town still there? From what little Granno could tell of the history, before even the Prax invasion which had occurred decades before he was born, Singletary doubted it; the northern hemisphere was said to be a wasteland of burnt geography and wild creatures. The people only referred to the time as "the dark years." Somehow, he figured the US would be gone and along with it Dayton, Ohio. Still, he wanted to make a try for it. But Skip wanted them all together for as long as possible should the Captain try to make it back to them. Skip argued that if it were possible, the group would much rather return to 2029 than disperse in this timeline to an uncertain fate, assured that their loved ones were long dead.

The idea of it created a tightness in Singletary's chest that wouldn't go away.

He thought a lot about Myra; they had been set to be married that coming Spring of 2030. Her parents had been thick in the planning already on August 21st, the date the Bonhomme Richard had left that world behind, courtesy of these horrible aliens. It had only been a month or so since their last kiss, but he was already forgetting her in the immediacy of survival in Rat City. He wished he'd kept a photo of her, but everything had been on his phone which of course was still aboard ship in the desert out there, battery long-dead anyway.

He sat against the stone wall and pondered his tattered sandals; they'd given up the boots too. His feet were raw and in constant pain. *No Tylenol in the med bag*, he thought grimly. *And no med bag.* He looked across the dimly lit hovel they were lying low in today at Commander Chandler, who was flat on his back with eyes open staring at the ceiling of burnt plaster-like material. Beyond Skip and the clump of other Navy men sleeping sat Seaman David Witmer and Missile Tech Karl Lamb, idly rolling a smooth stone someone had picked up between them. One of the rebels, an old man whose name Singletary thought was Deiter—sounded German somehow—watched the two seamen with narrowed eyes. He expected the native to tell them to stop the noise momentarily. This was their existence.

Chandler was sure that the Skipper had gotten away; he pointed to the fact that the Prax had all zoomed off and left them alone as proof. Singletary could agree to that, but whether Halloran or anyone else on that shuttle was still alive was an open question. He rested his head on his knees, the position he spent most daylight hours recently.

"Terry."

He looked up again to see that Skip was no longer in the same position. The sun had moved as well; the light in the room was different, lower. He'd slept. Chandler was standing in the crushed doorframe, motioning to him.

With a glance to see that everyone else was still in their places—Witmer and Lamb were sleeping now—he grunted to his feet and padded over to follow Chandler through into the next room of the dilapidated house.

Most of the rebels were here, cradling their weapons between their legs in a way as to prevent it from being stripped from them in their sleep. Eyes followed the two Navy officers as they approached Granno and Jailar where they crouched in the center of the rough floorboards. Not that they looked much like parade-ground spec anymore; long beards and unkempt, dirty hair hid their features. Lack of consistent and proper food had taken a toll on their bodies as well.

How long had they been creeping through this terrible place?

Singletary noted the huge hole blasted in the far wall; this house had been the center of a battle at some point in the past. These rebels knew all the abandoned squatter locations to hide. They had to.

Granno nodded to the floor next to him. When the two were seated he smoothed out the dust where he'd been doodling and drew an oblong circle with his finger. He tapped the edge near his line. "We are here."

Chandler edged in. "Close to the outskirts of the city."

"This word outskirts does not translate in my device."

"The edge. Of the city."

"Yes, yes, edge. One night's crossing. There is protection field here too."

Chandler nodded. "Makes sense." He looked at Singletary. "Must be a massive power generator somewhere."

"It is the Center which holds energy generator," answered Granno. "We know this is where the Prax concentrate their…resources."

Singletary was hopeful. "Can we get out?" He asked Granno, feeling Chandler's eyes still on him.

Granno shrugged. "There are tunnels. Prax know this too. They patrol heavily here." He drew a line away from the circle, tapping one side. "Water here. And land here."

Chandler was thinking. "So if Tom wanted to find us, what's the best place to effect a pickup? Inside or outside the city?"

Singletary felt the urge to shout, but kept his voice soft at great effort. "Anywhere but this hellhole, Commander." He deliberately used Skip's rank to make the point.

Chandler exhaled slowly, then looked at Granno. "What do you want to do?"

Granno shrugged again; he did that a lot. "Your people, they are strong and healthy. But no weapons. Some day you tell me where you come from, agreed?"

"Agreed."

Another shrug. "For now, we can be team together. But you need weapons."

"Are there weapons out here?" Chandler tapped the land area noted in the dust.

"There is a station Prax keep, many kilometers up the coast. But it is an outpost and not so well-defended I hear." He looked carefully around the room. "Before I don't think I have the men to plan attack." He pointed at Chandler and then Singletary. "With you, I say we try." The brown-skinned man's disgusting teeth showed as he attempted a grin.

Jailar spoke up for the first time. "We *all* go. Not separate." There were three women in the group; Singletary could understand her desire to stay together rather than be left behind in this city.

After a moment of looking at her, Granno nodded. "It is better if we travel together."

"When do we go?" Singletary asked eagerly.

Granno frowned at him. "Tomorrow night we will try the tunnel best remaining no Prax."

Singletary heard the other rustling around them; the rebels understood what was happening. They were excited—fearful?—of the prospect of leaving the city.

Get me out of here, Singletary thought. *I'll kill any red alien I need to to see a country road again. Or a ship's deck, free to sail.*

Chandler smiled thinly at Singletary's obvious enthusiasm. "Tomorrow night it is. I'll pass the word to the men." He patted Singletary on the shoulder as he got his feet.

"You ready to fight, Single man?" asked Granno.

Singletary stood and looked down at him. "Watch me."

Chapter 24

Tavar, Struve System

Three hours and twenty-six dead later, the humans had gained the upper hand. Max and his unit had linked up with Halloran's and together the large human contingency had pressed the Prax defenders into a series of small caverns. The confined spaces had lent themselves to the defending side, however, and the human casualties quickly mounted. Max called a halt to the advance and their people took up positions guarding the cavern openings. The leadership gathered in the main cavern liberated by the humans. Halloran wondered at the myriad of massive machine units installed; they must have been carried in piece by piece over months…or years. Max, Anders and Lonergan moved amid the equipment with much greater familiarity. Eventually Max returned to where Halloran stood over a badly injured Frank DeBartelo; Corpsman Whitney and a Tavarran medic worked to stabilize the big sailor, who'd been hit in the gut by a plasma bolt.

Max looked down at the wounded man. "What's his condition?"

Halloran replied, "Critical. The shot took out a section of his bowel."

"Can we move him?"

Whitney looked up from where he was holding pressure on the prostrate Navy man. "We'll have to. He won't last two hours down here."

Max frowned. "We should get him going, as well as those other two wounded. We can spare the manpower to give them a dozen helpers."

Lonergan was there. "I'll organize that now, Max."

Max nodded, then looked at Halloran with a wave encompassing the cavern. "They've built a miniature version of our smelting and rolling mills. This equipment is basically a very close copy of Tavarran technology."

Halloran nodded. "I understand they're very good at that."

"Well, at this scale they'd be working at a small fraction of our production. One of the teams found a cut passage for the rolled product to be hauled to the surface. I'll wager that there's a hidden hangar somewhere that they used to move the steel off-world when no one was scanning that sector."

Anders walked up. "I found the control room, Max. Just like you guessed, it's a small version of our level four monitoring facility."

Max shook his head. "This operation has been bleeding our power source for at least a year. We should re-examine the data to see when the first noticeable drop-off occurred. Who knows how many months they've been finishing the metal? And also, what exactly are they using it for?"

Halloran thought of his ship orbiting over their heads but said nothing. Max would know soon enough of their request for help to install Tavarran steel on their ship.

One of the security team trotted up. "Max, excuse me."

"What is it?"

"Scans down here are a mess as you know, but we think we see nineteen Prax life-forms in their defensive position."

"No way for them to try to blast their way out?"

The man shrugged. "They could try, but we've got three guns to every one of theirs. If they had heavy weapons, they'd have used them by now, I would guess."

Max looked around the cavern. "This place isn't rigged to blow, is it?"

Anders spoke up. "My men have been looking; so far, no signs of that."

"Casualty count?"

The Tavarran medic looked up from DeBartelo. "Twenty-three Prax, all dead. Twenty-six Tavarran dead and fifteen wounded, some mortally."

Max fixed Halloran with a sad look. "A bad business."

Anders said with a sense of awe, "They didn't go down easily."

Max pointed at DeBartelo and said to Halloran. "You oversee Lonergan and the wounded back to the upper levels. We'll wait the Prax out down here; they can't last forever in those holes."

Halloran nodded. "Take care of yourself." They shook hands and Halloran realized how much he'd come to like the Tavarrans.

As Halloran moved off, Max called Anders back over. "You go with the Captain and stick with him. Get him what he needs for his men and keep an eye on him for the Governor. He may be a citizen now but it's our job to watch for threats to the rest of the colony. You go where he goes, understand?"

Anders nodded and trotted off after Halloran, who was now following the makeshift stretcher his man was laid on and being carried by four Tavarran policemen.

His security officer said at his shoulder. "You don't trust those offworlders, do you?"

Max put his hands in his pant pockets. "Jackson made the call; they're citizens now. But that doesn't mean trouble won't follow them." He jerked his head to indicate the Prax equipment around them. "Look what we found once they got here." He looked at the man with a shrug. "What's next?"

Parker and Kendra were back in the hanger, watching as six Tavarran handlers positioned the slab of steel destined for the Serapis on a towing sled. Petty Officer Wilson—recently returned from below in the caves—was in the midst of the gaggle of locals, watching the process closely and asking questions loudly every few minutes. In addition to the huge chunk of metal, half a dozen box-shaped contraptions were loaded into the sled where they promptly locked down in place. Wilson shook one hard and looked over to where Parker was watching, shrugging mightily before turning away.

Eventually a worker trotted over. "The product is secured for transport. The requested welding units are attached as well."

"That those boxes over there?" pointed Parker.

The man nodded. "They will detach on their own once commanded to initiate."

"Tell me again how this works."

"Your ship, when you get this piece in place to where you need it, the bots receive the instructions from the ship's computer as to the exact locations of the hull repairs. Your job is to watch it."

"Why should we bother to watch if the freakin' computer will do everything for us?"

The man seemed amused by Parker's language. "Because the computer isn't perfect."

Kendra intervened. "Don't worry, Chief Parker. Travers will be there to assist the bots; he's used similar tech in Fleet repair situations."

"Okay, then."

The Tavarran was still there. "May I ask a question?"

"Shoot."

The man smiled again. "Your language. I see that you speak a language that is not Standard. I have heard this language before, what it is called?"

"English."

"I am most interested in this language 'English' as my family elders also can speak it. Where do you know this language from?"

Parker heard the Skipper's admonition in the back of his head. "We are from Earth."

The man's eyes went wide. "Earthers?" He looked from Parker to Kendra with astonishment.

"Not me, my home is Coloran," Kendra raised a hand in protest.

The man was not dissuaded. "Earthers who speak English! My elders will be pleased to meet you."

Parker shifted his footing. "Yeah, well, we're aiming to shove off as soon as we get re-organized here."

The man's face fell. "I am sad for that."

Wilson trotted up to the grate they were standing on. "Seems like we're ready here. Any word from the Captain?" He looked quizzically at the Tavarran, noting the odd expressions on everyone's face. "What'd I miss?"

The Tavarran said, "Another Earther who speaks English."

Parker smiled. "Yep. We got a few here and there."

The man's face brightened. "I wish to visit your ship! I can assist with the repairs; I know this material very well."

"Um," Wilson looked at Parker with a 'what are you doing here?' look.

Parker said, "What's your name, friend?"

"Cassis."

Parker shook his hand. "Chief John Parker. Thanks for your help, Cassis."

"Then I may go to your ship?"

Wilson stepped between them, back to Cassis. "Thanks but we have to go regroup with the Captain. Ma'am?" He indicated to include Kendra in the conversation.

"Ma'am... Why do people keep saying that around me?" Kendra asked Parker as they left a crestfallen Cassis and began following Wilson up the gangway into the colony proper.

"It's a term of properness. Back on Earth. Toward women. Guess you don't use that out here?"

She shook her head as several workers passed them. "I don't remember that term. It is military in origin?"

"No, ma'am—sorry. It's been around for a long time. English, I think."

"Yes, I understand that it is the language."

Parker held open the hatch door for her. "No, I mean the English. A country…the UK? United Kingdom?"

She looked pointedly at his held-open door. "And this, is it also a properness for women?"

Embarrassed, Parker let her pass through. "Sorry. Habit."

She paused inside the door as he closed it. "The only united kingdom I know of is the Telarian Kingdom. But they are not of Earth."

"Yeah, well, my Irish ancestors weren't too fond of the English, anyway."

"I do not understand."

"I'm sorry, Captain."

"I much prefer *that* title to your 'ma'am' term, Chief Parker."

"Aye…Captain."

Wilson called back from up the hall. "What are you gabbing on about back there, Parker? Ma'am, we need to move out if that's okay with you."

Kendra looked at Parker, who shrugged apologetically.

As they caught up to Wilson Kendra answered. "We are behind you, *ma'am.*"

Wilson half-turned mid-stride with a raised eyebrow.

"Don't ask, Gerry; I'll fill you in later," Parker offered.

The group gathered in the colony's medical facility where Patredes was laid up. He was awake and greeted the trio as they entered.

Wilson shook the Seaman's hand. "Looking better, Rick." He glanced at the female medtech, then at Kendra. He bent over and whispered, "Just don't call her 'ma'am.'"

Patredes frowned. "Um, yes, sir."

Parker motioned to the medtech. "Any word on the situation down below?"

The woman looked him over critically before answering. "The medical director is returning with a number of casualties."

Patredes added, "There's been a lot of activity here. Looks like a bunch of wounded on their way."

The woman looked at Patredes like he should be sedated, then nodded. "We are expecting sixteen patients."

"Any from our party?" asked Parker.

The woman turned away. "Please stay out of the way once they arrive, thank you."

Wilson was still next to Patredes' bed. "Friendly one, that."

"I will return." Kendra had her hand on the door latch.

"Where are you going, Captain?" Parker had a concerned look on his face.

"I will return." And she was gone.

"Another friendly one," offered Wilson. "What's with the 'ma'am' issue? And why are you chatting up the locals?"

Before Parker could launch into a defense a commotion sounded in the hall outside. In a flash the woman tech was there, shooing Parker away from the entrance. "They are here."

Kendra found Jackson in the control center, watching the planetary defense monitors. He acknowledged her presence. "Just come from the medical center? I understand the wounded have returned."

She shook her head. "I left just before they arrived."

He waved at a monitor. "Another Fleet ship just entered orbit. Transponder says it's the Valor. Apparently Captain Orris felt the need to—what?"

Her face had gone pale. "That's the ship I was last on."

"So? Something I should know?"

Kendra composed herself with a slight shake of her head and a glance away. "That Captain and I have a history."

"Heres?"

She nodded.

Jackson looked exasperated. "I need to focus on protecting this colony. Your prior relationships are *not* a priority, Captain—hero status or not." He pointed at the monitor. "Tell me about this."

She rallied her expression before answering. "The Valor was in pursuit of Captain Halloran's vessel. Luyten system."

"So…"

"I expect their mission hasn't changed."

"So they're looking for you? Where exactly *is* Halloran's ship, Captain? I know he's holding out on me but I expected that. But you—I need straight answers here."

Kendra felt the pull of conflicted convictions. "Governor, as you know, the Captain of a ship is the absolute master of it. And as a member—."

"You're not going to pull that one, are you?" With a sudden burst, Jackson took Kendra by the upper arm and steered her toward a door nearby. Before she could mount a resistance, he had her into a small conference room and was closing the door behind him.

She tugged free and crossed her arms defiantly.

He glowered. "I've been more than fair with you and Halloran to this point. In fact, I've boxed myself in by bestowing Tavarran citizenship upon all of you."

"I declined that offer as a Coloran citizen."

He waved a hand in front of her. "Either way, he now has the *right* to decline to answer my questions. But I think he's more than that. What I *won't* get is the straight talk I need when it comes to his ship and crew; like I said, I understand that." He pointed at her. "But you're a member of the Fleet—the same Fleet that's up there defending Tavar as a war asset. You need to understand your responsibility here. Or should I just call up Orris or the Captain of this Valor and ask *them* about you?"

She was beaten. "What do you need from me?"

Halloran was just regrouping in the medical center with his team when the entrance flew open and Jackson was framed in the doorway. His dramatic appearance drew the attention of everyone except DeBartelo, who had slipped long ago into unconsciousness.

"Captain Halloran," The Governor said loudly with clearly-restrained anger. "A word in private?"

Halloran looked around his gathered men. "Where's Captain Kendra?"

Parker looked cowed. "She took off shortly after we got here, sir."

"All right—."

"*Now,* Captain?" called Jackson from the door.

Halloran lifted a hand in acknowledgment but didn't look over. "All right, you men see about transferring Patredes and DeBartelo to our shuttle once Kendra returns. Parker, get the Tavarrans ready to go with the metal. I'll be right back."

In the hall Jackson stalked down a few meters and opened a door across the way for Halloran to follow him into. The space inside was an examination room.

Jackson turned on Halloran. "You're on the run from the Fleet for kidnapping their officers! You are the *Captain* of an advanced Prax warship! And now you've conveniently come to Tavar and I've granted you *citizenship*!!!" He pounded a close-by cabinet with a meaty fist.

Halloran took a few steps to the side to open the space between them. "I see you've been talking to Captain Kendra."

Jackson glowered. "I knew she'd do her duty at *some* point. But I didn't expect what she told me!"

Halloran had put the examination table between them. "It's true that our ship is a 'liberated' Prax warship; Lord knows we can't understand half the controls aboard her."

"Where's the Prax crew? Or are they hiding aboard your ship like I've had here for months, apparently?"

Halloran was serious. "They're all dead; some virus killed them all before we came across her."

"Her who?"

"The ship. She was called the Trellixan by the Prax, but I rechristened her the Serapis."

Jackson shook his head as if to clear it, then stepped forward and leaned his balled fists on the exam table, looking directly at Halloran. "Your ship possesses advanced cloaking technology that renders it invisible to sensor activity," he growled. "A small fact that you have omitted to date. What exactly are you hiding, Halloran?"

Halloran met his glare. "Oh, it gets better, Governor. We're not only renegades who got our ship from those people—what were they called?—'Haulers,' that's right. We're not only kidnappers of Fleet officers. We're harboring a Praxxan member of their royal family."

Jackson's eyebrows shot up. "Why am I not surprised?" He banged a hand on the table. "Come on, there's *got* to be more, Halloran. Try to *really* impress me! I've a mind to lock all of you up and call a Fleet shore party down to retrieve their prize. What's his name again? Oh yes, Captain Heres of the Valor…"

Halloran sighed with head lowered, then looked up at Jackson. "All right. There's a good reason my crew speaks English as natives…"

Chapter 25

Chief Reyes was back with his unit of Tavarrans from the lift. Parker saw the short, stocky Cuban walking with the others, rifle slung over a shoulder as if he'd been part of their crew for years. But it was the somber silence of the men as they passed that struck Parker. When Reyes looked up and saw Parker he slowed, patting a few of the Tavarrans on the back as they walked by. Several of them spared Parker a suspicious glance without a word.

"Chief, what happened?" he asked quietly. "You look a bit rattled."

Reyes saw the others inside the medical bay over Parker's shoulder. He made a head motion. "Inside."

Wilson stepped forward and shook Reyes' hand. "Good to see you back, sir."

Reyes nodded at him, his eyes taking the short party in. "Rick, good to see you awake." After a moment he asked Parker, "Where's the Captain?"

"The Governor stormed in a while ago and took Skipper for a walk. He was pretty unhappy. What's got you, Chief?"

Reyes looked around the group. "Captain asked me to keep watch on the Prax after he left with your bunch."

"Right."

"Well, my team and I were waiting them out where they'd holed up. Nowhere to go, understand? Then, not that long ago, we hear plasma shots going off and everyone dives for cover. But nothing, none of those nasty rock chips come flying." He rubbed a cheek where a bright red cut sat. "After a while one of the braver Tavar people goes to look and calls the rest of us in to see." He blinked—a veritable outburst for the Chief.

After a moment Parker prompted him. "And?"

"And they'd blown each other's heads off, that's what. The mess was incredible." His eyes took on a vacant look. "What that last poor sod had to see just before he put the barrel in his mouth…"

"Sounds like they got what was coming to them."

Everyone turned to Patredes, who'd uttered the words from his bed.

Reyes nodded. "I'm feeling like it's time to get back to the ship." He looked around one more time, turning for the door. "I'll go an' find the Skipper."

A Tavarran policeman stopped Reyes outside. "You and your men come with me."

Reyes eyed the man's rifle, cradled in his arms at easy reach. His own was slung over a shoulder. "Sure, you here on behalf of someone?"

The policeman read his thoughts. "You can keep your rifle. Governor wants to see you right now, up top."

"And our Captain?"

The man looked unperturbed. "I expect he'll be there. Either way, the Governor wants you, so that's where you'll go."

"Sure." Reyes turned and reopened the medical center door. "Guys, Governor wants us all hands on deck. Follow us."

The group obediently kept up with the policeman who shepherded them through passages that were beginning to feel familiar after several days at the colony. A cargo lift took the men up to the control level.

"I don't like leaving Patredes and DeBartelo behind, sir," said Whitney under his breath to Reyes.

"They're in good hands. Let's look out for the Skipper and Captain Kendra now."

The door opened, and they paraded down a well-appointed passage lined with offices and banks of screens displaying cameras tuned to various points within the colony levels. One in particular caught Reyes' attention; the medical room where Patredes sat, staring at the wall from his bed.

At the end of the corridor they were turned left and down another, even nicer hall. Numerous people dressed in the gray and orange attire of the police watched them pass. Reyes was nodding in greeting to them as appropriate from his position behind their shepherd. Finally, they arrived at a door made of wood—not something seen much on this rock planet— and the policeman opened it for them, stepping aside with a nod to Reyes as if to say *thanks for not making my life difficult.* Reyes returned the nod and walked in.

The Governor and the Captain were sitting at the far end of a long conference table. "Come in, gentlemen, and have a seat," waved the Captain.

Reyes walked left and halfway around the rectangular table before pulling out a chair and sitting. Parker, Wilson and Whitney followed suit, everyone looking a little bewildered. Reyes set his rifle on the floor but within reach.

Jackson looked like a man who'd just finished throwing up his lunch. "There are the two in the medical unit."

Halloran nodded. "Them and Captain Kendra."

"She's on her way."

Halloran caught Reyes' glance and shook his head microscopically. *No trouble.* With a last check of his rifle's location Reyes set a thin smile on his face and clasped his fingers in front of him on the conference table, which he noticed was made from wood as well. In fact, it had a familiar feel about it…the smooth lacquer marred by scratches, yet…

"These men are all from the military you describe. The 'US Navy' circa 2029."

Reyes saw Parker across from him start with surprise.

Halloran took no notice. "Yes, and the two in the medbay. Plus another dozen or so aboard the Serapis. There are several others…still on Earth as I described earlier."

So the Captain had told the Governor everything, Reyes realized.

"And the Prax—they devised this time machine? Do you agree with this account?" The Governor addressed Parker.

"Yes, sir."

The door opened and Captain Kendra and Max from Tavarran Security entered. Kendra looked from Halloran to Jackson, then sat next to Parker on Halloran's side of the table, which did not go unnoticed by the Governor, who shifted in his chair. Max walked around and sat next to Reyes, looking from the gun on the floor to the Chief with a slightly raised eyebrow as he did.

"Now that we're all here, Governor, I think it's time we discussed our departure from Tavar."

Jackson had his own hands on the table and he lightly drummed his fingers before answering. "Captain, there's a matter of accountability I must broach with you…and your men here."

"Go on." Halloran pushed back a bit from the table, one hand on its edge.

"The record shows that you swore an oath to the Republic of Tavar. I understand your desire to return to Earth as you related to me, but I would contend that you and your vessel should be held accountable, at least in part, for the defense of this planet."

"Your assistance in arranging the materials and equipment to facilitate the repair of my ship is greatly appreciated."

"A ship that is constructed, by your own admission, of Tavarran state property—now captained by a Tavarran citizen as well," Jackson countered.

"The Captain and crew of the Serapis owe Tavar a debt—of this I am not in dispute." Halloran smiled.

"As do the people and government of Tavar do to you, in your aid rendered to discover and flush out the Prax infiltration. But, as Governor I feel obligated to clarify this matter before allowing your party to leave."

Halloran's eyes narrowed. "You didn't say that earlier. You're going to hold us hostage?"

Max said, "A debt is owed. The steel and services—."

"—Are more than repaid by the sensor scans and personnel assistance rendered," finished Halloran. He leaned in. "We have two men down for you, Governor."

The room was still as the two leaders glowered at each other. Finally, Kendra broke the tense silence. "Look, it's my fault that we're here now." When the two looked her way she continued. "When the Valor entered orbit, I knew that we needed a new plan. Heres isn't that stupid; he'll smell something is up right away when we lift off with a load of steel and then disappear somewhere in mid-orbit." She looked around the table. "Does everyone remember what happened last time we faced him?"

"We need a distraction."

Everyone looked at Reyes, who'd blurted the words out uncharacteristically.

Halloran responded first. "The Chief has a point. We need to effect the repairs on the ship, and you need a reasonable exit strategy with regard to this Prax incursion on your territory; when the Fleet hears about it they'll be down here in force to protect their investment."

Jackson had the look of someone who'd already come to his conclusion. "All right, Halloran. You can have your repairs *but* you need to shield Tavar from any consequences from the Fleet once they find out about the Prax here." His shoulders slumped somewhat. "And they will; this place is not airtight with regard to Fleet informants."

Halloran stood; the meeting was his now. "Chief, got any ideas in your mind?"

Reyes was looking at his rifle again. It was in his hands now. "Yes, sir…I think I do."

After the men had hurried off with Max to work on Reyes' idea, Jackson, Kendra and Halloran lingered in the conference room. Halloran bent under the table. "This is an old Earth furniture piece; where'd it come from?"

"The first colonists—my family among them—brought relics of their old life on Earth. I don't know much about it except that their world was badly damaged by the ancient war."

Halloran ran his hand over the tabletop. "See this inlay? It's called 'leather' and it's skin from an animal called a cow."

Kendra rolled her eyes. "How barbaric."

Halloran tapped the table. "It's very ornate. Must have come from an important place on Earth."

Jackson nodded. "Telos would know. He probably has the original records."

"Telos?"

"He's an archivist."

"An archivist?" Halloran was surprised.

"Yes, an archivist collects information of historical—."

"Right, I know what they are, Jackson. Who's this guy you're talking about?"

Jackson shrugged. "Only the elders know much about him. He operates one of the oldest archives in humanity. Those of us from old families periodically use him for research of claims against other families."

"Is he on Earth?"

Jackson laughed. "No, I should hope not. The Prax would've gotten him right away. He and his bots renovated an old orbiting station not too far off, in the

Perses system. The Fleet knows about it but leaves him alone. I hear the Haulers keep him supplied."

Halloran was thinking. "So this archive has a lot of ancient historical Earth data?"

"More than any other I know of between Earth and Coloran."

Kendra spoke. "What are you up to, Halloran?"

Halloran put a hand on both of their shoulders. "You can both call me 'Tom' if you ever get around to remembering that. But not in front of my men, thanks."

"Two names," Jackson said to Kendra. "How strange."

"Once we get out of here I might want to pay this Telos fellow a visit. Can you get me the coordinates for our navigational system?"

Jackson stepped to the door. "Will do that right now. You two should prep for your flight." And he was gone, bald head reflecting the light of the outside hall as he walked off.

"I like him," Halloran announced.

"Hmph. At least you don't call him 'ma'am.'"

Halloran opened the door for her. "What is *that* about?"

With a grunt, Kendra pushed by him and took off at a quick gait.

In the hangar bay, the Tavarran lift engine was ready to go and Kendra was waiting for the group in the Serapis shuttle.

Max shook Reyes' hand. "Safe travels, Abran."

"Take care of our adopted home planet, Max. And take care of my two men 'till I come back for them."

"Will do. I expect your little diversion will stir up some interest from the Fleet gang. We'll keep your men out of sight if it comes to it."

"Keep your head down."

Max grinned. "I like that. 'Keep your head down.'"

Reyes joined Parker at the lift engine. "So you've got this all planned out, right Chief?"

"Absolutely, Master Chief. What could go wrong?"

Reyes slapped him on the back. "Let's not keep the lady and our two replacements waiting."

Once the remains of the shore party were aboard, Kendra fired up the ship's main engine and they lifted into the air. As they watched, the lift engine followed them, its onboard nav computer programmed to track them all the way to the Serapis. Inside it was Anders, who had volunteered to go with the Americans along with…Cassis.

Halloran watched Reyes strap in. "That thing will fly back by itself?" He asked Parker. "The Governor promised me those two men as replacements for Patredes and DeBartelo."

"Yes, sir, they'll EVA over to the ship while repairs are underway with the bots. Cassis—the dock guy—has experience with those things. Then the lift will autopilot back home."

As they rose, they passed a series of viewports in the levels. At one, Halloran caught sight of Jackson standing with his hands behind his back. He pointed the figure out to Kendra with a tap on her shoulder.

"Watching us go," she commented.

"Man's got some resolve. He runs quite an operation in what amounts to the middle of a war zone." He was silent for a moment, then, "Makes me want to return to Earth all the more. We've got things to make right."

She looked over her shoulder at him. "Jackson's not the only one with a resolve of steel."

"Serapis shuttle…hangar control. shell opening. safe journey and send us back our lift and bots."

"Will do, hangar control. Shuttle out." Kendra closed the comm. "No point in any further advertising over the comms."

"Time to ship?"

She checked the readouts. "If they are still in the same orbit, we'll link up with them in twenty minutes."

Halloran leaned back and said to Parker. "Chief, twenty minutes to shipside. Then who knows how much time we can give you."

The Chief nodded. "Give me another thirty beyond that and we'll be ready to jump out of here."

Chapter 26

Aboard Valor

"**Has** it moved?" Heres stopped behind Renno.

"Hard to tell from this position in the atmosphere, sir. As you noted, the anomaly is carefully positioned on the far side of the planet from the rest of the Fleet ships."

"Captain," said a tech nearby. "Captain Orris for you."

Heres sat at his station and pulled up the monitor in front of him. The face of the older Captain lit it up. "Captain Heres, may I ask what you are doing?"

Heres nodded to the tech. "Please switch us to the secondary channel." The Fleet kept a rotation of alternating comms in order to confound listeners. When the tech nodded back, Heres smiled at the screen.

"Captain Orris. I am moving my ship closer to a scanning anomaly currently in low orbit."

Orris frowned. "Can you be more specific?"

"May I have permission to conduct this maneuver beforehand?"

"So I understand this; you've identified an anomaly in orbit and want to maneuver closer to it—just not in the normal fashion of adjusting to match?"

Heres paused. He was placing a lot of stock in Renno's hunch that the "anomaly" was being identified by the targeting computer as matching the readings shortly after the Prax warship had disappeared off their sensors back in the Luyten system. Computers were known to be wrong in their target designations before—actually quite often at longer ranges or when conditions weren't optimal. But—and this was a big but—if that was indeed their prior quarry renegade Captain, Heres knew that simply dropping into a lower orbit and adjusting velocity to match would spook him and send him off to yet another system. Suddenly, Tavar itself and the drudgery had been replaced by the thrill of the chase once again. No, it just *had* to be Halloran. "Captain, unless there is another more pressing concern to address my crew to?"

Orris' face revealed that he was perfectly aware that there wasn't anything else, and that Heres would get his way. "You may proceed with your...*maneuver*," he growled with frustration.

"Thank you, sir. Oh, and please, no open-comm communication until we advise otherwise?" He flashed another smile.

"Orris out." The screen went dark on the annoyed senior Captain's face.

"Now we're committed, sir," observed Renno dryly.

"Sir!" called another sensor tech. "Picking up two small craft in ascent from the colony."

Heres leaned over the armrest to see the tech. "Heading is the spaceport?"

She shook her head. "No, sir, the vector is taking them in the opposite direction...one is ID'd as a Tavarran lift engine towing a cargo. The other is..." She looked at him with confusion. "Uncategorized."

Heres smacked the armrest with a fist. "Renno! Pick up the pace. Weapons powered up and ready to engage!"

The weapons Lieutenant turned to him. "Sir? We're in orbit with three other Fleet units…what are we powering up for?" She wasn't in on the "maneuver" yet.

"Just do it, Lieutenant. Renno, talk to me!"

She was flicking between screens, making adjustment furiously. "I think we got them, sir. The vector is a perfect match to a geostationary path to the anomaly."

Heres stood up, excitement coursing through his veins. "That just *can't* be a coincidence. Prepare to—."

"Sir!" The sensor tech was looking at Renno for confirmation. The latter saw her stare and went back to her instruments. "Confirmed. Captain, there's been a massive explosion on the planet surface."

"Sir, Captain Orris on the comm."

Before Heres could move, the senior Captain's voice filled the Valor's bridge. "Valor, abort your current maneuver and prepare to close with the rest of the flotilla. Governor Jackson is reporting a Prax attack on their refining facility!"

"What!" Heres stormed over to Renno expectantly.

Renno pointed at a display. "Readings confirmed, sir. There was a factor-six internal explosion within the colony's secondary facility."

"Captain Heres, acknowledge my directive," Orris said over the comm.

Heres looked from the sensor image of the rising small craft to the other of the expanding cloud of debris that was already dissipating in the harsh surface winds. He squeezed the back of Renno's chair. "It's a distraction," he fumed. "It's too perfect."

"Try telling Orris," Renno offered.

He stalked back over to his station and hit the comm control. "Captain Orris, may I point out the two small craft in the middle atmosphere?"

Orris came back on immediately. "Yes, we're aware of them, Captain. A shipment to the spaceport gone off-course. They'll correct…the priority is the Prax, Captain. Or have you forgot?"

Heres' cheeks reddened as he looked around his bridge. Not a face was angled in his direction.

"Close *ranks,* Captain. Prepare an armed shore party for departure in ten minutes to join shuttles from the other ships. I want your sensor team focused on the planet surface with everything they've got until further notice—is that clear, Captain?"

Heres gritted his teeth. "Yes…sir. Preparing shore party. Now." He smacked the channel closure control hard and exhaled angrily. "Old fool."

Renno turned in her chair. "Sir, I've taken the liberty of informing Major Dillarn to activate his unit." Dillarn commanded the detachment of soldiers stationed aboard the Valor.

"Very well, Lieutenant. Thank you."

"Will you be accompanying the Major to the surface, sir?"

"By the stars, no!" Heres dropped into his chair. "What next?"

"Sir, the two small craft have disappeared from the sensors."

Heres crossed his arms. "Of *course* they have."

USS Serapis

"**Shuttle** 1-5, Serapis. You're a welcome sight. And I see you come bearing gifts," Antonov's voice boomed inside the shuttle.

Halloran tapped the comm. "Captain, good to hear your voice. I'm assuming our channel is secure?"

"And you as well, Captain. Correct, this frequency is the one recommended in the Prax operating instructions for Hidden Claw comms. Opening shuttle bay door now."

Halloran briefly outlined the plan of action. "We saw the explosion on our underpowered scans; it must have been massive."

Reyes said, "Sir, Max promised one big bang when that fuel storage was triggered."

Antonov replied, "Lieutenant Travers is on the bridge and pointed out that the explosion was a 'factor-six' which is apparently an atmospheric event."

Halloran frowned at Reyes. "I hope they didn't overdo it."

"I don't know, sir. He only promised a big bang that would accompany the report of Prax on the surface."

Antonov said, "Lieutenant Carruthers points out that the Valor has aborted a 'suspicious'—her word—series of course corrections and is taking up station at the far side with the other Fleet units."

Kendra nodded as she angled the nose of the shuttle toward the opening bay below them. "They'll likely send troops down."

Antonov called again. "Sir, the Tavarrans have exited their vessel and are moving to deploy the repair robots. Lieutenant Travers has linked the ship's computer with them."

Halloran smiled. "On autopilot."

"Not me," Kendra replied.

Halloran leaned close to her ear. "You wish you were with them? The Fleet ships?"

She stared out the viewscreen for a moment, then shrugged without looking at him. "They don't need me; your sorry bunch certainly does."

"No argument there, Captain. I need you."

Now Kendra looked, her raven hair rustling as she shook it from her eyes. "Even if I'm frumpy?"

He sat back. "*Especially* if you're frumpy."

Behind them Parker poked Wilson in the rib. "You hear Skipper call her 'frumpy' just now?" he asked softly.

"Nope. Did she haul off and punch his lights out?" Wilson looked half-amused, half-incredulous.

"No, she even laughed it off," Parker whispered.

Wilson shrugged. "No understandin' it, Chief."

"Guess not."

"Captain on the bridge!"

Halloran walked onto the bridge and immediately felt the sense of satisfaction wash over him. He realized how close he'd been holding his expectation of failure; that there was no way everything would work out. But he'd found a critical ally in Governor Jackson and—among many miracles—that had made the difference. So he again got to stand on his own bridge, looking over the expectant faces. *His* people. Even Djembe at the pilot's station had a small grin on his face when Halloran caught his eye.

He drew in a big breath and exhaled, smiling. "Feels good to be back. Thank you to everyone who held the fort while we were away." He saw Axxa standing in the corner, as always, and walked over to him.

"My understanding is that you uncovered Prax on the planet," the big alien said quietly.

"Yes, Commander."

Axxa frowned at the title but ignored it. "Please know that I was unaware of this."

Halloran felt as though he was seeing Axxa for the first time; so much had happened in the last few days. The Prax was marooned on a stolen warship, stuck with a human crew. Even if the guy professed sympathy for their cause, he still had to be alone and rudderless. Then, as if to counter his budding empathy, the image of his best friend being beheaded by this creature leapt into his mind unbidden.

He nodded stiffly. "Understood." There seemed nothing else to say so Halloran turned away to his own kind.

Antonov and Lieutenant Travers were at a station across the bridge, bent over a monitor. Halloran came up behind them looked over their shoulder. "Travers. XO."

Antonov looked up. "Watching the robots work, Captain. Incredible."

Travers was excited. He pointed to something a bot was doing. "That's cold welding in action. Something you don't see much outside of a shipyard. Excellent! They're moving very fast."

Halloran's brow creased. "Are we rushing this?"

Antonov stood and crossed his arms. "The guy Cassis from Tavar seems to know what he is doing with the robots. The other individual is aboard ship and being checked out by Wilson's team."

"He knows Anders well. Won't be a problem."

"The Valor bothers me, sir. They know who we are. Perhaps their computer kept our drive signature somehow? Similar to what we do with enemy sub reactors back on Earth." He blinked. "You know to what I refer."

"No offense taken, Captain. With the current tech anything is possible. Carruthers?"

She turned. "Captain?"

"Does our computer retain drive signatures for target designates? Like the ASIC10 would do back home?"

"I'm sure it does, sir. Just haven't figured that out yet. Sorry, sir."

"Thanks, Lieutenant." He turned to Antonov. "Let's say that they 'see' us somehow. Would that make some sense of their movements since entering orbit?"

"To be honest, Captain, I don't know. This is all very new to me." Antonov made a face.

Halloran thought about it. "Well, he's been recalled to his group either way. He's got to be pissed."

"Yes, sir. I'm sure he is."

They shared a silent chuckle together before Travers spoke. "I think the bots are finishing up."

Halloran leaned in again to see the bots floating away from the ship's hull, gathering in one area of space about fifty meters away from the Serapis. "Call Chief Parker and see what his assessment is."

Parker's voice came on the comm line. "Parker here. Cassis tells me that the repairs are complete. Twenty-four minutes by my time, sir."

"I owe you a coffee, Chief."

"Luckily, we happened bring along a crate of the stuff in the shuttle, sir. Your treat."

"Any time."

"There's another thing, sir. Cassis says that the bot analysis of our hull is that it's ninety-four percent grade Tavarran steel."

"Meaning?"

Cassis came on the line. "Well, just that it's not exactly the same material The Prax seem to have done something to it."

"Mr. Cassis, is our hull integrity restored?"

There was a short lull wherein Halloran could hear Parker in the background saying something sternly that sounded like 'no editorial comments to the Captain,' making Halloran grin. Finally Cassis came back on. "Yes…Captain. The bots report that the patching mated perfectly to the Prax steel material."

"And the ship's existing hull is different in composition somehow?"

"Yes, the metallurgy scan shows that the material has been coated with something that enhances energy absorption. Nice formula; I'd like a sample if possible."

"For the Hidden Claw, sir," Carruthers offered.

Halloran nodded. "Thank you for that report, Cassis. Chief Parker will fix you up and find you a berth. Chief, round up Anders as well and have the two of them assigned by Chief Reyes ASAP."

"Aye, sir. Now, if we—."

"Captain! Sir!"

Carruthers' urgent call drew Halloran away from the comm unit. "What is it?"

"Sir, sensors are targeting nine new contacts, designations of Charlie One through Charlie Nine. Range two hundred eighteen thousand kilometers, in decel approaching Tavar."

Halloran strode to his command station as Antonov took Travers' seat and pushed the young man toward the entrance. "Get down to Engineering now, Lieutenant!"

Halloran leaned forward to study his screen where Carruthers was repeating her main monitor view. The ships were clearly heading to Tavar. "They just jumped into the system?"

"I believe so, sir. The computer just started telling me about them."

"And the target designations?"

"I added those a day ago. Feels more familiar, sir."

"That it does, Lieutenant. Nice work." Halloran studied the pattern of the ship formation. "That lead one—Charlie Three—seems bigger?"

"The computer is trying to call it a friendly, sir." Almost apologetically she added, "It still thinks we're Prax."

"Okay."

"It's calling out names to each of the signatures. Look at your screen now, sir."

Halloran saw a scrolling set of ship schematics. "So that's the Faraxxan. It does look big."

"Aye, sir. The rest are below if you scroll down."

"Any chance they will recognize us even if we're cloaked?"

"No way to know, sir."

"Well, we'll find out in…eleven minutes, when they come out of decel."

Aboard Argon

"Can we get the shuttles back in time?" Orris demanded of his Lieutenant Commander, a heavyset man named Danyal.

"Unlikely, sir. They were just touching down at the site. The visibility is reported to be near zero and sensors are severely compromised at the surface."

"We'll have to leave them. Instruct Usar and Saranin to break orbit with us. We'll form up between the Prax and the planet in wedge formation. Have Valor break above us as the high position. Borelin and Vanguard stay back to plug a hole if needed."

"Yes, sir." The officer began relaying orders to others over the comm channels.

Orris went to the communications station. "I want Grisa up here now."

"He's on his way, sir."

"Prepare a jumpdrone communication to Fleet Command, priority one action. My authorization."

"Go ahead, sir."

"From Orris, Tavar stationkeep, urgent action needed. Nine-ship flotilla inbound Prax medium-class warships, estimated arrival 2365 local Struve time. Argon, Usar, Saranin and Valor preparing to engage with Borelin and Vanguard in reserve. Reinforcements requested. Repeat urgent, action imminent." He reread the transcription and nodded to the tech. "Send that *now*."

"Yes, sir."

"Captain! The Prax lead vessels are exiting decel early."

"Let me see!" Orris stormed over.

Lieutenant Treela was showing the trajectory data on her screen, looked up at him. They both knew the maneuver; it was designed to cut the time available for a defensive force to form up against a decelerating attacker. The extra-hard decel put a lot of stress on a ship and threw off the navigational and targeting computers on all but the very newest classes. Plus, a ship executing this maneuver close to a planetary body ran the risk of overshooting and slamming into it. If done correctly, however, and with a dose of luck, the attacker could successfully disorient the defenders and open fire much sooner.

She rechecked the rapidly changing data. "Four—no, six—vessels are exiting decel and will enter mid-orbit. They are trying to get behind us, sir!"

Chapter 27

Aboard Serapis

"**Captain** Kendra." Halloran was watching the unfolding tactical situation on the Serapis' sensors but was having a hard time of understanding.

Kendra came on the comm. "Kendra here."

"Leave Engineering and get up here on the double."

"On my way. I'm assuming that means quickly."

"It does, Captain. You're needed on the bridge." He felt his voice rising somewhat in concern.

"May I, Captain?" Axxa was by the command station.

Halloran waved at the display, inviting the Prax to look at it.

"Something is wrong," Axxa announced.

"What do you mean?"

"It is well-known among the Prax that this planet—this system—is firmly in the hands of the humans. Now we see an infiltration and an attacking fleet. Something is wrong within Prax command."

"I don't see how that helps us here, but thanks for the heads-up."

Kendra burst onto the bridge and went straight to Halloran's station. She was out of breath. "Captain? What's happening?"

"Nine large Prax warships just jumped in and are entering our sector. They seem to be maneuvering rapidly. The human ships have broken orbit and are forming up somehow. Can you interpret all this?"

She studied the display for a long half-minute, then jumped over to Carruthers. "Let me see the tracks."

"Report, Captain," prompted Halloran. He could feel Antonov's eyes on the group from across the bridge.

"The Prax have pulled off a rare maneuver called—by us—a high-gee decel exit. They must have practiced this to get it so close to the gravity well of a planet…impressive."

"So it's a surprise attack?"

She straightened. "Well, surprise attacks are pretty hard to do in space, with modern sensors. What this commander did was split his forces with the lead six dropping in below the Fleet formation, essentially placing themselves between the defenders and the planet. The other three will come out further away and put the Fleet ships in an exposed position defending on two axes initially."

Halloran processed what she had explained to him as the sounds of machinery hummed through the silent bridge; everyone waiting expectantly for what would happen next. "What does the tactical situation look like for our side?"

She shook her head. "They're going to get hit hard."

Halloran watched the six Prax ships turning and lining up behind and below the Fleet ships. "Mr. Antonov."

The Russian was there in an instant. "Yes, Captain."

"Our mission is to protect the colony," Halloran said softly.

"Aye, Captain. What are you considering?"

Halloran placed an elbow in a palm and cupped his chin in the other palm. "What if we dropped in ahead of the human column and fired everything we had at that lead Prax, Charlie Three—the big one named the Faraxxan? Then head straight for the outer three enemy ships and push through their formation doing maximum damage." He looked at Kendra. "Would that give Heres and the other's assistance?"

"Sir, that would of course expose us to both enemy and friendly fire," Antonov pointed out.

Halloran was still looking at Kendra.

She nodded slowly. "Yes, if we could disable the Faraxxan, that might allow the others to take on the remaining ships. Would give them a fighting chance. But," she nodded at Antonov, "he's right; we'd be giving everything away."

After a curt nod to them and a few strides he tapped the comm on his station. "All hands, this is the Captain. We're about to engage a numerically superior enemy force. Sorry Chief Parker, but we may poke a few fresh holes in your hull. Everyone do their best; I know we're new at our jobs, but I'm proud of what each and every one of you have done to make Serapis a fighting ship. Now, let's show them what we're made of. Captain out."

"That was good," Kendra whispered.

Halloran shot her a hard glare as he pointed to Axxa. "You, back in your seat. Antonov, I want you riding shotgun with Carruthers on the sensors. Kendra, we will want to jump the moment we get a clear path beyond the incoming Prax formation. The coordinates are logged in the navigation system." He fixed her and Antonov. "By me personally. If I am disabled you execute on those coordinates if all possible, clear?"

Both nodded automatically.

Everyone bustled about the bridge as Halloran retook his seat. "Djembe, fire up the mains and move us out ahead of the Fleet formation. I want a clear shot with the plasma cannons at the Faraxxan, understand?"

"Perfectly, sir. Leaving orbit now along the necessary thrust vector and acceleration."

Aboard Argon

The formation was setting up too slow for Captain Orris. He was taking turns berating the other Captains over public channels. Now, Captain Jollo of the Vanguard was the subject of his ire. "Your ship movements have been sloppy! Was your pilot asleep? You should be abreast of Borelin by now!"

"The same engine trouble as before, sir," explained Jollo with a clear edge of frustration in his voice. "If we don't follow the modified procedures during startup the same reactor issue—."

"You should have been working around the shifts to fix that, Captain. I don't want to hear about it now as we go into battle. Match our velocity!" He closed the channel.

"Captain, the enemy ships are all out of decel and forming up in standard staggered line. They'll be within firing range in three minutes."

"Thank you, Lieutenant Treela." He walked behind the pilot and glanced over his shoulder, reading the instruments.

"Captain," called Commander Danyal from his post at the back of the bridge. Orris stepped to his location. "Damage-control reports ready. All compartments report sealed and ready, sir," "Valor and Saranin are within formation, ready in all respects. Usar reports that they will be in position in one minute, thirty seconds. Borelin is in position for reserve with Vanguard two minutes, forty-five seconds back."

Orris frowned. "That bumbler Jollo. They weren't ready."

"Sir, I think we should bring Borelin and Vanguard up while we still can. It's six on four with another three inbound on our flank."

Orris nodded at the man's suggestion. "Trust me, I understand the tactical situation. But we can't leave Tavar without a reserve. We'll just have to make a dent with what we have at hand."

"Yes, Captain."

"Captain," The lead Prax in the first phalanx is firing. Correction, they're all firing!"

"Brace, everyone!" Orris grabbed a rail near him.

The Argon's arti-grav fluctuated violently, the intensity of it driving him to his knees with a grunt. Lighting flickered.

"Plasma hit in Life Support!" yelled a tech.

Orris held onto the rail as his eyes met Danyal's. "Nice shot. Return fire, Commander."

"We'll be within effective range in ninety seconds."

"Return fire, Commander Danyal."

Danyal leaned into his station, sending the command to all ships. "Fire at maximum range—now!"

"Captain! Something's happening!"

Orris struggled to his full height, planting his feet and making his way across the bridge to his own station as damage reports began lighting up screens and comms all around him. He felt the satisfying lurch of the ship as their own weapons fired. He dropped into his seat. "What is it, Treela?"

"The targeting computer is reporting a new contact directly ahead. But then it changes its mind and cancels the contact!"

"Well, what *is* it?" Orris demanded, scrolling through his own repeater screen menu.

"It's nothing, sir. Empty space. Look!"

The Pilot, Treela and Orris looked at the forward display at the same time. The Pilot said, "My system is telling me to avoid colliding with the mass in front of us."

But Orris was staring at what appeared to be a rearranging of the stars before his eyes. The normal panorama of lights seemed to elongate, then collapse on itself. Something wasn't right about it. "Lieutenant, range to this new target?"

"The computer is saying twenty thousand, Captain, but that can't be right…"

Orris had glanced to her as she reported but now saw something different on the screen. The stars were now missing. Something big and black was blocking them from view. Whatever it was was absorbing the light. "Lieutenant…"

"New contact! Um, unknown vessel."

"Unknown?"

"The hull is unclassified, Captain."

"Commander!" Danyal called. "Targeting has acquired the new contact."

"Bring all forward batteries into the attack."

A tech called, "Captain, Usar reports heavy damage in their second reactor compartment; evacuation of that level underway. The ship has lost maneuvering!"

Orris was focused on the new contact. "Treela, what are the sensors telling you?" He prompted at her silence as she frowned over her console.

"It's a light cruiser class in size. Maybe a large frigate. It's not in the Fleet registry, either public or classified. Sir!" She turned to him. "Reactor output is identified as Prax in signature."

"Fire on my command! It's too close and can shoot right down our line."

Danyal called back. "Target is firing!"

Too late, Orris fumed.

"Direct hit on the lead Prax vessel! Great broadside."

"What?" Orris jumped to his feet despite the disproportionate gravity that tested his leg strength.

"The new contact fired on the Prax lead target," Danyal confirmed.

"They're shooting at each other?" Orris stamped over to Treela's station, sick of his repeater. He was an old sensor tech himself and craved the larger displays. "Show me."

The comm tech called out. "Incoming hail on open fleet frequency, Captain!"

Orris looked up. "Let's hear it." The artigrav surge relented and he could stand more comfortably now.

A buzzing sound filled the bridge, followed by the sound of someone clearing their throat. Then, "To Commander human Fleet, do not fire on the target at the head of your line. Repeat, do not fire! This is Pyotr Antonov, Executive Officer of the USS Serapis, at your service." After a moment's pause filled with confused looks passing between the Argon's bridge crew, the man continued. "We're on your side, commander."

Orris pointed at Treela. "Get me an identification on that *ship,* Lieutenant."

Danyal cried out. "Prax are firing projectiles, Captain!"

"Return fire!"

"At the new target, sir?"

"At the ones *shooting* at us, Commander!"

"Yes, sir."

Then everything descended into a chaos of sound and fury.

Aboard Serapis

"**No** answer?" Halloran glanced Antonov's way. The Russian shook his head.

"Sir, the lead human ship just took a heavy broadside of projectiles."

"Anything coming our way yet?"

"Nothing yet, sir."

"Can we get another shot into Charlie-three?"

Djembe answered. "Our velocity needed to get ahead of their formation is carrying us well beyond the battle, but I think I can adjust our orientation and get off another plasma broadside targeting Charlie-three."

"Do it now, pilot. Weapons, prepare to fire on the Pilot's mark!"

"Aye, sir."

Aboard Valor

"**I** knew it!" Heres stormed across his bridge. "He's shown himself!"

"The ship just announced its identity as the 'USS Serapis.' A commander I don't recognize by name," called Renno. "They just hailed the Argon."

"It's Halloran. It *has* to be the same ship."

"Sir, fire on the crew deck is expanding into adjoining sections; the suppression system was punctured by a projectile."

Heres hit the comm near him. "Engineering, status!"

"We took a hit down here, Captain, but repairs are being made. You have full capability."

"Excellent. Renno, close on that ship. Grisa, return fire on the Prax line; pick one ship to target."

Renno turned in her chair. "Sir, we'll be pulling ahead of the Argon—."

"Just do it, Renno," Heres said in a low tone to her as he walked back and forth. The ship shuddered as the main battery let loose its barrage of plasma bolts.

"New target has a velocity that is taking it ahead of the formation. It is adjusting course now…no, spinning on its axis. Firing again!"

"Their target?"

Renno looked up at the Captain. "The Prax line, sir."

Grisa called out. "Our last attack hit the number-two Prax ship hard; split through an engine nacelle. That will had to have caused serious damage to their maneuverability, sir."

"Excellent. Are we in range for a round of projectiles?"

"Yes, sir—midsize recommended."

"Fire midsize now. And check in with the 'blinders' to see that they're on target."

"Fire projectiles, yessir! Directed energy stations report targeting locks on several enemy sensor nodes."

Heres rubbed his chin vigorously. "Assign the forward stations to the new target dead ahead of us."

He was still near Renno's station. She said quietly and urgently, "That ship is *helping* us, sir."

Heres turned on her. "It's a Prax ship and under the command of a renegade we have orders to locate and destroy." He pointed at the image of the mystery ship's main engines flaring out ahead of them. "And there it is, accelerating away from us!"

"Forward directed energy batteries report two targets isolated. Execute?" Grisa was looking over.

"Yes, execute!"

"Yes, sir."

"We can hit them with batteries one and two, sir," offered Renno without enthusiasm.

"Captain Orris on the comm, sir!"

"Fire out of control! Lieutenant Erodan's team one is offline!"

Heres ordered, "Get team two over from Engineering to the crew deck and team three to back them up."

The ship shuddered violently as Orris' voice boomed over the open channel. "Valor, report! Why are you accelerating?"

Heres replied, "Taking the lead position, sir. I have orders to track that ship out in front of you."

"Orders from whom?"

"Mars Command directly. That's what we were doing in the Luyten system."

"We don't have *time* for this, Captain! My bridge just got annihilated by the *Prax* flotilla. I am countermanding any existing orders you have under section 32 of the—."

"Acknowledged. Heres out."

"Should I slow us down?" asked Renno after thirty seconds of frustrated silence by Heres.

He exhaled. "Keep us ahead of Argon and ready to accelerate the moment we can. Grisa!"

"Yes, sir?"

"Go down and look over the fire damage and report back. Find Lieutenant Erodan."

"Going now, sir."

"Two Prax ships are boxing Usar in, sir!" Renno wiped a bead of dripping sweat from her brow as Heres watched. It was getting warmer on the bridge. Ventilation must be knocked out from the fire… "They're concentrating fire!"

"Reposition us to bring all batteries to bear. Fire everything the moment you're locked. Target the most active Prax ship hitting Usar."

"Yes, sir. Argon just hit the lead ship hard; the Serapis looks to have stopped it in space with their last salvo. Nice shooting both!"

"Serapis," Heres muttered in a low breath. "What's a 'Serapis' anyway?"

The ship once again made that sidewise shudder as the big projectiles were expelled from their guns. Then it gave a larger lurch and gravity went out momentarily.

Heres was half-in his seat and managed to grab the restraint. Almost as quickly, gravity came back.

"That was a hit, sir!" called a tech. "Aft C deck near the shuttle bay. Compartment isn't answering my call, sir."

"All right, get me a report from the first crew that arrive there. Are those batteries still online?" He looked over.

The man checked, then nodded. "After batteries report ready to fire."

Heres noticed when he turned back that Renno was sweating profusely now. So was the Pilot. They all were. "Get environmental control back in line." He glanced up at the screen to see the tail end of the Serapis pulling away from them. "You go, Halloran," he muttered to himself. "We'll catch up when we can."

Chapter 28

Aboard USS Serapis

In Engineering, Trigg Wyatt huddled with Machinists Mate Bruce Brown in their seats before the master control console. Lieutenant Travers was across the equipment bank from them. Mark Hummel made his way carefully between their area and the back of the compartment where Jack Stacey was watching his reactor panels. The ship's heart was only a few short bulkheads away to the aft, thankfully shielded against the gamma radiation filling the main reactor chamber. The hum was pervasive and dulling to the senses.

Hummel paused by Stacey, hanging on a grab bar designed for that purpose. "Seeing what you need to see, Jack?"

The other man glanced over. "Yessir, Lieutenant. I think I've got this." He looked around his station of gauges and monitors appraisingly. "Really, it's not all that different than riding shotgun on the S9G kettle in Bonny Rich." He grinned lopsidedly. "Except that only pumped out one-fifty megawatts; this thing is ten times that output…then of course there's the gamma radiation."

Hummel nodded in the direction of the reactor compartment. "Definitely don't want to be back there right now."

"Don't want any of that bad stuff up here, either, sir."

"Well, we're in the middle of the action now, so keep on your toes until we hear different." Hummel turned away from Stacey and made his way back to the main area.

Wyatt looked up at him as he approached. "Looking good, sir."

Hummel nodded in acknowledgment, the stress showing on his face.

Five long minutes of silence later, Travers stopped monitoring his instruments. "What is the tension in the air?"

Hummel put both hands on the console and just looked at him.

Travers tried Wyatt. "What is it?"

Wyatt slid his eyes to Brown before leaning in. "It's bad luck," he answered at last. As quietly as he could.

"What is? What's luck?"

Wyatt looked at Hummel with a raised forehead. *You tell him, you're closer, sir.*

Hummel edged closer to the Fleet officer. "So you're at eight hundred meters and you've been pinged. Active sonar. They've got you dead to rights. The skipper has us on silent running, pulling the plug to drop to fifteen hundred. Then the techs pick up splashes as the torps hit the water."

"So the enemy has targeted you and sending guided munitions. Your shields…"

"Ain't no shields in the ocean, Lieutenant," added Wyatt. "You have to outrun them; change depth, launch countermeasures that distract their targeting computer with noise. And mostly pray."

Hummel nodded. "It's the guys in the nuke gang that have it the worst; they're plugging away at their posts, just meters away from the reactor. No facts, no updates from the conn. They just keep quiet and do their jobs until the torp hits or they get out alive."

Travers' serious face showed his processing of the narrative. At length he nodded. "I understand."

Brown finally spoke up. "Stop talking, please. Bad luck."

Missile Techs Karen Flagler and Bob Cochran, on the other hand, were anything but quiet. They pounded along the starboard passage from Battery A toward Battery B. On their heels was the Tavarran, Anders.

"You take the relay panel by the hatch, Bob. I'll try the subpanel that's set along the gun itself!"

"Does this happen often?" called Anders from behind the two.

"Heck if I know, boss," said Flagler. "This is only our second engagement with these things, and last time we got our butt kicked ASAP."

They reached a lift to the upper deck but instead popped down the hatch leading to the inter-deck ladder. Anders looked longingly at the closed lift door.

"Don't bother, they're down too."

"Down?"

"Broken," clarified Flager as she waved Cochran up the ladder. "Non-functional."

"Hmm. Both the lift and the projectile battery are non-functional?"

Flagler pointed up the shaft where Cochran's boots were receding. "You next."

She came up behind Anders. The decks were separated by five or so meters of layered electronic conduits, structural components and general bundles of wiring and piping leading somewhere. Cochran popped the hatch on B Deck and clambered up, waiting for the other two to join him.

Flagler dropped the hatch and stepped on the lock mechanism, sealing the tunnel. "This way."

Anders followed them up an ever-tightening corridor that grew shorter until they were running fully bent double. At last Flagler stopped at an oval hatch and worked the manual release.

Anders touched the opening hatch. "Hmm."

Cochran caught his sound. "What?"

Anders looked at him, face yellow-tinted in the overhead amber lighting. "Lift, locking mechs, electromag guns all out."

"Get *in* here, Cochran!"

"Let's go."

Inside the two ship's crew went to work attacking their respective panels. It didn't take long for Flagler to report. "My tester is calling this box clean."

Cochran was frowning over his own test. "This one, too."

She huffed for breath—the run had taken it out of her—and put her hands on her hips with a curse. "I don't friggin' know, Bob. What is it?"

"We've checked the mains as soon as the panel went green—stupid Prax colorations. The computer says the short is on B deck weapons." He pocketed his tester. "Got me, Karen."

"Skipper needs to know we can't find the issue." She headed for the comm unit mounted by the hatch.

Anders had his hand on the huge gun barrel. "I have an idea."

Flagler paused with her hand on the comm panel. "Shoot." The Tavarran had both their attention.

"Well, on Tavar in the mines my family used heavy electromag drilling units." He patted the gun. "Not much smaller than this thing. When it shorted it threw fuses for half a kilometer in every direction."

Cochran said, "But Flagler checked the gun's relay; it looks nominal."

Anders stomped his foot. "Our drilling unit had a subpanel, too; but that was a slave to the control panel, which was located directly below it in the housing."

Flagler looked dubious. "But this is an alien spaceship."

But Cochran had shoved Anders' boot out of the way and was on his knees, feeling around the base of the gun for something to lift. "Call it in, Karen!" He spared Anders a glance. "Get down here, will ya? I sure hope you got this right."

Djembe was manning the comm on the bridge as Halloran, Kendra and Antonov conferred by the Command station. He took Flagler's report and half-turned. "Captain."

"Yes, Pilot?" Halloran broke from the trio and looked his way.

"Weapons team reports that the electrical short is still there in the system, and that the B Deck Starboard projectile battery is offline, but they may have a solution. Sir," he added as he turned back to flying the ship.

Kendra was serious. "That's an important battery if we're going to proceed with driving straight into an enemy line."

Halloran considered. "Alright. We got very lucky that we haven's taken a hit yet, probably thanks to the Hidden Claw. Somehow I don't think our luck will hold for the next thirty minutes uncloaked."

"Re-engage the Claw, sir?" Carruthers was hopeful.

"We want the power to weapons, Lieutenant. And engines. No, we've played our hand, now we see what the other guys have."

Antonov asked Carruthers, "time to firing range of the outer Prax line?"

"Seven minutes twenty-five seconds if I'm reading this right, sir," she promptly answered without turning.

Halloran tapped his chair. "If I go down remember the plan, ladies and gentlemen." He got up and left them to approach Axxa. "A word, Commander?"

Axxa looked surprised but obediently followed the Captain to the rear of the bridge near the entry.

"The odds are steep against us getting through your countrymen unscathed in the next few minutes."

The Prax said nothing.

"You've been a patient passenger to this point, Axxa, but I'll need you to step up in the event that we take significant casualties." Halloran's eyes were hard. "You have claimed repeatedly to be on the human side of the equation, and you *did* defect. But now I'm looking to you to walk the walk; you're a Commander-level officer in your own military structure."

"I was not a flect officer, but ground forces. But I understand the reference, Captain." His red features were flushed dark crimson with emotion at Halloran's earnestness. "I will not fail this ship or crew or…" He nodded in deference. "…You. I owe you personally."

Halloran tapped the giant on his chest. "Yes, you do. See to it you make me proud."

"Bridge says we got six minutes to get this bugger online." Karen Flagler closed the comm channel and turned to the men who were on their hands and knees, feeling around the projectile cannon.

"One benefit of this short is that the port won't open and suck us out, at least." Cochran was following a thick conduit underneath the barrel base. He grunted as he chased it over a large servo box that was part of the attitude adjustment system—they'd learned that much in the research sessions on these weapons.

Flagler went to the opposite side and reached under the base of the loading mechanism. The gun was fed with projectiles by the computer from the in-between deck munitions storage. A long ramp and piston system that vaguely reminded her of watching a video once of the old Missouri-class sixteen-inch gun loading rams. These guns used intense magnetic bursts instead of huge powder sacks, however. *We might get sucked into space but at least we won't be blown to kingdom come,* she thought as she patted the sides of the loader chute.

Something caught Anders' attention. "Flagler, feel a bit to your right." He was pointing over the gun at her hand.

"What do you see?" But even as she asked she felt a thick conduit the size of her fist. "I can't see it from my angle."

"I'll follow it." Anders wedged himself under the guns breach and twisted. Cochran stopped hunting to look. "I've got it. It does lead to the relay box."

Flagler stretched to slide around the gray-painted metal of the chute. She was exactly in the line of the rising munitions now; if it turned back on it would autoload and crush her instantly. Trying not to think about it, she looked down into the chute where the 'tween decks was dark as space, the power out. "Sure could use a light right now," she gasped.

There was a larger relay box on the underside of the gun deck. As her eyes adjusted to the dark, they followed the conduit into the rectangle.

With some exertion she levered herself back upright. Cochran offered her a hand to her feet. She wiped her hands, looking at them with professional admiration. "Aliens sure keep a clean ship."

Anders was trying to see the box. "How do we get down there? We can't fit through this chute and this space has got to be twenty meters from the ladder through a maze of mechanicals."

"Plus, we only have five minutes to fix this thing. Did I mention that Djembe said this battery was key to our first barrage on those aliens we're supposedly going to reach in five?"

"I'll go."

Anders and Flagler looked at Cochran.

"I'm small. I can squeeze down there."

Flagler stamped her foot. "And then what? You'll be in the way of the munitions flow?"

Cochran made a show of bending and looking into the narrow hole. "There's room in there to stay out of its way."

Anders pointed at the shut port. "When they ready this gun, that'll open and you'll lose atmosphere."

Cochran wiped his brow. "So get me a breather. This can't last that long." He tested the opening; it did seem as if his body would be able to get down in and twist underneath the relay box.

"Bob…"

He looked up at her. "Karen, there's no time for this. You know I'm the smallest."

She sighed, shooting Anders a frustrated stare.

Cochran looked at the Tavarran. "I'm going down. You have four minutes to find me a breather…please."

"All batteries report online according to the computer, sir," called Antonov from his station. "Except the starboard Battery B."

Halloran slid his eyes to Kendra at her borrowed seat nearby. She shook her head slowly. "No update from weapons?"

"Wilson went down two minutes ago to check."

Halloran nodded. " Time to firing line?"

"Three minutes, sir," Djembe answered. Accelerating to three-quarters sublight, which we'll reach approximately twenty thousand kilometers from their line."

"Steady as she goes, Pilot."

Gerry Wilson dropped the distance from A deck to B using the ladder rail as a slide. As he emerged on B deck, he shoved up the balanced hatch and heard it click loudly into place.

Anders the Tavarran guy run up. "Sir."

"What is going on up here?" Wilson demanded. "We need that gun back online *now*."

Anders shied away from the burly Petty Officer's wrath. "I am looking for a breathing unit."

"A *what*?"

"Mr. Cochran found the electrical short but needs to get in a tight spot to effect the repair. He won't be able to get out, he suspects, before the activated system is needed by Mr. Halloran."

Wilson grasped the situation, but there was almost no time. "Follow me!" He thundered down the passage to a locker thirty meters away, near the medical bay entrance where Whitney was prepping for casualties. He wrenched open the door of the locker and leaned in, rummaging through racks of life-support gear. Presently he yanked out what looked like an old-school scuba unit with mask and mouthpieces. "Here!"

Without thanking him, Anders grabbed the unit and started back up the corridor. Wilson followed him back up past the inter-deck tubes and into the forward part of the ship. He knew that the bridge was actually not too far away above them; they were at the leading edge of the knifelike forward hull.

Anders put his shoulder to a hatch that Wilson knew went to the Battery B emplacement.

"About time," he heard Karen Flagler on the far side of the hatch as Anders passed the rig to her. "Oh, sorry sir," she corrected as Wilson stuck his head in. Without further comment she passed the equipment to a hand that was extended up through the loading chute for the projectile ammo.

He leaned over. "Bob, you in there?"

"Yessir, Petty Officer."

There seemed like nothing worth saying of note. "You take care in there; stay out of the way of those things." It sounded lame to his ears.

"Yessir."

"We'll be back for you the moment we can secure this gun, Bob."

"Thanks, sir."

Wilson turned to see that Anders was in the hatch and Flagler waiting. Her eyes were wet.

He pushed at her gently. "He'll make it, Karen. Let's go."

Part Five - Sacrifice

Chapter 29

Aboard Faraxxan

The human ships reeled under the power of his fleet's weapons. Their aggressive attack at close range had taken the filthy aliens by total surprise.

Had that been the end of the battle, it would have been glorious. But a new ship had appeared and placed several perfectly-aimed salvos into his flagship, crippling it.

Now, Horax could only fight the growing structural failures dooming the Faraxxan. The crew worked feverishly to shore up sagging decks, their integrity stretched to the breaking point by the fires burning out of control—suppression systems were down along with most electrical support. He also knew that life support was dead already. Their time was growing short.

"Commander Horax, are you able to transfer to the Braxxar?" The Captain of that ship was calling again on the inter-ship comms.

Horax wiped the black electrical soot from his eyes, feeling the raw burns on the side of his head. "Tell the Captain the same thing again."

As the wounded Prax manning the bridge comms opened the reply call, another voice cut in. "Horax, you will not leave, will you?"

The Commander slammed a red fist against a dead instrument panel, yelling. "There are six hundred crew still aboard this ship! My job is to save them."

"Your job is to do the will of your Lord, Commander," came the placid voice again.

A limping junior officer stepped up to Horax with a report, but he brushed him aside and stormed to the comm panel, startling the wounded bridge tech in the process. He leaned on the console with both hands, speaking deliberately into the microphone, glad for a moment that the arrogant son-of-a-Mugpa on the other end couldn't see his loss of control. "The will of my *Lord?* I regret the day I arrived at the Sol system. May you rot in the deep recesses!"

"You are ordered to abandon your crew and take the shuttle to the Braxxar at once, Commander."

"Lord," cut in the Captain of the Braxxar," I believe his shuttle bay is destroyed."

"Silence! Horax, the Premier has need of your political influences on Prax. You are to—."

"The Premier! He's an illegitimate son-of-a-Mugpa like his son!"

"You will pay for that."

"Commander," the junior officer tugged on his ripped sleeve. "Commander, the main hull ribbing is failing below this deck."

Horax sighed, shaking his head with all fight leaving his tired body. "No, Calxen, you and your father will pay. By the stars it will come to pass."

The Captain of the Braxxar came on. "Good fight, Horax."

Horax looked into the face of the terrified junior officer, then laid a consoling hand on the Prax's shoulder. "It is well."

The deck below them collapsed in a groan of tortured, superheated metal.

Calxen watched the Faraxxan's upper section implode in spectacular fashion. After that the mid-hull twisted and gave out, unsupported by the rest of the structure. And an instant later the collapse reached the reactor and a burst of pinkish flame burst out of the wrecked ship in all directions, snuffed out almost as quick by the vacuum of space. Where a Prax ship-of-the-line had been only moments before, now only an expanding cloud of debris and a crumped hulk remained.

Calxen turned to his ship's Captain. "I am assuming formal command of the flotilla at this time."

"As you wish, Lord."

"Get me a damage report on the rest of the ships. And get me the commander of the outer group!"

A minute later the face of the Captain leading the three ships making up the incoming flotilla popped onto the screen. "Lord Calxen, the Faraxxan—."

"—Was destroyed without honor. That ship—that stolen Prax ship fired on Horax with dishonor!" Calxen's voice rose. "You *must* destroy that ship, Captain. It is Prax technology but crewed by filthy *humans*."

The Prax on the screen looked shocked. "Lord, this ship approaches our coordinates and is accelerating. I think it means to break through."

Calxen pointed at the monitor. "You shall not let him pass!"

The Captain looked confused. "Him?"

Another voice in the background begged the faraway Captain's attention. "What is it?" he snapped offscreen. Then, "Lord, patching an incoming inter-ship transmission to your screen."

The view of the other ship's bridge morphed into the face of...Axxa, son of Krex.

"Greetings, fellow Prax. I ask you to hear my claim."

Calxen pounded on the console. "No! Destroy him!"

But the traitor was droning on. "In one minute this Prax ship will enter your protective zone. We have succeeded in destroying the enemy-held Faraxxan and now ask for asylum with your flotilla…"

Calxen heard the Prax Captain's confused voice. "The Lord Calxen said to destroy your vessel, Commander Axxa. How is it that you are—" Then the feed faded away.

"Get them back! It's a *trick*!" Calxen spit in rage at the tech manning the comms.

The Captain of their ship announced flatly, "The unknown ship has reached our outer flotilla."

"Get them back!!!" Calxen shoved the tech hard, drawing his Xu blade.

"What, Lord, will you kill your own crew?" asked the incredulous Captain, even as he distanced himself from the enraged warrior.

The screen flashed to life again and the three Prax saw a new face—a human in an odd greenish-patterned uniform. The man's eyes locked on the Xu standing alone before the monitors, blade drawn. "I see you, Calxen. I'm coming for you and your father. Thomas Halloran—remember that."

"The unknown ship is firing into the flotilla at point-blank range." The Captain kept his distance.

Calxen stabbed his blade into the monitor and the human Captain's face. The device flashed with sparks and the crew nearby jumped for safety. He withdrew the sword and pointed it at the now-quavering Captain. "Get our ships *out there now!*"

"Our first salvo took them without response yet, sir," Carruthers said from her station. "Looks like your ruse worked."

"Hit them again." Halloran had cut the video feed on the furious face of that assassin. Apparently he'd survived their last encounter… He felt a little guilty about the display but felt it had needed to be said. Or else he might have gone slowly mad leaving the words inside much longer. Now he caught Antonov's disapproving look from across the bridge. But both Kendra and Axxa nodded at him, each for their own reasons seeming to be okay with it. "Fire!"

"Battery B has overloaded again," Djembe reported. "They got two rounds off. I think both were direct hits, sir."

"We're in their midst, sir! Incoming from several vectors." Carruthers braced her hands on the console in front of her. "This is gonna hurt," Halloran heard her say clearly under her breath.

The ship took a severe hit and everything seemed to move at the same time; the gravity went out, the bulkheads vibrated and everyone was thrown against their restraining belts. The lights went out.

"Get the lights back on!" Halloran wanted to get up, to go help belowdecks where his people would be struggling right now. He'd been dragged into this war and knew that this could be the end of their quixotic journey. *Lord, don't let this be the end.*

The lights flickered to an amber color rather than white light.

Axxa spoke up. "This is the natural color spectrum to a Prax."

Halloran shot a look at him.

Then the Master Chief was on the comm, calling for Halloran. "Captain, it's a mess down here!" The sound of escaping air filled the airwaves, almost obscuring the raised voice on the other end.

"Where are you, Chief?"

"Life Support, sir! There was a clean plasma hit in the compartment…and…we're venting atmosphere!"

"Lock it down, Chief, and get out of there."

"Aye, Captain." A pause. "We've got men hurt."

"Do what you can, Chief." Halloran cut the channel.

Djembe spoke up. "Sir, the jumpdrive is reporting damage. Exact nature unclear."

"Can we fight?"

"Most of the projectile batteries are offline. You have all but one plasma cannon available to you!" Halloran heard the suppressed excitement contained within the Pilot's voice.

"Target the ships we missed the first pass…and fire."

The ship shuddered again. They were taking more hits.

Carruthers yelped. "Sir! We've knocked out one of their ships!"

Halloran turned to Antonov. "Can you take Axxa and back up Reyes?"

The Russian unclasped his restraint. "Going now, sir."

Halloran pointed to the XO's station, looking over at Kendra. "Captain?"

She was almost to the seat when the ship lurched again and gravity went out. With both hands gripping the seatback, she was thrust up at an angle toward the overhead. Halloran suddenly wanted to unclasp his own belt and jump for her, but knew the foolishness of the act. His voice came out strangely level. "You hanging on?"

"I've got this," she turned fierce eyes on him.

"Excellent. How do we turn the gravity back on?" The words sounded so odd.

Djembe was pointing at a control in front of Carruthers, making the tapping motion. "That one! It will reboot the subsystem—if it's still functional."

Kendra had reeled in the seat and twisted herself into position using only her arm strength. She strapped in and leaned forward to the weapons control. "Still have all plasma cannon but one, Captain!"

"Target whatever's close, Kendra. Sensor status of enemy units, Lieutenant?"

Carruthers looked back. "Target designate Charlie Six is apparently heavily damaged; course and speed consistent on a vector away from the scene. Significant debris field. Target designate Charlie Seven shows signs of life-support loss and hull damage amidships. Target designate Charlie Nine appears to have full operational capacity; the last two hits came from their projectile weapons, Captain."

"Damage report, Pilot?"

"The hull sensors report sixty-two breaches ranging from twelve centimeters to sixteen meters in normative diameter. Main engines are online and reactor function appears nominal, however the jumpdrive is offline and the extent of damage is unclear."

Halloran fiddled with the comm at his station. "Engineering, report your status."

After several repetitions Trigg Wyatt came on the channel. "Sorry, sir, I could hear you but this console suffered damage. We're here." He coughed heavily. "We've got several shorts that are throwing off sparks."

"Fire?"

"No, sir, just a foul atmosphere."

"What can you tell me about the jumpdrive?"

Wyatt coughed again. "Lieutenants Travers and Hummel are working on it, sir. Mr. Travers says it's a break in the grid between the reactor and the field generator."

"Very well," Halloran answered. "Get that atmosphere cleared and have Mr. Hummel report in once he has something figured out. In the meantime, keep the ship moving forward."

"Aye, sir."

The ship jerked and tweaked Halloran's neck muscles painfully. "What was that?"

Kendra replied, "Batteries fired, Captain. Without full gravity it feels worse."

Halloran knew the time had come to get out. "Full ahead, Pilot. Take us out of here."

"Yes, Captain."

Before a minute had passed, Carruthers spoke up. "The two remaining Prax ships are altering course to pursue, sir."

"Very well, Lieutenant." He turned to Kendra. "Can you raised anyone in Life Support?"

She shook her head at him.

He unbuckled himself and stood on shaky legs, his body protesting the light gravity. "I'm going down. Captain Kendra has the conn," he announced to the bridge.

"Be right back," he said quietly to her as he passed. "Shoot whatever you have to."

"You shouldn't go." She was grasping his sleeve in an iron grip as she whispered the words. Her eyes were like fire, haunted.

He faltered. "I need to."

"A Captain…just don't go, Halloran."

He shook his arm free, gently. "I have faith in you."

She shook her head. "That's not it."

He pushed off her toward the exit. "You keep her safe."

Resolve Of Steel

Chapter 30

Aboard USS Serapis, Struve System

By the time Halloran reached the medical center on B Deck he knew there was trouble. The lights were flickering a green-amber color; some kind of warning tint to the Prax, he surmised. The air was thick with choking electrical smoke. The moment he dropped out of the ladder tube his ears were assaulted by the roar of broken equipment and his feet slipped on debris strewn in the passage.

He dodged a thick pipe that had split and bisected the passageway with its bulk. Beyond that a man lay on the decking in the midst of the wreckage, facedown and unmoving. He was about to bend to the man when he heard his name called.

Wilson was down the passage, waving at him. "Come on, sir!"

With a last look at the dead man but unable to place him, he chased after the Petty Officer while trying to compensate for the light gravity and avoid smacking his head on the ceiling. Wilson passed the medical center at a bound and Halloran had a glimpse of bloody tables through the clear plexi.

"Down, sir," cautioned Wilson as he ducked under another disjointed piece of structure. "Very sharp edges, sir, be careful."

"Life Support?"

"Ops Center and Life Support both, sir." Wilson slowed and put his lips near Halloran's ear. "They're close together and the shot cut the place to ribbons in a second!"

"Plasma?"

"Projectile! It was a *big* one, sir." Wilson's face betrayed his amazement.

They stumbled over some electrical debris that shifted and grabbed at their boots as they crossed it. The Operations Center was just ahead, but blocked by a massive section of the deck above that had collapsed into the passage. But Wilson shimmied through an impossibly narrow gap against the bulkhead. Without pausing, Halloran followed the other man through with an eye for edged chunks of metal that seemingly protruded everywhere. His pants were slashed through by an unseen sharp section and his forehead caught the frayed ends of a wire bundle, scratching deeply.

The Ops Center was torn open as though with a giant can opener. The bulkhead had been crushed down by the force of the collapsing deck and smoke poured from the hatch that Halloran remembered led into Life Support control adjoining. Two men wrestled in the opening with fire-extinguishing equipment. The Prax version of the firehose was a series of tubes emitting a suppressive foam product that no one had been able to figure out the origin of. Even Axxa hadn't known how the system worked. But now there was the big alien reaching out a hand from the burning area, grasping at the hose being unrolled by Reyes. The Chief looked up to see Halloran approaching over the broken metal. "Sir, we've got three dead in there and several more wounded. Antonov took those to the doc before the deck finished falling in on us!"

Halloran stooped to the Chief. "Glad you're still with us, Abran! What's the status of Life Support?"

Reyes passed another hose kit to Axxa, whose grime-stained face Halloran now saw framed in the opening. Wilson stepped between them and through the hatch to join the Prax.

Reyes watched him go before turning back. "Who knows, sir? This ship was impossible to figure out *before* they blew it all to shreds."

"Are we going to suffocate?"

Reyes exhaled with a huff. "We need to get this 'lectrical fire out first, then we can assess damage."

Halloran took him by the shoulder. "You've got this, Chief?"

Reyes nodded. "You get back to the bridge, sir." As Halloran nodded and began to turn he grasped the Captain's arm. "And stop in the med center for a minute—but no more, sir." His eyes said the rest.

Halloran squeezed through the tangled wreckage and made his way to medical, pausing to compose himself before opening the door.

The scene inside shocked him. Half a dozen crew were spread around the room in various states of injury. Blood was everywhere.

Whitney saw him from where he was planted over someone working on what looked to be a chest wound. "Captain." His clothes were bloodstained and his voice stretched with exertion.

Several eyes turned his way. There was Flagler, holding an arm with blood soaking the sleeve. Cassis the Tavarran was next to her on the floor, and Halloran immediately saw the glazed-over eyes that signified shock. Also, there was Seaman Don King, laid on a table and holding his hands over his abdomen. They were glistening red. Halloran couldn't see the face of the man on the table beneath Whitney. Halloran felt the weight of these people's lives weighing on him. It wasn't a new sensation by any means, but the new circumstances frustrated him. He was out of control, out of his depth in space.

"Sir, you're bleeding," observed Flagler, her dark eyes fixed on him.

Halloran felt his forehead and the slickness on it. He forcefully wiped the blood with a sleeve. "Everyone keep it together, we're almost out of harm's way."

Back in the noisy passage Halloran paused to suck in several lungfuls of air. His crew was dying in front of his eyes. And what for? He felt sickened by the stunt he had pulled with Calxen in the adrenaline of being near him again.

The man on the floor groaned and rolled over. It was Antonov. He looked up at Halloran in confusion. "Captain, you're down here…who's got the conn?"

"Kendra. Are you okay?"

He sat up and held his head until Halloran reached him and levered him to his feet. "I had dropped some wounded off at the medical unit and was returning to the bridge when that," he pointed to the collapsed piping and mechanicals, "Fell on me."

"Get back there and have your head checked. Then go help Chief Reyes figure things out."

Antonov stumbled on a chunk of metal. "Our ship is a mess."

"Tell me about it." Halloran felt the clenching of anger in his gut tighten yet another notch.

"We're not going to outrun them, Captain."

"We need to jump but we can't."

Carruthers looked back at Kendra. "Could we jump with our damage?"

The latter nodded. "Yes, if we had that much damage we'd know it." She checked the engine system logs. "Looks like they're working on it down there. I can see that they've already run-tested the drive." She looked up resolutely. "They'll fix it."

"The enemy ships are closing to firing range, Captain," said Djembe. "What are your orders?"

Kendra felt trapped by their situation. This wasn't *her* ship. But Halloran had been clear. Do what you think is right. *And what if Halloran never came back to the bridge?* She got out of her seat and moved behind Carruthers, leaning in to see the primary sensors. The two Prax cruisers were closing in but the one was damaged and lagging behind. A gap was opening between them...*hmm.* "Can you pick up the situation toward Tavar?"

"There are several destroyed ships based on their energy readings. Uncertain as to which side took the most damage." She pointed to the indicated sensor. "Three ships appear to be heading our way from that engagement."

"If they're all Prax, we're in trouble." Kendra rubbed her chin. "We need to—." The ship shuddered on its long axis. "Long-range shot?"

"Only one hit—somewhere aft. The rest passed ahead of us."

"We need to punch back without sustaining any additional damage."

Djembe looked over. "With all respect, we need to exit this sector as fast a possible."

Seaman Chapan come into the bridge. "Chief Parker sent me up…er, Captain," he stumbled upon realizing that Kendra had the conn.

"Take the Executive Officer's station, Chapan," ordered Kendra.

"Aye."

Kendra turned back to Carruthers. "Weapons?"

"Still have ten out of twelve plasma cannon but only three projectile batteries back online, all on the port side."

"That's the left."

"Yes, Captain."

"And thrusters?"

Djembe rechecked. "All operational."

Kendra had stalled enough. "Here's the plan…"

Aboard Valor

The ship was out of danger for the moment. Heres returned to the bridge to find that the crew had cleared the damage away from the command station and pilot's console. The bodies had been removed—what had been left of them from the projectile that had decapitated Grisa and crushed another tech on its passage through the ship.

Renno was still at her station, one of the only crew unscathed by the destruction that permeated the bridge deck. She brightened visibly at his reappearance. "Sir."

"All clear in engineering. Gallorn has things well in hand. Status?" He avoided his seat and stood behind her instead.

"We're still at max sublight, following the vector laid out by the Serapis after leaving orbit."

"And the three Prax out here?"

"One is twenty-five thousand kilometers off, basically destroyed. Sensors aren't picking up life signs. Unclear whether they abandoned ship."

"They don't abandon ship."

She nodded slowly, then turned back to her station.

"What is our range to the target?"

"One hundred thirty-six thousand kilometers. Between us are the two Prax ships pursuing them."

"Their jumpdrive is damaged; otherwise there's no reason to still be in this system."

"That was my estimate of the situation as well, sir."

He grinned behind her. "I'm sure it was."

"Glad you're back, Captain."

His grin widened. "Give me every bit of power we have, Renno. I want to catch him."

"Sir!" called a tech from across the mangled bridge. "Captain Orris wants you to know that he is busy with the remaining Prax ships and won't be lending aid to the Valor who is being pursued by two remaining enemy ships."

"How far back are they?" Heres asked Renno.

"Fifty thousand, and losing ground. I think they're actually retreating in our direction rather than pursuing us, sir."

"Very well. Keep after Halloran."

"Oh, oh…" Renno was staring at her screen.

"Now what?"

"The Serapis just performed an emergency decel."

"Let me see!" Heres burst forward and leaned over her for a look.

"They are overtaken by the Prax pursuers."

"No," mused Heres with a tight smile of admiration. "They're sucking them in. It's a turnaround from what the Prax did to us an hour ago."

"Serapis is bracketing the lead pursuer with plasma, sir. Nice shooting."

"That was a rarely used old Fleet maneuver. Impressive, Halloran…"

"We're now only eighty-four thousand away. They're accelerating on a new vector."

"Stay with them, Renno. I don't want to lose them again."

A Tech spoke up. "Sir, new inbound contacts dropping out of jumpspace near Tavar. I'm counting fourteen."

Heres leaned heavily on the broken bridge ceiling section. "And?"

The man looked up. "Sir, it's Fleet."

Heres pounded a fist on the wreckage in satisfaction. "Excellent! Orris has his flotilla. Now we go back to our original mission…" He wiped his face, suddenly overwhelmed with the tension of the past few hours. His hands were shaking.

"Sir, are you well?"

He slid his eyes longingly to his comfy chair, wishing for a quick nap. Holding his third officer's hand as she died in Engineering had taken a lot out of him and Heres realized that his crew was beat, both mentally and physically. The medical techs would be busy for hours more. *Perhaps we should attempt to shadow this ship and see what transpires before launching into another battle.*

"I'm going to check in on the wounded, Renno. You have command. Where they go, we go. But maintain our distance."

"Yes, sir." The flash of concern on her face passed and was replaced by that look of determination that Heres so appreciated about her.

"And get a repair team up here to start working on my bridge."

Halloran pounded into the bridge on a mission. "What just happened?" His face burned for some reason and he put a hand to it self-consciously.

Kendra was leaning over Djembe, pointing at some instrument. She straightened at Halloran's approach. "Sir?"

"What maneuver did this ship just execute?"

"Sir," Carruthers got his attention with her wide-eyed stare. "It was amazing."

"Lieutenant?" He looked from one woman to the other expectantly.

"Captain Kendra pulled a rapid-decel maneuver with the main engines—it dropped us right in between the two targets, sir."

Halloran looked blankly at her.

"She hit the enemy at point-blank range." Carruthers shook her head as if to herself. "I never would have thought you could do that with a ship this big and no friction."

"Sir," Kendra said, "The maneuver is in the Fleet tactics book, it's just not used often because you don't typically see one heavily armed ship being pursued by several others." She shrugged in an apologetic way. "Just so happened that the Prax didn't know that."

"Damage?" Halloran's stare moved to Djembe, who was sitting back in his seat to take in the conversation.

"Minimal, sir," replied the Pilot with a nod. "It *was* an excellent defensive move."

Halloran suddenly had the distinct sensation of being a third wheel on his own bridge. It wasn't something he was used to. He had a sudden flashback to his first command dive as a Lieutenant, aboard the old trainer USS La Jolla. With Captain Sears watching his every move, every command from the rear of the bridge. The sensation that he could be replaced at any moment by half a dozen more qualified officers aboard. The clench reminded him of its presence down deep.

He looked from one to the other again, then turned to his own station with "Very well, then. What's our current heading?"

Djembe leaned forward. "Five-five-six mark two-zero-four." He looked back at Halloran. "The coordinates you wanted me to return to."

"Sir," called Chief Reyes from the intercom at his elbow. "Captain."

"Chief, glad to hear your voice. Status report."

"We've got the fire under control, but the comms in the lower and after decks are still down. Brown just came running up from Engineering, though. He wanted you to know that the jumpdrive should now be operational."

"That's good news, Chief; I think we've worn out our welcome here. Governor Jackson will have to hold his own with the Fleet now."

"Aye, sir. I'll check with Whitney and get you a casualty report. Any more shooting coming up?"

Halloran sat and rubbed his warm face again, feeling somewhat dizzy. *The archive.* We're done here," he said more to the whole bridge than just Reyes on the comm. "Pilot, jump us to the coordinates indicated."

"This will be a short jump, Captain; plan on four hours seven minutes."

"Very well."

"Where'd they jump to?" Heres was in his usual spot behind Renno. Several crew were almost done removing the chunk of wreckage. He spared his poor command chair a glance but saw that it was beyond repair.

Renno smiled up at him. "We got him. They were tracking on a specific vector—a pattern—twice in the last engagement. When they jumped they stayed on it."

"Tell me."

"Perses system."

"What's in that system which jumping to?" Heres frowned. "How are you sure?"

"Because," she explained with some affectation of patience for his attitude; she had seen the chair, too. "That's the only system in the line of jump unless they plan to overshooting into Prax-declared space."

Heres' frown deepened. "A possibility, yes?"

Renno shrugged. "Perhaps."

"So. Halloran runs. He's trying to hide. Why Perses?"

"It makes some sense, Sir," said the pilot from his station.

"Why?"

"Perses is where Garvin is. The abandoned station." He studied his report onscreen. "Records indicate it was occupied by a private citizen."

Heres wagged a finger in the pilot's direction. "Sounds like a perfect hiding place."

The communications tech called. "Captain, Captain Orris is hailing us."

Heres, about to order the jump, relented. "I'll take him privately." He leaned over Renno. "Be ready to jump to this Garvin the moment I give you the go-ahead," he whispered as he turned away.

Chapter 31

Reyes was standing outside Medical as Halloran approached. The look on his face was solemn. "Captain."

Halloran laid a hand on the Chief's shoulder. "Bad, Abran?"

The Cuban nodded his thick jaw. "Bad, sir." He looked over his shoulder. "Captain Antonov wants to be here before we do this." He had a tablet in his hand, which Halloran saw was shaking.

"You alright, Abran?"

Reyes tried to meet his eyes and failed, glancing away. "It's…it's a lot of the men." After a moment he did make eye contact. "You grow closer together, through this, you know?" He blinked and Halloran felt a stab of compassion for the thick-skinned man before him. Reyes might be the unflappable Master Chief, undisputed ruler of the crew, but he too had a breaking point. Halloran remembered the tense minutes back on Earth, when Reyes had been just over the breaking point. He'd have to watch the man carefully now. *I don't know what I'd do without him.*

Antonov came out of Medical and let the hatch close behind him slowly.

"Pyotr."

"Sir." He looked at Reyes and nodded tightly. "Chief." He swayed as he said it and put a hand out against the bulkhead for support, blinking.

Halloran realized that his crew had *all* passed the breaking point. He exhaled. "Let's have it."

Reyes lifted the tablet. "We started out with two Tavarran replacements for Patredes and DeBartelo. Post engagement, the report is five KIA; Kauffman and James in Electrical, Baker in Ops."

"They were in the Ops Center when it was hit?"

Reyes nodded before continuing to read. "Also one of the replacements, name of Cassis. And Cochran in Battery B." Reyes' eyes had reddened when he glanced up; He and Cochran had served together in prior boats.

"Go on."

Aye, sir... Six wounded, including Captain Antonov here."

Antonov lifted an arm to show the wrap around his midsection, under his shirt.

"How is it?"

"Puncture wound, missed the vitals but hurts like a bear."

"King took a bad hit; he's unconscious now. Flagler tore up her arm trying to save Cochran, sir."

"I'm sorry, Chief."

Reyes swallowed. "Monahan has burns over most of his lower torso. And the alien got hit by a falling chunk of debris."

"Don't call him that, Chief. Call him Commander Axxa."

Reyes' frown said volumes about what he thought of it. "Aye, sir."

Halloran crossed his arms, feeling the tension. "Eleven casualties against a roster of twenty-nine. That isn't good."

"At least Engineering missed getting hit. We're under full propulsion. I was down to see Lieutenant

Hummel, sir; the jumpdrive is working fine now that they've isolated that electrical issue."

"Other damage? Hull?"

Antonov sighed. "Actually, it's not as bad as it looks."

Halloran's brow rose. "It looks pretty bad."

The Russian nodded. "I have Chief Parker and Yeoman Butler combing over the outer compartments looking for breaches we've missed like last engagement, but by and large the hits were sealed by this incredible Tavarran steel. I am glad he repaired the hull when he did."

"But the interior…"

"…Ain't great, sir," completed Reyes. "We've got life support and operations in shambles. Lieutenant Travers managed to re-patch some of the life support functions through Engineering backups, but our atmosphere is going to begin declining within hours. Deacon got banged up during the gravity loss but did okay…for an 'air breather.' I put him on the job of monitoring the remaining life support equipment with orders to call me if anything looks off to him. There's not much to monitor, though," he added with a face.

"Will we need to evacuate?"

"You'll need to ask Lieutenant Travers that, sir. He knows this ship's systems better'n anybody." He made a face. "Food processors—really the entire crew compartment—destroyed too, sir."

"Weapons status?"

Antonov took the tablet and scrolled. "We can get all batteries back online eventually, but right now there are failures reporting in seven of the twelve projectile batteries. Three of the plasma batteries had their power cut by incoming fire, but Parker believes he can repair them fairly easily." He handed the tablet back to the Chief. "I sent Petrey and Wilson to scrounge any other spares that they can find—the two of them know the layout of the storage best." He shook his head. Halloran saw that the usually-implacable Russian was rattled. "We don't have enough crew left on two feet to complete repairs in a month, assuming we even understood how the equipment went together."

Halloran leaned against the bulkhead. "Let's work one problem at a time. So, we can maneuver and fight, but our air is limited and we're down a third of our complement."

Reyes tapped the tablet as if to make a point. "We'd probably be a lot worse off if Captain Kendra hadn't pulled off that stellar attack back there. Sir."

So word had spread from the bridge about that, Halloran noted. "Alright, we're several hours out from our destination, so I'll check on the wounded and talk to them. Antonov, you get yourself sorted out and take my cabin to be closer to the bridge as we come out of jumpspace; we're still not sure what to expect at the other end." He ended with a meaningful look at the other officer. *Get yourself together, I need you.*

After a few moments of silence filled by the sounds of machinery humming loudly, Antonov slowly saluted with a nod. "We're heading to that abandoned world you mentioned, correct?"

"That's right. There's an old archive on some Fleet station that's out of service."

"Expecting anything?"

Halloran straightened and stretched his neck. He was more tense than he'd ever felt in his career. "I'm expecting anything, Pyotr."

Reyes was only half-listening; Halloran could tell that his mind was already on the repairs and wounded. "Sir, we need to do a service. I'm having Brown come up and help me with the bodies." The broad-shouldered man's red eyes looked bloodshot.

"I know, Chief. I'll work on that." He placed a hand on Reyes' shoulder. "We need to keep moving. We can rest later. No looking back or down."

Reyes nodded in appreciation and adjusted his cap with two hands. "And sir, you should know that Commander Axxa really did well. I'm sorry about that earlier crack."

"Thanks, Chief. I'll stop in and see him."

The Medical bay was worse than the last time he'd seen it. Bloody bandages and clothing were everywhere, on every surface. The floor was streaked with red from the passage of the wounded. The space wasn't that big to begin with; Halloran figured that the Prax didn't plan to save their own as much as let them die in battle.

At the far end of the well-lit space Elias Whitney was bending over a crewman whose face Halloran couldn't immediately see. Blocking his view was Stan Richards from the mess; Richards had been assigned to the medical team at general quarters by Chief Reyes.

A voice at his elbow said, "It's Don King, sir. He went into shock from blood loss."

Halloran nodded. "Thank you, Yeoman. How are you?"

Flagler held up a splinted arm. "Feels okay now that Stan shot me full of painkillers. It was a gash when I...I..."

Halloran put a hand on her shoulder. He saw Axxa watching the exchange from across the room where the alien sat against the wall.

Flagler's eyes were thick with emotion as she looked up at Halloran. "I couldn't reach him, sir." She swallowed heavily, then cleared her throat and batted at an eye with her free hand. "He was trapped in there after the battery got hit. I managed to close the outer doors, but there was a fire below him."

He tightened his grip. "Bob was a good sailor."

Flagler nodded up at him as another tear ran slowly down her black-stained cheek. "He was always so stubborn. Cassis did what he could, too—before he got hit by some chunk of metal like I did—but Bob wasn't getting out of that hole." She looked down at the deck. "He's still there, sir."

"We'll get him out, Karen." He felt Axxa's eyes on him again and looked over. The Prax displayed no emotion but his gaze was hard. Halloran gave Flagler a brief hug. "You take care of yourself and connect with Gerry when you're able. I need the two of you on the weapons systems ASAP; we're on our way to a new star system I hope will be quieter but one thing we've learned out here is nothing seems to go right for us."

"Aye, sir. It sure doesn't." But Flagler had straightened somewhat at the business talk and was tugging on her uniform shirt in a new effort to recover her dignity. She'd be okay.

Halloran patted her on the shoulder again and walked over to Axxa. He watched Halloran approach and stood up before he got over. "Captain." He was favoring one side and there was blood on his pant leg.

"What's your status, Commander?"

"I believe I am fit for duty, but the surgeon ordered me to stay until he is done with Mr. King. He would like to inspect me."

Halloran turned to watch the surgery. Whitney was attempting to guide Richards' hands to something on the table. "The Ops Center is out of action?" He looked sidewise at Axxa.

"The fire destroyed much of the equipment, Captain. I find this all quite interesting."

Halloran raised an eyebrow up at the alien.

"I don't think the translator is correctly conveying my comment. What I mean is that, on Prax…in our way…the dead are honored for generations. To perish in battle is preferred. As a result, we do not seek to heal our wounded." He put his hands together with a slight grimace of pain that Halloran picked up on. "Our way is to fight and die together. No surrender, as you discovered in the mines on Tavar."

"We have similar sentiments, Mr. Axxa." Halloran folded his arms across his chest. "When the time comes, we humans will rally to each other to fight a common enemy—to the death if need be. The Alamo."

"Alamo?"

"It was a fort in Texas where defenders of all sorts banded together to hold off an overwhelming invading Mexican army. They knew they weren't going to make it but they stayed and fought anyway. No one survived."

Axxa dipped his head in understanding. "This sounds like the Prax way."

Halloran studied him for a moment. "But we seek always to save the wounded at great cost to ourselves. Our military has a 'no man left behind' policy."

"This is not our way, Captain. But I also perceive how it makes your race stronger."

Halloran was still staring at the alien thoughtfully when Whitney came over. Halloran saw the man's exhaustion. "Sir."

"How is Seaman King?"

Whitney pulled off a bloody glove. "He's stable now. We managed to get blood…" He glanced at Axxa, "From an unlikely source."

Axxa actually looked embarrassed. "It is known among our people of the similarity in blood chemistry. Mr. King would have died anyway."

"Well, that's true," noted Whitney. "The Prax typing kit ID'd Axxa as a likely donor and I frankly didn't have time to search for a human match."

"I was the wrong type, sir," added Flagler from where she sat.

Halloran grasped Axxa's elbow. "Good work, Commander."

"Well, we'll see what the long-term effects of the transfusion are," Whitney said. "Stan is finishing his suture up now; he's actually good at that. Better'n me." The Corpsman dabbed a cut on his cheek.

"You're tired, Elias. If everyone here is stable you should grab some shuteye. We're coming out of jump in a new system with an as-yet unknown reception."

Whitney dropped the gloves he'd been holding into a bin and tugged on a fresh set sourced from a pocket. He shrugged at Halloran's raised eyebrow. "Sorry sir, we're doing the best we can." He took Axxa's arm and lifted it. "Now let me see where those ribs are broken, sir."

Axxa turned to let Whitney examine him and addressed Halloran. "I shall return to duty shortly, Captain. I assume we are understaffed…"

Halloran sighed. "That's an understatement." He included Flagler with a glance. "I know this is hard but I need everyone back at their posts and helping out ASAP. I want Richards to join the damage party the moment he's done with King. Elias, you too. There are some bodies to be dealt with; the Chief is working on that."

Whitney looked up from his examination. "Aye, sir."

"How many did we lose, sir?" Flagler had stood.

"Too many, Yeoman. Too many."

Chapter 32

The Perses system and the planet that suddenly appeared on the forward screen was truly beautiful. Everyone on the bridge was struck silent by its majesty of purple-blue swirls. Even at hundreds of thousands of kilometers away its beauty captivated.

A full minute passed wherein Halloran allowed himself to be taken in by the vision of it, letting his crew see it and appreciate the moment, before speaking softly. "Can I assume we're there?" The silent enormity of space hadn't stopped making a profound impression on him. He'd spent a restless hour in his cabin attempting to sleep but failed miserably.

Djembe nodded. "Outer Perses system. That's Garvin, sir. We'll make orbit in…one hour, fifty minutes from our exit point. Nice and close."

"Carruthers, get me a detailed scan of the vicinity and locate this orbiting station."

"Aye, sir."

Chief Reyes came onto the bridge and over to Halloran's chair. He still looked haggard even after the Captains-orders shower and shave. "You called, sir?"

"Not a lot of people left to mount a proper landing party should we need to, Chief."

"I'll go, sir. Let me bring one other man and Captain Kendra in the shuttle."

Halloran considered it. He had planned to lead the shore party once again, but with their severe lack of staffing the ship was becoming difficult to operate. Repairs from the battle were barely underway. The life support situation had been attacked first and Parker had figured out a workaround to bypass some of the fried electronics. But it was far from permanent. What if the ship experienced a major concern while he was away? Halloran trusted Antonov, but the man was hurt and could develop complications. Kendra would be off-ship.

But Reyes was the glue that kept the crew—what remained of it—together. If Halloran were to lose him, the men would never be the same as a unit. Chief Parker was a mechanical expert, but not a Chief of the Boat. Outside of Halloran and Antonov themselves, Reyes was the only other man aboard comfortable with running a crew.

"Sir," called Carruthers without looking back. "Sensors are detecting a large mass on the far side of Garvin. Appears to be in orbit."

"Engage the Hidden Claw. It's still operational?"

"Aye and yes, sir. Engaging now."

"How long before we can get a better read of this object?"

"Unclear, sir. Still scanning the planet and surrounding bodies. Some of the damage affected the power source for the sensor arrays." She sounded tired, too. *We're all a mess,* thought Halloran. *One more push and we may not bounce back.*

"Very well." Halloran looked up at Reyes. "Thanks, Chief, but you're needed here. While I'm away, the priority is effecting every critical repair we can pull off."

"Aye, sir. May I recommend Lieutenant Hummel for your team? Wyatt has Engineering under control, and you may have the opportunity to forage for supplies." As the supply officer aboard Bonhomme Richard, Hummel had displayed considerable initiative in securing hard-to-find items while in port.

Halloran agreed. "Very well. Is the intership fixed?"

Reyes looked pained. "No, sir. I'll send someone to inform him."

"Have him report to the shuttle bay in shore party gear immediately. And find Captain Kendra, too. Same orders."

"Aye, sir."

After Reyes had gone to find his runner, Halloran stood. "I'll be in my cabin." He nodded to Carruthers. "You take the conn."

Once the door to his cabin closed, Halloran leaned against it and closed his eyes, running his fingers through fuzzy hair. The cut had grown out microscopically and he suddenly felt unkempt. He had a sudden flashback to being berated about his longish hair once, at boot camp in Michigan. The DI had insisted he'd amount to nothing with his lack of discipline. *Maybe the jerk was right after all.*

Halloran stepped forward and dropped onto his bed. The mattress—if it could be legitimately be called that—was very hard. Even after weeks in space, he hadn't grown accustomed to it. Perhaps it was because the bed was so big.

Doubts and concerns filled his head. Once again, they approached a planet with unknown capabilities. Jackson had said that this Telos Archive was benign, lacking integral defenses. But the Haulers were known to trade with this Mr. Telos. Halloran was sure that an undamaged Serapis could handle a Hauler ship in a fight, but with the current situation he feared that even a lucky shot from an enemy could cause critical damage and they'd lose the ship in the process. Let alone if anything properly armed would show up. Fact was, the Serapis was ill-prepared to survive another pitched battle. *At least the Engines and shields were operational,* he reminded himself grimly.

And he was down to a skeleton crew. Halloran was proud of every one of the Americans; each had become subject matter experts on their Praxxan systems to the best of their ability. There just wasn't enough crew left to even minimally man the ship, let along fight.

"Captain to the bridge!"

Halloran sat bolt upright. He was on his bed. He'd heard the speaker blare the request; they must've fixed the intership. His eyes felt like they had lead bags underneath them. The short nap hadn't apparently helped much.

The bridge was the same as he'd left it with the exception of Axxa, who was back in his normal position. The alien inclined his head as Halloran noticed him. The damaged ribs were tucked inside a wrap that covered his upper torso.

"Sir, we've got a problem." Yusef Malone, part of Gail's tech team, was speaking from his station to his right.

"What?" Halloran marched up behind him.

"Two Prax warships."

Halloran leaned in with nerves on fire. "Where? Was that the mass initially scanned?"

"Yes…that and some kind of orbiting station."

"Can we get it onscreen for visual?"

Carruthers spoke up. "Yes, sir, but they are in a geosynchronous orbit and the planet rotates slowly." She looked at Djembe. "How long did you estimate?"

The Pilot glanced at them. "A day cycle of forty-two hours."

Malone muttered, "That's a long workday."

Halloran touched the young man's shoulder. "What?"

"Sorry, sir. Surface scans indicate a toxic atmosphere and high surface temperature; no life signs."

"How far are we from orbit?" Halloran asked Djembe.

"We are done with decel, Captain. You can enter orbit at any time."

"Captain."

Halloran straightened and turned to the source of the voice. "Yes."

Axxa said, "I should point out that to find Prax ships here is highly unusual."

"You said that about the last planet we visited, Commander."

"True."

"Can we ascertain the type of ship?"

"Computer is crunching on it, sir. Heavily armed cruisers are all I've got right now."

"Wonderful." Halloran sat in his station. "Djembe, put us in orbit on the opposite side of the planet. Then move us around to close on the target. Slowly and deliberately." He hit the intership transmit button. "All hands, this is the Captain. We're arriving at our destination but it seems to be guarded by two Prax warships. We're cloaked and will approach with care to assess the tactical situation." He hesitated. "I know some of you are wounded and all of you are understaffed to man your stations; my hope is to find us a haven to rest and effect repairs." *And hopefully find some answers.*

"Confirmed targets, now designated Zulu One and Zulu Two, sir. Zulu one is a class or heavy cruiser. The computer says twenty-six plasma batteries, eighteen projectile batteries. Should I describe Zulu two?"

"No, thank you, Lieutenant. We're outgunned but we have the element of surprise." He watched the mesmerizing swirls of light blue pass beneath the ship on the viewscreen. "Can we take them?" He said the thought aloud, not entirely intending to.

Djembe shook his head. "Even a very damaging first-salvo would fail to critically wound something that big. We'd take several full salvos ourselves."

"Which we can't afford. Can we lure them away?" He looked at Carruthers. "Anything on the station?"

"Minimal readings; there are some bodies there, just not many. No targeting emissions to be concerned about. It is four hundred meters in length and a hundred fifty meters at its widest point, sir." She looked back. "Zulu One is anchored in a matching orbit a thousand meters from the station. Zulu Two is in a similar orbit but ten thousand meters on the opposing side."

"They're screening each other. Very well. Let's move up inside Zulu Two and target the Zulu One and the station. See what presents itself."

"We're in orbit, sir," announced Djembe. "No signs that the Prax have detected us yet. Initiating movement toward the station now. ETA in…twenty minutes at current projected course."

Why am I doing this? We're severely outgunned. Every principle in the book says turn away and find a safer harbor to effect repairs.

"Mush Morton wouldn't." *He'd go in under the destroyer screen, damage and all.*

"Sir?"

Halloran had spoken his thought aloud. He shook his head at Djembe. "Nothing, Pilot. Sound General Quarters, Lieutenant. Target Zulu One with a full broadside of plasma cannon at point-blank range. Prepare to fire on my command." The tension between his shoulders was blazing.

"Aye, sir."

Trigg Wyatt and Chief Parker picked through the wreckage of the Ops Center, moving shred of metal structure aside to create a path to the main bank of controls for life support. Bits of insulation littered the compartment, torn free from the projectile hits and atomized by the high heat of the fire. They stirred up into the air around their booted feet and got in their noses.

Parker coughed. "This stuff is intolerable."

"Aye, Chief." Wyatt lifted a large piece. "A little help here, sir?"

The two of them managed to move the chunk out of the way, exposing more of the controls. Parker immediately went to the panel and studied it. Wyatt crowded in next to him, careful to avoid all the sharp edges sticking out around them.

Parker tapped a panel that was melted; the controls bent in several directions at once. "Yep, Nunez's the expert on this system but I'd say your readings down in Engineering are correct."

Wyatt wiped the screen on the panel, but it was clearly dead. "This thing'll need a complete teardown and rebuild."

"Which time we don't have." Parker sighed. "This ship's life support system is on life support."

Wyatt looked at Parker. "What about Mr. Axxa?"

The older man shook his head, removing his cap and running his fingers through his hair. "No go. I asked the skipper to talk to him. The guy doesn't know anything about this kind of tech, even if it's his own race."

Wyatt cleared another panel off. "This looks like sensors. They're still working, right?"

Parker looked. "Yup. Gail says no issues other than the power reroute when I checked with her."

Wyatt grunted at the Chief's use of the Lieutenant's first name. "How're you two holding up, now?" Parker and Carruthers had been an item on the Bonny Rich at one point. Since the 'incident' bringing them here and Carruthers' promotion to officer, Wyatt and others had noticed their separation.

"It's tough, Trigg." Parker crossed his arms. "I mean, she's an officer now. What do I do with that?"

Wyatt didn't look up. "Oh, I don't know, I've done things with officers before."

Parker heard the grin on the Engineer's face. "Yeah, well, it's weird."

"I don't remember it being weird."

"Cut it out."

"Yes, Chief." Wyatt straightened from the panel he was examining. "This section looks cooked too."

"Trigg, are we gonna make it home?"

Wyatt paused at Parker's sudden question. He pulled back from the panel and massaged his temples after wiping grime from his hands, more to gain a moment to think than anything else. Finally he let his hands fall. "Chief, the Skipper knows best. Don't ask me these questions."

"But what do you think?" Parker pressed.

Wyatt put a hand on the older man's arm. "Dude, you should marry her. That's what I think. You're good for each other." He waved at the bank of gear. "Now what have you got me away from my precious engine for?"

"We're seven thousand meters from the Zulu One, sir, with the orbital station between them and our position. Zulu Two is continuing on its orbit without signs of seeing us."

"We practically ran right under their stern, Carruthers." Halloran leaned forward. "Do we think they're waiting for us or are they worried about hitting the station?"

Malone spoke. "No signs of engine activity from either enemy vessel, sir. No indications they have learned of our presence."

"What do you think, pilot?" Are our chances of doing damage better now?"

Djembe shook his head. "No. In my experience the Prax do not hesitate to attack. We're so close…they *clearly* don't know we're here yet. Yet, even if we get off a solid broadside, they'll have the range and be able to hit us from both vectors."

Halloran felt as though he was trapped. They'd done the best they could to get into a good tactical situation but now he had to commit his wounded ship and crew to another action with a superior enemy vessel. Or, he could succumb to the nagging desire to slink away and lick his wounds. But where would he go? They needed help. They'd gone as far as they could go with this ship, awesome tech or not. *What I need is a drydock.*

"Carruthers, keep us in position opposite the Prax ship. Anything new from the station itself?"

Malone said, "No, sir."

Halloran stood up, crossing his arms. "Djembe, open a channel. Let's see if we can talk to someone aboard it. Maybe they have weapons we don't know about."

The pilot half-turned. "But sir, the Prax will be monitoring…"

"I know, Pilot. Can't be helped. Get ready to maneuver."

"Channel open, Captain." Halloran could tell from the old man's tone that he disapproved.

If we have to fight, we fight. "Attention orbiting station, this is Captain Thomas Halloran of the United States Navy. Respond, please."

A minute passed in silence. "Am I transmitting?" Halloran asked Djembe.

"We're being hailed, sir. It's the Prax."

Halloran sighed. "Let's hear it."

"Video capable. Onscreen."

With a start, Halloren jerked his eyes up as the figure of a large Prax officer resolved into view. His voice boomed into the Serapis bridge. "Human ship, we have ascertained your position based on your transmission."

Halloran cursed. "Cut our feed." When Djembe nodded in reply he ordered him, "Back us up five thousand kilometers."

The Prax on the screen was still talking. "We are in full control of your station. Prepare to defend yourselves!"

"Sir!" Malone was calling out. "Zulu One is moving forward, around the station! Closing fast! Zulu Two is turning toward our location."

Halloran said resignedly to Carruthers. "Prepare to fire on Zulu One as planned." But now he felt a meaty hand on his forearm and looked in surprise. It was Axxa.

"Allow me to speak to him."

"What? Why"

"I know him."

Halloran felt the pressure of his inner conflict over this alien boiling over inside, and then it left him. He exhaled through tight lips and nodded to Djembe. "Put us on."

"You're on."

But they hadn't needed the Pilot's warning. The face of the Prax on the screen was all the confirmation they needed; his eyes went wide and he leaned into his camera lens.

"Axxa?"

"Yes, Commander Grysx."

"You are aboard a human vessel?" The man's eyes had now narrowed with suspicion.

Axxa glanced at Halloran. "I am...assisting...this human Captain. We seek *your* assistance now."

"What!?"

Halloran nodded minutely at Axxa. "Commander, we are in need of—."

But the alien on the screen was stepping aside to make room for another figure. Now it was Axxa's turn to gasp in surprise.

"Ryax?"

"Brother, it is so excellent to see you alive." Halloran's translator couldn't get the terms right.

Axxa's hand on Halloran's arm tightened and he was silent for several uncharacteristic seconds. Halloran was about to nudge him when he finally spoke, and the words came slowly and with great emotion—for a Prax. "And I you, brother."

"Tell them to stand down, Axxa," Halloran whispered urgently.

Axxa stepped forward away from the human. "Ryax, we need your assistance with our ship."

"What, why?" The Prax on the screen frowned.

"It's one of ours. A Prax stealth warship."

Ryax shook his head. "I...I am familiar with this vessel." He bowed his head. "I am not honored to discuss these matters. But I think there are some Prax aboard our ship who will be honored to see you." He smiled in that odd Prax fashion.

The older Prax stepped back into view. "Captain, we will hold our position until your identify is verified. It is apparent you are using some new technology to hide your vessel from scans."

Halloran felt the first easing of the tension in his gut. "Actually, it's *your* technology, Commander."

"I do not understand."

"Then let's get together and I'll show you. Just don't shoot us first."

Chapter 33

Perses System - Telos Station, orbiting Garvin

Kendra eased the shuttle onto its landing skids with perfection.

"Nice." Halloran put on his borrowed Navy cap and tugged it down low and tight.

She tapped through the power-down sequence. "It's hard to believe."

"What?"

"That we're on Telos. I've heard my father mention it before, over the years. Even when I was a child. It must have meant something to him. I'm finding it interesting that we're actually landing on it."

"Sir, let me go first." Gerry Wilson hefted a plasma rifle as he reached for the hatch.

With Kendra, Axxa and Halloran were Chief Reyes, Wilson, Djembe, Yeoman Flagler and Bruce Brown from Engineering. All carried plasma rifles from Tavar as well as Prax sidearms originally from the ship. Antonov had felt recovered enough to take the bridge while they traveled to the station. Despite the severe loss of hands to the ship by staffing this shore party, Halloran wanted to project as much of a show of force as possible given the situation.

Halloran had considered that the Prax decision to move the meet to the station could be a trap. Anything could be a trap right now…The aliens had been tight-lipped after the initial emotional outburst between Axxa and the other guy aboard the enemy cruiser.

As Halloran stepped and looked around, he found himself wondering. *Are we the enemy here? Or are they?* The sensors couldn't read anything unusual about the station interior. There was definitely humanoid life already aboard somewhere, even before the Prax cruiser had detached its own shuttle prior to theirs.

There were several other small craft in the bay. Most looked to be older, boxier designs to Halloran's untrained eye. Kendra pointed out the Prax shuttle nearby. "That's them."

Almost as if in response to her comment, a Prax soldier stepped into view around the other shuttle, a weapon held in front of him. Everyone froze and Reyes looked at Halloran. "Orders?"

"Stay with the plan. Kendra, lock the shuttle up. Like we figured, their shuttle will hold twice as many troops. We need everyone together."

Djembe whistled. "It's as big as the Imani."

"Missing your ship, Djembe?" Halloran asked.

"Yes. Sir." The older man's tense face turned to his.

"We'll get you home. Although I don't know if I really want to part with my crack pilot."

Djembe's expression relaxed somewhat. "Yes, Captain. We shall see." And he cracked a small grin. "Mr. Chapan has performed admirably in his lessons."

"Alright everyone, button up and Let's find this meeting place."

The Prax guard watched the group pass by without making any provocative moves. Reyes caught Halloran's eye several times; the Chief didn't like any of it.

Beyond the Prax shuttle, an entry hatch similar to the one in Tavar's hangar stood. Kendra took the lead and keyed something into the system. The hatch slowly opened from within.

"Secret code?" Halloran waved her in after the others had gone. He was half-watching the Prax guard behind them.

"Open. No secret. You'd know the command if you were from this century, Captain."

"I'm still learning."

She shot him a look before stepping over the hatch coaming and into the station.

The group was arrayed in a wide passageway beyond. Halloran saw the station immediately as something not kept up the way that Tavar did their colony. Or any of the warships for that matter. There was oxidation on the metal railing running the length of the wall nearest him. He ran a finger over some absentmindedly. *No, not well-kept.* He felt close to something big. Jackson's word came back to him; *Telos would know. He has the original records.* Halloran hoped this trip had been worth it. "Kendra, any idea on where to find the control room of this bucket?"

Reyes spoke up. "Sir, I don't think we need to look."

Halloran turned at the Chief's warning tone. Several Prax soldiers rounded the far corner of the hall, guns drawn down on them.

"Everybody down!"

"Halt!" Called a voice from the gaggle of Prax, who had quickly closed the gap between the opposing forces.

"Don't fire!"

Halloran recognized the voice as coming from Axxa. His team had gone to their knees but now Axxa was rising, striding forward toward the enemy team. He saw him holstering his pistol and showing his palms. And then there was another Prax stepping from their group and the two embraced, the emotion rolling off the two aliens as they struck each other on the upper arms in a sort of a greeting, then back to the crushing bear hug and back slapping.

Reyes was at Halloran's ear. "I see that they know each other." Halloran read the unspoken question in the statement.

He slowly got to his feet and lowered his pistol. "Okay, everyone. On your feet. Stay sharp but lower your barrels for the moment."

Axxa pulled back from the other Prax and gestured to him.

"Careful, sir," whispered Reyes.

"Keep a gun on my back, Chief." Halloran walked forward, clearly holstering his own pistol as he went. He could feel the sudden tension in the air and see it in the eyes of the assembled Prax soldiers. "Axxa…"

"Stand down!" Said the other Prax with Axxa, turning to his troops.

Guns drooped but not all that much.

Halloran reached the two. "Friend of yours, Axxa?" He nodded at the other Prax.

Axxa gripped the Prax's arm. "Captain, this is a longtime comrade of mine. Ryax." Again, the translator seemed to have trouble understanding the words. Halloran wondered if they were some sort of terms of endearment not added to the lexicon of the translation software. The two certainly seemed comfy enough together.

He bowed just a bit at the waist, the way Axxa had taught him. "An honor, Ryax."

Ryax was looking him over from top to bottom. "You are a large human."

Reyes had appeared at Halloran's elbow. "Is that supposed to be a compliment?" He asked quietly to him.

Ryax skewered the shorter Cuban. "And you are not."

Axxa laid a hand on Ryax's shoulder. "This man is the Chief of their ship. A respected leader of his crew."

Halloran caught the compliment and smiled. He slid his eyes to Reyes and saw the other's eyes flinch. *Wow. How long had Axxa been holding that in?*

Ryax bowed in response. "An honor, then." He looked at Halloran warily. "I meant no disrespect."

"None taken, Ryax." He extended a hand. "He gets called short all the time."

Ryax studied the proferred limb warily.

Axxa stepped in again. "Grasp and shake."

Ryax complied gingerly for as big as he was, glancing from Axxa to Halloran. "A human custom." He looked distinctly uncomfortable, as if the touch of a human was somehow dirty.

Halloran nodded. "To honor another."

Ryax pursed his lips. "Then grasp you I will."

Halloran didn't think the translator got that right, either.

But Ryax was ushering Axxa toward his soldiers. "Lead us," He ordered them. "Human, I must insist that your, um,"

"Crew?"

"Your crew surrender their weapons."

The outburst from the humans nearly caused a firefight right there and then. Guns came up on both sides with the three officers caught in the killing zone.

"Belay that!" thundered Halloran, letting the stress and tension out with his bellow.

All eyes, both human and Praxxan, turned to him.

Halloran blew out a breath and turned back to Ryax. *Focus.* "Mutually assured destruction."

Ryax—and Axxa—stared at him.

"We keep ours, you keep yours. One side starts shooting and we all die. Detente?"

Ryax nodded slowly. "I understand." He made a lowering motion toward his soldiers, then motioned with his head at the humans.

"Match their movements, people," Halloran warned.

Once the guns were down toward the floor again, Axxa spoke. "Ryax, these humans have traveled far in my company. I would say…I would say that I trust them to…act with honor."

Halloran nodded in appreciation. But Kendra's snort was obvious from the back of the gaggle of humans all the same.

The group moved off on the heels of the Prax troops, with Wilson taking up a rear position to keep an eye on the two armed Prax that had magically appeared in the corridor behind them. The hall widened into a large atrium and the Prax soldiers led by Ryax headed across to the far wall. Kendra was nearby now and leaned over to Halloran. "This is the station core." She motioned up with a finger.

Halloran looked in that direction. The central structure of the station was a massive cylinder, the ceiling of which was far above where they stood. Dozens upon dozens of stories separated their deck from the topmost of the station. He heard several others of his group gasp in amazement. "It's much bigger inside," was all he offered. But he was impressed.

At the same time, he saw the telltale signs of neglect. Even on the decking below their feet the oxidation was everywhere. Flaking surface coatings were apparent, as were the haphazardly scattered crates around the space. Several of the containers looked big enough to house a tank. Or a shuttle. Halloran wondered how stuff this big had gotten through that typical passageway behind them. The whole area felt…dusty.

The Prax never stopped to look, however, and presently the group of soldiers fanned out and turned their guns back on the humans. Ryax came to Halloran and Axxa, who had conspicuously stayed at the human's side as an obvious show of allegiance and protection. "Commander…Captain," He began, spreading his arms. "I must request that your crew relinquish their weapons beyond this point."

Halloran began to protest but Axxa cut him off. "Ryax, why is this? Explain yourself."

Halloran realized with sinking heart that another dozen Prax had appeared around them. *So this is where we end.* He fingered the trigger and caught Reyes' eye.

Ryax speared his friend with a hard gaze. "You will understand more in a moment. We have a duty."

Axxa's eye's widened just a bit. He turned to Halloran. "You should comply."

Reyes interrupted. "What? No way, sir." His gun came up ever-so-slightly, and Halloran could immediately see the Prax soldiers tensing up. Kendra had a stray lock of black hair over her right eye. She blew it away with her lips and nodded at Halloran meaningfully.

No. He gently pushed the Chief's weapon down again. "I'll be back momentarily."

"What are they so skittish about, Skipper?" Halloran heard the man's accent slipping in—his Chief was nervous.

"I don't know, Chief. But I…trust Axxa." The tension was still there, wedged in his gut, but that admission caused a sudden loosening that allowed Halloran to breathe that much easier. He *did* trust Axxa.

Axxa nodded gravely. "I hold the Captain's security in my honor, Chief Reyes."

After a long moment, Reyes dipped his head and stepped back marginally. "You be careful, Captain."

Kendra just looked mad.

"Always, Chief." Halloran motioned to Ryax with a reassuring nod in her direction. "Lead on."

"Your weapon, human."

Halloran passed it to Reyes instead, with a sweet smile for Ryax as he did so. Reyes hefted both guns easily, flexing his substantial biceps and smirking at the Prax nearest him. "Bandito," he offered the alien, who looked unimpressed.

After an appraising stare that encompassed all the human team, Ryax turned and motioned for Halloran and Axxa to follow him. The trio passed through the gauntlet of well-armored Prax troops and Halloran knew that his crew wouldn't stand a chance against these aliens in combat. He had a fleeting memory of the Prax he'd killed on that space station, seemingly years ago. The body bleeding out with that unusual red color, hanging in the broken glass of the door above him. The blood.

Ryax was at a door. "Show honor and do not speak, human." He nodded to a soldier who opened the door firmly, somehow without losing his grip on his rifle held at attention. Ryax led the way in and Halloran followed.

Inside was a large meeting space, similar to a base briefing room on any Naval shore installation. Several more Prax soldiers lined the wall, weapons at the ready and eyes straight ahead. At the front of the room a small group of Prax stood stiffly at attention, looking their way with consternation written all over their faces. Halloran felt Axxa suddenly tense up at his elbow, and a gasp fell from his lips.

And then Axxa was striding across the room. "Maxlan! Crex! What are you doing—?" The translator descended into Praxxan terms that it couldn't properly render.

Ryax stood next to Halloran now. "These are servants in his family household." Halloran could plainly hear the pleasure in the Prax's voice. He was enjoying this moment.

Axxa had stopped dead, a meter from the group. Another Prax came out of the group and Halloran realized that this Prax was...a female. He'd never seen one before. "A female," he said to himself.

"She is the consort to the Premier, human," corrected Ryax. "And Axxa is her sire."

"Her...son?"

"True."

And there was Axxa, embracing the female in a loving way that warmed Halloran's heart. It felt good that *someone* was getting their reunion. He found himself dreaming of Cindy. *To hug her, hold her again...* The anger threatened to flare up again. *Extreme bad timing,* he forcefully reminded himself.

"Human, approach." Ryax was nudging him out of his reverie.

Halloran refocused on the scene. Axxa was bowing before another Prax, one dressed in obviously-the-boss garments. Not quite a king, but definitely a prime minister type. Ryax had said 'Premier.' He went toward the imposing figure, suddenly aware of the gravity of this moment. If this guy was indeed a high ruler of the Prax, and here he was a human—this just *had* to be big. He found himself wishing for Kendra at his side, to talk him through this from a Fleet perspective. To offer some moral support…no, she'd probably want to go for it and try to kill him.

Halloran kept his feet moving, words rushing through his head. The Navy taught its senior leaders how to interact with foreign dignitaries. What would the book say now? Aliens?

Axxa was turning to Halloran, a grave look on his face. *Conflicted.* Still Halloran came on. He forced himself to exhale slowly as he closed the distance deliberately, watching his steps. *No tripping now, human,* he told himself.

The Premier watched him with cold, hard eyes. The outfit was military, but festooned with jewels that glittered in among a variety of colored sashes. Halloran remembered Axxa talking about the sashes they had found aboard the Serapis. Denoting family affiliations within the Prax culture. *Maybe this Premier wore all colors of families to show respect to them.* The high collar of his top exhibited several adornments of rank. Halloran saw the claw symbol prominent among them.

And then he was bowing stiffly before the alien leader, sensing the tension in the air around their group. Carefully, he kept quiet and eyes lowered.

A long, *long* moment later the voice said, "This human shows…honor, Axxa. You have trained him?"

"A little, my Lord. But mostly, it's his way." Halloran heard the slight injection of humor into the response and risked a glance up. The Premier had his arms folded casually in front of him. He was tall, even taller than Axxa. Still he said nothing but nodded slightly to the Prax.

Axxa cleared his throat. "Father, this is Captain Thomas Halloran of the human Earth Navy. Captain, this is Premier Lord Krex of the Praxxan Empire."

Halloran bowed again. "It is indeed an honor, Premier." And he meant it. The clench in his gut loosened ever slightly more. *To face your enemy.*

The Premier nodded. "And it is well to meet the human who rescued my son from the schemes of a dishonored family."

So something is wrong after all. Something about families dishonored, on Earth.

Axxa tapped Halloran on the arm. "You realize that you make history today, Captain. You are the first human to be in the presence of a Prax Premier."

Halloran swallowed. "I figured as much. I feel like a diplomat, only I'm not one."

The Premier chuckled. "Diplomats." The Prax word for it fell with some clear bitterness from his lips. "I have no use for them. An honorable warrior is what I desire to treat with."

Axxa nodded with appreciation as the Premier half-turned away. "Good answer, Captain," he whispered to Halloran.

The Premier had the female with him now. "I present my consort, Sar'yana of the Sight."

Halloran nodded to her. "Ma'am."

Her eyes…he saw them dancing with light and fire. So unlike the males. She was captivating in her gowns of red shades. Her hair was oddly radiant in the nasty artificial light of the room. So alien a presence. And yet, he knew her.

"You, Captain Thomas," she smiled at him. "You are the man of my dreams."

Halloran frowned slightly, concerned about the translation he was hearing. "Umm."

The Premier patted her on the elbow. "My consort has visions. You…" he looked with feeling to Axxa, "…and you were in them in recent ones."

"You." Halloran felt mists clearing from a corner of his memory. "I saw you. In my dreams." He found himself smiling inexplicably.

"You," the Premier looked incredulous. "You, a human, have Sight?"

She ignored her husband and stepped forward to lay a hand on his arm. "I am truly sorry for your pain, Captain Thomas. Your family."

He smiled faintly. *She'd seen it.* "Thank you, ma'am." He felt slightly ashamed.

"Call me Sar'yana." She backed up and turned a sharp eye on her husband. "This human has earned much, my Lord. Honor and respect."

"A dishonorable race." The Premier was studying Halloran closely. "But you showed honor."

Halloran breathed in deliberately, feeling the tenseness. *Focus.* "I would contest your assessment of my people, Premier." He straightened to his full height and the room went up a few degrees as Prax shifted. Halloran knew some guns were pointed at him. But he was *so* close. If he just had a long knife…

Axxa intervened. "Father, how come you to this remote human facility with only one ship?" Halloran heard Axxa's tone and use of the familiar title and his brain translated for his slow-witted body. *This is Axxa's father, and he's here relatively unguarded; pay attention you idiot.*

The Premier held Halloran's eye for a moment longer before turning them slowly to his son. He straightened, shooting a glance back at Halloran. Clearly something was holding his tongue. Halloran bowed on a sudden instinct. "Allow me to return to my people while you conduct your discussions and continue greeting Axxa."

The Premier's chin dipped. "Honorable response, Captain." But the eyes were still hard. Halloran read the command behind them. *Dismissed.*

Halloran risked offense and spun on his heel, stalking back up the room to where Ryax was standing. As he made to pass, the big Prax reached out a hand and gripped his own forearm, halting his progress. Their faces were close.

"It is good for you that you have returned Axxa to his people, human." He glowered.

Halloran's eyebrows went up slowly. He flexed his forearm and pulled it away with brute strength from the alien. *Ouch.* His lips curled up slightly, letting the attempt at intimidation wash over him. "Not exactly how we thank each other where I come from."

At the door he paused between the two guards and glanced back. Axxa was among his family, hugging and clapping arms in an emotional display Halloran felt he might be the first human to witness. With his hand on the latch, he realized that something big had happened here today…Halloran felt the weight of the galaxy upon his shoulders. But, the burden felt strangely light. He caught Sar'yana looking over and saw the understanding in her eyes as she nodded to him.

Some sacrifices may have been worth it.

Chapter 34

Prax Homeworld

Talxen stood with his father and surveyed the closing day of the Rite, the ceremonial robes of the Premiership weighing heavily on his shoulders. He fidgeted a bit with the thick garvite chain that secured the cloak around his neck.

His father was concluding his address to those assembled. "To the future glory of the Conquest we will march. With my son leading us, the glory is assured!"

The world representatives' reception was cool—the applause didn't quite thunder and lasted only long enough to pass muster on the loyalty scale. But Talxen didn't care. He'd have the clans under control within months; his own clan was one of the most wealthy and powerful, as his father had proven through the recent days. Many key supporters of Krex had been eliminated along with their clan representatives. Even now, Prax warships loyal to his father were fanning out toward those colonies to 'pacify' them. The rest would fall in line or die.

Talxen's only wish was that Krex himself and his consort would be found and destroyed quickly. He shot a sidewise stare at his father, feeling a tinge of frustration and…disappointment…in the older Prax's failure to destroy the one family that most needed to be dealt with.

There had been no word from Calxen at Tavar as of yet, after the initial reports back via drone courier that the battle had been joined with a relatively small flotilla of human ships there. He hoped for the best but planned to deny everything and place blame on his First Advisor should the attack fail. If there was one thing that would bind the Empire's resolve tighter it would be a decisive human victory in the war.

The war. He smelled the scent of the thousand attendees and inhaled it deeply. To be among his own people instead of the filthy humans and their stinking planet…he reveled in it. No, he did not want to return to Earth. That system would burn under his concentrated assault next. Mars would be obliterated once the new weapons were deployed in mere days. His last report from scientist Elexxan was that the Prax version of the missile was almost ready for loading onto his latest warship. And others in the Sol flotilla, reborn without that old, insolent Prax Admiral. He rubbed his hands to together in satisfaction.

"And I present to you, our Premier!" Terxan was stepped aside for Talxen to come to the center. Now the applause did seem thunderous as he lifted his hands to receive the adulation he so richly deserved.

**Outside The Perimeter
Rat City, Earth**

The water was beautiful. To Terry Singletary, anything outside that horrid city would be forever beautiful to him. As he removed his sandals and stepped into the cool sea lapping against the shoreline, Singletary closed his eyes and imagined himself sitting on the wood dock of his grandparent's cabin, splashing young feet in the water and enjoying the summer sun on his back...

"Okay, Terry, enough of a break. Granno wants to keep moving and I agree with him. Only another hour or so before the sun comes up and exposes us. We need to find cover."

Singletary reluctantly opened his eyes and peered at Skip Chandler, barely visible against the gloom of the night. "Was thinking about my kid days on Lake Michigan. When I first learned to love the water."

"Granno says the sea is full of creatures that will suck the life out of you. Nasty things." He could hear the chuckle in the Commander's voice.

With a sigh, Singletary trudged up onto a rock shelf and sat to put his sandals back on. His feet throbbed with the exertion of the previous two nights. After making their way in the pitch black tunnel from within the city—thankfully without discovery by the Prax guards—they had trudged up the coast for endless kilometers, hiding during the daylight in the thick reeds that choked the shoreline.

Skip stood over him as the others passed behind them, the group making little noise and seeming to be ghosts on the dark landscape. "Granno says another twenty klicks and we'll be in the area of the target."

"So tomorrow night."

"Sounds like it."

"I wish we could just keep walking. Maybe if we go far enough we can find a place untouched by the war."

"Wishful thinking." Skip laid a hand on Singletary's shoulder. "You holding it together?"

Singletary could hear the concern in Skip's voice. He shrugged and said, "Seems like we got the short end of the stick, that's all. Halloran's out shooting around the galaxy while we slink around our own world with sand in places it don't belong."

Skip moved close, glancing around. "Or," he whispered, "Skipper's long dead with everyone else and the bunch of us is all that's left to organize a proper resistance. You ready to give up, buddy?"

Singletary stared at Chandler for what felt like a very long time.

"Exactly. Let's get moving. God willing, there'll be time to play in the water later."

Singletary followed the Commander up the beach to a reedsy hill where the rest were squatted. Men looked up, pale faces shining dimly in the dark night.

"Have a nice swim, sir?" joked Missile Tech Arrie Hester.

"Not long enough, Arrie."

"Roger that, sir."

As the men came to their feet, Granno passed by Chandler and Singletary and whispered, "No talk. We must go now."

"Roger that," muttered Chandler to the thin man's retreating back.

Vice-Captain Chen was there. "Commander, while I am glad to be rid of that city, I find myself with the desire to make my way to my own country."

Chandler said, "China, sir? I doubt it's even still there."

"I would supremely doubt that, Commander."

Chen had been helpful and positive the whole ordeal; there was nothing that any of them could say bad about the lanky Asian. Singletary spoke up, "If he wants to go we can't stop him, right? He's Chinese Navy, not US."

Skip looked dubious. "Sir, I would advise against it. You don't know what the world is like now. Plus, there are bound to be Prax patrols everywhere. And China's a long way off." He tilted his head. "Plus, if I don't say so, you've been a great help here."

Chen nodded. "Thank you for that honor, Commander. I would not separate without your approval. I only ask that you consider releasing me."

Chief Brown was there. "Sirs, Granno's gettin' pretty antsy at us just standin' here out on the beach."

Skip waved a hand in the gloom. "After you, Chief." Singletary could sense the dawn coming; Skip's hand was that much more visible than when they had started talking.

As Chen passed them Skip said, "I'll give it some thought, Captain Chen."

"Thank you, Commander."

Singletary followed the group of sailors dressed in rags and felt the sand weaving its way around the tin sandals and into the crevices of his feet. The salt water had stung the cuts, but felt wonderful. Now the grit was filling them up again.

Two rebels walked behind him, watching and waiting for the inevitable alien attack or ambush. Singletary had a hard time imagining what an entire life could be like spent under occupation. He didn't want to.

Granno led them to an abandoned complex of buildings that he seemed to know about. They took their time scouting around the half-caved-in structures before selecting a mode of entry. A door that had been blown off its hinges. There was room in a long, dusty hall for everyone to find a spot and little light entered save from the doorway, which Chandler assigned Arrie Heister to watch along with a rebel Granno had pointed to. Heister got one of the guns from another of the natives—something Singletary had noticed was unusual.

Chandler motioned to him and together they cornered Granno. "How far to this installation?" asked Chandler pointedly.

Granno made a vague motion with his hands. "I have not been here in many time."

"Years? Months?" Singletary was frustrated.

"Yes, yes. Many."

"Guess, then," offered Chandler.

Granno considered. "Very close, I think."

Chandler looked at Singletary. "There may be patrols."

"Do we post someone outside?"

Chandler thought, then shook his head. "Those drones we saw flying around in the city—I don't want to risk getting caught in the open."

"I'm sure they have infrared. Won't matter if it's day or night should they come looking."

"Well, they haven't so far," Chandler noted. "Or they're watching us to see what we do."

Singletary smacked the fire-streaked wall with a fist. "If this is all a game, I think I'll go nuts."

Granno had been following the interchange. Now he raised his hand. "No, no, Prax do not watch; if they did, we be dead already."

"Well, there you go, Terry."

"Reassuring." Singletary deflated, feeling exhausted. "Permission to get some shuteye, sir?"

"Two hours, then spell me."

"Aye, sir."

When Singletary had gone down the hall, stepping over the legs of sprawled men and women, Granno leaned over. He motioned with his head in the Singletary's direction. "Your man, he is weak."

Chandler stared at him. "Thank you for your opinion."

Granno slid down to a seating position. "All I say is the truth."

Chandler ignored him and went to look for a spot of his own, knowing that the rebel leader had indeed put his finger on something troubling. He'd have to watch Terry.

"Thoughts?" Chandler and Chief Brown were prostrate, mostly buried atop a rise in the dunes. They had painstakingly dug themselves up the last fifty feet to the crest, making every effort to stay completely out of sight should an errant drone burst overhead. Literally every crevice of Chandler's body was sand-packed. But they had—by all indications—made the journey undetected. Now they peeked over the lip at the distant structure.

"Sir," Brown whispered. "I don't see no activity down there." The Chief had the best eyes of the Americans, and Chandler wouldn't allow a local with him to assess a tactical situation. "Think it's abandoned?"

"Unlikely, Chief." Chandler spit some sand from his mouth in disgust—quietly. He thought of the rest of the sorry excuse for an assault team back in the dunes. They had traveled only a few kilometers before seeing the first signs of alien presence. Then Granno had a revived memory, and they'd taken to hiding despite the dark night. "See the lights inside?"

"Sure, Commander. But they look like nothing. Like a night light at home. You know."

"Never had one of those. Let's watch a bit more."

But an hour or so passed without any movement whatsoever. The Prax facility was comprised of three low buildings, two with openings—windows—that emitted light as though something was within. The third structure was dome-shaped with no apparent openings. "A radar installation?" offered Brown suddenly.

Chandler saw the parallels to a twenty-first century station. "Could be. Automated?"

"That Granno fella hasn't been in a long time. Maybe they converted it and left?"

"Seems too easy."

"You're the officer, sir."

Chandler frowned. They had to be at least thirty kilometers from the edge of the city with its protective shielding. They had seen almost no enemy activity since exiting the tunnel out. Perhaps the Prax had gotten lazy, automated some systems in the decades since the invasion?

We've come this far. The only option is to go in and check it. "Alright, Chief, we go back and get some guns and see what there is to see."

Brown's sigh was audible. "No more hiding, sir. Let's do it."

Prax Sol Center - Rat City

As soon as the comm signaled an incoming connection First Advisor Vellerx jumped at the tablet, pulling to him across the table. "Yes?" His practiced calm veneer made the words sound casual.

"Advisor, the ships have returned," reported a somewhat breathless tech on the other end.

"Get Horax on as soon as you are able."

"Lord Calxen is in command now, Advisor."

So Horax was dead. With the Flotilla commander out of the way, Vellerx had moved that much closer to the new Premier's inner circle. The Xu son was an annoyance—a dangerous one at that—but only Conquest veterans made the jump to Prime status. With Axxa and Horax dead, and Admiral Xylan locked up beneath his feet, Vellerx as First Advisor was the obvious choice for Prime. He'd served the clan well, and spent many cycles here on this disgusting planet. *Perhaps as Prime I could take pleasure in squeezing the remaining life from these pathetic humans.*

"Advisor? Are you connected still?"

"What? Yes, put the Xu on when you can."

A moment later the line beeped. "Sol Center, Sol Center."

Vellerx felt a flash of annoyance. "Yes, you son-of-a-Mugpa, yes!" He knew it wasn't Calxen on the connection; even he wouldn't be that brash to a Xu.

"This is the Captain of the Braxxar."

"Where is Lord Calxen?"

"He, er, has retired to his cabin."

"Then report, Captain."

"Lord, we have returned four ships to the Sol flotilla."

"What!" Vellerx suddenly felt the weight of possible shame lay across his shoulders. "Explain!"

"Advisor. The human defenses of the Struve System were vigorous. Commander Horax and his ship were destroyed, and additional human reinforcements arrived to box us in. In all truth, Advisor, I was fortunate by the seven suns to be able to withdraw with three other vessels. All sustained significant damage, and two ship's jumpdrives failed after the first jump, delaying our return as we defended them during their efforts."

"And the humans?"

"They did not pursue, Advisor. This is my report."

Vellerx didn't speak for some time.

"Advisor? I would like to request that I attend to my ship."

"Sol Center out." Vellerx cut the channel and rose, feeling many time heavier with the responsibility. His would be the task to inform the Premier of the Sol fleet's failure.

Horax should have taken more ships. If it wasn't for the need to keep Xylan's loyal Captains and their ships boxed in near Earth, he could have. The Admiral had some staunch supporters and the stalemate was going to wear thin. Vellerx knew that the traitorous Captains knew of Xylan's imprisonment and would refuse to leave him in the hands of the Terxan clan. Could he negotiate something with them—offer to release the Admiral? Then trap them during the transfer?

The comm signaled again, and he leaned over the tap it. "First Advisor."

"Advisor, science officer Elexxan reports that he is transferring weaponry to the fleet."

"Now?"

"Yes, Advisor."

Vellerx frowned. He knew that Elexxan and Talxen were close confederates. Until recently, he had never given serious consideration to the scientist as a potential rival. *But…* "What ship?"

"The log reports it as a new arrival in the system."

"What? Why wasn't I informed?"

There was hesitation on the line. "Advisor, I do not know. This is the first we are seeing this ship here in the command center. Most unusual." Someone said something in the background that Vellerx couldn't make out. "It couldn't just appear on the scan. Check those calibrations," ordered the Prax to the other person. "Advisor, it seems…it seems there is a technical difficulty with the sensors. I will investigate. But the log shows that Elexxan and members of his team have requisitioned several large transport shuttles."

Vellerx slammed down the tablet and stormed out to pay a caustic visit to the command level. By the seven suns, he would not be overshadowed by a…scientist.

Part Six - Fulcrum

Chapter 35

Perses System - Telos Station

"**Sir,** I don't think we're going to get out of here without a fight. But the ship needs us. Bad."

Halloran stopped his pacing near Reyes and whispered fiercely. "Don't you think I *know* that, Reyes? Try being *useful* with your comments instead."

The hurt look that jumped into the back recesses of the Chief's eyes shamed Halloran, but he ignored it and paced off, feeling the guilt within for what he'd said. The anger and helpless pain he felt allowed no room for sympathy.

After the initial possibilities that the meeting with the alien leader had seemed to create, things took a turn for the worse when the humans had been summarily hemmed into a tight space and relieved of their weapons forcefully. At first, Halloran thought it might just be a security measure but when the group was herded into this room—cell, it seemed—his anger had returned in full force. And Axxa…he had *not* returned.

They were trapped.

And Reyes was right, the ship needed them. Needed *him*. With a skeleton crew and several wounded men—some badly—the Serapis was in trouble. And if Parker hadn't fixed life support, the jerry-rigged system might have already collapsed.

He caught Kendra's eye. She was angry with him, he could tell. *You got us into this,* he seemed to read on her face. But maybe he was imagining it.

Wilson and Flagler sat against the bulkhead, heads down and seemingly asleep. Djembe conferred in low tones with Bruce Brown, and Halloran caught a surreptitious glance from Brown. *They think I've lost control. Well, I have.*

Why had he thought coming here was a good idea? They should have limped off and found a safe place to patch up the ship and tend to the wounded. But even as he thought that, the cold anger returned and washed over him like a bucket of cold water splashed in his face. *It's my job—my mission—to keep going into the unknown and subdue it.* He needed to deal this uncertain future a blow from his past. Their past. If that meant dropping in unannounced on the ruler of the Prax Empire then so be it. An image of the woman from his dreams leaped into his mind unbidden. *She's been following me all along.* What was it called…the Sight, his translator had termed it? Some kind of connection that he found completely incomprehensible. But the general gist was that beings could be interconnected somehow. He snorted quietly at his own ridiculousness.

Halloran believed in God, always had. He saw the Earth, the sea as obviously too delicate and balanced a thing to be the product of random chance—there had to be a creator. In recent months, though, he'd questioned his own faith. The days following Cindy and the baby's death had been hard, even with Tom Junior and Laura there at the house to keep him company. He'd tried going back to the church they'd attended in town in past years, but the sea of unfamiliar faces punctuated by several well-meaning but too-insistent counselors had blunted his interest. Fact was, he'd fashioned a life around a series of steel tubes filled with crew who loved their roles—despite all the complaining that was the ritual. Cindy and the kid's life ashore had been comfortable but disconnected from his intense profession.

The thought struck him that there was a bond—an interconnection—between the crew. One generally didn't look at it from a metaphysical angle but a well-trained and comfortable crew worked as a true unit, anticipating the others' words and movements smoothly. In fact, that was the goal all the leadership strove for. In battle and stress situations, it was that intuition and reaction that would save the ship and, ultimately, the crew within her.

"Hmm." Perhaps, if he opened his mind a bit, this concept of interconnectivity would make more sense to him. He exhaled and found himself feeling more relaxed. He felt some peace with what he had to do.

Reyes was standing there. "You better, sir?"

Halloran took the man's hand. "I'm sorry, Chief."

Reyes slow-grinned up at him. "It'll take more than one chewing-out to break us up, sir."

The door opened and a Prax guard stood there. He looked around the expectant faces in the room. "You, come."

The guards herded the humans into a large lift and up they went. Halloran leaned casually against the wall and crossed his arms, thinking. Kendra paced back and forth. Reyes stared from one of the two guards to the other. Bruce Brown was down on his haunches. Karen Flagler, Djembe and Gerry Wilson stood stiffly, clearly more afraid in the presence of the armored aliens. Halloran glanced over his group, taking them in. He found himself missing Skip Chandler. His XO would be in firm control of the tactical situation by now. In fact, Halloran was certain that many of his decisions in the past months would have been far better executed by the taciturn Kansan.

But Chandler was stranded on Earth and that had to remain Halloran's priority. As much as he despised the Prax for what they did to his best friend and crew on Earth, he needed to keep threading through the fabric of this war, making his way to Earth to rescue his people.

His eyes rested on the Prax guards, whom Kendra was now standing in front of, staring. They were the enemy of humanity, but Halloran also had the stirrings of a new interest in them.

The Premier—he had seemed…a lot like Axxa, if Halloran had to be honest. More formal, older but still with the careful appraising attitude that radiated from the younger Prax. Axxa hadn't become part of Halloran's crew despite shared action. He had made a contribution, to be sure, but the divide between human and Prax seemed as wide as ever. Halloran looked at Kendra. *Especially with her.* She was a product of this century and all its violence. Hatred.

As if hearing him, Kendra paused in her pacing close to Halloran and put a hand on the wall next to him, coming close. "Aren't you worried about where they're taking us?" She asked with an edge of frustration.

He regarded her impassively. "Of course."

"So?"

His brow twitched. "I came here to find answers, Kendra. I intend to."

"The archive, yes. I remember. But we're *prisoners.*" She tilted her head and her black hair spilled onto a shoulder as she emphasized her words. Halloran blinked, some of his impassiveness lost in her dark eyes and closeness.

He held up a hand with a lowered chin to ward her off. "We aren't done here yet. Let it play out."

She kept her proximity. "You are a fish out of water, aren't you."

"Very much so. I've been running off instinct for a while now."

She exhaled and lifted her eyes to his with a half-smile. "So what are your instincts telling you now?"

He took an extra few seconds to answer. "That we're close to a breakthrough."

Her eyebrows rose. "Is that instinct or wishful thinking, Captain?"

He leaned in close to her and whispered flatly. "The Captain is always right."

She straightened and pushed off the wall with a frown. "With the Prax nothing can be trusted. Nothing."

The lift finally slowed its rise and stopped. Brown was up and the others alert as the door slid open and the Prax stepped out. The aliens motioned for them to follow.

This new level was low-ceilinged and the corrosion less apparent. Walls were painted some kind of tan color and the floor had a pattern to it. On a whim Halloran bent and touched the pattern. "Huh."

Reyes stamped. "If I didn't know any better I'd say this was carpet, sir."

"I think you're right, Chief."

Brown was looking around. "This place is weird, sir."

The guards were pushing them to move so they did. The hall ran around the station—circling the central hub Halloran had seen from below, if he had to guess. Doors passed on both sides, all closed. No labels presented themselves.

"I feel like we're in an office building back home, sir," offered Yeoman Flagler as she fidgeted.

Halloran nodded but said nothing.

After it seemed they would circumnavigate the station given how far they had walked, the leading guards paused at a large double door and one opened it cautiously. Satisfied, he stepped in and his partner waved Halloran to follow.

The room that lay in front of them was…amazing.

The ceiling was at least thirty feet high, and at the far end of the roughly hundred-foot on-a-side space was an immense glass wall displaying a mind-blowing view of the planet below. Halloran heard someone's sharp intake of breath behind him as the group followed him in

It was impressive.

He felt drawn into the place, tearing his eyes from the view to take in the rest of the surroundings. It was a lounge, with cushioned couches scattered in groups around it. He saw a lone guard standing just inside to entrance.

"Captain, look." Reyes was pointing.

At the one side of the room was a bar. It looked almost real—like a twenty-first century one. It was long, perhaps thirty feet. Behind that bar was a man—a human. He was in the act of pouring a bottle but had stopped mid-motion to stare open-mouthed at them.

The Prax who had come in first took the inside post in relief of the prior guard. Then the others stomped out and closed the door loudly. Halloran matched stares with the guard, who kept a stony face beneath his visor.

Reyes was approaching the bar. "Who are *you*?" he asked the man.

The man had recovered and was finishing his drink. He leaned forward on the bar with wide eyes. "I am Telos. And you…you are a ghost, I assume? An apparition?"

The Cuban snorted. "Hardly." He turned to Halloran who was now walking over with the rest. "Sir, permission to pour myself a stiff one."

Halloran shrugged. "When in Rome, Chief."

The man's face had gone pale. Halloran held out a hand. "Captain—."

"—Thomas Halloran." The man finished in a high-pitched voice. "My God." He looked genuinely scared. He looked at Halloran's hand as if it were about to bite him.

Reyes had selected a bottle and was looking at the label. He nodded at Halloran while glancing at the man. "Not good manners, old man."

With reluctance changing to resignation he took Halloran's hand and grasped it. His strong grip surprised Halloran. "Telos, proprietor of this archive."

Halloran held his grip. "You know me."

"No—I mean, not really. I…I know *of* you." He shook his head defensively.

"Why?" Halloran released the man and placed his hands on the bar.

"Sir?" Bruce Brown was hefting a bottle as a question. Halloran nodded, quickly turning back to the man Telos.

"You drink, Captain?" The man's eyes shifted from one corner to the other nervously.

"Bourbon and water, if you have it." Halloran suddenly wanted the drink. He waited until Telos had filled the glass and passed it to him. "Now tell me."

Telos looked at the others. Kendra in particular. He addressed her. "You're not with them."

She leaned on the bar next to Halloran. "I most certainly am. And I know of *you*. My father—."

"—Is Admiral Kendall of Coloran," Telos finished.

Reyes snorted again from his seat nearby. "Do you always do that?"

"How do you know that?" Kendra demanded.

Telos spread his hands. "Captain, your reputation precedes you. Struve Six? The Goliath? As well, I've known your father since we were young together in the service. Many years ago. Did you know, I actually transited on the Goliath once during the eridani campaign? I was a fresh recruit at the time." He looked over at Djembe who stood beyond Reyes. "You, sir, served as well in those days unless I miss my guess."

Djembe watched him with narrowed eyes but said nothing.

Halloran lifted his drink with one hand while he lightly pounded on the bar with the other. "You haven't answered my question, Telos."

The old man turned back to him. "No, I have not. A word alone, Captain?"

Halloran set his drink down without having tried it. "Now would be good."

Telos sat him down in front of the massive wall of glass. As Telos lowered himself into an adjoining soft chair he leaned forward, elbows on knees. Halloran had noticed his dress. "You're wearing blue jeans," he observed as he watched the old man settle in.

"The fact you even know what they are astounds me, Captain."

"Why?"

The man waved a hand at the planet below. "Beautiful, isn't it? Perses system was once a thriving hub of activity during the first expansion. After the war with the Prax broke out, the high command decided that this system was too far toward the enemy-controlled systems and pulled everyone back. Once the battle of Struve System was over, the Prax scare drove the rest of the colonists toward Coloran." He patted his knee. "That's when I brought some other wounded veterans over to claim this station and the archive, which the Command in its infinite wisdom had decreed wasn't 'necessary material' worth relocating. Been here ever since." He puffed and watched Halloran with a slight grin.

"So the archive is real? It's here?"

"Oh, yes. This station is the single largest repository of human artifacts outside of Earth itself, which I hear has suffered greatly in the last century of occupation. That occurred several years before I took command of Telos."

Halloran wiped some dust off his knee. "So about me…"

"Admiral Kendall requested information on a Captain Thomas Halloran, United States Navy, circa

2000 to 2050. Any military documentation or imagery. News stories, etc."

Halloran was leaning forward. "And you found something in the archive?"

Telos didn't look at him but kept his face toward the space vista. "499."

"What's that?"

"One more year—less than a year—and we arrive at a new century."

Halloran leaned forward. "You're saying this is the year 499?"

"Precisely. But they changed the dating system. For you and your people, it would be 2499. At least I think so." Telos looked at him with sadness on his face. "The last turn of the century was one of celebration across the light years from Earth to Coloran. Humanity was at peace, and the stars were being explored. I was fourteen. Five years later the Prax attacked Pelenam Station and killed all forty thousand inhabitants. *This* turn of the century, the war rages on."

Halloran perked up. "Wait…that means you're over a hundred."

The old man smiled lightly. "Of course."

Halloran did more math in his head. "470 years. We've jumped 470 years."

Telos nodded slowly. "Your photograph and military record. Nothing detailed since most of that goes too far back. Perhaps in a bunker buried somewhere in what's left of the old United States." He looked off wistfully.

"That all you found on me?"

"I found the news stories in the communications records."

"Of what?" Halloran felt a dread knotting in his gut.

"Oh, your promotion to Captain. Then, in 2029…"

"My family. The accident."

Telos nodded. "May 13th, 2029. Tacoma, Washington."

Halloran flinched. "You do you remember that?"

"It's what I do." Telos shrugged, staring at Halloran. "So it really *is* you. I was still wondering…"

"Wondering what?" Halloran wished he had brought the bourbon over with him.

"Never mind." Telos leaned forward. "You disappeared on August 21st, 2029, along with your entire warship and crew from Pearl Harbor, state of Hawaii. On board your ship were several foreign diplomats."

Halloran sat back with an exhalation. "That's right. We ended up here. The Prax." His voice hardened.

Telos whistled. "Unbelievable. They possess time travel technology."

"They do. At least one-way."

"Your ship was armed with advanced twenty-first century weapons of incredible destruction. These were, logically, the target of their project? The Prax are nothing if not ingenious in destructive ways."

Halloran nodded. "I need to get back. To stop them."

"You do. But I don't see how. Time travel is beyond my feeble mind."

Halloran frowned. "What?"

Telos looked confused for a moment. "Umm. You wish to return to stop the war, yes?"

"What war? I want to get back to Earth, save the crew I left behind and stop the Prax from using the weapons against the humans."

"Oh." Telos' eyes were lowered for a long minute while Halloran stewed and gazed out the at the magnificent view of the planet. Now the nearest Prax warship was sliding into view as the station rotated.

"Captain."

He awoke from his reverie. "Yes."

"I need to tell you something. Perhaps it will be useful in some way, perhaps not, but you are clearly a man who leads and understands the need for those in command to possess all the facts."

Halloran leaned toward him. "Go ahead."

Telos cleared his throat. "When I was researching your name and saw the name of your last command—the USS Bonhomme Richard—something struck a memory in me. When I found the record of your disappearance, it all came together."

"What?" Halloran was growing impatient.

"This…this is difficult to tell." Telos swallowed, then lifted his eyes to meet Halloran's. "But the disappearance of your ship caused the Great War which destroyed much of Earth in 2030."

Chapter 36

Outside The Perimeter
Rat City, Earth

Terry Singletary stared at the two dismembered bodies that lay in the sand. The horror of seeing people die in front of him lay around his shoulders like a heavy, wet blanket.

The group had gone out of the way to crawl cautiously and take the safest path upon entry to the compound. When it had become clear that the place was unmanned and no proximity alarms—that they could hear—had sounded, their painstakingly slow pace had relaxed ever so slightly. And the result were two more dead humans.

Granno's people had inadvertently discovered a network of cutting lasers patterning the ground just inside of a low concrete-style wall about twenty meters from the structure. After their choked screams faded, Brown had swore and leapt to the wall top, scanning the area before jumping as far he could. Thankfully, his range had exceeded the killing beam's coverage area. The group now waited by the wall as Chandler and Brown nosed around in the structure.

It was pitch-dark now, the middle of a warm and moist night. The sounds of the sea nearby did nothing to calm Singletary's misgivings, however. He was concerned for the people, fearful that the Prax had been alarmed and might be bearing down on them even as they stood helplessly in the dunes. Singletary was ashamed of his fear. As he heard the humans around him stir quietly, he forced himself to remember that the people of Earth in this time were hardened, and if they felt fear they were either too tough or too tired to show it. Their sun-browned skin and hooded eyes under mops of stringy hair, combined with the general emaciation of the population that tended to blend the genders together, made them as a group very hard to read. Humans were a demoralized mob, yes, but when a few—like these—began to move with new purpose, the mob took on a determined sense that lifted the funk upon them all. Rebels.

The light in one of the structures blinked several times through a window. Moments later a set of hidden exterior lights flared into brilliance, caused many in the group at the wall to shield their eyes, including Singletary.

Vice-Captain Chen stood next to him. "I believe they have found something."

A voice boomed from the light. Chandler's. "Okay, Terry, the defensive grid is off!"

Chen looked at Singletary in the gloom. "Commander?"

Singletary hesitated. He imagined the sight of the mutilated humans in the daylight. He imagined himself among them and cowered at the thought of it. *I'm not ready to die. Not here.* He had wanted so to try to return home, even if it was—.

Chen had grasped his shoulder. "It's all right, Commander." The Chinese climbed onto the wall and shouted at the building. "Coming now, Commander!" Without further deliberation he jumped lightly into the area of sand where the bodies lay. Singletary's breath shot of his lungs in concern.

Chen began walking toward the building. Granno got to the top of the wall and began calling softly to his people.

Chandler hollered again. "Terry! Get everyone moving our way!"

They stepped gingerly over the killing area and jogged the last distance to the low-slung building. Chandler was waiting and motioned to them to follow. They passed between two textured walls that were rough against Singletary's hand as he ran it along the surface out of curiosity.

Chief Brown was framed in a doorway, arms crossed and clearly waiting for them. "Sir, all the indicators are dark now."

Chandler nodded, his face pale in the ghostly light emanating from the room. "Good. It's hard to figure anything out in their language, and the colors seem all wrong from what we're used to. But if we don't see a sentry landing in the next few minutes, I think we've done something right." He looked up between the two buildings to where the sky was dark. "Best be ready for anything."

Chen fingered the trashed lock mechanism. "Did you?"

Brown shrugged. "Let's just say I took out some aggression on the door latch."

"I might have helped," observed Chandler. "Shall we?"

Chen ventured into the lit space as Brown stepped back inside. Granno followed. Singletary was about to do the same when Chandler barred his way and said softly, "Terry, why'd you let Chen go first? That was *your* order."

Singletary just stared at him, face suddenly reddening with heat.

"Keep it together, Terry. I need you." And then Chandler removed his arm and stepped into the room.

Granno was pointing at a set of characters on the wall. "This is language of Prax."

Brown shrugged at the smaller man. "Figured."

"It says guard station. I've seen it many times in the city."

Brown turned away to study a bank of electronics. "Figured that, too."

"All right, Chief." Chandler stepped up. "What are we looking at?"

Brown waved a hand over a row of black-levered controls. "Some of this looks very old. Even for this future-stuff," he made a face at Chandler. "My guess is that some of this is obsolete tech and this," he moved his hand over another rack of equipment, "is the newer-installed stuff."

"We took a guess and threw these switches." Chandler showed them a segment of the newer instrumentation that was marked with a yellow square around it. "Seemed like a perimeter control bank."

"It worked," offered Brown.

Arrie Hester called from the doorway. "Sirs, there is a landing pad in the center of this complex. Clearly marked. Lamb has got the locals out that way, resting against the wall of this structure."

Chandler looked over. "No signs of life, right?"

"None, sir. Witmer and Morales are scouting the edges now…hopefully no more lasers." Hester made to duck out but Chandler's call stopped him.

"Sir?"

"Have them gather up the remains and hide them. Make it look as normal as possible before dawn."

Hester nodded gravely. "Ain't no normal around here, sir."

When the Missile Technician had gone, Chen got their attention. "This is a communications tablet of some sort." He held up the device in his hand.

Chandler remembered seeing something like it when they had been making their group escape from the enemy headquarters monstrosity. He took the tablet and examined the edges. "No buttons."

Brown reached out. "May I, sir?"

Chandler handed it over.

"Like this, sir, if I had to bet." Brown grasped the edges of the tablet naturally as if he was about to read from it. Immediately, the ceiling was bathed in the light from the device's screen.

Singletary burst out, "Don't set off any alarms!"

Chandler took it back from Brown with a raised eyebrow at Singletary. He tapped the screen. "Looks like it's unlocked at least. Maybe they don't do that sort of thing now. On the other hand, I can't read a thing."

Chen said, "Perhaps Commander Singletary is right; we should avoid inadvertently alerting them to our presence."

Chandler nodded and put the tablet on a shelf. "So, we are holed up in an outpost. Didn't we come for a weapons cache?"

Granno nodded enthusiastically.

"Well, let's find it."

Fifteen minutes later they found it.

The heaviest door in the toughest-looking of the four structures was judged to be the likeliest location. And, the magic tablet, when held up against the lock, turned the mechanism. The door swung open lightly, and the group stepped inside. Brown found a light switch.

"Wow," exhaled Hester.

Row upon row of Prax pulse rifles lined one wall. Racks of smaller weapons and equipment were arrayed along the opposite side. Chandler stepped to a rifle and pulled it from its cradle with a popping sound. He examined it.

"Dusty." He blew and the stuff coating the weapon exploded into a small cloud. "Can't keep the sand and earth out even if you wanted to."

"This equipment has been here for a long time," observed Brown as he handled a weapon himself.

"Will it still function?" Asked Singletary. "These are energy weapons."

"You're the expert, Weps," Chandler pointed out. You've got an hour to figure all this out and report before we have to deal with the coming dawn."

"They aren't Mark 48 torpedoes but I'll see what I can do."

Brown set the weapon back and stared at the officers grimly. "Sirs, something's got to give. We need a break."

Chandler tossed him his rifle. "We might have just gotten it, Chief."

Prax Sol Center - Detention Area

Xylan paced his cell relentlessly, ignoring the hard cot offered to the prisoner and opting instead to stay on his feet. Dozens and dozens of cycles spent pacing ship bridges had steeled him to the activity, and in fact the movement put him in a frame of mind to think best, to analyze.

He found himself reliving the death of Hrodax in the Prime's office again and again. The senselessness of it. The glory of the Empire seemed to be crumbling in front of the old officer. The glory of the Conquest.

Or was it? Talxen and his father's clan were nothing if not warlike. There was no doubt that their leadership of the Empire would portend a renewal of the war against the humans. A war that had dragged on longer than any other in Xylan's memory. The tenacious aliens were resourceful and determined; witness their fervor to reclaim the very planet he was currently interned on. The other species that the Prax had vanquished had eventually given up the fight and capitulated…or been extinguished.

That was the difference under Krex's Premiership. Krex was a hard Prax, but loyal and true to those he served the Conquest with and…to those he vanquished. Honor lived with Krex. Xylan reminded himself of all that he owed to Krex. All that his family owed to both Krex and his consort Sar'yana for their support of his career in the military.

Xylan stopped by the cell door and regarded it. No, he would not join the clan of Terxan and its head the megalomaniac Talxen. *My only Premier is Krex,* he announced to himself as though to cement his loyalties.

He resumed pacing.

The ships—how many had survived the purge? What was their disposition now? Had the humans seen the disarray around Earth? So many questions.

He counted off the Commanders in his mind, ticking each one and considering if they had been able to use the warning given in time to stop the mutiny. He came up with a best-case of eleven. His most loyal officer was Commander Loxanna of the dreadnought Dexellan; the two had served together for a generation and Loxanna was incredibly cunning. There had been times when Xylan himself had wondered about the Commander's loyalty. But the Prax was true. Then there were a number of junior ship captains who either Xylan or Loxanna had groomed over the cycles. Some were more adept than others. It was anyone's guess which had managed to forestall the predicted takeover attempts from their ranks aboard ship.

Then there were the planetary defenses. Earth's population had long ago been pacified. Had the prior Premier been in power, every last human subjugate would have been either executed or shipped to the mining planets and the planet razed. But Krex had notoriously chosen to spare the human homeworld from annihilation. Those on Prax speculated. Was it natural resources? A slave labor source? Certainly, many millions had already been shipped off to other systems destined for hard service in untold numbers of "project planets" claimed by the Empire. Those that remained had posed little threat. An ongoing program of pacification had blunted any budding attempts on behalf of aggressive humans to organize. The planet had been a training site for Xu recently—including the

Prime's own son, Xylan remembered—and human life was cheap.

This planet, among all others in his memory, had proven the single largest stumbling block in the Conquest. He paused, nodding to the resilience of the humans and granting those who faced him across space their due of honor.

His thoughts returned to the problem of Talxen and his loyal forces. He weighed his options and evaluated possible scenarios, but much was hard to ascertain since he'd been imprisoned very shortly after the revolt. He found himself wondering if Krex and Sar'yana yet lived.

How long had he been in this cell? Other than the occasional use of the waste removal system mounted in the wall, all he'd done is pace. No food, but that mattered little. Xylan was accustomed to hardship; once he'd been trapped in a chunk of destroyed frigate, the only survivor, for long enough that by the time he was rescued he'd lost much of his weight. But he'd stayed alive be keeping his focus on persevering and he would do so again, unless the traitors—the true traitors to the Empire—came to execute him. And if so, then he would face them with honor.

Resolve Of Steel

Chapter 37

Perses System - Telos Station

Telos stood. "Follow me."

Halloran looked over to where Reyes was watching them like a hawk. The Chief knew something was being said of importance to his Captain. "Are we going far?"

Telos followed the direction of his nod. "Not far." The old man hesitated. "Captain, I hesitate to share this information with any of your subordinates before you have had your own time to ponder its significance."

Halloran caught Reyes' gaze and tapped his chest, indicating Telos and holding up five fingers twice. He almost chuckled at the suddenly narrowed look the Cuban shot Telos. With a shake of his head he stepped over to where the door was being held for him. "A good COB is hard to find."

"He is a senior non-commissioned officer, yes?" Telos let Halloran past him.

"He is the senior non-commissioned officer, yes."

Telos led the way in the passage. "In my time in the Fleet, we relied upon such men in battle."

"Then not much has changed." Halloran noticed the Prax guards standing at the lift nearby, watching them with narrowed eyes. "Are you under some sort of house arrest here?"

Telos paused at another entrance, looking at Halloran with furrowed brow. "'House Arrest?' I have not that expression, I think. But if the English terminology connotes what I believe it to, then it would be an accurate assessment."

Halloran smiled tightly. "So, that's a yes."

Telos frowned as he held open the door. "I believe that I said that. Am I conveying my English correctly? I have so little practice."

Halloran shook his head as he followed the stooped man into the room.

In marked contrast to the spaciousness of the lounge across the way, this compartment was low-overhead and packed with equipment and storage containers. Telos threaded his way between two large crates and motioned for Halloran to follow. It was clear that he knew the layout of the maze well as he led them down a series of twists and turns through piles of metal boxes and racks holding bins made from some sort of yellow plastic. Eventually they came out into what appeared to be a central station where a series of work monitors and chairs were arrayed in a circle.

"My hovel, Captain. My inner sanctum. Did I convey that correctly?"

Halloran put his hands on hips and surveyed the messy area. "I get what you're saying, Telos." He saw the cot against the bulkhead. "So you sleep here, too."

Telos sat at a workstation. "Since they came, yes. Frankly, I was surprised that they let us live."

"Us?"

Telos glanced up. "Yes, I have several assistants here as well. They are being held in chambers beyond yours. I see them daily and there appears to be no overt action taken toward any of us…yet."

Halloran came over. "Why are you not with them?"

"The work, Captain. The work. Here, sit." The old man held out a chair next to him.

"What work?" Halloran asked as he dropped down.

"Backing up the archive, of course."

"What?"

Telos stopped to look at him. "I must attempt to save as much of the digital information as I can, in the event that the Prax elect to destroy us." He had taken on the officious air of a lecturer, causing Halloran to wince.

"Tell me what you meant, Telos."

"About the war."

"Yes."

Telos pulled up a screen and pointed to it. Halloran leaned in.

The news stories flashed before them on the monitor. It was a parade of headlines. The word WAR and DESTROYED figured prominently among the titles.

"Wait, stop there," Halloran commanded. Telos stopped and scrolled the display back.

It was a New York Times article. The headline screamed RUSSIA, CHINA READY FOR RETALIATION. The photo beneath the headline was what had caught the Captain's eye, though. It was that photo—the one of him looking down at the photographer from the sail of the Bonhomme Richard. The subtitle read, "Nations unable to reach accord in the disappearance of Navy sub. Accusations escalate."

Telos tapped the photo. "You."

Halloran nodded.

"Amazing. That here you sit."

He exhaled through pursed lips. "I wouldn't use that word."

The archivist tapped the photo again. "The records we have of that period are like this; tension between the old Earth nations. Then the exchange of fire and destruction of military installations. But, within a year—if I remember my dating—one of the nations launched a strike with their nuclear weapons. The dangers of escalation."

"Which one?"

Telos shook his head. "Unknown. The records end abruptly. To the best of my knowledge, the major nations simply ceased to exist in a very short period of time."

Halloran sat back, the enormity of it all washing over him like a freezing river.

Telos said, "I'm sorry, Captain. You can see why I didn't want to discuss this in front of your crew."

Halloran found himself staring at the old man. "And if we go back…can we stop…" He waved at the frozen monitor of headlines. "…This?"

"I'm sorry, I don't know the answer to that. I'm not even clear on how you came to be in this time."

Thoughts came unbidden to Halloran's mind. *The Prax stole my ship from the past and by doing so caused the destruction of much of humanity hundreds of years ago. This same humanity then rebuilt itself and reached into space, thereby encountering the Prax and sparking a war that brought the aliens to Earth. But what if I and my crew hadn't left? Would humanity have discovered space and traveled beyond the solar system?*

Telos was handing him a glass. Halloran hadn't noticed him leave.

"Sorry. You fell into a reverie—is that that correct word in English? I took the liberty of assuring your people that you were safe. Kendra is very insistent, isn't she?"

Halloran took the drink and downed it, wincing and nodding. "Yes, she is."

"Much like her father."

"You know him? Kendall, right?"

Telos sat in his chair. "Kendall and I were young recruits together. I was a year older than him—twenty, and him nineteen—when the Prax first attacked and the Fleet organized. It all happened very fast, mind you. Before that, no one worried about war. We'd had hundreds of years of peaceful expansion."

"There's that word again."

"Expansion? Yes, we called it that, when I was a boy. After the war began, nothing was the same. Kendall and I, we were together at Eridani." A faraway look came over his face. "Only a few of us got out of that alive."

"Ground forces?"

"Yes. The Prax overwhelmed us with their superior numbers. That was before our space fleet had built itself up to reasonable strength to hold their own against those things."

Those things. Halloran understood. "You didn't know."

"Know what?" Telos cocked his head.

Halloran thought of the mother embracing Axxa. "That the Prax had families, too. Sons."

Telos snorted.

"I'm just saying—."

Telos held up a hand. "Son, don't. I might be an old, broken-down soldier but *don't* talk to me about them like they were people too!" The fire in the man's eyes flared.

Halloran sat back and sighed, regarding his empty glass. After a moment he sat it on the monitor station and crossed his arms. "It's all so unreal."

"It's *very* real." Telos tapped a key and the screen with all the horror stories from the twenty-first century went dark.

Halloran pointed at it. "I'm going to want to study this. I have several crew members who will want to dig, too. We may find out about our families."

"There's no going back."

The flat finality of what Telos said slapped Halloran, and he blinked. "Why do you say that? We don't know—."

"You're *here* now. Even if the Prax possess the tech to send you back, they won't. It's not their way." Telos stood up, his small frame looking even frailer than it had when they'd first met. An hour ago?

Halloran leaned forward, elbows on knees as he thought about that. Finally he looked up. "You may be right. I don't know." He got up, stretching. "But I do know that we've got the Prax Premier on this station and need to do something about it."

"What!" Telos was as shocked as a man could be. He staggered a bit, reaching for the top of the monitor to steady himself. He looked like he was having an attack. "What are you saying, Halloran?"

Halloran turned away. "Time to request an audience and work some things out."

Telos followed. "You can't be serious. The Prax Premier? On my station?"

Halloran paused by the nearest bank of equipment, turning back. "Want to meet the ruler of the hated enemy, and his wife and kid? Let's do it."

Chapter 38

Aboard the Valor - Entering Perses System

Heres paced the bridge as Renno checked the scans. "He's there, sir."

The Captain pounded a fist. "Excellent!"

"But…"

"What?" They had jumped out the moment that the Fleet command in the Tavar sector had given them clearance. Heres had used the delay to effect as many repairs to the Valor as possible; there was no telling what tricks Halloran had up his sleeve. The crew had located the Telos Archive and Heres had immediately pieced it all together. Now, as they approached the planet Gavin and the station came into range, it was taking everything Heres had to stop short of an all-out assault on the smaller mystery craft.

"Two decent-sized Prax cruisers, sir. All assembled around the archive."

"I knew it. They're rendezvousing."

Renno ran another scan. "Their weapons systems are significant but we have comparable firepower." She looked up. "If we drive straight in with a strong decel we could hold the initiative."

Heres pondered. "It's three on one. Is the station armed? Missiles?"

"System doesn't say, sir. That place is ancient."

"Let's approach cautiously, Renno. Place us on alert status."

The alarm sounded through the ship as Heres paced to the weapons station. "If they try any communications drones, target them and shoot them. Clear?"

"Yes, sir."

Heres lapsed into his hastily rebuilt seat and fidgeted, eyes on the overhead grating. He, like everyone else, had to now wait until they drew close enough to engage.

Heres was hoping to split the enemy, that Halloran would run and give him an opportunity. An extra ship would have come in handy, but Heres knew he'd been lucky to be even himself detached by the Tavarran command.

So he fidgeted.

Finally Renno turned in her seat. "Approaching fire position on the station, sir."

Heres sat up. "Range?"

"Ninety Thousand."

"Why haven't they moved?" Heres had been expecting some repositioning of the enemy units.

"No signs of engine activity, sir. They're cold."

Heres stood up. "All right, then. Target the closest Prax cruiser first, then move the next plasma salvo to our mystery ship. Then—."

The communications tech called. "Sir! We're being hailed."

"By who?"

"By the station, sir."

Heres lifted both eyebrows in surprise. "Accept."

The monitor lit up and there was the human, Halloran. The man still wore those odd green mottled colors. His cap was the same material.

"Captain. Heres, correct?"

Heres crossed his arms. "Prepare to be fired upon, sir."

"How about not?"

The rogue captain wasn't behaving according to plan. "I have orders," Heres began.

Halloran held up a hand. "Wait, Captain. What if I…what if I told you we had an, um, historic opportunity here?"

"You have ten seconds, Halloran."

The other nodded. "I have made contact with the Prax Premier—their leader. We have reached an understanding." Halloran looked offscreen and nodded again. Moments later, a large Prax in a very official uniform joined him in view. "Heres," Halloran said, "This is Krex. He is the Premier of the Praxxan Empire."

Renno gasped from her seat, as did several others on the bridge.

"You're not serious, Halloran." Heres was stunned.

"Captain, he is quite serious," spoke the alien who dominated the conversation with his deep voice. "Your Captain Halloran is an able representative of your people. He has prevailed upon me with the notion of a combined effort to rectify an internal struggle within my people." He lifted a hand at Heres. "A struggle that you and your crew would earn much honor across the galaxy for assisting us with."

"Um," was all Heres could manage.

"Heres," came a new voice from offscreen. Then, incredibly, Kendra was standing there. "You know you want to get into the action."

"Kendra, what—."

She pointed at him. "Get over here and listen to this! You *know* me, Heres…" Then, that maddening grin split her face. "…And I know *you*."

"Is this all..real, Kendra?" Heres was staring.

She shrugged. "You know me, always finding trouble."

Heres thought and thought—at least a minute while everyone patiently waited. *One thing was for sure, and that was that Kendra was telling the truth when she says she's always finding trouble.*

Heres made a "why not?" face at Renno. She was on the edge of her seat. He glanced at those waiting onscreen. "I'll be over, Halloran."

He motioned for the comms tech to cut the transmission. "Stand down from alert. I'm taking the shuttle over to the station. I'll take—."

"Sir, take me."

Heres paused in mid-sentence. "Why, Renno?"

"I just want to go this time, sir."

Heres frowned, then nodded. "You're with me, Renno. Haster has the ship, inform Engineering."

Renno joined him at the bridge hatch. "Sir, this is going to be big. I can feel it."

He snorted as he opened the hatch. But he, too, felt the tug of a new adventure, even if the Prax were involved. The Premier? How could that be, out here in the dead regions of space. There would have to be some serious trouble in the Empire to bring a Premier all the way out here.

Okay, it *did* sound like fun.

"Let's go with your gut feeling, Renno. I just hope we're not getting in over our head."

"But if Captain Kendra is there, sir…"

He pointed at her as they tromped up the passage toward the shuttle hangar. "If Kendra is involved, we'll want to watch our backs every step of the way."

Mars - Inner System Sensor Array 231

The planetary skimmer left a drifting wash of red dust behind as it moved across the plain at high speed. The pilot pressed the small vessel's speed to the max as though he or she were late for an appointment.

To Commander Kaela, who stood atop the sensor array superstructure with four techs and a junior officer, the approaching craft indeed represented an appointment. After one more long look at the captivating swath of rust-colored dirt, she turned to the group gathered with her and motioned to the man in charge.

He came closer, and she could see his ashen face behind the transparency of the EXP suit.

She tapped his shield. "He's here. You and your people take care of the work while I go down."

He looked nervous, and Kaela thought she caught a glimpse of sweat matting the man's hair to his forehead. With the cooling system built into the exposure suits, overheating shouldn't be a problem. She leaned in close so he could see her face clearly. "Are we clear?"

The man coughed, unnecessarily, into his suit mic. "Yes, Commander. The team…has been thoroughly briefed."

"Fine. And you…any concerns? Problems?"

"Well, Commander…"

"This is a private channel," she reminded him.

"No. No concerns. It just…feels…wrong."

She understood and tapped the visor again. "You and your team just do as you're told." Without waiting for an answer she turned away, the Martian atmosphere distorting her body's movements as she stepped lightly down the metal grated stairs to the lower level. As she did so, she switched to another private channel. At the base of the array station, she waited and watched as the skimmer slowed during the last several hundred meters. Even the pilot's deceleration was precipitous and Kaela had to fight the sudden urge to leap back up the stairs and out of the path of the careening craft. With moments to spare, however, the ship turned and decelerated, ending up mere meters away from the structure. A wash of redness rose around Kaela, matching the redness within her helmet as she experienced a flash of embarrassment. *He's toying with me,* she found herself thinking. *Seeing if I have the guts to stay standing here.* But, thankfully, her feet had remained rooted in place. But had it been terror or bravery?

Not unexpectedly, Krug himself emerged from the craft's cockpit. With a laborious show of stepping down to the surface, he ambled over, looking lopsided in his EXP suit. Kaela remained standing as he covered the last few meters; either one of them could have spoken on the reserved channel, even at several kilometers with the point-to-point transmission. But Kaela had decided that if Krug wanted to talk, he'd have to open the conversation. She wondered idly if the work party above had stopped to watch the showy entrance by the Senior Commander.

The man placed his hands on his hips before her. "A pity. A body like yours shouldn't be all bottled up in a bulky suit like that."

Kaela ignored the comment. "Don't you think this is suspicious? Why couldn't we have this conversation back in Command?"

If Krug could have shrugged through his suit, he would have. "I don't see any reason to be overly cautious beyond the measures we have already taken. Unless, there is something you know that I don't?"

"No, nothing. So why here?"

He leaned back and she could see him lowering the tinting of his shield. He was looking up at where she'd come from. "Your crew taking care of things?"

"Yes." She had one gloved hand on the stair's metal tube rail, finding herself interested in getting away from Krug. Again.

"Excellent." He leaned in toward her. "The timetable has been revealed to me."

Kaela felt her breath sucked away, despite the continuous flow of air around her face within the suit.

"The Prime has communicated, now we have only to put the final pieces into place for him."

"Please share, Commander."

He waved a careless hand. "Need to know, Commander. Need to know."

She was feeling the shield steaming up from her rising temperature. Although it wasn't. "I think I've put as much into this as anyone…you, even."

"Yes, yes, your dear father, the great Admiral Kendall." She heard Krug's derision clearly. "He and his fellow bureaucrats will get their war—down upon their heads."

"When, Krug." Her mic amplified the flatness in her tone.

He relented, attempting to place a hand on her shoulder. She pulled back from sudden disgust. "Now, Commander, your efforts have indeed been instrumental and those you have turned to our cause will all be recompensed."

"As you promised."

His helmet bobbed slightly. "As promised. All is in readiness?"

She considered. The three teams of co-opted personnel had been through all the main sensor relays, reprogramming the CPUs and setting failsafes in the guise of routine maintenance. The initial trial runs—on the Lunar sensors, which were of similar equipment—had gone flawlessly. So much so that it had landed her in a disciplinary process.

"Commander?"

Kaela nodded within her helmet. "We will be ready. Timeline?"

"Days, Commander. No more than a few days. Be ready."

"And our people will be protected?"

"That, my dear, is up to you…and me." He pointed at her, the leer clearly visible inside the shield.

She stepped back. "Then I'll put the last pieces in place and wait for your notification."

She heard his chuckle. "Very brave of you, standing here stock-still as I came crashing up. I didn't think you had it in you. More your sister's style, no?"

"If you mean reckless disregard for her life and those around her, then yes."

He turned back toward his skimmer, where a timid-looking pilot was now poking his head out. "I know you have a soft spot for your Kendra. You don't fool me for a minute." He reached the hatch and turned back to her, but she was unable to see anything inside the helmet at that distance. "Just remember, I can bring you down with one word, now, *Commander.* When the time comes, you execute on the plan. Or your pitiful showcase career will end in infamy and the undying hatred of your own race." He climbed into the craft and Kaela heard the channel close with a chirp in her ear.

As Krug moved off in a burst of billowing dust toward the red horizon, Kaela grasped the metal rail as if for strength and support, despite the lack of Martian wind. Every time she interacted with the man, she felt drained of all resolve in her own competency. The hard work she'd put into getting here.

No, she didn't hate her sister. In fact, it was quite the reverse. But, she was ready to embrace her own destiny as humanity's savior.

"Commander?" The junior officer called down. "We're about ready here."

"Good. Get everyone back in the shuttle—I want to be at Command in time for the evening meal." And to start her final-countdown planning, if Krug's warning was to be taken at face value.

When the fleet of Praxxan warship began their stealth bombardment, the humans here will never know what hit them, she thought as she made her way to the waiting ship. *It will be glorious.*

I hope you enjoyed "Resolve of Steel." please leave me a review where you purchased it! This really helps my readership grow.

The die is cast. Treachery runs deep as the century-old war between humans and aliens boils over. Will one rogue time-transplanted Captain and his beleaguered crew tip the scales in favor of victory? And at what cost will they find their way home?

Watch for the thrilling conclusion to the "Halloran's War" first Trilogy from author J.R. Geoghan!

Keep up to date with tips and (maybe) spoilers by joining JR Geoghan's reader community
At www.jrgeoghan.com/join1

Resolve Of Steel

Do you want to read more of Tom Halloran? Kendra? Axxa? Join my reader community at jrgeoghan.com/join1 to hear about the latest free story downloads and more news!

Plus, you'll get an exclusive subscriber-only account of the battle that made Kendra famous among humanity!

About the Author

J.R. Geoghan resides in Lancaster County, Pennsylvania with his family and loves writing and fast motorcycles. He grew up on Long Island, New York in the roaring seventies. Somewhere along the way Jeff picked up a knack and a love of writing that decided to reassert itself after the lingering effects of a management MBA wore off…many years later.

www.JRGeoghan.com

Printed in Great Britain
by Amazon